'Beautiful, shattering, and deeply affecting. Patsy's story ultimately makes for a novel that is destined to endure.'

Chigozie Obioma,
Man Booker-shortlisted author of *The Fishermen*

'Dennis-Benn is a prodigious world-straddler, and not just geographically; her characters are memorable and fully drawn, and the devastating meta-legacies they conjure are all too real.'

Vogue

'*Patsy* is a portrait of black queer women grasping for self-determination, and a challenge to the conventions of what is expected of good mothers and good women and good immigrants. In writing beautifully about that unending struggle, Dennis-Benn finds a way to extend to black girls and women some of the love that the world may never offer.'

The Atlantic

'Dennis-Benn has the uncanny ability to create characters that feel deeply, painfully real and the people in her second novel are no exception... A compulsively readable book that deftly grapples with maternal ambivalence.'

BuzzFeed

'*Patsy* methodically and unapologetically engages with the choices women do and should be allowed to make, and...does so with nuance and grace... Ultimately, *Patsy* is a deeply queer, sensitive and vividly written novel about a woman's right to want and a child's right to carve her own path.'

Washington Post

'Dennis-Benn has written a profound book about sexuality, gender, race, and immigration that speaks to the contemporary moment through the figure of a woman alive with passion and regret.'

Kirkus

'A beautifully layered portrait of motherhood, immigration, and the sacrifices we make in the name of love from award-winning novelist Nicole Dennis-Benn.' *Chicago Review of Books*

PRAISE FOR *HERE COMES THE SUN*

Winner of the LAMBDA Literary Award for Lesbian Fiction

A finalist for the New York Public Library Fiction Award, the NYPL Young Lions Fiction Award and the Center for Fiction First Novel Prize

A BEST BOOK OF 2016 ACCORDING TO
NPR • *Entertainment Weekly* • *BuzzFeed* • *Bustle* • *San Francisco Chronicle* • *Kirkus*

'An expertly timed examination of race, class, gender and sexuality, weaved seamlessly into an engaging narrative...brilliantly written.'

Guardian

'Stuns at every turn... It's about women pushed to the edge, Jamaica in all its beauty and fury and more than anything else, a story that was just waiting to be told.'   Marlon James,
author of *A Brief History of Seven Killings* and *Black Leopard, Red Wolf*

'[A] lithe, artfully-plotted debut... Margot is one of the reasons to read this book. She is a startling, deeply memorable character. All of Ms. Dennis-Benn's women are.'   *New York Times*

'*Here Comes the Sun* was the first Jamaica-set book I read. As a Jamaican woman, that was really exciting. It follows three women: two sisters and their mum. The older sister is navigating sexuality and being a queer woman, the younger is battling identity, being a darker-skinned girl, bleaching. It's really addictive.'   *Observer*

'The book vividly captures the fraught dynamics of familial and romantic relationships... Poignant.'   *The New Yorker*

'There is a richness to the way [Nicole Dennis-Benn] writes about Jamaican culture and identity, along with the New World colonialism that has cropped up along the nation's shores. [...] This book treads into brave territory. The struggle is not a beautiful one. But it is deeply powerful.'

Refinery29

'A compelling exploration of exploitation, sacrifice, tourism, poverty and the drive for freedom, *Here Comes the Sun* will transport your mind – and heart.'   *BuzzFeed*

PATSY

NICOLE DENNIS-BENN

ONEWORLD

A Oneworld Book

First published in Great Britain, the Republic of Ireland and Australia
by Oneworld Publications, 2019
This paperback edition published 2020

ISBN 978-1-78607-710-3
ISBN 978-1-78607-658-8 (eBook)

Printed and bound in Great Britain by Clays Ltd, Elcograf S.p.A

Oneworld Publications
10 Bloomsbury Street
London WC1B 3SR
United Kingdom

Stay up to date with the latest books,
special offers, and exclusive content from
Oneworld with our newsletter

Sign up on our website
oneworld-publications.com

MIX
Paper from
responsible sources
FSC® C018072

In memory of the unsung stories of undocumented immigrants in search of trees with branches.

*"Maybe home is somewhere I'm going
and have never been before."*

WARSAN SHIRE

BOOK I

BIRDIE (1998)

1

JUST TWO YEARS SHY OF THIRTY, PATSY HAS NOTHING TO SHOW for it besides the flimsy brown envelope that she uses to shade herself from the white-hot glare of the sun. The envelope contains all her papers—from birth certificate to vaccination records. But most importantly, it carries her dream, a dream every Jamaican of a certain social ranking shares: boarding an airplane to America. For the destination, and for the ability to fly.

So when Patsy got the second opportunity to interview at the U.S. Embassy, she went. She hadn't mentioned this to her family and hadn't stopped to consider what they would think. This morning she slipped out of the house early—before Mr. Belnavis's cock crowed, before the scent of Miss Hyacinth's baking bread replaced the damp smell of morning, before Ras Norbert started chanting,"*Believe me! Believe me not!*" about gold buried in their backyard. Patsy scribbled a letter to her daughter in her best handwriting and left it next to Mama G's Singer sewing machine in their modest two-bedroom house in Pennyfield—a working-class neighborhood contained by a hill and a gully. "*Have a good day at school. Remember to look both ways before you cross the street and do not talk to strangers. Also, tell Miss Gains I will pay at the end of the month.*" It wasn't yet hot and humid when Patsy left, which made the light brown tweed blazer and olive polyester skirt that her best friend, Cicely, sent from America years ago seem like a sensible choice. Once upon a time they were too big when she tried them on, but now they fit snugly. Patsy had hung them up outside the wardrobe days before her interview to get the camphor-ball smell out the fabric, since she has never worn them. She wanted to appear confident, though when she stepped off the bus on Half-Way Tree Road she started to sweat. She stood still for a moment and looked back down the long stretch of road from which the bus came, wondering about how, when she left, her daughter simply turned on the squeaky queen-size bed they share without questioning. In the dark, as Patsy got dressed, she felt—or did she imagine it?—the eyes of the child peering at her from the bed, knowing and watchful. Patsy always dresses in the dark since she never looks in mirrors, is unimpressed with what she catches glimpses of: an average moon-shaped face, broad nose, full, down-turned lips, the way a child looks who has lost something, save for the perpetual deepened dimples in each cheek. She has eyes men compliment her on, though her large breasts upstage them, and dark brown skin that emphasizes the whites of her perfectly aligned teeth. Her hair she simply straightens with a hot comb every Sunday evening after dinner and brushes back into a tight bun with a slab of gel. When she felt Tru's eyes this morning, she readied herself to put her index finger to the child's lips in the dark and explain. But she didn't have to. For Tru tends to squirm and sigh in her sleep anyway, as though she has already discovered Patsy's betrayal. Not since Patsy hid the letters with the Brooklyn address inside a locked briefcase, which she keeps on top of the wardrobe, had she felt so dubious and guilty at once.

In the embassy line, Patsy fiddles with the small tiger's-eye pendant around her neck—another gift from Cicely—for good luck. *"Ah bought it in Chinatown. Yes, m'dear! Dem 'ave a place name suh! Dem 'ave good, good deals. When yuh come we can go together."* A liquid-like sensation shoots through Patsy's veins underneath the tweed jacket. Though she's early getting to the embassy, there is still a long line stretched all the way up to Knutsford Boulevard by the Jamaica Pegasus Hotel. The bright June morning is a merriment of blues, greens, and yellows. The sun is already approaching its hottest at seven o'clock, and the scents of Julie mangoes and crushed worms fill the air—remnants of last night's shower. A flock of white, triangular birds fly south the way they do when fleeing the cold from North America.

But Patsy doesn't pay attention to any of this. She clutches the large brown envelope under her armpit, where sweat blooms down her sides. Cicely told her to wear a suit. *"Dey will tek yuh more seriously dis time."* But standing in a suit in the hot sun only makes the heat feel worse. There's no way Patsy can take off the blazer, since the blouse underneath is soaked by now, hugging her like a wet T-shirt, too scandalous for the gaze of the Americans inside the embassy.

Aside from the few women dressed like they're going to church on Easter Sunday, in hats and pastel-colored dresses with perspiration visible on their backs, many people, like Patsy, are dressed formally in business attire—some of the clothes borrowed, some bought, most too dark and heavy for the mocking heat. Patsy beckons a boy selling frozen bag-juice, hoping it will relieve some of the heat and maybe numb her nerves as she thinks of the questions the American will ask in the interview.

"Twenty dollah, miss-th," the boy says with a lisp. He's also selling whistles hung with strings around his thumb for people who, though in line to leave the island in droves, might want to join the evening celebration of the Reggae Boyz making it to the 1998 World Cup in France. Everyone in Jamaica is getting ready for the match this evening between Jamaica and Argentina. Nothing brings Jamaicans together like an international sporting event where they'll be represented. Strangers embrace in Half-Way Tree. Gunmen lay down guns, grab barflies, kiss their proud, laughing mouths, and spin them like battling tops into the street. Young people open kitchen cupboards to fetch Dutch pots and metal spoons to bang with. In Pennyfield, men started making bets as early as last month, digging deep inside shallow pockets at Pete's Bar, where there's a big TV. Miss Maxine, known in the community for her cooked food, is prepared to snatch the fattest fowl from her coop to make brown-stew chicken and white rice for the occasion to sell with her special malt-liquor concoction—good for women wanting to conceive and men desiring energy, especially on a night of predicted victory.

Patsy pauses and looks at the young haggler with the bag juice and whistles around his thumb—a scrawny young man no older than sixteen in a mesh marina and a pair of knee-length shorts that don't cover the scars on his legs. "Twenty dollah fi one bag juice?" she asks him.

"Yes miss-th."

"Yuh t'ink people 'ave money like dat jus' because dem inna embassy line?" Patsy asks.

The boy doesn't respond, knowing his market. Just as he's about to move to the next customer, Patsy says. "All right, gimme di orange."

The boy hands her the juice and takes her money. He swiftly counts it, using his free thumb. Patsy watches him, impressed, as her mind spins and loops around the numbers. She lifts her tongue to the edge of her lips as she too counts in her head. Math was her favorite subject in school—the only subject that she excelled in. For there is nothing more certain than numbers. When the boy gives her the exact change, she tells him to keep it. It is easy to believe each penny will go toward his future; it is easy to believe he has one—that he will live out his days not selling juice and whistles, but working in someone's bank as a senior accountant. Or owning one himself. But this moment of optimism lasts no longer than the line stretched around the corner, full of people who have discovered that certain seeds the land will not nurture. "T'ank yuh, miss-th," the boy says, slightly bowing his head as though in resignation.

Patsy thinks of all the money she has wasted, investing in a passport and an American visa application. She was turned down two years ago with no explanation. People say it's because she doesn't own property in Jamaica. Aside from the seed money she gets from Vincent, the married businessman she sleeps with, there are no real assets she can tell the Americans she owns. *"Dey tend to give you a visa if dey know yuh have assets to come back to. Dat way yuh won't run weh fah good,"* said Ramona, one of the other secretaries in a cubicle next to Patsy's and the only one Patsy eats lunch with. *"Also, dem tend to be lenient if yuh own yuh own business too,"* said Sandria, the other secretary, who tends to butt her nose into people's business, then go back to tell their boss, Miss Clark—a witch of a woman who scowls at everyone below her rank.

Pricked by the hopelessness of her situation, Patsy considers her story—one that lacks the drama inherent in, say, an asylum story, which she heard guarantees acceptance anywhere. She read in the *Jamaica Observer* a few months ago about the man who got chopped up with a cutlass by four men who found him in a *"compromising position"* behind a bush with another man. How he hauled himself, not to the hospital or police station, but to the Canadian Embassy and got a visa on the spot. *"Dem funny man can mek anyt'ing 'appen. Even part di sea an' walk 'pon wata. All dem haffi do is cry wolf,"* Ramona had said, wrinkling her nose and folding the paper. Nonetheless, Patsy practices in her small cubicle at the Ministry, sitting upright in her swivel chair, legs crossed at the ankles, facing the blank wooden partition. And again, last night in her bed, lying on her back and staring up at the gaping hole of blackness in her bedroom, her daughter snoring softly beside her. *"I am going to visit a friend"*—simple as that, though she still lacks confidence saying it. She plans to follow it up with her rehearsed story—one that would convince them that she has no inclination of running away, because— *how could she*? She'd tell them that she owns land in Trelawny where she plans to build a house. (The land really belonged to Papa Joe, Mama G's father and Patsy's grandfather, a sugarcane farmer. He was forced to sell it to developers, who bought it for chicken feed and turned it into a stadium. Papa Joe died from a broken heart shortly afterward.) The embassy officials won't know whether it's true.

Most times Patsy stops herself mid-practice, worrying about being struck by lightning for lying, like Mama G always warns. But then again, Mama G has warned against other things that Patsy has disobeyed. Her whole childhood was spent with her mother at church or on street corners handing out *Jesus Saves* flyers and praying for "sinners" who refused flyers because they were in a hurry to work or school. Almost always Patsy would find herself repenting for sins she committed. But to lie for an American visa won't be so bad, she reasons, since God will understand that it's for the good of her family. She will go to America and send money home as soon as she finds work. This much is true—as her daughter's name suggests. It's a nickname that has stuck—a casual and spontaneous utterance when Patsy was too exhausted one day. Or was it for a whole week? A month? A year? She tends to lose count of these periods, too weak from the dark, heavy thing she cannot see but knows is always there, quiet and waiting. Mama G calls it the Devil's cold, because it has a tendency to creep up like a thief in the middle of the night. How often has Patsy gone through periods where she feels like it's pressing down, down on her chest? There are times when she can barely breathe because of it, much less lift the sheet to get out of bed. It was during one such spell that she willed herself to utter her daughter's name, Trudy-Ann, which rushed out with an exhaled breath as only Tru.

Without pausing to correct herself, Patsy let the name carry on, since it drew her daughter to her anyway. She looked into her child's large brown eyes that day. Her open moon face, which is similar to Patsy's, lacked the earnestness of a curious toddler. When the thing finally lifted and Patsy regained her ability to breathe, she repeated the name, seeing something take shape in her daughter's eyes. Mama G, whose head remains in the clouds, surprisingly caught on to the name as well, since to her the name sounded like the sort of name that would make the child less sinful. When the little girl began to write her own name, she spelled it as TRU—the name her school friends and teachers used, the name Pastor Kirby called her when he asked Patsy if she would send her to Sunday school like the rest of the children. *"She might even learn to be a girl then,"* he pressed. Only Tru's father refuses to use the name or acknowledge it.

Patsy thinks about all this as she sucks on the cold bag juice, relieved to feel both its cooling and numbing effect. The embassy line begins to move steadily. In the shade of the palm trees Patsy pays more attention to the other people around her, wondering about their lies—how creative they might be. Take the man in a dark suit, who looks like he's on his way to his own funeral. Like Patsy, he clutches his documents in an envelope, constantly adjusting the blue tie around his neck with the black callused fingers of a laborer, maybe a farmer. What might a man like that say to the embassy official? That he owns many acres of land? That he uses it to plant produce? That the produce doesn't remain untouched, sitting bruised and overripe in Coronation Market, the only market where his things might sell, since his country can't export them? Or maybe he's going away for a few months, maybe a year, to farm, like most Jamaican farmers, who have lost the ability to profit from their own land. And then there's the family of four behind him—a mother and her three small children. The oldest is a girl who watches her younger siblings as their mother scurries over to a food cart made of bamboo painted black, green, and yellow like the Jamaican flag. Peeled Julie mangoes and June plums dangle in transparent plastic bags from its awning. The children should be in school, Patsy thinks. What might the mother say to the embassy official? Patsy imagines the mother lifting up the two younger children for a smug-faced official to see—perhaps even handing them over like the bag of June plums to assess their worth. *"See? See?"* the mother might say. *"All t'ree assets right 'ere."*

ONCE INSIDE, PATSY SITS AND AWAITS HER TURN, UNABLE TO revel in the reprieve of the cool air coming from the air conditioner. She feels hotter all of a sudden. People are seated next to her on plastic chairs, waiting their turn. Each time the attendant calls, "Next!" the person at the end of the front row gets up and goes to the available window. People move down accordingly, reminding Patsy of a game of musical chairs. Patsy prays that the window she gets called to will have someone nice and in a good mood. The Americans are protected behind a glass partition, their heads bowed as they take notes or review questions. Some seem distracted by things other than the person in front of them, perhaps unable to understand the patois spoken by the men and women from the rural parishes—country people who have left their villages before the crack of dawn, squeezed against vendors carrying produce to sell at the markets in town. Perhaps the Americans are equally frustrated, because no one can understand them either, especially when their *t*'s sound like *d*'s and their vowels are sawed in half, making simple words sound complicated or completely swallowed. "How many *rums* do ya have in the house *yur* building?"

A confused interviewee might respond with, *"But sah, me is a Christian. Me nuh drink rum."*

Once she makes it to the final seat in the front row, Patsy overhears the interview of a middle-aged man who is dressed in a pristine white suit and powder-blue shirt, looking like he's on his way to a banquet. "Repeat wha yuh jus' seh, Officer. Me cyan't hear yuh good." The man presses the left side of his face to the glass partition, smearing it with his cheek. "Dis ah me good ears. Come again." Patsy cannot hear the interviewer's question, but by the look on the older man's face—crumpled like the handkerchief that he pulls from his back pocket to wipe perspiration despite the cool air—he's still unable to comprehend the interviewer's question. Just then Patsy hears, "Next!"

She almost leaps out of her chair, the *clack-clack* of her wedge heels too loud in her ears on the concrete tiles as she hurries to the window, adjusting her blazer and steadying her hands by squeezing the brown envelope. Like Patsy, the interviewer to whom she's assigned is on the chubby side. Not that this fact eases the pressure inside her in any way.

She just has a tendency to find something in common with people. Patsy doesn't know the details of her interviewer's face. All she knows is that it's flushed pink by the heat and sun, which he has undoubtedly gotten a lot of in Jamaica. Even his eye color misses her as they greet, since she doesn't dare meet his gaze. She fixes her eyes instead on the center of the man's forehead, just like Cicely tells her to. *"Americans like direct eye contact, suh mek sure it look like yuh staring dem in di eye."* Patsy notices the man's striped shirt and khaki slacks, the color of the uniforms the schoolboys wear. She's sure he smells like cigarettes and coffee, since American men on television, especially the detective types, like coffee and cigarettes. She can almost smell it through the glass partition that separates them. Patsy always wonders why glass partitions are necessary at the embassy. It's not like it's a bank where there are vaults of cash. And even with banks one can just walk in and sit down with an associate. But then again, the desperation contained within the stiff grins and the too-tight metal clasps and neckties worn by the visa hopefuls might get out with a force hurling them over tables and onto the legs of the American interviewers like dogs in heat. *"Please, sah. Please, madam. Me ah beg yuh fi a visa. Me pickney dem haffi eat. We have nothing out 'ere. Di government nuh like poor people."*

"Tell me your occupation," the interviewer says to Patsy, silencing the bloodcurdling cries of desperation in her head. He's looking down at Patsy's documents. Or he might be reading a script. She's not sure. She would have thought any other person who fails to raise his head in greeting impolite.

Patsy clears her throat. "I'm a civil servant, sah. A secretary at di Ministry."

The man scribbles something on a sheet of paper. "Sounds like a good job."

Not when is minimum wage an' yuh have a dawta fi send to school, an' a retired mother living undah yuh roof fah free since she give all ah har pension to di church, Patsy wants to say. But she keeps this to herself in case it might jeopardize her chances. Also, she got the job because Pastor Kirby knew someone who knew someone else who had a second cousin in HR. For at the time no one wanted a high school dropout.

"What's the purpose of your visit to the United States?" the man asks. He raises his head and pins her with his eyes. Aside from her wanting more out of life, and more resources to take care of her daughter, the possibility of her and Cicely together again in America looms so large in Patsy's heart that she almost trembles, having to compose herself before she utters the first answer aloud to the interviewer. Though she has all of Cicely's letters saved, she carries around the one she favors most in her purse. It was written months after Cicely vanished from Pennyfield. Not a word about where she went until the letter came. Patsy read it so many times that she has memorized it:

Dear Patsy,

I am writing from Brooklyn, New York. I was going to write sooner, but I had to get settled first. Please don't tell anyone you heard from me. Not Roy, not Mama G, not Aunt Zelma, and especially not Pope. America is everything that we dreamed about. There is so much here. It's cold and snows a lot in winter. If you see me again, I'll be so light. I am more comfortable now. But I miss the sea. I miss the hills that surrounded us. I miss gazing up at the sky at nights and seeing stars so close that I could grab them. I miss the smell of breadfruit roasting and saltfish cook-up. Now I have to go to a restaurant to pay for it. But that isn't so bad. I always pretend that you're here too. I like to imagine us, free without your mother, my aunt, Pope, Roy, and everyone else in Pennyfield. Like I said, don't tell a soul you heard from me. Now that I am here, my memory of you and our special friendship will live forever. You have always been my home in this world.

Yours, Cicely

"I'm going on vacation," Patsy blurts out, forgetting to say she's visiting a friend. Vacation by itself sounds idle—something white people do. Like the ones she sees on the island, lazed and sunburnt on the beaches. But before Patsy can correct herself and continue about her elaborate plans to build a house on the land she forgot to mention, the man says, "I can never understand why you Jamaicans go to America for vacation when you live in this paradise." He chuckles to himself and shakes his head.

"Is really for a wedding," Patsy hurries to add. Since sickness and death are two things one can't lie about without jinxing oneself. It isn't what she rehearsed, but she'll go with it. She's stunned by the ease with which the lie flies out of her mouth. Cicely got married years ago to a man she only married for papers. *"It was jus' so-so,"* Cicely said over the telephone. Normally, they would dance around each other's dating life—Cicely never asking about Roy, and Patsy never inquiring about Cicely's love interests or offering information about hers. Patsy had cradled the phone between her ear and shoulder, listening to Cicely above the noise of squawking fowl in the backyard and the drumming of her own heartbeat as Cicely said, *"We did it at the courthouse. Before we blink it was ovah. Di hardest part was convincing di immigration officer. He wanted proof. But thanks to those acting classes we did in school, ah showed him. You woulda think our relationship was real."* She cackled. Patsy was comforted by her friend's comedic account, picturing Cicely tongue-kissing her play-husband under the bored gaze of a white man fiddling with his pen. But there is no way that this interviewer at the embassy could possibly research this detail.

"Wonderful," he says. "Who is getting married?"

"M-my best friend."

"When is the wedding?"

"October."

"May I see the invitation?" The man asks.

"Sah?"

"The invitation. I need proof."

"Oh! Yes, yes, di invitation."

Patsy feels faint all of a sudden, making a production out of fumbling in her handbag for something she does not have. All the time and money and practice that went into preparation for this interview flash across her mind. Her head spins. She's about to lose everything because of one stupid lie. She cups her mouth. In her best English she says, "Please forgive me, but I forgot my invitation."

"I get stories all the time," the man says, looking away from her pleading gaze to the paperwork on his desk. He taps his pen lightly on the table. Patsy watches his fat fingers curl, holds her breath as the pen hovers. In one stroke he could write her off. Stamp DENIED on her paperwork. Quietly tell her that she can apply again next year when there'd surely be a wait-list for interviews that might take another two years to get. Patsy focuses on the pen, which is in charge of her destiny.

"Why should I believe you?" the man says, pausing to look at her.

"The friend who's getting married is—" Patsy stops herself and searches for the right words. The memories of them together make her smile. Usually she reserves these thoughts for nighttime, right after everyone goes to sleep. She lowers her eyelids and dabs at the sweat on her top lip, hoping the man behind the glass cannot read her mind and see an image of Cicely lying naked in sunlight inside the house on Jackson Lane, soft and fleshy as ripe roast breadfruit. Pastor Kirby preaches against such evil, his mouth foaming like a rabid dog every time he shouts fire and brimstone on the damned souls who have such desires. Mas' Jacobs—a slight, friendly man with a lisp who used to call Patsy *Passy*, was chased out of his mother's house for it when Miss Roberta, the town crier, claimed she saw him put a little boy on his lap.

But Patsy cannot help it. With a visa she wouldn't have to rely on memories any longer.

Patsy lets out a sigh that fogs the glass in front of her, "She's like a sistah to me, sah. My dawta's godmother, who ah haven't seen in years."

She swallows, feeling all the other lies that have been stored up inside her go down with the force of a whole chicken bone in her throat. She almost chokes before the man says, "You have a daughter, you say?"

Patsy pauses again, confused, when she notices the smile on his face. His first.

The interviewer she had two years ago wasn't satisfied with that answer by itself. Her having a daughter meant nothing to them then. Clearly, the embassy had begun to figure out that people would leave ailing parents, spouses, and newborn babies if they have the opportunity to live and work in America. It reminds Patsy of the Rapture. Mama G always talks about the Rapture—how Jesus will return for the good Christians, the chosen ones, leaving loved ones behind to be destroyed by cannonballs of fire. Though in Jamaica the chosen ones are the pale-skin people on the hills living in mansions. Since they're so far away from everything, tucked up there near Heaven—away from the hot, dusty city, and black faces slicked with sweat and creased under the weight of daily burdens. They have no reason to escape.

"Yes," Patsy replies. "Ah have a dawta."

She opens her wallet to show a picture of a smiling Tru in a red plaid uniform—one taken on the first day of basic school.

"She's beautiful," the man says. "How old?"

"Five going on six in October."

Patsy quickly closes her wallet. Hiding the photo takes the sin out of lying, out of wanting.

"My wife just gave birth to a girl. Our first!" the man confides, lowering his voice. "And would you know, she hired a Jamaican nanny. Nice woman." It's Patsy's turn to smile. But, upon realizing she's already doing so, smiles broader—this time feeling it touch her eyes. She leans in farther toward the glass partition to see the picture the man holds up of a sleeping, bald-headed baby. "She's lovely, sah," Patsy says.

The man smiles again, reminding Patsy of a glistening penny caught in sunlight. "Thank you," he says, flushing pink. Patsy realizes that what she sees on the man's face is pride—a pride that saddens her for no earthly reason, at least no reason that anyone would understand had she told them, and no reason that Patsy herself understands.

She focuses on the man's color, amazed how white people can change color in an instant. Cicely changes color like that too—an ability that made Patsy's best friend the most worshipped girl in school. Teachers spoiled Cicely because of it. They made it known that girls like Cicely, the pretty ones, were worthy ones. She was quiet, an angel that had fallen, stunned and flushed by the jarring descent. Whatever she said in class or on the playground was taken, in a sense, as biblical. Never mind that the whole community knew that her mother, Miss Mabley—a peanut-colored coolie with hair so long that it touched the high mounds of her swaying backside—slept with men who paid, and that Cicely never knew the man who put white in her blood.

They were ten years old when Cicely chose Patsy. Patsy happily took on the coveted role of Cicely's best friend—a role that came with certain privileges, like playing with Cicely's long, silky hair, which went past her waist and shimmied with every movement, and the bliss of confessional friendship filled with intimacy and gossip. Patsy also did Cicely's homework, helped Cicely with math tests by scribbling answers on Wrigley's gum wrappers, and protected Cicely from jealous bullies, who used the shame of Cicely's mother's death a couple years later as ammunition. Patsy's drive to help Cicely was an impulse that was as mindless as a blood cell that spends its whole life providing oxygen to a tissue.

You have always been my home in this world. Patsy pictures Cicely as pale as the father she never met, pale as the princesses in those fairy-tale books she sends Tru with her initials, *CM*, written in perfect script on the inside, her beauty preserved like a carved ice sculpture in that cold weather.

"She's my everything," the interviewer at the embassy is saying to Patsy, still musing about the baby in the picture.

"Mine too," Patsy says.

✔

Patsy hurries to Tru's school, trying not to fall in the wedge heels she wore to the interview. She's even more aware of the weight of the promise inside the bag she carries—her stamped passport. Her lungs fill with excitement, like she has narrowly escaped something. She finds herself looking over her shoulder, half expecting the embassy representative to chase her down and take back her visa. When Patsy sees no one behind her, she slows her pace.

The schoolyard is quiet when she gets there. The grass blows wave-like on the wide, open field that is used for PE and fetes put on by the school. Saints Basic School, which Tru attends, is on this side; and Saints Primary School, which Patsy hopes to send her when she starts first grade, is across the street. Vendors have already set up their tables full of sweets for the outpour of children as soon as the last bell rings. There are cars parked in the dusty parking lot where parents wait, some leaned back in their seats with their radios tuned to the soccer match between Italy and Cameroon or to Barry G for the latest music. The World Cup theme song, "Rise Up," is on replay in one car, with various Jamaican singers telling other Jamaicans, *"There's a winner inside you . . . be the best that you can be."* Just like the Reggae Boyz. Patsy smiles to herself, the too-optimistic song finally resonating with her after what she just accomplished. She sings along. The man in the vehicle with the music must think she's smiling at him, so he winks. Patsy politely nods in solidarity and turns away. The afternoon sun glistens off the top of the band shell, where the children gather for devotion each morning before streaming to their classrooms in the two-story school building, painted blue and white.

It's after one o'clock. When Patsy gets to Tru's classroom, Miss Gains is standing in front, watching over the children saying their after-school prayer. Tru, who must have sensed her mother's presence, spots

Patsy and keeps her eyes open as she mouths the words to the prayer. "Our Father, who art in Heaven, hallowed be thy name . . ."

She's smiling at Patsy and bouncing in her chair, unable to concentrate. Patsy mouths, *Close your eyes.* But Tru is already too excited, quickly forgetting her obligation to Miss Gains. Miss Gains looks up and sees Patsy. The teacher gives her a stiff smile meant to reprimand her for showing up too soon.

". . . forgive us our sins, as we forgive those who trespass against us . . ."

Patsy steps aside and waits patiently by the door of the classroom for the class to finish the prayer.

"Remember you have homework!" Miss Gains says above the chatter and screeching of chairs, bringing Patsy back to the classroom.

Tru waves, and Patsy smiles. Miss Gains gestures to Patsy to come inside. To Tru, she says, in the practiced diction that every teacher at the Catholic school uses, "Tru, will you step outside for a second? Mommy and I need to talk."

Tru obeys, taking her lunch box and book bag with her. Miss Gains waits until she's out of earshot before she says to Patsy in patois, "Dis can't continue."

"I know. Ah was early."

"It's not dat."

"Oh?"

"It's only a mattah of time before di school look at di roster an' see—"

"Look," Patsy says, a sigh escaping her. "Ah told Tru to tell you dat I'll have di money by Tuesday."

"You said dat last month."

"Dey had a payment freeze at the Ministry. Yuh know dat. I'm trying my best."

"Your best is not enough when it's har education. I'm not di one making di rules here."

"Yuh t'ink ah don't know dat? We come from di same place. Yuh know how it guh."

Miss Gains folds her arms across her chest. She's a handsome woman, more handsome than any woman Patsy has ever seen, with high cheekbones and a wide, square jaw. She wears her hair natural, plaiting it into two neat French braids at the sides of her head. Her dark brown skin—an anomaly in a school of nuns—is flawless, which makes it hard to guess her age. She has lived in Pennyfield on Newcastle Lane as long as Patsy can remember, with her foster mother, Miss Myrtle (God bless her soul), and her younger sister, Bernice. Miss Gains also goes to Pennyfield Church of God Assembly for the Righteous, where Mama G has been going for years. She is not Catholic, but she lives like a nun. No man or children to call her own, although it has been speculated that Bernice is really Miss Gains's daughter given to her by her own father, since the girl is retarded. Patsy doesn't care one bit. Not like the other women in Pennyfield— women who wrap the bones of their many children like shawls just to say they have them, unable to feed them. To those women, it's suspect that a woman above the age of twenty-five doesn't have a child. Either she's tragically barren, or, to those convinced that Jamaican men are the most desirable men on earth, she's *funny*—the latter impossible in a place like Pennyfield, where everyone knows your business, can look right through the veranda into your living room, peer through a side window into your bedroom or kitchen, or look over your zinc fence and see you bathing in the outdoor bathroom, naked as the day you were born. No corner for hiding in a place like that. And while people would pardon convicts, drunks, and men who fuck goats, cows, dogs, and children, they are suspicious, almost terrified, of a woman without a family and no religion. Jesus is the only viable excuse a young woman can use to deny the penis.

"I'LL GIVE YOU TO NEXT TUESDAY," SAYS MISS GAINS, WHOM THE elders in Pennyfield still refer to as Miss Myrtle's foster daughter. "After that I can't have her in my class. I could get in trouble with the school. I'm only doing dis because she's a good student an' you're my neighbor—"

"I will take care of it."

Miss Gains nods. "All right, then. Give yuh mother my regards."

Patsy turns to leave, letting Miss Gains's last request fall between them on the deaf concrete tile of the classroom.

✦

"MOMMY 'AVE SOME GOOD NEWS!" PATSY SAYS TO TRU AT THE Tastees Restaurant in Cross Roads, where Patsy takes her after school. Workers from local businesses sit on benches near them, devouring beef patties and cocoa bread. Tru and Patsy sit at one of the plastic tables that face the road. Tru is looking at her, blinking away the dust in her eyes from the construction work at the gas station. Her eyes are a lighter brown than her skin, bright as though the sun is at their centers. She has been studying Patsy like this lately—with the wizened observation of a woman with experience. Miss Gains has suggested that she skip the first grade when she starts primary school in September. Patsy has given it much thought, fearful that her daughter might be too small to exist among the bigger children, though her intelligence is the same as theirs, if not higher. But that is all Patsy fears. Deep down, she welcomes the idea of Tru skipping a grade. It will only make her mature faster, leapfrogging over milestones that will relieve Patsy of the burden of raising her. She's quickly overcome by guilt for feeling this way. Her daughter's face holds within it a conviction—a darkness and a mystery that Patsy fears, which sometimes causes her to look away or fix what doesn't need fixing. Like now. Patsy reaches her hand across the table to wipe the patty crumbs from her daughter's mouth. For good measure, she smooths Tru's bushy eyebrows with a finger and tugs at the tips of her plaited pigtail held by white bubbles and clips shaped like bows. When she runs out of things to fix and touch, Patsy's movement slows.

"What is it yuh want to tell me, Mommy?" Tru asks, chewing with her mouth open, a space visible where her two front teeth used to be.

"Is a surprise."

"Yuh got me a football to play wid so I can be like di Reggae Boyz?" Tru asks, her eyes getting larger.

"No. Is a biggah surprise."

"Albino Ricky say dat nothing is biggah than di Reggae Boyz," Tru counters.

"Dat's Ricky's opinion. And how many times I tell yuh not to call di dundus boy dat? Dat's not nice. I hope yuh don't call him dat to him face."

"No, Mommy."

"And I hope yuh not letting nobody tell you what to think."

"No, Mommy."

"I want you to grow out of dat tomboy ways of yours. Good girls keep dem self neat an' clean. Like those Wilhampton High School girls. Dey don't play wid boys an' dirty up their nice white uniforms. Dey are well behaved an' obedient. Can you promise me dat? Promise me dat you'll—" She catches herself when she notices her daughter's eyes fall away from hers. Patsy takes a deep breath and changes the subject. "All right. If I tell you my secret, promise me dat yuh won't seh anyt'ing to Grandma."

"I promise!" Tru says, animated again, bobbing up and down in her seat with the excitement of holding a big secret.

"Yuh sure?" Patsy asks, half smiling.

Tru nods with such vigor that her plaits shake.

"I don't t'ink yuh big enough to handle secrets." Patsy leans back and playfully folds her arms across her chest. "Only big girls keep secrets," she says, echoing what her Uncle Curtis used to say to her when she was Tru's age.

"I'm a big girl!" Tru shouts.

Patsy laughs despite the uneasiness knotting inside her stomach.

"All right. I'm going to America," Patsy says finally, crushing the napkin in her palm. "I got my visa today."

Tru's eyes widen. She springs from her seat and comes around the table to hug Patsy tightly. "We going to America!" Tru shouts, drawing attention. Some grudgingly turn their heads and shrug, their voices lowering to whispers; others raise their brows and smile with admiration. Patsy allows herself to sit with her daughter's arms around her—her daughter whose only glimpse of America is through the Walt Disney fairy tales she watches on television when Mama G is not around to talk about the Devil in cartoons—or the ones she reads in books Cicely sends her. And there was that snow globe Patsy picked up once from the Woolworth downtown—an unusual treasure amid the Virgin Mary and Jesus figurines that sit on the whatnot inside the living room. Tru, like Patsy, delighted in shaking the thing to see flurries of snow fill the glass and settle on the beautiful two-story house and the surrounding pine trees inside it. "*Snow!*" Tru would say, giggling while tilting her head back and fluttering her eyelids as if she could feel the snow on her face.

One day the globe disappeared. Tru admitted to taking it to school to show her friends and somehow misplacing it. Patsy almost fell on her knees the moment her daughter confessed. She grabbed her then and gave her two big slaps on her buttocks. "*Me did tell yuh to tek it to school?*" But it was Patsy's eyes that were hot with tears. "*How much time me warn yuh to be careful wid it!*"

Inside the globe was the secret promise of a life without worry or care or want. When Tru lost it, Patsy felt like she lost *her* fairy tale—something her daughter didn't understand. Tru's cheeks were dry while Patsy's were wet.

Closing her eyes in this moment—the sun on her lids creating a yellow void inside her—Patsy regrets the scolding. She squeezes her daughter in a tight embrace, wishing she could be satisfied with the simple pleasure of feeling the sun on her eyelids and the embrace of her daughter. But as she inhales the smell of the Blue Magic hair oil she uses in Tru's hair, which mingles with the smell of beef patties and exhaust fumes from the traffic, and as she listens to the sounds of rush hour on Half-Way Tree Road clamoring around them, Patsy only feels her secret yearning for more deepening.

Truth be told, she never loved her daughter like she's supposed to, or like her daughter loves her. Tru's love for her—an unconditional love that Patsy didn't have to earn or deserve—seems unfair. Everything Patsy does and says to Tru is taken with wide-eyed acceptance. Sometimes Patsy finds herself wanting to crush the image of herself that she sees at the center of her daughter's eyes. The day Tru lost the snow globe, Patsy struck her hard, finding for a moment a reprieve in her daughter's anger, and hoping the frozen image would drown in her daughter's tears. But Tru didn't cry, coming to Patsy moments later with those wide brown eyes that seem to take up her whole face—bottomless wells Patsy is careful not to look into for too long.

After the loss of the snow globe she began to plan and dream without Tru, writing letters to Cicely about staying with her in Brooklyn, applying for a passport and a visa. The rest she'll consider when she gets to America—a place where she hears jobs and opportunities are abundant. Cicely told her that they have things like job agencies to help people find work. *"An' good jobs too! Yuh can mek triple what yuh making at di Ministry in one week!"* Patsy always imagines them walking hand in hand in America, trying on clothes in boutiques and zipping up each other's dresses like they did as girls, and shopping for household items together, like real couples do, for their house—a two-story brick house. She didn't tell Mama G or Roy, because she wanted to see if she would get the visa. The visa solidifies for Patsy that she could have a life with Cicely; that all her unhappiness would be rewarded; that all life's mistakes would make sense in the end. Now she has to figure out a way to tell Tru that she's going to America without her. As if Tru already knows this, she holds on to Patsy tighter. A lump rises steadily in Patsy's throat.

"God nuh 'ave no room in Him army fah di coward at heart," Mama G always says. Patsy swallows.

2

PENNYFIELD WAS ONCE A MIDDLE-CLASS NEIGHBORHOOD UNTIL the original owners, with some means, fled in the 1970s thinking Jamaica was on its way to becoming a Communist country like its neighbor, Cuba. Panicked, they leaped back into the arms of Mother England. They left faded colonial houses, stripped of paint and stature. They left mango trees, pear trees, ackee trees, and guava trees susceptible to the stones of hungry children. Each house now stands weighted down by poverty and Mother Nature. Pennyfield, which is positioned under the foot of the hills and spreads all the way to the sandy gully, got its name from the Englishmen who once buried pennies in the area for good luck, according to Ras Norbert, the old Rasta man who lives in a shack down the road. He says the Englishmen buried generous amounts of gold coins. *"Believe me, believe me not!"* the old man would holler before beginning his tale, his one good eye roaming to find the steady pair of anyone who would listen. This supposedly happened before the upper-middle-class Jamaicans flew away like exotic birds to seek refuge, certainly way before Mama G's gaze moved heavenward. And before trigger-happy young boys drew invisible lines across the gully, marking their turf with sanguine spray paint, their cryptic crab-toe writings scrawled across buildings and walls: PNP VERSUS JLP; ONLY BATTY MAN WEAR ORANGE; KEEP JAMAICA CLEAN, VOTE GREEN; WE WANT FREEDOM.

During election season, politicians come to Pennyfield in BMWs with tinted windows. They carry crates of Guinness to hand out to people, as if that will fix things. To the young boys in the community—boys who don't go to school, boys Patsy has known since they were just tots—the politicians give guns.

Patsy and Tru pass Ras Norbert sitting on an empty D&G crate by Pete's Bar, in the shade of the big lignum vitae tree—the one on the corner of Walker Lane that attracts so many yellow butterflies in May that it seems that the leaves themselves are yellow and fluttering. Ras Norbert is telling his tale to Miss Foster's runny-nosed, picky-picky-head children—all of whom never seem to own a pair of shoes or ever go to school. Though the children vary in age, they are the same height and look identical. Even the girls, with their hair picked out and simple cotton dresses draped over their bony shoulders, look like the boys in their khaki shorts and torn T-shirts with names of places they would never see—France, Brazil, Italy. The children are sucking on their fingers, quietly listening to Ras Norbert. The brooms Ras Norbert makes and sells for a living are leaned up against the bark of the tree as he talks about a time when men in trousers and high socks squatted in the blazing heat at the foot of the hill to dig holes and plant gold. No one ever asks Ras Norbert how he knows such things, just like no one ever asks him how his dreadlocks, peppered with gray and matted together like a big tree's bark made up of smaller trees, got to be so long. He has to carry it all over his shoulder like the anaconda snake at Hope Zoo so that it doesn't sweep the ground when he walks.

"But if dey plant go'al, why dem call it Pennyfield?" a child, who is not one of Miss Foster's, asks. Ras Norbert stops his story to locate the source of the small voice. It's Miss Ida's dundus grandson, who is hard to miss with skin as pale as a ghost and hair the color of dried-up weeds. He hides behind his grandmother's floral skirt, which only enhances his paleness, save for the bright pink tongue he sticks out at Tru. Tru retaliates by sticking out her tongue too, both children looking like two croaking lizards sparring in a yard. Patsy pinches her daughter on the forearm. "What me tell yuh 'bout sticking out yuh tongue? Is not lady-like." Tru folds her arms across her chest and pouts, shooting daggers with her eyes at the dundus boy. Miss Ida, a cook at the basic school on Molynes Road, doesn't seem to notice her grandson's antics. Like Patsy, Miss Ida has stopped to listen to Ras Norbert too.

"Only fools t'ink a penny is jus' a penny," Ras Norbert says to the boy. "But a wise man know di worth of a penny. Problem is we too lazy an' downtrodden fi stay an' search we own backyard fi find we blessing."

Miss Ida and Miss Foster laugh and fan Ras Norbert away, grabbing the hands of the wide-eyed children to haul them in different directions. "Is wah di backside him talking 'bout?"

"Come, children! Time to go! Me haffi cook dinner before di match start! Di Reggae Boyz g'wan delivah we go'al!"

"Who yuh telling! M'dear, is foolishness di ole man talking!"

"If go'al was really in we backyard, Nelson woulda find it by now. No treasure nor money can't miss dat wutless brute of a landlord."

Patsy is the last to walk away. The other women's cackles grow faint around her. All the elation she felt earlier is suddenly gone, replaced by sadness—a sadness she has always felt, but can never pin down. "Come," she says to Tru in a joyless voice, averting her eyes from Ras Norbert and his reprimands.

M AMA G'S PLANTS CROWD THE FRONT YARD ALL THE WAY UP to the veranda. The rented two-bedroom house they share is a low powder-blue box with a shingle roof, louvered windows with burglar bars, a veranda, and a TV antenna sticking out from the side. Most of the houses in Pennyfield look like that. The yards are separated by barbed-wire or zinc fences with holes bored through them, giving neighbors immediate access into each other's business: *Dat Peggy get a new man again. Hope she can keep dis one!* Or, on days before the end-of-the-month's paycheck when a dollar fails to stretch to the last penny, ingredients for cooking: *"Beg yuh a dash a salt, nuh Jerry? Beg yuh two ginger head, Miss Berta. Come sip dis soursop an' tell me if it taste right. It want more sugah, nuh true? Beg yuh likkle?"* Children spy on each other bathing outside, laughing and pointing at their peers with outie-navels or misshapen birthmarks in odd places. Rubbing soap from their eyes, the shamed children yell, *"Leave me alone! Wait till me tell yuh mother! Yuh not g'wan see di light ah day again if me evah catch yuh! G'weh!"*

But all the noise and chatter give way to sighs during quiet moments. Or sometimes, during turf wars, they give way to the sound of gunshots. From her bedroom at night Patsy hears them. But in a place like Pennyfield where these sounds are common, people are unafraid but never unprepared, sleeping with doors shut and bars on the windows. And, quiet as it's kept, they can be at ease because of Pope. Patsy knew Pope as Peter Permell, when they were schoolmates at Pennyfield Primary— the oldest of Miss Babsy's three sons, who grew up on Melrose Lane. Cicely dated Pope in secondary school. Patsy always thought he was bad news, though his mother gave Patsy food and invited her to their dinner table when Mama G stopped providing. He became Pope when he was deported from America. Presently, he presides like God Himself over Pennyfield, more powerful than any crooked policeman or politician. His younger brothers, Keith and Leroy, who now go by Bishop and Cardinal, are his right-hand men.

"One day ah g'wan buy you a big house," Patsy says to Tru, who is holding her hand. With her other hand Patsy opens the gate. From one of the plants comes a sweetish smell that reminds Patsy of something painful. She lifts the latch on the grille.

"Will it 'ave a upstairs?" Tru asks.

"Yes," Patsy says.

"Wid a balcony?"

"Definitely wid a balcony."

"An' a big yard where ah can play football an' practice to become good like di Reggae Boyz?"

Patsy pauses before she says, "Yes. Wid a big yard where yuh can play yuh football an' be our first woman football star."

"But where will it fit?"

"I'll build it on di hill. Like those." Patsy points, and Tru follows her finger toward Miss Ponchie's ackee tree, all the way to the highest branch, above which she can spy the big houses on the hill overlooking Kingston like grand castles. "Dat's where it'll fit," Patsy hears herself say in a near-whisper. "Dat's why I'm going to America. To mek t'ings bettah fah you. Fah all ah we." She wants to add, *Suh dat yuh neva have to rely on Pope fah anyt'ing*—but decides against it.

T HEY ENTER THE HOUSE, WHICH HAS NO SCENT OF COOKING OR cleaning like the rest of the houses, just a sickening smell of rosemary oil. The long pink curtains with red flower prints cover the louvered windows, which are closed. Patsy moves to let in some fresh air. Dust motes dance in the rays and settle on the Jesus figurines that crowd the whatnot and the old stereo box Mama G used to play Motown records on before she stopped listening to the "Devil's music." Patsy averts her eyes from the waxed faces of the Jesus figurines in the small living room. She came of age under those same frozen querying gazes, awkward with fear. Their quiet judgment seemed to sift down like the dust they collect, dulling the room, choking the life out of it and the whole house.

"Evening, Grandma!" Tru calls out as soon as she drops her book bag on the plastic-covered couch to find Mama G.

Exhausted, Patsy moves slow behind her, checking the mail—mostly bills piling up—on the dining table. She sifts through each of them like a stack of cards, whispering, "Dat can wait. Dat can wait. What is it dat me owe dis one again? Dem so t'ief!"

She drops the stack and shakes her head. It's only a matter of time before Mrs. Tyson will come knocking at the gate for the rent money. Patsy swears the old woman only leaves her house uptown in her chauffeured vehicle to assault them for rent money. She's one of the few landlords who refuses to give up her property to Pope. Most landlords have stopped coming into the area. They end up abandoning their properties altogether, fearful of retaliation of some sort, or extortion on other properties or businesses they own. Mrs. Tyson's father was one of the upper-class people who lived at the house when Pennyfield was a well-to-do place. He died in the late sixties and left Mrs. Tyson the house. Instead of selling it, Mrs. Tyson rented out one side to Mama G—who was then a young helper who was pregnant with Patsy—and left the other side of the house boarded up with her father's things still there covered in dust and cobwebs. Mrs. Tyson's body has since shrunken with years, her pale face set in a permanent scowl. She has a tendency to look around the yard, walk through the house with her cane, and peer inside cupboards and pots on the stove when she comes, her nose turned up.

"Dat woman is Satan," Mama G used to say when Patsy was a girl. And Patsy believed it. Mama G used to tell Patsy to tell the woman she was out—the only lie Mama G stuck to even after being saved. But there was a time when Patsy, barely eleven years old, disobeyed and let the woman inside the house. It was Mrs. Tyson who peeled off a twenty-dollar bill from a stash of rent money to give Patsy, discreetly pressing it into her open palm. *"Go buy yuhself groceries wid dis."* The woman's eyes had slid to the bare cupboards Mama G had forgotten to stock during one of her many fasting periods, which could last for days, sometimes weeks. It was a rare act of kindness displayed by Mrs. Tyson, who has yet to make repairs.

"Ah can't afford all dis right now," Patsy says aloud, her eyes eventually landing on the figurines. She wants to smash each and every one of them, then crush the splinters with her heels.

Just fifty years old, Mama G has long since renounced her life, waiting patiently for the Day of Judgment, too caught up with scriptures and collecting these damn figurines to concern herself with bills. *"Di Lawd will provide. Remembah di loaves of bread Him multiply?"* Mama G always says. But it's Patsy who has been providing, multiplying, and dividing—dwindling to a frayed thread. It's her punishment, she tells herself, for getting pregnant by a man who already had his own family. A fact Mama G has never let her live down. Patsy constantly repents those sins by working overtime to feed not only Tru but Mama G, whom Jesus has called to testify full-time and therefore makes no money for the house.

Mama G is now sitting on the small back porch that Uncle Curtis built before he left. He was really Patsy's stepfather, but Mama G said to call him Uncle. She didn't like the idea of Patsy calling him Papa, and Mr. Willoughby sounded too formal. Uncle Curtis was too much of a jealous man to put up with the idea of Mama G loving another man, even if the man in question was God Himself. Uncle Curtis continued to drink his rum and smoke his cigarettes despite Mama G's protests. He liked to sit in his armchair in the living room at nighttime, his big feet resting on a stool, and listen to old hits on the stereo. The music drew Patsy out of bed to his side. *"We use to dance to dis,"* he would say when he sensed her presence. His sad, drooping eyes would find Patsy's face hidden in the dim light. *"Remember, Gloria?"* The years between them evaporated like the veil of cigarette smoke when he looked at Patsy, curious about what had gone wrong, bewildered when the veil cleared and he still could not see her young face, but Mama G's.

Then one day he left, unable to take Mama G's newfound religion anymore. *"Me is a grown man! Nuh tell me what fi do! Me nuh tek talking to from no 'ooman!"* Mama G didn't flinch. *"G'long, then!"* she said. She helped him by putting out the rest of his things in the middle of the yard.

Without the drama of casting out sin, Patsy suspects that her mother wouldn't know what to do with herself. She is wholly animated by her contempt for the secular world. Here she is wearing her usual housedress, a bright orange tent that covers her full-fleshed legs, the languorous calves that used to make men stop and say, "*Howdie,*" before she uttered a single word, the liquid roundness of a body Patsy caught glimpses of as a girl under sheer nightgowns. It used to seem so sure of itself, that body, when it moved to wave for a bus, jump over a puddle, or reach for food inside the cupboard. Now it's covered, closed to the rituals and passion of love. The frail hope died in her eyes long ago, just before she folded up her youth and sealed the grip, a hole closing up beneath her. Without her Bible she's a broken thing, as empty as the dust-yellow rooms she once cleaned out in a fit, purging to fill with Jesus figurines. Patsy stays back in the dark kitchen and watches her mother pat Tru gently on the head.

"How was school?" Mama G asks, closing the Bible.

"Fine," Tru replies, looking up at her grandmother with those large eyes.

They seem almost perfect like that—grandmother and grandchild tenderly exchanging stories about their day. Mama G's laugh is as murmurous as water. A contrast from the shrill yet gravelly condemning cries capable of grating meat from coconut.

"Jus' fine? What did you learn?"

"How to add an' subtract!"

"Oh? So yuh can teach me."

Tru nods.

"Yuh know, yuh mother was really good in maths."

"Really?"

"Come first in har class. Teacha neva see a girl so good in maths suh. Dey say she did 'ave nuff potential."

"Potential?" Tru asks.

"Yes. Potential."

"What dat mean, Grandma?"

"Somebody who could be great."

Patsy looks down at her own hands in front of her, her fingers clasped in painful motionlessness, unable to hold on to the thing that slipped from their grasp, streaming in the sea of dark that embraces her.

Tru leans in closer to Mama G and whispers, "Mommy told me a secret."

"What kinda secret?"

"Dat she'll move us closer to God on di hill."

"How so?" Mama G's voice drops an octave with a hint of laughter.

"She got a visa!"

For a moment it appears Mama G doesn't understand. Her eyebrows hold questions too heavy for Tru to bear as she lifts her gaze above Tru's head and finds Patsy standing behind the mesh door.

"Go get yuh homework suh dat ah can help you," Patsy says quickly.

Her mother doesn't drop her gaze. Patsy unfolds her arms, lowering them to her sides as Tru runs into the house for her homework. "Walk!" Patsy calls after her. "I'll be there in a second."

Mama G takes the left leg she favors off the stool. Lately it has been bothering her, but she refuses to get it checked out. Another miracle left for Jesus to work. The glimpse of silver under her mother's black head-wrap eases the tension in Patsy's back, but only a little.

"Mama, ah want to talk to yuh 'bout somet'ing," Patsy says, though she wonders now if it would've been easier to just quit everything without saying a word. She wishes to skip what's coming and go to bed, to sleep deeper than when she took her first swig of rum from Uncle Curtis at ten; deeper than the pits of mangoes, steadier than a john-crow's flight, and more tranquil than the fresh bloom of hibiscuses outside. Until it's time to board that plane.

The spell, which comes and goes often, passes through like a heavy breeze, shifting things, slamming doors shut in its wake, then standing there in her periphery, watching and listening. It uses air from her lungs to breathe, to expand, to crowd the room; bulging into the hall, the two bedrooms of the house, onto the veranda, into the street, and flaunting its black in the face of the sun. The Devil's cold is as vicious as it is overbearing, and Patsy would sink under its weight, fade within its shadow, invisible.

She faces her mother in this moment to disclose the one private thing that has kept her happy and alive for years. "I'm going to live in America," she says.

Mama G puts down her Bible, her dark face stern. "Yuh was in labor for a long time delivering dat baby," Mama G says.

Patsy narrows her eyes. "What does dat have to do wid anyt'ing?"

Very slowly Mama G takes off her spectacles and rests them on her Bible.

"Dis one came out alive. Di Bible seh children are di heritage from di Lord. Di fruit of di womb. Yuh reward! Ah hope yuh not t'inking 'bout leaving di chile God bless yuh wid."

Patsy pauses to compose herself, to quell the rage that flows through her as if a faucet has turned on somewhere inside her brain. She knows she won't win a battle once Mama G brings up the Bible or God.

"Mama, I want more," she says.

"Look, Patricia, mi nuh come yah fi hear horse dead an' cow fat. What yuh saying?"

"I'm saying dat maybe—maybe if I go away, I can . . ." Patsy's voice trails as she loses courage.

"So, is me did lay dung an' spread me legs, don't?" Mama G asks, tilting her head, her teeth a sturdy cage. "Whose fault was it? Yuh evah hear di saying when coco ripe it mus' buss? What yuh t'ink woulda happen when yuh lay dung next to a tick, eh?"

"Mama, don't."

"Don't what?"

"I'm tired."

"Yuh listening to yuhself?" Mama G says, wincing as she lifts her weight out of the rocking chair. "How many woman yuh hear talk 'bout dem want more an' lef' dem pickney? Is we carry di belly fah nine months. Suppose I did leave yuh saying ah want more?"

Patsy laughs—a genuine one.

"What suh funny?'

"If it wasn't fah Uncle Curtis, ah woulda starve to death."

Mama G's face seems to fall as if all its muscles give. "Don't you dare bring up dat ole drunk." After a strained pause, Mama G speaks. "So, yuh jus' g'wan leave Tru wid me?"

"I know bettah than to leave har wid you," Patsy says.

"Then who you g'wan leave har wid? Dat wutless bwoy who t'ink because him own a gun him is somebody?"

"He's her father," Patsy says.

"Suh yuh can't ask him fah money, but yuh can ask him fi raise di chile? But yuh see me dying trial! Patricia, where's yuh head?"

Patsy hasn't mentioned any of this to Roy yet, and now she feels sick. She sits on the edge of the chipped blue wall that surrounds the back porch, the reality of her decision not to consult with him sooner descending like crows to feed on every bit of joy she had earlier. The scent of cooking is strong in the backyard, as if all the neighbors have swung open back doors to air out their kitchens. Patsy rests both hands in her lap. She allows all the other sounds to fill the space between her and her mother in their silence—barking dogs, and the distant cackling of neighbors getting ready to view the World Cup match at Pete's Bar or on their televisions. No such joy and noise happen at 5 Rose Lane.

"You jus' g'wan sit there like yuh jus' discover Jesus left di tomb?" Mama G asks.

"Jesus Christ, Mama! Done wid dat foolishness!"

"Don't you dare call di Lawd name in vain!"

"Does everyt'ing 'ave to be about yuh stupid God?" Patsy says, realizing too late that she said this out loud. Mama G's eyes widen like she has seen Satan's shadow slant across Patsy's face. Mama G's hands fly to her covered head and she begins to pray, mumbling something about forgiveness and the curse of her only child being possessed by the Devil. Something shifts inside the old house. Tru must be waiting impatiently. Mama G stops praying suddenly. "Him send you a angel in dat child," Mama G whispers. Her face tightens, the black so definite, so unequivocal, it astonishes and awes Patsy. A hard wetness veils her mother's eyes. "Tell me yuh wouldn't dare leave dat child," she says again. "Jus' like you would neva curse our living God an' expect Him to bless you."

"Mama . . ."

"In God's name!"

"Mama . . ."

Patsy is unable to discern whose voice she hears saying, *Mama*: Hers? Or Tru's? Suddenly the old smell returns. In this house with open Bibles and crucifixes in every room, and the Virgin Mary and Jesus figurines condemning her on the whatnot, old burdens replace the new one. Patsy, too nauseated by the smell of stale blood and rosemary, can no longer take it. She pushes pass her mother and hurries to the bathroom.

"Mama?" Tru calls after her.

Patsy slams the door in the girl's face and bends over the rusted toilet, where she sees her own face in the base of the bowl.

❦

SHE WAS FORBIDDEN TO HAVE AN ABORTION, THREATENED BY HER mother to be thrown in jail, since it is illegal in Jamaica and deemed an abomination by the Church. It was unheard-of for a woman to willingly end a pregnancy—even if it was her rapist's child that swelled her stomach; or even if, like Patsy, she was no more than a mistress unable to tell her lover of his child. More common were the women locked up in a ward in Bellevue Hospital on Winward Road because they went mad and buried newborns in plastic bags or mounds of sand. There were also the young girls, barely fourteen, with protruding guts that embarrassed their families, who ended up sending them off to the country to have babies; and the ones who secretly drank concoctions, convinced that salvation was as easy as a gulp. Those were the ones too whose babies came out with no limbs or overgrown heads, abandoned on the steps of churches, back doors, or group homes. The *good* ones remain with Miss Foster, who clothes and feeds them until the visitors, mostly men in cars with dark-tinted windows, come to get them. Patsy has seen the cars pull up to Miss Foster's yellow house plenty of times, then depart as quiet as night before dawn, rolling down the graveled path of Rose Lane, leaving Miss Foster with one less child and a fistful of cash she stuffs inside her brassiere.

Patsy's rage had soared unbounded, encompassing not only her powerlessness but the accumulated resentments she had for her mother—the pain of her mother's loyalty and affection for Jesus. Patsy had to be restrained once by the church sisters, who had come to pray for her. They clamped their hands on her shoulders and belly—hardened hands callused from washing clothes and scrubbing floors, hands used to comfort grief-stricken mothers and catch those who throw themselves about, eyes rolling, swept up in the Holy Spirit. Those were the hands preventing Patsy from harming herself. Her head was so foggy that she had forgotten that those women with their minted breath and church hats and starched dresses worn proudly on Sundays were the same women she was taught to respect and fear, the same elders who scowled at any expressions of youthfulness with stern faces, the same elders who spoke of the end of the world at the mere sight of a young girl wearing too little clothes or a young boy smoking loosies, the same women Mama G feared for their judgments.

Patsy had forgotten who they were when she wailed at them to go to Hell, her desire to fling herself down the steps outside the porch Uncle

Curtis built, before he left for good, swelling more than the child in her belly. But they were too strong, too determined. They wrestled Patsy to the mustard sofa inside the living room, held her down, and prayed. Mama G prayed too, devoid of real emotion, her eyes receded in their sockets, fixed on Jesus. When the baby was born, Patsy didn't try to kill it. It was too late. There were times when it cried and cried and she didn't stir, not even a twitch in her fingers or nipples. She sat there inside the stale light of the room, propped against pillows on her bed like a rag doll with thin, rotted thread aged by time, her gaze traveling the room, lingering on each Virgin Mary and Jesus figurine that Mama G had placed on the vanity as if they could help her.

One day when she was left alone with the baby—no church ladies darting in and out of the house with wet rags and a bucket to wash the sour milk from her breasts and wipe her down—the baby wailed. Patsy wouldn't, couldn't, move to stop it. Then, out of the blue, the crying ceased. Patsy remembers the relief she felt. It was like a waft of fresh air filling her lungs that had been flattened for months by the dark thing that weighed on her. But the relief was short-lived. The quiet became frightening. Panic set in, as if she had screeched toward an edge, unable to stop herself from toppling over. She had a sudden burst of energy that put movement in her legs toward the baby's crib. There, she caught a glimpse of the small dark face surrounded by a halo of thick black curls. It was not at all like the doll babies Patsy played with as a girl—the ones that Cicely reminded her of with her nice fair skin. Tru was quietly sucking her thumb, staring up at Patsy as Patsy experienced a small burst of regret. It was as though the child somehow knew, even before she had started to live, that she would have to soothe herself.

3

Roy sits back in the leather swivel chair at what Patsy believes to be his desk at the police station—the only place where Patsy agrees to meet him to discuss their daughter. He runs his hand over his recently cut hair—a modest, police-force-friendly fade with two equal parts on the left side of his head. A 1998 National Housing Trust calendar hangs on the bare beige wall marred only by the faded marks of nails and tape. Even if this were really Roy's office, it wouldn't have been shocking to find it bare. Roy is a man who believes in essentials. He would never spend a penny on frills or anything extra. He only owns three pairs of everything, in brown, navy blue, and black. *"Why would a man need more than dat?"* Several dates are circled on the calendar, the only personalized thing inside the office—maybe court dates, birthdays, days off duty. Patsy is relieved by the ambiguity of the office, by the fact that there are no pictures of his family pinned up on the walls like the other secretaries tend to have at her workplace, as if they need to be reminded why they work eight hours in a freezing office, subjecting themselves to paper cuts, leg cramps from too-small cubicles, and the condescension of the higher-ups.

From this angle where she peers at Roy, he seems to her like a boy adjusting the collar of a baggy uniform, his head raised as if to match the height of his ego. He looks the same as the day she met him at her secondary school fete: tall, dark, and good-looking in a boyish way. Patsy knew who he was—Roman Phillips Secondary's beloved track star. He was seventeen and she was fifteen. He was more put-together than the other boys, with his stone-washed jeans, dress shirt with colorful patches, and gold chain. He wore a fade, the top of his hair tall and squared like a pencil eraser. And when he approached her, he came

over smelling like lemons. With age—and a rigorous boot-camp rou-
tine, which he still adheres to before the break of dawn every morning
since his track-and-field days—his lanky body has transformed. What
remains of the boy Patsy once knew is the prominent dimple in his chin,
the full lips, and the pinpointedness of his light brown eyes capable of
bursting any doubts about him. He gave their daughter those eyes. It's
those eyes that look right through her now as she awaits his response.
Roy's pause is beginning to seem endless, as though he has forgotten
that she had said anything or that she's even there in his office. All night
Patsy agonized over telling Roy, aggravating the worn-down spring mattress with her tossing and turning.

"Yuh not g'wan mek me feel guilty about this," Patsy says in a hushed
voice. "Not again."

"Not again? Have I ever?"

"Yuh wasn't exactly happy when I told yuh I was pregnant."

"Yuh waited months to tell me."

"Dat's because I wasn't sure yuh could handle it. An' so far, yuh
haven't proven dat yuh can."

She knows that Roy's coworkers—especially Johnny, who looks like
a red rat, and his sleepy-eyed sidekick Raymond, who calls himself a
lieutenant—probably have their ears pressed against the door, listening.
Hardback clowns, who drive around areas like Pennyfield in their police
car to look at women or poke young boys with their rifles to see if they'd
wet their pants.

"Trudy-Ann need har mother," Roy finally says, clasping his hands
on his desk. "An' if dis is about finances, no one tell yuh to send har to
dat Catholic school."

"Dat school is di only way she g'wan learn. Yuh want har to fail?"

"I didn't say I want har to fail. What I'm saying is fah you to be
more practical an' send har to Pennyfield Primary like everyone else.
It's cheaper."

"Says di man who probably gambled on di Reggae Boyz last night!"

Patsy hisses. "Listen, Roy, ah don't normally ask yuh fah anyt'ing. I've been taking care of our dawta since birth. So, I need you to do dis one favor . . ."

"If you g'wan talk about gambling, then talk di truth, Birdie," Roy says, dismissing her last statement and calling Patsy by the pet name he gave her. "I don't get it." He leans forward, his eyebrows drawn together. "How yuh g'wan even afford to move all di way to America an' survive, much less provide?"

"A friend is helping me."

"Which friend is dat?"

"Cicely."

"Cicely?"

"Yes." She meets his gaze.

Roy's face creases into many lines. "Di same Cicely who—"

"Dis is about Tru," Patsy says, cutting him off.

Roy chortles, shaking his head and stroking his chin with his right hand, the long, nasty scar visible on the back of that hand. It glistens in the fluorescent light. Patsy looks away from it, and down at her hands in her lap.

"Why yuh don't jus' change dat to say you, Birdie?" Roy says. "Dis is about you. Not our daughter. Jus' say dat."

"Roy, don't turn dis into something else."

"I have three boys living undah my roof right now. Where is Trudy-Ann going to stay as har mother leave har fi go play house in America? Tell me!"

"Get outta my face wid dat, Roy. Have you ever tried to raise har?"

"A girl-pickney need har mother. How else she g'wan learn fi be a woman?"

"Don't you come to me wid dat foolishness. She need har father too."

"What about Mama G? Why yuh don't have dis conversation wid her? Why don't you leave Trudy-Ann wid yuh mother?"

Patsy retreats, her back hitting the chair hard like Roy has just shoved her with his suggestion. She blinks several times, her thoughts firing in rapid succession, from light to dark. She had counted on Roy. All the planning and paperwork she had done was with the expectation that Roy would step into his role as parent to their daughter. For Patsy knows that, as hard as he tries to portray himself to be, their disagreements on any matter come from the same place that once moved him to whisper, *"Birdie,"* in her ear.

His question remains suspended between them. Through that hazy distance, they glare at each other, two strangers over a life.

"I'd rather ask Pope to raise our dawta than Mama G," Patsy says, her chest aching after expelling those words with all the breath she could muster.

"Don't you dare bring up dat criminal when it comes to our dawta."

"Yuh give me no choice. All I'm asking for is yuh help. If yuh was half di man ah t'ink yuh was, I wouldn't have to beg like dis."

"You didn't care who I was," Roy says. "Ah shoulda left you alone fi roam di wild. Jus' admit it, Birdie. Yuh don't belong in a cage."

She knows that he despises her as much as he admires her for the easy way she gave herself to him the first time. More than anything else, she remembers, with embarrassment, the panic that coursed through her at the sight of his semen on her red sequined dress, not because this had never happened to her before, but because the dress belonged to Mama G—a dress she found in a pile of discarded clothes that Mama G had stopped wearing when she found Jesus. Roy dipped inside his back pocket like a gentleman and handed her a handkerchief. His voice was soft, like the wings of the moths bombarding the single light that shone from a pole behind the school. *"Yuh didn't have to do it."* How Patsy felt ashamed, wiping herself, her back turned to him. But she relaxed when she heard the smile in his voice—*"Ah neva expected anyt'ing, really. You're a sweet girl."* Like the scar on his right hand, it tugged at something inside her. And to think it all started by him whispering, *"Birdie, ah t'ink I'm in love,"* over the boom box. His words made her cheeks warm as though someone had taken two sun-baked stones and pressed them against the sides of her face.

Now, in his office, when Patsy lifts her head to look at Roy she sees a glint of affection lance his eyes—a burst of passion similar to the one that created Tru long after they had broken up as boyfriend and girlfriend, and long after Roy had moved on and started his own family. But just as quickly, his resentment shades all the tangled emotions. Patsy sees his eyes hardening and his face shutting like a slammed door. "Ah will talk to Marva to see if she'll be all right wid taking on yuh responsibility," he says.

Patsy gathers herself and all her regrets. *Her responsibility? What about his? And how could he let Marva determine whether or not he takes his own daughter?* Patsy shuffles out of the small, sterile office, managing a faint goodbye, afraid she might say something that could ruin her chances. But Roy stops her:

"Yuh know, Birdie. I'm not di one yuh g'wan have to answer to at di end a di day."

Patsy pauses by the door—where red-faced Johnny and droopy-eyed Lieutenant Raymond are probably listening. She doesn't dare to look back at him. She doesn't want to give him the gratification of seeing the pain rippling across her face. Without another word, she opens the door and closes it softly behind her.

P ATSY STANDS OUTSIDE WITH THE THIN STRAP OF HER PURSE slung over her shoulder. She stares at the marquees at Carib Cinema, which faces the police station. She considers taking a robot taxi from Cross Roads to work, but decides against it, since she is in no mood to be piled into an old, smelly Toyota Corolla with ten other people by a desperate taxi driver. She needs to clear her head anyway. She walks east, down the busy stretch of Slipe Road, past Tivoli Gully, toward Heroes Circle. The late afternoon sun squats above her head, exacerbating the smells, the heat, and the humidity. Deaf to the horns, Patsy slows midstride near the roundabout at Heroes Circle—a dry open field with nothing but stray mongrel dogs and roaming goats nuzzling brown grass and weeds that spring up near the monuments of the country's heroes. Big black flies maul the rotting carcass of a mongrel dog. The pedestrians on the sidewalk hold their collars or handkerchiefs to their noses to avoid the foul smell.

At work, she stares at the blank partition that separates her cubicle from Ramona's, unable to concentrate. She pulls out the envelope containing Cicely's latest letter and runs her fingers along the crease and each line. Cicely writes often, asking Patsy about her days working at the Ministry. Patsy writes back, telling her about her coworkers; her supervisor, Miss Clark; the case of the missing lunches from the office kitchen. No one ever catches the gluttonous thief. Patsy suspects that it's Aubrey, the skinniest woman in the office, who sounds like a mouse when she talks. Those are the ones to watch—the *sneaky* ones. The stories flow out of Patsy like an open tap. She laughs out loud as she writes—something that would've been pitiful had it not felt like she was talking to Cicely in person. Cicely replies eloquently, as if she takes her time to agonize over each sentence, thinking long and hard about each experience she thinks Patsy would find amusing. She shares entertaining anecdotes that make Patsy laugh even harder when she reads them at her cubicle or at the dining table under a dim lamp when Mama G and Tru are asleep. Like how the old white woman she once worked for insisted on calling her Eunice, though Cicely corrected her many times. Or how in her biology night class Cicely falls asleep to the drone of the old professor, who also puts himself to sleep. Patsy keeps each letter safely tucked inside the briefcase on top of her wardrobe with other things, like Tru's birth certificate and rent receipts. Cicely's letters always end with, "*There's so much here that I want to experience with you. I miss you so much. Yours, Cicely.*"

Patsy puts down the letter and surveys the manila budget folders piled on her desk, stacked precariously like Jenga blocks. All the budget records, which Patsy deals with since she's good with numbers, are hard copies despite the new Microsoft computers the supervisors have at their desks. Patsy should be the one with the computer, since she does all of Miss Clark's work for her. Miss Clark has been promising to send her to a computer course, but every time Patsy asks about it Miss Clark brushes her off: "*It's not in our budget.*" Perhaps the woman thinks Patsy is stupid enough to believe such a lie, when she's the one crunching the numbers for her. Mr. Crawford, who is head of the finance department and who is Miss Clark's boss, praises Miss Clark for her sharp mind and even gave her a raise (which Patsy noted in the newest budget proposal). Yet Patsy has the same salary she started with and is told the computer course is once again on hold.

As she folds Cicely's letter and puts it back inside her purse, she overhears Ramona cooing on the telephone at her cubicle. She has been on the phone for at least forty-five minutes. Miss Clark's door is closed. She has been out sick with the flu for the past couple days, and for that Patsy is grateful. "When can I come over?" Ramona whispers, thinking no one can hear her. Patsy doesn't have to look over her partition to know that Ramona has slipped off her pumps and is wiggling her stockinged toes as she sips Tetley tea from her bright red mug. Patsy wishes she could be as content and comfortable at her small cubicle. She wishes she could constantly decorate like Ramona, accepting that this is her place—a cubicle where she will spend most of her prime years working, appeased by employee-of-the-month stickers—until it's time to collect a pension. Patsy glances at the stack of folders on her desk, feeling like the walls of her cubicle are closing in on her. She gets up, grabs her purse, and leaves.

❦

A N HOUR LATER, SHE LIES ON THE BED, LISTENING TO THE SOFT sounds of Vincent's clothes dropping to the floor as he undresses.

He never has to hide his wedding ring with her. He's a local business-man who works at an insurance company downtown. They have passed through the stages of formality and seduction and come to a kind of easy intimacy, though Vincent is older than Patsy's mother. Vincent is sixty-three—thirty-five years older than Patsy—but in good shape, except for the loose skin around his once-sturdier muscles. What single mother in Kingston wouldn't jump at the opportunity to share an extremely generous man like Vincent? He was the one who gave Patsy all the seed money she needed to convince the American Embassy that she has assets to return to. It had surprised Patsy a little and saddened her a good deal when she found herself in his car, heading over the Causeway Bridge to a hotel on Backroad in Portmore.

It's habit that keeps her coming back. The sounds they make in bed whenever he takes her from behind—she on all fours, her loosened hair clumped inside his fist like he's riding a racehorse. Their sounds remind Patsy of worship—of the shouts of spirited men and women in church, caged within an angry maw of judgment, their shrill cries shafting the air, pleading for something, someone, to save them before it destroys them. For Patsy, sex is a reenactment of fantasy, a rebellion against the fear of impending doom that has shaped her. She cannot help but echo those cries, boisterous and uninhibited, bursting full as a hand mercifully reaches from the air, raw with the smell of sex, and relieves her.

When they're done, the heavy silence, which loomed earlier in Vin-cent's Lexus on their way over the bridge to the hotel, returns. Patsy gets up from the queen-size bed to relieve her bladder. She covers herself, mostly her belly because of the scar she's had since as long as she can remember. She touches it, coarse, dark, alive, her fingers on the slightly raised flesh shaped like a branch with no fruits. She has managed so far to make love to men, and before that, boys, making sure to keep light from hitting her belly, or keeping it covered. Most times she lets them take her from behind without an explanation. Though sex with boys was horrid, daunting, and a little demeaning, with no warmth, no closeness, no pleasure, she got used to it. It was attention she got, and not because of Cicely. Cicely, whom all the boys used Patsy to get to; Cicely, who never had to give herself for boys to like her more; Cicely, who stood up first when Roy approached: *"Birdie, can I have dis dance?"* Schoolboys were the worst, since they gossiped about Patsy's freakiness, waiting for her after school or church so she would prove what their friends had already told them. She welcomed the attention, and the associated label, since it was better, safer, than the truth.

When she returns from the bathroom, she sits on the edge of the bed and stares at the canary-yellow wall. Except for the one frame of a green banana leaf, the walls are bare, blank canvases intended for the murals of lovers' silhouettes mounted on them daily when the sky goes purple and the sun glows blood orange. The small hotel, which looks like a two-tiered wedding cake on the outskirts of Portmore—twenty minutes away from downtown Kingston—is called Lovers' Paradise for this very reason. Patsy grapples with whether or not to ask Vincent for help with Tru's school fee like she has done in the past, but today the words won't come. She knows Vincent watches her back—the horizontal lines from the sun's rays squinting through the louvered windows cutting her in parts. Half of a woman. In the faint shadow created on the wall, her shoulders rise with each breath she takes. She's careful not to breathe in too deeply, fearing sorrow might slip sideways beneath her rib cage.

"Care to say what's on your mind?" Vincent asks in that studied university diction of his. Sometimes he speaks that way, but then slips into patois unannounced as if he's two different souls. After graduating with a bachelor's in economics from the University of the West Indies, Vincent studied business at Harvard (the only American university Patsy has committed to memory) on a scholarship.

"Haaarvard," she repeated, imitating his nasal emphasis on the first syllable.

"*Did you like it?*" she asked him.

"*How yuh mean? Loved it!*" he replied.

"*What was it like?*"

"*What? You interested?*"

When she nodded shyly, he laughed so hard that he nearly choked on his own spit. His return to Jamaica was a triumphant one, since he became the poster boy for success—country boy turned business mogul. He laughs whenever he tells Patsy the story, with a glint of nostalgia and something sad veiling his eyes. Patsy met him long after the buzz, but at the height of his success with the insurance company. She spotted him four years ago in the bank. She liked how he stared. But unlike other big men, who only pick up young girls like her to impress them with nice things, Vincent has confessed that Patsy makes him feel less out of touch with the type of people he grew up with. When she asks him what *type of people* he's referring to, he reminds her that he used to eat tin mackerel for dinner, study under a kerosene lamp, and walk barefoot to school every day because he didn't own a pair of shoes. "*Yuh mek me remember di good ole days. When ah didn't take anyt'ing fah granted.*"

Though slightly offended, she held on to his admitted dependence. Replayed it in her mind every chance she got—the way Mama G meditates on her favorite Bible chapter, her crooked index finger caressing each word. She never asks Vincent about his two grown children or his uptown wife—a woman much lighter than him, she's sure, whom she imagines sits like a preening bird inside his big house on the hill. However, he has a tendency to ask her what she's thinking, as if her silence is something he fears.

"Ah got a visa yesterday," Patsy blurts out despite her intention to get dressed and leave. She sits still, glancing at their rumpled clothes on the carpeted floor.

"Congratulations," Vincent says softly. She feels him move closer to her on the bed, but doesn't respond as he kisses her right shoulder. "You've always wanted this." He nuzzles her neck. She tenses.

"How long did they give you?" Vincent asks, pausing.

"Six months."

"Yuh don't look too happy 'bout it." He turns her gently to face him.

He seems to be looking right through her now. She hears him cracking his toes beneath the sheet—a habit that makes her cringe, though she's not around him much to complain to him about it. She busies herself with covering her breasts with the sheet. "I plan to leave at di end of summer."

"And when yuh coming back?" Vincent watches her with a frown.

"I'll be leaving fah good."

"What?" He sits up so that there is enough distance between them.

Patsy is reminded how small and aged he looks without his sharp tailored business suits. "Couldn't dat create problems wid U.S. Immigration?" he asks. "And what about your daughter?"

He never calls Tru by her name, which makes Patsy believe that her life is an abstract portrait to him—evasive yet attractive from a distance. She takes in his face—the broad nose, the thick eyebrows peppered with gray like the coarse coils on his head, the contours of angular bone under deeply browned skin the color of coffee beans—and determines that even with his blackness, his well-molded status has created a void between him and the past he describes so fondly. A past which by now is a strange, unfeeling world that he continually seeks in the well between her thighs, but imposes himself somehow on its stilted image. How many nights has she lain in bed, staring at the hills, at the mansions looking like tea lights in a sea of black in the sky, thinking of him in his big house, sleeping next to his wife in his big bed?

"Vincent, ah didn't come here to t'ink 'bout dat," Patsy says, feeling cold all of a sudden even with no air-conditioning inside the room. At some point it stopped working. Patsy thinks there might be a power cut. JPS has a tendency to cut the electricity at odd times of the day.

"I come here to tek my mind off t'ings," Patsy continues, pulling on the sheet to cover more of herself.

"All right." Vincent holds up both hands. "Ah jus' want you to be careful. They turn down a lot of Jamaicans for visas because of dat. You know how many guys I can't send to training because the embassy won't even grant them a work visa? Also, can you imagine how many students are denied scholarships like what I got because half of them neva return back to the island?"

"Dat's not my problem," Patsy says.

Patsy is a little hurt that Vincent's main concern is potential problems she faces with U.S. Immigration. He doesn't beg her to reconsider because of how much he would miss her. Can't he see that she's doing this for better opportunities? That if she doesn't leave now she might end up like her mother—hopelessly clinging to a distant glimmer of salvation?

She should shower and leave. It's nearing the time for her to pick up her daughter from school anyway. God knows she's not looking forward to seeing Miss Gains again, but what can she do? In a matter of months, it will be fine. For the first time in her life, she feels somewhat hopeful—that all the loveliness and beauty of life is at arm's reach. Vincent pulls her close and rocks her back and forth. "I didn't mean it dat way. I'm very happy for you. Whatever you need me to do to help . . ."

He pulls the sheet off her and she doesn't protest. She tilts her head back, seduced by promise.

4

THE NIGHT PATSY TELLS TRU THAT SHE ISN'T TAKING HER WITH her to America, there's a power cut. Mama G went to a night service, leaving them alone. It's one week before Patsy's departure, which means she cannot delay telling Tru any longer. She holds her dream in a tight clasp at the dining table as the child peers at her in the dimness of the flame from the kerosene lamp. Patsy can vaguely make out the expression on her daughter's face. "It will only be for a few months," she says to Tru, unable to look straight at her.

"Why?" Tru asks. "Why yuh going without me?"

Patsy sighs. She quietly praises JPS in this moment. The darkness is helpful as she struggles to find the words behind the veil. What can a young woman on the brink of defeat say to the questioning face of her five-year-old daughter? Where is the honor in her daughter knowing she owns nothing? Not her dreams. Not her life. Not herself. What can she give her? What could her repression of desires, which she has resisted for so long, achieve other than resentment that could potentially destroy Tru?

But the words stall in the back of her throat.

The night is still. Not even the sounds of gunshots cracking in the distance can fill the silent void. A moth hits the lampshade and falls on the table. Patsy watches it wiggle its way across the wooden surface. Tru is quietly watching her, waiting for a response. Their day had begun simply, shopping for school supplies at Woolworth, picking out fruits and vegetables from the market downtown, Tru counting the change from the vendor. "*Good girl!*" Patsy said, caressing Tru's shoulder.

"I will send nice t'ings. You will have dat football yuh always wanted an' more," Patsy tells her, unable to disguise the hesitation in her voice. "Yuh like pretty t'ings too, don't? Girls like pretty t'ings. I'll send yuh so many pretty t'ings dat you won't know what to do wid dem."

Patsy's tears come when she sees the soft trust in her daughter's eyes dim. That lingering trust might have been the kerosene flame playing tricks on her. When she blinks again, it's completely gone. Tru starts to cry, her little body trembling. "Ah don't want pretty t'ings! You lied to me! Yuh tell me I could come!"

Patsy moves to comfort her, but Tru shoots up from the table and dashes inside their bedroom. Tonight, Patsy's desire turns to ash inside her. She lowers her head in her arms on the table and sobs.

❧

THE DAY IS WARM AND BEAUTIFUL AND ALIVE—THE KIND OF DAY Patsy has always imagined for boarding a plane to America. The kind of day when life opens up like all sensations are meant to be felt. Lived. It's a fantasy she has kept to herself beginning before her daughter was born. And now, on the last Saturday of August—an August that seems to have flown by—when Patsy is finally getting the chance to experience the fantasy, the weather seems to mock the sorrow around her. Tru is clinging to Patsy, and Mama G is busy prying the little girl's tiny hands off Patsy's skirt.

"Mommy, don't go!"

"Ah have to leave, baby. Or else me g'wan be late fah my flight."

Patsy gently nudges her daughter, who looks like a wilted flower compared to the floral pattern on her skirt. But the little girl is stronger than Patsy thought, her grief an incorrigible force.

"She soon come back!" Mama G says to the girl above the noise of the intercom calling for passengers. Patsy wonders if her mother really does believe that.

"But when?" Tru cries.

"Before yuh know it," Patsy replies. "Jus' be a good girl. Remembah what I told you good girls do?"

Tru nods. "Good girls keep dem self neat an' clean."

Patsy smiles. "An dey are obedient. Can you promise me dat? Be a good, obedient girl an' I promise I'll be back fah you."

And just like that Tru lets go of Patsy's skirt, the release as startling and unsettling as the whoosh of breeze outside the airport that picks up all the dust and dry leaves in a mini-tornado, forcing everyone to cover their eyes and mouths. The area of Patsy's skirt that was crushed in Tru's tiny fist is now wrinkled and stained with snot. Patsy doesn't mind this. She bends one last time before Tru, who is wearing a pink dress Patsy forced her to wear with a bow—*"Jus' fah me. Jus' dis once"*—and matching pink ribbons in her two pigtails. Her brown face is open, a mysterious hope gleaming from it—or it could be the thin layer of Vaseline Patsy rubbed on it this morning.

"I promise . . ." Patsy repeats. The wind starts up again and hair blows in Patsy's face. She cusses. "Lawd, look at me crosses! After me done fix me hair nice, di wind guh blow it out!" She pauses to brush the loose strands back in their places. Meanwhile, Tru watches, unmoved by her attempt to sound lighthearted. Patsy bends down again to hug Tru and kiss her on the forehead.

"Yuh father will take good care of you."

She uses her thumb to wipe the berry lipstick she wears—only for this occasion—off Tru's forehead, her own eyes blurred again with tears. The lipstick won't rub off properly. Since Tru is going to live with Roy, who eventually agreed to take her—saying that his woman always wanted a girl-child anyway—Patsy doesn't have to worry about Mama G dragging her daughter to every church service. She fishes a handkerchief out of her purse, wets it with her spit, and wipes the stain off Tru's face. "There. Now yuh look like *my* child." She says this with a nervous, tear-filled laugh, pinching Tru's cheeks before raising herself up. "I'll be back," Patsy says again, this time more to herself. "Ah promise."

Tru's face closes as though she has already figured out that promises are merely sweet lies.

Patsy quickly turns from her daughter and meets her mother's gaze. Mama G's mouth quivers as if she's not sure whether to smile or speak. "You is a grown 'ooman. By now yuh mus' know what is right from what is wrong. Can't say ah didn't—"

"Mama, please. Not now."

Mama G nods. "All right, all right. Me dun' preach. Jus' let di good

Lawd guide you on yuh journey," she says to Patsy. "Nuh forget who's in charge. An' nuh forget yuh family."

Patsy nods. "Yes, Mama."

They don't hug. It's not in Mama G's nature. Her way of showing love is pressing a small Bible into Patsy's palm. "Dis will carry yuh through." Patsy takes it without protest, though she knows that she'll never open it. She puts it inside her purse and picks up the one suitcase she packed. Her coworkers have told her there was no need to bring much luggage if she's going to a place where she can get better things. Her office at the Ministry had thrown a big going-away party, Ramona the mastermind behind it. People Patsy had never interacted with held her hand and squeezed it, saying, *"Don't forget we."* Miss Clark gave her the tightest hug, as though she had always regarded Patsy as her equal, and said, *"Now I'll have a place to stay when I visit New York!"*

It doesn't seem so bad now, watching Tru reach for Mama G's hand, the both of them standing there as though they've always stood this way, just the both of them, together. Because of the sun's rays, a bluish orange halo surrounds the two figures. Patsy blinks. It's hard to see her daughter's face behind the sheer golden curtain. She thinks to herself, a good mother would have snapped a photograph of a baby girl not quite six with a mouth fixed like her father's and eyes that seem to contain many moons that threaten to eclipse the sun. A good mother would have taken the time to use the very last second to inhale her daughter's scent of Blue Magic hair oil mixed with baby powder. But she's late to catch her flight. The farther Patsy gets, the more Tru fades. Until the little girl completely vanishes in the sunlight.

BOOK II

AMERIKAH

5

WHEN THE SLIDING DOOR OPENS ONTO THE STREET TO LET Patsy out of John F. Kennedy International Airport, her first sight is not of the tall buildings she saw when the plane was landing, but pigeons. A group of them are huddled by a lone baggage cart, picking at bread crumbs, the whites of their shit staining what Patsy imagines were once pristine sidewalks. They are not skittish and frightened, but bold, waddling like they belong among the people waiting in line for the yellow taxis driven by black and Indian men. The cataclysmic swirl of different languages spoken over car horns is jarring to Patsy, since she knows America to be mostly white and English-speaking— from the TV shows she watched back home, to the people working at the embassy, to the tourists on the island. She stands alone amid the chaos and joy of families reuniting with each other. She watches other Jamaicans who were on her flight greet their loved ones. *"Lawd, me glad fi see yuh!"* Standing by herself with her one suitcase, she feels more alone than she has ever felt.

"Taxi, oh?" asks a man with a thick African accent. There are two scars on each side of his dark face. Patsy shakes her head. All she has in her purse are two crisp American hundred-dollar bills. She hopes that will hold her until she finds a job. Cicely had told her to wait inside the airport, but Patsy has been waiting for two hours since her flight landed. In those two hours, Patsy has taken regular trips to the ladies' room, fixing this, adjusting that. Maybe Cicely is lost inside the airport, looking for her. Maybe she doesn't remember what Patsy looks like. Or maybe Patsy has forgotten what her best friend looks like and has passed by her several times. They occasionally have mailed pictures to each other, but they haven't done so in years. The one suitcase Patsy carries is packed mostly with goods for Cicely. Luckily the immigration officer didn't open her bag to see the cans of Horlicks, Milo, frozen beef patties from Tastees, banana chips, fried escoveitch fish, with lots of onions dipped in vinegar, ackee, frozen and wrapped carefully in newspaper and plastic to keep it insulated, Shirley biscuits, star apples (Cicely's favorite), and Appleton rum. Of course, Patsy didn't have to carry this much food, but since she'll be staying at Cicely's house, she thought it would be nice as a housewarming gift.

"Patsy?"

When Patsy hears her name, she turns. The woman standing behind her is dressed in a manner as close to Scarlett O'Hara as Patsy has ever seen anyone pull off in real life—in a black straw hat that covers one side of her face, a black-and-white polka-dot A-line dress that flares at the hips, red pumps, and a red handbag that she carries on her left forearm. She attracts the glances of women and men—young and old, black, white, and in between. When the woman takes off her dark shades, Patsy immediately recognizes those blue-green eyes. *Cicely!* She looks the same way she had looked in school, except her long hair is covered under her hat. Patsy throws herself into Cicely's arms. Seeing her friend again makes her think of their sun-washed days as girls in the schoolyard, sitting among tall green grass, their legs folded under them, giggling with secrets. Patsy presses her face into her friend's neck, overcome by the sheer joy and loveliness of their reunion.

"Ah miss yuh so much," Patsy whispers into Cicely's neck, her friend's perfume stuffing her nostrils and tickling the base of her throat like a sweet ache. Cicely pulls away from the embrace and holds Patsy at arm's length. Looking her up and down, she says, "Girl, yuh need a jacket! But I'm not dat familiar wid plus-size stores!"

Patsy doesn't wonder at her friend's put-down. She is quickly reminded that Cicely can be abrasive. But since Cicely is the only person who makes Patsy laugh, and the only one Patsy trusts with her secrets, Patsy has always forgiven this flaw. Patsy follows Cicely to a shiny black car and nearly stops in her tracks when she sees a man sitting in the driver's seat as if he came with it. Patsy assumes he's the play-husband Cicely mentioned, who still buys her things—the Yankee who made Cicely's life as easy as the sliding doors Patsy had just walked through. The man doesn't get out of the car to help with the suitcase. Patsy and Cicely lift the luggage inside the trunk.

"What is inside dis t'ing?" Cicely asks, noticing Patsy noticing the man as a solid figure in the driver's seat. She adjusts the suitcase next to a wrench and a toolbox.

"Goodies for you," Patsy replies. "Ah carry bulla, Shirley biscuit, Tastee patties, cocoa bread. Remember how yuh did love cocoa bread—"

Cicely stops her. "Ah watching my weight. All dat food good fi ah army. In America thin is in."

Patsy hides her disappointment as Cicely holds the car door open so that Patsy can sit in the tan backseat that smells like new leather. The man appears to be cut from one of the Sears catalogues that Patsy used to browse at the seamstress's—with a neatly trimmed mustache, smooth brown skin, and hair with a waxy gleam to it, like shoe polish. He's older than Cicely. Maybe in his late thirties, early forties. Nothing play-play about him. He barely smiles when Patsy enters the car, his green eyes (something Patsy has never seen on a black man that shade) look right through her.

"You must be Marcus!" she says to break the ice. "Nice to finally meet you."

"Same," he says, barely glancing at her in the rearview mirror. He pulls away from the curb and cuts into a lane, inciting a chorus of screeching wheels and beeping horns. He simply holds up his middle finger, pushes hard on his horn, and keeps driving. "Damn immigrants don't know how to drive." He puts his right arm possessively around Cicely's seat as he maneuvers the steering wheel with one hand. Cicely does all the talking.

"How does it feel to finally be in America? How was your flight? Did they give you something to eat? We really need to go shopping for a fall jacket. It's unusually cool this year for the last week of August!"

Patsy cautiously observes the driver, who snatches his gaze away when their eyes meet in the rearview mirror. Cicely talks and talks, her chatter oddly turning Patsy off. So many words coming at her at once. She has no time to process her own thoughts, miss her daughter, or peacefully observe the loops and bridges on the highway, and green exit signs with names of neighborhoods that Patsy wishes to explore on her own someday. But more upsetting to Patsy is the strangeness of her friend's accent. How Cicely curls her tongue when she speaks. Like an American. An accent Patsy never picked up over the telephone or the moments before they entered the car. Cicely grins a lot too, sneaking sideway glances at her husband, wholly animated by his silence. It's as though he's keeping tabs of her performance to reward or critique her later.

"So, how was your flight?" she asks Patsy again with that strange accent. Its peculiar quality puts a salty taste in Patsy's mouth like stale saltine crackers, forcing Patsy to sieve her words—to placate Cicely's new American optimism with a filtered, surface response. "It was all right."

Patsy feels as though she's answering to a stranger and not her best friend of how many years. What she really wants to say is, *Ah couldn't really tell yuh since ah sleep di whole way.* The last thing she saw was the wet blue eye of the ocean as the plane took off. She stared at it until she couldn't see anymore. Now she trains her eyes on the dove-gray sky, where the sun is only a white, distant circle. She begins to miss home. She wonders if she's made the right decision leaving Tru. The car stops at an intersection, the *tick-tick* sound of the turn signal synchronizing with Patsy's heartbeat. It takes over, the impulse to run the other way nulled by the vehicle's steady progress in the opposite direction through a dark tunnel of uncertainty.

THE CAR TURNS ONTO A TREE-LINED STREET FACING A PARK.
"We're here!" Cicely announces, glad to have broken the silence in the car.

"This is where you live?" Patsy asks, beholding the handsome red-brown houses joined at the sides. They are about three stories tall, each with wide stoops decorated with elaborate black banisters perfectly lined in rows all the way down the street. The designs and gargoyle-looking things on the green roofs remind Patsy of mansions in vampire movies set in another century. Mama G would've undoubtedly linked them to the Devil. *"Yuh see. Di Devil deh everywhere. Is suh Satan army strong!"* A flight of black birds swirls from the rooftops like confetti onto the street. Marcus parks the car. When he gets out, he jingles the key to the house, still mute. The threads of resentment creeping toward Patsy from him are partially blocked by Cicely's quick move to help Patsy maneuver the suitcase from the trunk.

"Watch your step," he instructs them, leaping, on the way to his gate, over dog shit and what looks like a discarded needle. "Damn low-class black people won't curb their dogs or their habits!" he mutters.

"Marcus workin' hard to maintain di place. Him renovate it jus' last year," Cicely says in a whisper, sounding like herself as she lifts Patsy's suitcase out of the trunk. Marcus waits at the gate and takes the suitcase from his wife when she approaches him. The three of them hobble up the steps together. Patsy looks around and sees Caribbean flags in people's front windows, in front yards, and hoisted on the antennas of parked cars. One window has JUSTICE FOR ABNER LOUIMA taped across it.

"What's wid all di flags?" Patsy asks.

"The West Indian Labor Day parade is coming up next week. People like to show where dey come from."

"There's actually a parade like dat?"

"Of course! It 'appen every year."

Patsy is surprised that Caribbean people have their own parade and their own neighborhood in New York—a place she has always deemed *high-falutin'*, with its fashion and Central Park and Times Square. She first noticed this when they were driving—the Jamaican restaurants with their flags drawn on the awnings; the black and brown people with slow gestures and lingering gazes that indicated to Patsy that, like her, they had not long ago come from "home." If they have been here for a while, it surely doesn't look like it. Save for the paved roads and wide sidewalks and brown brick buildings, this could've been Half-Way Tree or downtown Kingston populated by dark, broad faces that are hard to read. Patsy doesn't remember seeing a neighborhood like this one in *Breakfast at Tiffany's*. "Weh di white people?" Patsy asks.

"You'll see dem from time to time," Cicely replies in patois when Marcus turns his back. "Yuh have to go to Manhattan. Dey tend to stay far from places like Crown Heights."

"That will soon change," Marcus says. It's the first time Marcus speaks to Patsy directly. She didn't even know he was listening to them. "Mark my word. In the new millennium, Crown Heights and Brooklyn as a whole will be the place people will want to invest."

Cicely doesn't say anything. She appears to grimace, but Patsy can't tell anymore. Her friend has changed too much for her to assume she can still discern her thoughts. Once inside, Patsy is greeted by the high ceiling and spacious foyer that leads to a living room with a fireplace, just like in the movies. She is almost afraid to step inside, feeling intrusive and out of place all of a sudden. Marcus excuses himself and disappears into one of the rooms. The place looks like a display—each piece of furniture arranged just so, as though no one has ever sat on them or touched them. The shiny wooden floors seem to mock her brand-new flats, which are shabby in comparison. The glistening chandelier above her head cuts her into pieces on the inside. Her friend has made it in America after all, and she's dragging Patsy through her castle, showing her just how far she has come from the girl who had nothing. So many pictures are displayed, but none of them showing Cicely's years in Pennyfield. All the pictures on the mantel above the fireplace are of Cicely, Marcus, and—"Who is di likkle boy?" Patsy asks.

"Our son, Shamar," Cicely says in the nonchalant manner of someone simply telling the time.

"Oh," Patsy says, the glistening shards cutting her deeper. She's stuck on *our*—a rock-hard word flung between her eyes. She blinks rapidly to quell the subtle headache from all the questions. "Where is he now?" Patsy asks, peering at the skinny boy in the pictures with lots of hair.

"Shamar is at violin lessons at the Brooklyn Academy of Music." Cicely says this as if Patsy is supposed to know the place. "I'll pick him up before dinner. Can't wait for you to meet him!"

Patsy follows Cicely down a long hallway with giant paintings on the walls, her heart dragging at her feet. In one of the rooms Patsy passes, this one filled with books, she spies Marcus on the telephone. Just the silhouette of his broad back as he faces the tree-lined street with the telephone in the crook of his neck. "Yes, yes, Max, I'm writing that down. One-thirty-two St. Johns Place. Got it! The building on Dean and Bedford would be a nice sell too. What you mean, the neighborhood is not there yet?"

"These buildings were built in the 1800s. So they're old," Cicely says to Patsy, getting her attention again, her voice lowered. "Marcus uses the word *historical* with his clients when he shows them the block. He says the day is coming when these brownstones will go on the market for millions of dollars. He's offering homeowners money to sell."

"An' what will happen to di people in dem?" Patsy asks, thinking about the dark faces peering at her with her suitcase outside, their Bajan, Haitian, Trinidadian, Saint Lucian flags waving at her in their front yards like peace treaties.

"Marcus plans to buy them out."

Her voice drops even lower when she uses Marcus's name, as if it is sacred and shouldn't be uttered out loud. Cicely takes careful steps down the stairs to show Patsy the spacious basement, which is set up like a living quarters, where she will sleep on a twin-size bed. She lowers her voice even more to explain to Patsy that Marcus hates to be disturbed.

"But yuh know I'm not here to bother nobody," Patsy says, offended that her friend is telling her not to be seen or heard. That it would be best that she not come up the stairs into the house, but use the door leading to the side of the house like a helper. "Only when him is here," Cicely says. "When him not here yuh can do as yuh like. I will let yuh know."

Disappointment drops like a weight inside Patsy. She would've rather seen her friend with that criminal fool Pope than this man. This is the man whom Cicely gives her whole self to, becoming someone else—a person Patsy knows with absolute certainty that she wouldn't have been friends with. And even if she befriends this person, she would have to accept that her best friend has changed. Jealousy looms large in her and makes Patsy turn from Cicely. To the bare, grayish walls inside the basement—where there's a washer and a dryer—Patsy says aloud, "I see yuh came a far way from Mabley." She hopes there's enough sarcasm in her voice to bring Cicely to.

Cicely's bangles stop jingling with the flash of her hands. "I have," she says in a near-whisper. "I have," she says again, louder.

When Patsy turns to look at her, Cicely is standing upright, the broad hat still covering one side of her face, her height elevated with the bright red pumps. Patsy remembers when they were girls, staring at each other face-to-face like this. They used to try on clothes they'd never buy at a fancy-looking boutique downtown, pretending to be grown women. They traipsed on tiptoes like they were wearing heels, the dresses draped around their pubescent bodies. They had the store to themselves, because the store owner—one of those Lebanese men who owned businesses on the island—took one look at Cicely and her fair skin and said she could be a model. His. He put the SOON RETURN sign on the door and told her she could try on whatever she wanted. He delighted in adjusting fabric around Cicely's narrow shoulders, smiling ever so gently, lasciviously, at the sight of a nipple or two. Patsy felt envious of the attention he gave Cicely, the suggestive remarks about her beauty, the way he stroked her like a pet when she sat on his lap. And Cicely was always calm, as sweet as a purring cat, as though she knew what it would get her.

"Yuh don't have to keep up di act wid me," Patsy says to her friend now, peering into the one eye she can see under Cicely's hat.

"Pardon?"

"Dat's what ah talking 'bout. Is not how yuh talk."

Cicely appears to be taken aback—eyebrow up, lips pushed out, nostrils slightly flared. Another learned expression, successfully executed by her friend who had always wanted to pull off this look—that same impenetrable expression she developed after her mother's passing.

"How yuh doing, Cicely?" Patsy asks.

"Can't you see?"

"I see yuh living large. I save all di letters yuh send, an' di pictures. But yuh haven't said anyt'ing 'bout yuh son, an' yuh husband . . ."

Cicely pauses as if trying to decide whether or not to divulge information to a complete stranger. She lifts her eyes to meet Patsy's. Perhaps. Perhaps not. But Patsy's frown convicts her. She visibly swallows. "I jus' didn't want to get into all dat."

"'All dat' is yuh life, Cicely."

Patsy retraces those letters in her mind—the ones she read over and over again. She doesn't recall a mention, not even a slip, about a child. The letters dwindled after the first two years, but Patsy assumed her friend was just busy with night school. Cicely really wanted to be a nurse. And when Patsy got pregnant with Tru, Cicely sprang to action and sent new clothes, books, diapers—things Patsy didn't even ask for, but needed—never once offering up the fact that she was going through the same thing. Shamar looks a few years older than Tru, from the most recent picture Cicely has of him. So surely Cicely could have mentioned her pregnancy, giving birth, becoming a mother. Did she too flinch at the first bite of the baby's teeth on her nipples and need Vaseline? Fuss over changing diapers and forget the baby wipes? Catch puke with the hem of a new blouse because she couldn't find a bib? Or how about the nontangible things? Had her limbs felt like they were tied to a chair or the bed, completely numb as if in a dream far from any she ever had for herself? Did she ever feel like the baby was pulling from her a thread of light until he took it all and left her with only the dark? To think Cicely kept this secret for so long . . . it makes Patsy wonder what else she has hidden from her.

"You could have told me," Patsy says.

"Patsy, I tried . . ."

"I don't understand. To have a whole child an' not say anything?"

"I—I jus' wasn't ready. I was afraid you'd ask too many questions."

"An' what was wrong wid di truth?"

Cicely shrugs. "Ah told you ah only married Marcus fah papers. Dat he was my play-husband. Di mention of a baby would've confused t'ings. Ah was supposed to be finishing night school. Ah was supposed to be going to nursing school right after. Everyt'ing ah said in those letters was what ah was *supposed* to do . . . what ah wanted to do. It sounded so nice to write dem down."

"So yuh lied to me about dat, too?"

"No. Ah jus' couldn't bring myself to mention how t'ings change."

"Is not like t'ings change fah di worse, Cicely."

"Ah was afraid to disappoint you."

"I'm not yuh pastor nor yuh mother."

"I know. But ah still value yuh opinion."

"Take off yuh hat. Ah want to see you."

Cicely obeys. Patsy is disarmed when Cicely takes off her hat, revealing long, fine hair, dyed yellow and flattened on her head. "Marcus talked me into it," she says with a sweet, ticklish baby-girl laugh that reminds Patsy of when they used to stick chicken feathers in each other's ears—an act that sent peculiar sensations between Patsy's legs. She wondered if Cicely felt it too, but never asked, deciding to keep this to herself. Long after they matured and before Patsy discovered masturbation, time stood still as Patsy spun the feathers inside her ears alone, the pleasure curling her toes.

"I'm not too sure 'bout it yet," Cicely is saying, touching her hair again and frowning at the split ends.

"If you don't like it, then dye it back," Patsy says.

"What yuh t'ink?" Cicely asks, peering into Patsy's eyes with her eyebrows arched.

"It doesn't mattah now what ah t'ink, Cicely," Patsy says.

"Don't be like dat."

"How else do you expect me to be?"

"You wouldn't have understood."

"You didn't give me a chance."

"Ah wasn't going to stay . . ." Her voice trails and her face darkens. "But Shamar came soon aftah."

"So, do you love him?" Patsy asks. The question sounds insubstantial in the fragile light and silence. Cicely takes a while to answer. Slowly she lifts her head, and when her eyes meet Patsy's they have inside them something abstract. Patsy breaks away from her gaze, too tired to figure it out, wishing to take the question back. Her next words rush out with her exhaled breath. "Is your hair," Patsy finally says. "Do what yuh want wid it."

If the primary school teachers could see Cicely now, they would delight in their accurate prediction of her fate. Her friend is a prized possession, after all. With a tinge of resentment, Patsy watches Cicely shag her bleached hair with her free hand. Everything else is the same—the face Patsy knows better than she knows her own—Cicely's thin nose that juts like the small outie navel of a toddler; those eyes that seem to pull you into view with interest, make you desperately want to see yourself in their lens. Maybe because they shine like blue-green marbles in sunlight, rendering one beautiful in their gaze. And finally, the scar on her forehead, just above her left eyebrow, which Patsy can still see, despite Cicely's efforts to conceal it with makeup. It forces Patsy to look away. For it reminds her of bloodstained shards of broken glass—hundreds of them that reflected bits and pieces of their girlhood that crashed down with the mirror that fell on them in the old, burned-down house on Jackson Lane.

Cicely steps closer and examines the tiger's-eye pendant around Patsy's neck in her palm. "You still wear it," she says, smiling. Her beauty, which had once stunned Patsy, is now made average with meticulously applied makeup that gives her gorgeous golden skin an ashen look. "Yuh don't need makeup," Patsy replies, her voice betraying the hurt she feels. "Did he ever tell you dat?"

Cicely lets the pendant slip from her hand. "Yuh want some tea or hot cocoa?" she asks without looking at Patsy. She begins to fuss around the kitchenette, opening and closing the cupboards, fumbling with the faucet, banging the cups, and upsetting the utensils in the drawer.

"Tea is fine," Patsy says over the noise. Cicely lifts up a shiny red kettle, fills it with water from the faucet, and puts it on a hot plate by the kitchenette area where there's also a miniature refrigerator and microwave. Patsy looks around the place. Everything is small. Or maybe she just feels too big and obtrusive inside this house.

"I bought groceries," Cicely says. She points to the beige cupboards above their heads. "Dat way yuh don't have to climb up an' down those stairs to the kitchen fah anyt'ing."

"You didn't have to," Patsy says, pricked by Cicely's efforts to keep her locked away in the basement.

Cicely carefully sets two empty cups down on the counter with her back still turned, as if she has read Patsy's thoughts and feels bad about the whole thing. "I miss you too," she says. She seems to be talking to herself at first. "Ah jus' had to run away from it all. Reinvent myself. Yuh know." She folds her arms across her chest and begins to look around all of a sudden as if she's lost inside her own basement.

"I know," Patsy says, regarding the side view of Cicely's face.

"How is di wicked witch Zelma?" Cicely asks.

"Dat auntie of yours nuh easy. Saw her a few times at di grocery store. She still don't talk to nobody blacker than she."

"I'm not surprised. She woulda love me if ah wasn't Mabley's child. She hated me so much dat she used to mek me kneel dung 'pon gravel in di hot sun, calling me a Jezebel an' saying ah was jus' like my mother— har own sister! Ah t'ink she still grudged Mabley for her beauty. Dat woman swore my mother's ways rubbed off on me an' punished me every day for it."

"I remembah," Patsy says, recalling those days when she had to rub *sinkle bible* over Cicely's sunburnt skin. She used a knife to access the gel from the plant. Slowly, she rubbed it between her hands and then, carefully, all over Cicely's back and shoulders. They were in the seventh grade when Cicely first slipped from her faded housedress, stepping boldly into a puddle of sunlight that strained through Miss Zelma's lace curtains to show Patsy her badly burned skin. Patsy remembered the shy yet curious way she regarded her friend's body, seeing for the first time the gentle shadow Cicely's breasts cast on her stomach that had no scar, the beads of perspiration that settled in the dip of her clavicles and navel, the raw cuts on her knees from kneeling on gravel in the sun. She felt the compelling urge then to heal and protect Cicely as she massaged her with the bitter balm.

"When you disappeared, ah thought she did poison you." Patsy chuckles.

Cicely chuckles too. "Me woulda kill har before she kill me. God know."

"How yuh g'wan mention God an' murder in di same sentence?"

"Chile, please." Cicely sucks her teeth. "Remember ole man Basil used to say di two important t'ings him carry wid him is him Bible an' him pocketknife?"

"Lawd, yes!" Patsy guffaws. "An' remembah him wife, Bertha, an' how she pop dung from all di beating him give har wid di same Bible in him hand? Father Jesus, I couldn't figure out how a likkle piyah-piyah man, dat look like breeze could blow him down, could beat a woman suh big."

Cicely half smiles. "Sometimes people have dem ways 'bout dem."

There's a disquieting silence after her statement; an unspoken confession, which pierces Patsy. Cicely's hands lift—as if in attempt to explain, to gesture, to declare what has not been declared. Or has it? Ultimately, she folds her arms across her chest, her right arm resting in the crook of the left, as if to hug herself.

The kettle starts to whistle, and Cicely wheels around as if relieved to take it off the hot plate. She grabs a box of peppermint tea bags. Patsy watches her friend's back. It forms a wall that separates the past from the present, a wall that closes protectively around her, though it looks vulnerable, narrow. Patsy drops her gaze. "I'm glad we're together again. Like old times," she says.

The sound of the spoon tinkering against the enamel cup dies down in the kitchenette area. Before Cicely can respond, Marcus's voice booms from upstairs.

"*Cicely!*"

Cicely jumps.

She hurries over to the table and puts a mug in front of Patsy, flustered. "Oh, Lawd, look how me down here running me mouth an' forget is time to get Shamar!"

Patsy stands. She watches her friend pick up her hat off the bed, and follows her to the foot of the stairs. Cicely stops suddenly, as if she has forgotten something. She turns to embrace Patsy, their reflection fitting together in the frame of a mirror by the small vanity—a mirror that seems to replace the one shattered many years ago that day on Jackson Lane. Patsy holds on to her, determined not to let go this time. But Marcus's bark frightens them both and forces them apart. "*Cicely!*"

"I have to go," Cicely says to Patsy. She touches Patsy's face—an intimacy Patsy has long missed. Cicely turns and runs up the steps with her high heels, "*Coming, honey!*" She closes the door behind her, blocking out all sounds from upstairs, where Patsy can only hear the *BOOF-BOOF* sounds of their footsteps—their world that excludes her.

6

TRU HAS NEVER SEEN THE TINY SUITCASE STORED ON TOP OF THE wardrobe put to use. She watches Mama G pack her things, folding them gently, the way her mother had laid out her good pink dress on the bed before she left—a dress Tru wouldn't have imagined wearing again had it not been for her mother coaxing her earlier. Her feet are imprisoned in shoes that squeeze her toes, and her hands are numb, squished underneath her legs. She aims to be on her best behavior, which means sitting still even if she might go blind from the pain in her toes. Mama G doesn't say much. She hums her church song from the base of her throat. She pauses, calm, almost pensive, folding Tru's clothes: framed by the light blue walls, her reflection held in the tall mirror. The sunlight leaves the room, taking the glint from the top of the mirror, dulling the pink in Tru's dress and Mama G's skirt. Tru puts her hands in her lap and crosses her legs at the ankles. By being good, she might be able to convince her grandmother that she won't be much trouble at all. Her back aches with tension, since she has been sitting upright on the stool for a good while, hoping to be acknowledged. To be told by Mama G that she has changed her mind. That she's a good girl after all and therefore doesn't have to leave to live with her father.

Maybe she's being punished for something. How many times has she stolen gizzadas and coconut drops fresh from the oven; stuck her fingers inside the brown sugar jar to eat it from her palms; severed the tails of lizards in the backyard to see them wiggle in the dirt; picked mangoes off Miss Grant's tree—the ones that hang over the zinc fence at the side of the house; thrown stones at Sore-Foot Marlon, the snotty-nosed boy with sores all over his arms and legs? Or how could she forget that time when she tried to pee up a tree trunk like the boys? How she got angry at God that day for missing the thing Albino Ricky pulled out of his pants to show her. How Ricky laughed at her for not having one.

"All right, dat's everyt'ing," Mama G finally says. She looks around the room, her dark eyes scanning everything except Tru. Tru has the same feeling she gets when she's on a roller coaster or a Ferris wheel just before it lowers from the top. Why is her grandmother no longer looking at her? "Yuh father will be here soon," Mama G says, as if to herself. Usually, when Mama G talks to herself, she's muttering to God. She keeps a picture of Him everywhere, even under her bed next to her chimmey. *"In case me mek a mistake an' draw fi di Devil."* From then on Tru started to believe that the Devil hides under the bed. So, instead of crouching to pull out the chimmey at nights when she wants to pee, she wets the bed, often annoying her mother who she shares the bed with. But who will she sleep with now that her mother is gone?

"Can I stay with you, Grandma?" Tru asks. "Ah promise ah won't wet di bed."

Mama G appears pained by something Tru cannot see. As if somewhere in the shadow of the room there might be the Devil waiting with a bow and an arrow to pierce her heart. "No."

"What did I do wrong?" Fresh tears spring up from Tru's eyes. Mama G pauses, holding the suitcase at her side. A purple scarf is tied around her head. The housedress she wears hangs off her body, since she's mostly bones from all the fasting she does. She meets Tru's gaze for the first time since they returned from the airport. "Nothing, child. You're not di one in di wrong."

"So why did Mama leave me? Why yuh sending me away?"

Mama G walks over to Tru with the pained look still on her face.

"Di money dat yuh mother g'wan mek in America will buy you more than grains a salt from those tears, yuh hear?" she says, anger starting to churn in her voice. "Undah-stand from now dat she only doing what's best for you. Money is di root of all evil, yes. But sometimes it mek t'ings easier. An' you see how yuh feeling right now? Is di same way Jesus feel every time we forget 'bout Him. So, jus' continue to be a child of God, yuh hear?"

When Tru nods, Mama G continues, "Yuh father will take good care of you."

"But why ah have to go? Why ah can't stay wid you?" Tru asks.

"Di Bible seh to honor thy mother an' thy father. Is di only way to Heaven. Now come here. Let me wipe dem tears from yuh face."

Tru closes her eyes as her grandmother wipes her face with a handkerchief and forces her to blow her nose. Just then they hear the crunching of wheels on gravel outside and then a car horn. Tru begins to climb down from the stool, but Mama G stops her. "You stay put. A real man should get outta him car, open di gate, an' say him greetings." Under her breath, Mama G utters, "Dat bwoy don't have no manners, but him g'wan learn it wid me."

Tru sits there under duress, listening quietly to her father (she's unsure what to call him to his face—*dat bwoy? wutless brute? Mr. Policeman?*—words her grandmother uses to describe him) blow his car horn, startling the sleeping dogs along the lane. They bark at the noise. Through the curtains with yellow flowers, Tru can see the tall, dark man, whom she has only seen three or four times before, getting out his car and slamming the door. Ras Norbert, who happens to be passing by with his brooms, chanting, *"Believe me! Believe me not!"* is suddenly still at the sight of the man. Tru observes the curious, tight way Ras Norbert holds his shoulders and neck. His mouth curves into an upside-down U as he stares at the police uniform—a striped blue shirt with three gold V-shaped patterns on the sleeves and a long pair of navy-blue pants with a broad red stripe down the sides of the legs. His face is still a mystery to Tru, hidden under the rim of the black peaked cap he wears. Something about his stiff demeanor strikes fear in Tru. The men outside, whom she knows as Johnson, Errol, Desmond, and Bo, pause their loodie-board game in front of Miss Maxine's gate, where they wait for her cooked food, to stare at the man with the same glares given to fowl thieves or visitors with cars they lock carefully before getting out. The man doesn't bother to say hello to the four men or to Miss Maxine, who comes out of her house with a dripping spoon to stare as well, her mouth a fixed O. The man's manner and police uniform seem to crowd Rose Lane, barging into living rooms where curtains are drawn, eyes perhaps wide behind turned-up windows; and into yards, scattering fowl and overturning buckets of water. Even the sun gives way, pushed behind the thunderclouds. He brings something dark across the faces of Tru's neighbors as if his presence has insulted them. The only one to say anything out loud is Ras Norbert. He lifts his hand and points a long, crooked finger at the policeman. "Babylon! Fyah bun Babylon!"

But Ras Norbert's outburst doesn't faze the man one bit. He walks like he's marching—left, right, left, right. Soon Tru hears banging on the veranda grille with what sounds like metal. Could it be his gun? She looks up at her grandmother, who seems unmoved by the noise, her jawbones clenched. When Mama G speaks, her words are measured. "Let's go. We let him wait long enough."

As soon as *dat bwoy* sees them appear on the veranda he stops knocking. His demeanor changes. Mama G says, "Good afternoon."

"Good afternoon, Mama G," he replies. He seems disarmed by Mama G's quiet tone. The silent exchange between the grown-ups seems to lay down a pathway for Tru to walk on—one foot before the other until she's next to the man Mama G calls her father. "She's all yours," Mama G says, granting *dat bwoy? wutless brute? Mr. Policeman?* permission to whisk Tru away. The ease with which this is done hits Tru harder than stones she and Albino Ricky aim at Sore-Foot Marlon from their slingshots. *She's all yours.* Until then Tru wasn't sure what she felt. A liquid wave of disappointment fills her chest. The man clutches her shoulder gently with a scarred hand. From the sides of her eyes she sees her neighbors watching. One by one they lower their shoulders as hers go up—an attempt to guard herself from their stares, their judgments, their pity.

❦

UPON ARRIVAL AT HER NEW HOME, TRU VOMITS HER BREAKFAST— the two eggs and crackers she ate before her father picked her up in his red Suzuki. His house is just over the gully that divides Penny-field, in a town called Rochester. So it's a mystery to her how he's such a stranger. Not even through the door, she bends and hurls the contents of her stomach, spraying the front steps, the brown welcome mat, the green walls, and her father's pants and shoes. She hears him mutter something under his breath. Her father makes a face as though tasting a teaspoon of something bitter.

"Marva!" he shouts, his voice booming in this neat and clean place that smells like furniture polish. Three boys appear, their varying heights making their flat heads look like steps up a flight of stairs, their brown faces closed up like cabbage as they stare down at the vomit.

"Weh oonuh mother deh?" *dat bwoy? wutless brute? Mr. Policeman?* barks. "Why oonuh stan' up looking like buffoons? Guh call oonuh mother! She deaf?"

"She roun' di back washing clothes, Papa."

"Call har now!"

They scamper off like mongrel dogs dodging a rock-stone. The television is on somewhere inside the house. Tru hears the voices of cartoon characters, soon drowned out by the *slap-slap* sound of a woman's house slippers on the concrete tiles. "Lawd Jesus, Roy," she says, out of breath. "Why yuh calling out me name suh like God a come?"

In this house, Tru's father is "Roy" or "Papa." The way the woman says his name makes Tru want to hold it on her tongue too. For *Papa* doesn't sound right. Marva stops short when she sees the mess. "Oh, dear!"

"Come help me clean dis mess," Roy says. "Yuh know how long me ah call yuh? If yuh did hear, why yuh neva answer?"

"Ah was in di back doing somet'ing, Roy."

Roy sucks his teeth. "Look wah she do me good, good pants an' Clarks." He holds up one leg to show Marva his shoes.

"Nuh worry," Marva says. "Me will clean dat likkle lata."

"Yuh see me crosses?" Roy sucks his teeth, a searing cheups that cuts into Tru.

"Roy, cool it. She's jus' a baby," Marva says. "Yuh pants an' shoes can wait." She turns behind her and calls out, "Jermaine, grab di mop wid some wata an' come help clean up di front step! Daval, come get yuh father shoes an' clean it off. Kenny, bring yuh father some clean trousers. When yuh done, put di welcome mat inna di sun an' help Jermaine wipe dung di walls."

"Yes, Mama!" the boys reply in unison.

Tru is still looking down at her vomit, tears blurring her eyes and streaming down her hot face. She wants her mother. Ever since her mother left, Tru has been feeling trapped in a space between dreaming and waking. When she came back from the airport, she expected to see her mother, searching the whole house to find her, thinking maybe, just maybe, she didn't really leave. That she was only dreaming everything. She can still smell the perfume her mother wore to board the plane. She can even feel the stroke of her mother's thumb on her forehead to wipe off her kiss.

"Come, sweetie," says Marva, taking Tru's hand. "Let me get yuh clean."

She leads Tru down a long hallway, and Tru wonders if she's taking her to a dungeon. She passes the living room, which is sectioned off from the hallway with glass bead curtains. Somebody turns the volume down on the television, but there is a ringing in her ear—a deafening silence. She passes by rooms with made-up beds, embroidered curtains, oversized furniture. She looks back, wondering if it's too late to run. Her father is slipping out of his shoes and cussing to himself, but Marva seems immune. "Nuh mind yuh father," she says to Tru. "Him undah a lot of pressure. Him not suh used to children dat way." Once inside the bathroom, she peels Tru's clothes off, fills the bathtub, and closes the door behind her.

"Hope yuh not coming down wid somet'ing," Marva says as gently as the water trickling down Tru's back in the bathtub. At home her mother bathes her in a yellow basin since they don't have a tub, often allowing her to blow bubbles from the suds. She prefers that to the vast white tub in this bathroom, which is the same color as the glowing white walls. Never before has Tru seen a place so full of light. Marva has big, broad hands and even bigger breasts that surge from the low-cut blouse she wears when she bends down to rinse dried-up vomit from around Tru's mouth. She's round and brown with a moon face, pointy chin, a small mouth, and large expressive eyes that remind Tru of the dollies the girls play with at school.

"Yuh not g'wan give us any trouble, right?" Marva asks as she wraps Tru in a towel that smells like flowers and then takes her into a room with a bunk bed. She strokes her hairline. "You is a big girl. Yuh mommy leave us in charge of you now."

Tru looks up at Marva. Marva knows her mother? And what does she mean by "leave us in charge"? Does that mean that Marva will become her mother now? She wants to ask this, but she's too overcome by fear and confusion.

"You an' yuh brother Kenny g'wan share dis room," Marva is saying. "You on di top bunk, an' him on di bottom."

Tru pulls her gaze away from Marva and looks around the room as Marva ruffles through the suitcase her grandmother packed. The room is so small that it only has space for the bunk bed made of bamboo, with steps going to the top that appears to touch the ceiling, much like the tall vanity—the top of which Tru isn't sure she can reach. There is no door to the room, just bare hinges, as if someone broke off the door and never bothered to fix it. Tru can still hear the litany of voices on the television in the living room, the laughter of her brothers cleaning up her vomit, and her father talking to someone on the telephone.

On the bottom bunk, her brother's toy soldiers and cars are scattered, his clothes rumpled. The window is open, and the breeze is blowing the sheer white curtain inward above a wooden chair that has clothes folded on it. She wonders how far her house is from this one. She sees the view of the same hill on which her mother said she would build a house.

"Dis is such a nice dress." Marva pulls out a red tunic. "Let's put dis one on."

A wave of terror passes over Tru, and her heart begins to pound hard. She pulls away from Marva, shaking her head. "What's di mattah?" Marva asks. She reaches for Tru again, and Tru slips from her grasp and runs naked out the door, through the hallway, passing the sounds of the television, her father's *hee-hawing* on the telephone, and her giggling brothers—into the big yard washed by the sun. The whole place is spinning like in a dream—the rosebushes, the fence with barbed wire on top, the oversized plants on the walkway, the leaning trees, the two dogs in the yard. She hears her name. "Trudy-Ann!" It's the sound of Marva's voice. It's too near. Too close in register to her mother's. It frightens Tru. Makes her believe Marva has powers to trick her into believing she's her mother. "Trudy-Ann, come here! Trudy-Ann, stop!" Marva's giant footsteps are chasing her.

In her panic, Tru cries, "Ah want my mama! You're not Mama!"

Roy's booming voice follows. "Trudy-Ann, get back in di house now! Yuh mother not coming back!"

Tru runs around the house, trampling the hibiscuses, and ditching traps of running Marys and macka bushes. She climbs the nearest tree—a cherry tree that seems high enough that no one can reach her. There are no cherries on the tree. A bird's nest sits not too far from Tru on another branch. Below her, her father, Marva, and her three ugly brothers are looking up at her in the highest branch. She trembles, the prospect of being caught scarier than falling. Here she is in a strange place with strange smells and strange sounds and strange people she barely knows. If her mother could up and leave her just like that, then what might she expect from her father, a man she hardly knows? And who's to tell if Marva, with her big hands and round face, is really a witch? "Mama!" Tru cries, swallowed into the cave mouth of fear. She looks up at the wide expanse of the cloudless blue sky that her mother flew into. A little bird swoops down just then into the nest. Two baby birds stick their necks out, their beaks wide open. Tru stops crying and stares at them, sniffling. The mother bird appears to glance in her direction, her side-eye fierce. Tru draws her breath, terrified.

"Trudy-Ann, don't move!" her father is saying down below. He's getting ready to climb the tree, taking off his shirt and throwing it to the ground. But Tru is in awe of the bird. She feels a sudden yearning to pet it. Just as she reaches for it, a good high wind shakes the quivering branches of the cherry tree. Not wanting to harm the baby birds in the nest, Tru reaches for another limb to break her fall like she does on the jungle gym at school. But what she feels is air between her fingers as she plunges. She lands smack in her father's outstretched arms.

7

ACROSS THE OCEAN, PATSY SITS ON THE TWIN-SIZE BED, HER bottom sinking into the mattress. She doesn't bother to unpack, still unable to believe that she's really here. In America. She puts her face to the surface to sniff the sheets, taking in a whiff of the perfume scent: Lavender? Roses? She can't tell. The pillows are fluffed atop the quilted comforter, which feels like it's padded with sponge. She squeezes it, then runs her fingers along the stitches and over the soft sheets underneath with more thread count than she's used to, considering Cicely's thoughtful preparation. *All fah me*, she thinks, warmed with affection. This is what she has always imagined freedom to feel and smell like. She stretches out on the bed, spread-eagled. She takes it all in, rubbing the surface of the sheets until her hands burn, and sniffing the sweetness until her nose tingles.

She turns her head and sets her gaze on an antique wooden desk by her bedside. Next to the lamp on the table is a feather quill without a pot of ink. Patsy figures that it's a part of the decor. She looks around the room, excited at the thought that outside this basement with no windows is a city waiting to be explored. Patsy sits upright at the thought of exploring, suddenly feeling the urge to take a shower, to wash with foreign soap. She rises from the bed and tiptoes across the hardwood floor—barefoot—to the bathroom. Cicely has left her with towels, a washcloth, and a basket full of toiletries. The bathroom is small, with a sliding glass door instead of a shower curtain. The toilet is a tiny chimmey that Patsy hopes can fit her rear end. And the sink is shaped like a small bowl. She peels off her clothes and steps behind the sliding door. She's suddenly conscious of her nakedness in a way she hasn't been before. How strange to feel naked in a room not her own, and not stepping in or out of a lover's embrace, but here, naked in the lavender-rose-scented basement of her best friend's house in Brooklyn.

The shower itself is a conundrum, with a knob that has an arrow between the colors red or blue. In Jamaica, there is only one way to turn on a pipe or a shower faucet. They aren't as fancy as this one, although Mama G used to come home in her helper's uniform gushing about how the people uptown have foreign things in their bathrooms like Jacuzzis and marble counters and pipes turning and twisting every which way.

Patsy stands there, the chilly air against her chest hardening her nipples as she stares at the knob. The branch under her navel itches. Cold and annoyance cramp her belly. She reaches out to turn the knob in the direction of blue. She reasons that she cannot go wrong with the color blue. She turns the knob, then stands back, only to feel ice-cold water pouring from the bottom faucet and not the showerhead. Patsy lets out a yelp. "Have mercy!" She frantically turns the knob in the direction of red until the water becomes lukewarm. But water still pours from the bottom, not the top, faucet. Too tired to figure out how water can come from the showerhead, Patsy squats to the bottom faucet, aware of her body filling the small space, her right knee pressed against the glass door. She performs her cleansing ritual—one she's accustomed to doing back home over a bucket of water when water pressure is low. If Mama G could have seen her now, squatting this way to wash her privates in America, she would have peered down on her like the glistening shower faucet above Patsy's head, her face fixed with scorn and some gratification. *What a disgrace! Yuh in a big-big country like America acting like a bush gyal.*

Patsy switches off the water and stands up so abruptly that her knee joints crack. She dries herself and steps from behind the sliding door, her towel around her. She tiptoes back toward the bed, stopping short when she sees Marcus, his back turned, dressed sharply in a pair of dark blue trousers and a white shirt, his shoe-polish waves shiny beneath the overhead light by the washer and dryer. Patsy lets out a shriek, which startles him. Their eyes lock—his unamused, devoid of the apologetic look Patsy would expect one to have upon walking in on her this way. All of a sudden she feels rotund in the towel wrapped around her nakedness. She hopes her large breasts will not burst forth from their restricted zone, and that her fleshy brown thighs will not explode into view to give the wrong impression. But then again, she's not the one intruding—he is. Patsy's entire body flushes hot.

"Excuse me?" she says, tightening the towel around her.

She clears her throat, unsure what to say to the man who owns the house. Cicely had stressed never to disturb him. She pleaded with Patsy in a way that reminded Patsy of how Tru, a child with no independence, would plead with her—whether to let her play in the yards of other children or to not give her vegetables. Now when Cicely isn't around—gone to pick up her son from violin lesson, perhaps rushing through traffic to finish dinner—the man does as he likes.

"The hamper is down here, so . . ." he says, as if reading Patsy's mind. But Patsy is only half listening to what he's saying. "Why yuh neva knock?" she asks, trying hard to take the edge out her voice.

"In my own house?" Marcus asks, his brows wrinkled to hold her question so that she can see how ridiculous it sounds to him.

Patsy fumbles with the towel, feeling as though she's the one in the wrong. The towel nearly falls, and in a panic she hauls it back up. Marcus doesn't immediately turn away to give her privacy. Her discomfort seems to fill him with some sort of reptilian assurance that leaves a smug smile on his face. "I'll finish up after dinner," he finally says. His footsteps are light going back up the wooden steps.

Patsy sits, stunned. What if Marcus tells Cicely that he saw her naked? Patsy cups her hands to her mouth and sits there for a long time.

❧

THAT NIGHT PATSY COMES UPSTAIRS. CICELY IS RUNNING BACK and forth from the sparkly kitchen with its granite island counter and stainless-steel appliances to the table that glows under the chandelier.

"Want some help?" Patsy asks.

"No, no. Sit," Cicely says, waving her away, her sterling silver bracelets jingling. She looks flustered, her face red and her voice breathy like she's been in a marathon.

Marcus and the little boy, Shamar, are now seated at the table, Marcus at the head. He smirks at Patsy when she sits. She avoids looking at him and focuses on the little boy. Again she is stung by the hurt that Cicely didn't even tell her when she was pregnant with the boy, who is now giving Patsy a curious stare. He's quiet and watchful even as Patsy smiles at him. In his pale eyes she sees an ocean she cannot cross, even with her American visa.

There are bowls of cabbage salad, smoked ham, macaroni and cheese, potato salad, and baked chicken spread out on the table like a feast. Patsy feels slighted by the fact that Cicely hasn't used the spices Patsy brought her from Jamaica. She's also resentful that Cicely has refused her help with any of the food preparation.

Cicely is too busy to notice the loud silence at the dining table. She's slicing up cucumbers, murmuring something about the chicken being too salty, apologizing in advance. Something in little Shamar's face, a sadness that reminds Patsy of herself at that age, makes her speak.

"So how is school?" Patsy asks the boy.

He looks at her, astonished. As though he never expects to be acknowledged, spoken to. "Fine," he says in a small voice. He is high yellow like Cicely, and shares her blue-green eye color as well, his hair standing up in massive curls all over his head.

"What grade yuh in again?" Patsy asks him.

"Fourth grade?" he says, the statement sounding like a question.

"Ah! So, you is a big boy now!"

The little boy smiles. But when he glances at his father, the quiet smile dies from his lips, wiped clean off his baby face. Cicely finally joins them at the table.

"Let us bow our heads," Marcus says.

Patsy holds her stomach muscles as Marcus says the grace, feeling Cicely and Shamar tense with awkward fear. When Marcus is done, everyone says a somber *Amen*, then begins to eat in silence. Because of this tension, Patsy eats too quickly, stuffing food without tasting it. "Dis is delicious, Cicely!" she says too loud. Marcus looks up from his plate.

"She's not the most creative cook. All we eat is unseasoned raw meat in this house."

"Di chicken is di best," Patsy says, defending her friend. Again, she feels the warmth of Marcus's resentment creeping toward her from his side of the table. But it doesn't hold against the secret smile Patsy catches on her friend's face. Patsy has seen this secret smile before—in the schoolyard when Patsy stood up to the bullies who teased Cicely about having white liver after her mother's death. Patsy didn't know then what *white liver* meant until she asked Mama G. Mama G twisted up her mouth and said, "*Is what di half-breed Indian girls have. It mek dem hungry fah men. Like dat girl I tell yuh to stay far from, an' har mother—may God deal wid har soul.*"

Patsy sees this smile again on Cicely's face. Feels validated by it—like it's the only purpose of her being in America; the only familiar thing that renders her envy harmless. It's easy to dismiss Marcus, easy to pretend not to see the little boy wilted in his chair under the frozen heat of his father's glance, his neck bent over untouched food. Easy to forgive Cicely for not telling her about her family. Warmed by Cicely's smile, Patsy hardly notices Cicely trip over herself on her way back to the kitchen, dropping the pot cover by mistake, a sharp breath escaping her in the stillness of her husband's contempt.

8

TRU IS SLUMPED AT THE DINNER TABLE WITH HER BROTHERS AND Marva. Now that the terror has passed, she is left feeling exhausted—too cried out to eat or drink. The curry chicken and rice Marva cooked remains untouched in front of Tru. Even if she were hungry, she wouldn't eat anything served to her by Marva. Marva pauses every so often to wipe her forehead, her eyes on Tru. "Ah not moving till yuh eat something," Marva says.

But Tru pushes the food away. In the light, Marva's shadow looms large and threatening, filling the whole house and blocking the front door, where Tru expects her mother to walk in at any moment. But each time she turns her head to look behind her, Marva's quiet devotion puts a strain in her neck. There's a constant battle raging inside Tru. The same instruction from her mother would have made her eager to please—the way she is eager to please her teachers at school by knowing the answer to every question. But she chills at the thought of giving this much gratification to Marva. There is a peculiar pleasure she gets in seeing worry mask the shiny, glaring face of the woman standing over her with her hands on her hips, her big chest heaving with enough air for the both of them. The attention clamps Tru's stomach tighter and curves her shoulders. And when Marva picks up the fork to feed her, there is profound satisfaction in shaking her head.

"Mama, can I get har chicken since she don't want it?" the middle boy asks.

"No," Marva snaps. "She g'wan eat dis food even if me have to force har."

"But she only wasting it, Mama," says the older boy, his voice low. "She waste everyt'ing we give har."

Tru doesn't respond. Her brothers finish their meals and clear the table, leaving Tru and Marva. Marva lifts the fork to Tru's mouth, this time cupping her chin. "Jus' open up," Marva says. The softness in her voice, which is as light as her touch, makes Tru want to. She opens up, giving into the soft fingers and steady gaze watching her chew and swallow. She begins to rely on the delightful effect of seeing a slow smile make its way up Marva's face. All of a sudden, her hunger returns. Unexpected. More aggressive than before. There is a calmness in being fed. It soothes the hurt in the tender place she can neither see nor touch in the bottomless cavity of her chest.

"Goaaaaall!" Roy exclaims from the living room. He's watching the Reggae Boyz on television, his dinner plate before him. Tru hears him loudly sucking the marrow out of the chicken bones. "Marva, beg yuh some wata, nuh?" he says without turning away from the television.

Marva suspends her feeding of Tru. She puts down Tru's fork and hurries to the refrigerator to pour water into a glass for Roy. Tru watches her move to the living room to take Roy's plate and hand him the glass. He doesn't thank her. But the quiet devotion Tru experienced from Marva earlier is now transferred to her father. With her hands, Tru shoves a fistful of rice off her plate. It lands on the floor. Marva spins around and gasps when she sees all her food on the floor. "Roy!"

Tru's father lowers his legs from the cushion and springs from the sofa, tearing his eyes off the Reggae Boyz' victory dance on the bright green field on the screen. He shuffles toward the table, sucking his teeth loudly, the way he does to rid meat from between his teeth. "What is it dis time?" Tru peers up at him, expecting him to strike her with his big broad hand with the snake scar she has grown afraid of. But he only lowers it to put it on her shoulder. "What is di mattah wid you?" he asks, his voice surprisingly low and tender, save for the words. "Yuh think because yuh mother in America yuh can waste food like dat? Yuh know how much children starving in Africa? Dis foolish behavior will only land you in di street."

"Ah want to go back home," Tru says.

"Dis is yuh home now. So get used to it," Roy replies. "If you insist on wasting we food then yuh bettah ask yuh mother fah every ounce a penny she earn fi pay we back. Keeping you here not cheap."

"Roy, yuh can't say dat to di child," Marva says.

"Then how else she g'wan understand dat we doing har a favor?" he hisses.

Marva and Roy continue to squabble, eventually disappearing into the other room, where Tru can no longer hear them. The fervor of the Reggae Boyz on TV mocks her as she sits alone at the table, looking down at her empty plate.

9

PATSY HAS SPENT TWO WHOLE WEEKS INSIDE THE HOUSE, TOO afraid to venture out by herself without Cicely. This morning she stirs awake to Cicely's touch. "Good morning, sleepyhead," Cicely says once Patsy opens her eyes. "I have something for you." She hands Patsy a newspaper with a list of jobs that Patsy should look at. "These jobs don't require any papers."

"Papers?" Patsy asks, rubbing sleep from her eyes.

"Work visa."

Patsy glances at the digital clock by the bedside. It's not even five in the morning, yet Cicely is sitting in a chair next to Patsy's bed, already dressed, a thermos of warm water in her hand, which she drinks first thing in the morning to speed up her metabolism, and a gym bag slung over her shoulder. Her hair is combed in a high bun, pulling her skin toward her temples; her face is almost bare except the light blush and lip gloss. How long has Cicely been watching her sleep? Patsy wonders. She smells like mouthwash. It's so strong that Patsy can almost taste it, the scent inciting a tingly sensation of betrayal—an inevitable truth that her friend, already dressed and ready for her group aerobics class at a nearby gym before she runs her many errands, has no time for her. All week she has been locked up in the house, guzzling Coca-Cola, orange juice, Hawaiian fruit punch, and gorging on potato chips, M&Ms, Oreos, gummy bears, Hershey's Kisses, microwave popcorn, Pringles—all the American snacks she could eat; foods which would've been overpriced at the supermarkets back home, the type where rich people shop. She has also been eating whatever foreign meals Cicely cooks and leaves in foil paper wrapping. Foods like lasagna, chicken potpie, honey-glazed ham, turkey, and provolone cheese sandwiches. Patsy has only known cheese to come in a bright red can.

"You have to check these out," Cicely is saying. "In dis place people don't jus' eat an' sleep."

Patsy rolls out of the bed and shoves her feet into a pair of fuzzy slippers. "Give me a minute."

Patsy feels Cicely's eyes on her as she walks to the bathroom. Self-conscious, she turns slightly away, since there is no door—something she never would have been concerned with in the old days. When she finishes she washes her hands and splashes water on her face to wake up.

"There's so many," Patsy says when she returns, squinting at the list Cicely gives her.

"In New York yuh have to cast yuh net wide," Cicely says. "I don't expect you to reach out to all of them today."

Patsy studies the "Help Wanted" ads Cicely circled for her in red ink in the back of the paper. It makes her dizzy. It's too soon, she thinks. And besides, whatever happened to the job agencies Cicely told her about that can help her find that dream job that will pay her lots of money? Most of the jobs Cicely shows her are menial work—cleaning lady, line cook, dishwasher, busboy, landscape maintenance, janitor, school night guard, day laborer, caretaker, dog walker.

"Dog walker?" Patsy frowns and looks at Cicely. "Who would pay fah dat? In Jamaica, dawg a dawg."

Cicely stamps Patsy with a look. "Here people treat dem dawg like a member of di family. So, get wid it if yuh want quick money."

"Yuh have anything else?" Patsy asks, sitting up on the bed.

"Hm. Figure model? It's forty per hour. A curvy woman in good shape an' flexible," Cicely says, chuckling.

Patsy moves to swat her with a pillow. "Seriously, Cicely. Yuh really t'ink I'd tek off my clothes like dat fah strangers?"

"Since when yuh dat picky?" Cicely laughs.

Patsy gives her a talking eye.

"All right. Here is one dat ah t'ink you should take." Cicely points to the ad that has a double asterisk. Patsy reads it: "Love children? Want a quick, easy way to make extra cash? Nannies needed. Email résumé and a cover letter to Candace."

She glances up at Cicely, who is smiling. But Patsy doesn't give the smile a chance to grow. It hangs there as Patsy studies the word *nanny*. The only time Patsy has heard the word was at the embassy when the official mentioned it. He said his wife hired one. A Jamaican.

"It's how a lot of women mek money here." Cicely goes on and on about what the job entails. "Ah know a couple people who . . ."

Patsy listens quietly. The job that she had at the Ministry in Kingston was by far a more dignified job than cleaning houses, wiping the asses of other people's children, walking a dog and picking up its shit. Even if she does apply and get the job as a nanny, the job title in itself might take some getting used to. That's what she will be called here in America if she follows Cicely and reaches out to these people. A nanny. But more than the name itself is the irony—to come to a place with so much freedom, only to take care of another child.

Cicely is still smiling. Perhaps it's hope—hidden and selfish, the way hagglers, men with erections, and loan sharks look at you. Whatever it is, Patsy hangs on to it, feeds into it. For the smile could quickly turn to disappointment. She feels obligated to show interest—to convince Cicely that she has begun to think about her independence; that mothering other children (and her own) comes more natural to her than her yearning to be swallowed up in the world beyond Pennyfield, beyond this basement—out there where small things seem large. Where foreign accents are spoken and could tickle your ears more than the tip of a chicken feather. Where pleasure is not just something felt in private, away from scrutinizing gazes of waxed figurines. Where you are never alone long enough to feel the spell overtake you, the darkness following you like an unmoving shadow. Out there, where a woman can walk free with not even a purse dangling from her shoulders.

🍂

WHEN THE WEEKEND ROLLS AROUND, CICELY OFFERS TO SHOW Patsy the city and take her to a job agency. It's nice outside and the leaves are starting to change color, reminding Patsy of that lignum vitae tree in Pennyfield where all the yellow butterflies flock to in May. In Cicely's company, Patsy is moved to smile at everything she sees—at the sheer loveliness of warm colors and people and the names of these foreign streets. She tags along with her best friend, almost running and skipping to catch up with her. Cicely walks full speed ahead, taking long strides on the big city streets that hum with traffic and the trains underground. She rattles off street names Patsy should know in Brooklyn—Nostrand, Atlantic, Flatbush. Names Patsy is sure she will forget, since she carries nothing to write them down. On the bus, Cicely points to landmarks. "Dat's di market ah go to. Dat's Prospect Park. Dat's di library." Patsy absorbs everything in silence. Mostly, she's happy to be in Cicely's company, their shoulders touching lightly as they sit on the bus seat. In this moment, Brooklyn fades away and Kingston emerges, rock-solid and flat. A place where two schoolgirls dressed in blue tunics are exploring downtown, holding hands. Two girls who thought life would be filled with giggles, infinite sun, and possibilities that wouldn't entail sacrifice.

Cicely presses a yellow strip next to their seat on the bus and it buzzes. The bus slows down. "Dis is our stop," Cicely says to Patsy, who is awed by the fact that Cicely didn't have to yell, *"Bus stop!"* to the driver like they would have to do back home. Everything seems so easy in America, with the simple push of a button—from microwave dinners to doorbells and buzzers.

"Where we going?" Patsy asks.

"Manhattan," Cicely replies.

"Times Square?" Patsy asks, giddy, seeing bright lights and giant marquees flash across her mind's eye.

"Aftah we find you a job," Cicely says. She leads Patsy like a child into one of the subway stations. In the train, Cicely points to the overhead board that lights up at each stop. "Dis train takes yuh from Brooklyn all di way to di Bronx," she says. "See? We got on right there at Atlantic Avenue. We g'wan take dis all di way to Grand Central, Forty-second Street. Yuh can't get lost if yuh know what direction yuh going."

Patsy nods as she memorizes her stop. *Atlantic Avenue.* People enter and leave the train at every stop, each one more interesting, intriguing to look at—the white guy with the T-shirt that reads DEMOCRACY TODAY and tattoos like sleeves down his arms, holding a lamp he probably bought just like that off the street; the young woman with bright red hair—is it a wig? Patsy can't tell—wearing a pink see-through dress that looks like a slip, her nipples like dark eyes glaring at Patsy; the black man with the Mets baseball cap who is fervently scratching off a lotto ticket with a dime and yelling, *"Argh!"* every time he fails to win. Many other commuters bury their noses inside books or newspapers. Some stare out into space. Most have placid looks on their faces. When Patsy gets bored of watching them (or paranoid when she notices that they stare back at her), she steals glances at Cicely. Patsy is taken by her—her maturity and her beauty; how she's in command of this foreign land where Patsy takes trepid steps; her ability to speak to shopowners, bargain prices, request a transfer on the bus, sit next to a white person on the train without apology, since here white people are natives, not tourists like they are back home, and here they might see Cicely as kin. And then there's her skill as a mother, how she seems so good at it; a real woman. She's everything Patsy isn't.

"What is it?" Cicely asks.

Patsy drops her gaze. "Nothing. Jus' remembering when we was girls."

Cicely smiles. "What yuh remembering 'bout dat?"

"How yuh always seem suh sure of everyt'ing. Even when yuh situation change wid Mabley's death . . ."

"Dat's because ah had you," Cicely says.

Patsy's face warms despite the cool air-conditioning inside the subway car. She looks up at a poster with a poem near the double doors: *Hope is the thing with feathers that perches in the soul and sings the tune without the words and never stops at all . . .* Underneath the poem is the name Emily Dickinson. She commits the name and poem to memory.

WHEN THEY GET OFF AT GRAND CENTRAL, PATSY IS IMMEDI-ately overwhelmed by the tide of people coming toward her, swerving this way and that way. She almost crouches to avoid being knocked over. "Come dis way." Cicely pulls her along, linking her arm with Patsy's toward the exit. Patsy admires the cosmopolitan vibe of the city—the women with high-heeled shoes, graceful even with the uneven sidewalks; the ones that hail cabs, holding out their pale arms like the beginning of a choreographed dance; the men with their hands stuffed inside their pockets, looking straight ahead like they are on a runway. Cicely was right. This is where the white people are. She instructs Patsy to move swiftly, to never make eye contact with anyone, to clutch her bag at all times, to look over her shoulders, to be nice to other people's children since here you can't scold strangers' children like you do in Jamaica unless you want your throat slit by the parent. Cicely also tells her not to mind the white people who may walk two paces quicker, glancing behind them, then crossing to the other side of the street; or the ones who may move away from her when she sits, or follow her inside stores. "Jus' know yuh place, be polite, work hard, an' get yuh money so dat yuh can tek care of yuh family. Dat's di only t'ing dat mattah. Be as invisible as possible."

On a corner, a group of black teenagers dance inside a circle. The people that crowd around them push dollar bills toward the smallest boy carrying a bucket to collect money. On another street corner is a group of black men dressed in purple and gold T-shirts. BLACK HEBREW ISRAELITES is written in bold black letters on a banner. One of the men pushes a flyer to Patsy. "That's the white man's sickness!" he says, looking at Cicely and Patsy with their arms linked. In the chaos, Cicely's arm feels good, safe. Cicely pulls Patsy along before the man can say anything else. "Asshole!" Cicely hisses, sounding American with those curse words Patsy has never heard her use, her face reddening with fury. She picks up her pace. Patsy's bubble breaks and disturbs her reverie of the city once she's aware of Cicely's annoyance. "Why should it mattah what he says? What can he do to us in America?"

The scar on Cicely's forehead, just above her left eyebrow, seems more prominent when she frowns, "We too old fah dis."

Patsy lets go of Cicely's hand midstride and succumbs to the roaring tide of expressionless faces on the crowded sidewalks. "What yuh mean?" she asks. Manhattan comes into focus, with its soaring skyscrapers, indifferent with grim, geometric faces; the wide, busy streets where taxis race to an indefinite finish line; the scaffolding around construction sites looking like bat wings arched toward the sliver of blue sky; the smell of sewer and hot piss rising with the steam coming from underground like a dragon's breath; the foreign tongues speaking all at once like on the tower of Babel, maddening with the honking of horns, the screeching of wheels, the high-pitched soprano of sirens; and above it all, the roar of Cicely's words. "*We too old fah dis.*" Patsy cannot take it all at once. She stumbles, blinded by daylight and bodies coming toward her. The sidewalk and street lift to meet her, and she can smell the molten tar spread across the road, hot with its blood smell.

"She all right?" someone asks. It's a man. When Patsy regains consciousness, she notices his white apron and the five o'clock shadow on his face, though it's midday. Both he and Cicely are hovering over her, their faces eclipsing each other. "Don't worry, I know CPR," Cicely says to him. A few people slow down to look at what's going on.

"You okay?" Cicely asks Patsy, scanning her eyes with her blue-green ones, the way she probably would've done with her patients had she gone to nursing school as planned.

"I'm fine," Patsy says as soon as she catches her breath.

Cicely pulls Patsy close and clamps her hands against Patsy's temples. "Just breathe with me," Cicely says, her mouth forming an O. She moves one hand and presses it against Patsy's chest. Patsy does as she is told, sensing their breath synching and the tightness in her chest go away as her heartbeat slows. "There," Cicely says, her voice gentle, soothing. "Just like dat. Don't scare me like dat again."

"I'm all right," Patsy says.

"Maybe dis is too much fah you today," Cicely says.

"I'm not ready fah dis by myself," Patsy confesses.

"Don't worry. Yuh not alone. Not while I'm here." Cicely takes off her fuchsia shawl and puts it around Patsy's shoulders. Patsy almost protests until she feels its warmth, unable to imagine another moment without it. Cicely stands and stretches out her hands for Patsy to take them. Manhattan with all its buzzing holds still, and the years rub away like smoke from glass as Patsy presses her palms into Cicely's.

T HE JOB AGENCY WHERE CICELY TAKES HER IS ON NINTH AVE-
nue. It's a hole-in-the-wall place sandwiched between a pizza restaurant and an office building, called Ray of Hope. There goes that word again—*hope*. It must be a good sign to see it twice in one day, Patsy thinks as she steps inside the place with bright purple walls. There are posters of people of different ethnicities posing in uniforms: a black woman wearing pink scrubs; a Spanish man in work boots, overalls, and hard hat; an Indian woman pushing a stroller on a pristine tree-lined sidewalk; an African man in a tuxedo holding the car door for a white man; a Chinese woman smiling with a whistle in her mouth, wearing a shocking-green vest as she directs traffic and pedestrians in the middle of what looks like a busy intersection. Above the images is the state- ment: WE ARE THE BACKBONE OF AMERICA. The receptionist is sitting at her desk, too busy toying with her horse-hair to hear the telephone ringing off the hook or see Cicely and Patsy standing there waiting to be acknowledged.

"Can I help you?" she asks in a faint Caribbean accent. Patsy can't place the island. It's obvious that she has been in the States for a long time.

Cicely clears her throat. "Ah, yes. We have an appointment."

The receptionist grudgingly opens a big book and flips through. "Your name?"

"It's for Patricia Reynolds," Cicely says.

The receptionist sighs as though it will take an exhorbitant amount of energy to tick off Patsy's name and hand her a clipboard with a form to fill out. "Answer all the questions and bring it back to me. They'll be with you shortly. You may have a seat." She flicks her wrist in the direction of the crowded waiting area filled with other foreigners. Patsy and Cicely take a seat on the padded chairs. There is a television mounted on a wall, playing the news on mute. President Bill Clinton is on the TV, talking to a journalist who seems to be challenging him on something. A photograph of a dark-haired woman keeps coming up, as do the words *Case for Impeachment* flashing across the screen as breaking news.

Patsy fills out her name, date of birth, country of origin, primary language, and her current address. She uses Cicely's address and telephone number. She also fills out a sheet asking for her work experience and educational background. (Though Cicely told her that no one would care about the two courses she took at Excelsior Community College. And certainly no one would care that once upon a time she solved a hundred math questions correctly in record time at Roman Phillips Secondary and was head of her class before things fell apart.) She pauses when the form requests her skills. Truth be told, Patsy isn't sure what exactly she could put down. *What am I good at?* She leaves it blank. She then signs an agreement form that everything she wrote is correct. When she hands the form to the receptionist she takes it, scans it, and gives Patsy a number. "Be seated till they call you."

Cicely and Patsy wait in silence. It feels to Patsy like they've run out of things to talk about. Perhaps Cicely's mind is still on what happened earlier with the man on the street. Patsy is almost relieved when a woman comes out and calls her name. She's young too, maybe in her mid-twenties, with dreadlocks—a hairstyle Patsy has never seen on a working woman, since most of the Rastas she knows back home are men; and if you do catch glimpses of their women, they're hunched over or squatting beside a stall of handmade things in the streets or craft markets, their long skirts sweeping the ground they walk on. But this Rasta has her dreadlocks twisted neatly into a style mimicking a coif. She's wearing a lilac cardigan and a green pencil skirt and clutching the clipboard to her chest. "Sorry for the wait, ladies," she says. "Follow me."

Patsy and Cicely follow the girl down a small hallway and into another section filled with rows of cubicles. There are computers set up where people are sitting with an aide—most of them young like the girl Patsy is assigned. Patsy passes by an open space with a white screen and a video camera where a man is practicing for an interview. The aide tells him to slow down and enunciate each word to lessen his thick African accent. The man acquiesces, sounding to Patsy worse than he did before—like someone took his tongue and severed it—"Please, nice to meet you"—yet the aide gives him a thumbs-up sign. "Good job, Kweku!"

"This way," the girl says. The aide waits for Patsy and Cicely to take their seats in a cramped cubicle before she sits. "I'm so excited that you chose Ray of Hope as your go-to place for job hunting," she says, sounding to Patsy like she's reading from a teleprompter. "Let's get you started."

The younger woman pulls up a blank screen on her computer. She begins to type the information Patsy wrote on the application. Her long fingers jump all over the keyboard like she's playing a church organ. Patsy is fascinated by the girl's dexterity on the machine.

"Where yuh learn to use dat?" Patsy asks the girl.

"In school," the girl says without stopping. She seems like a robot, with her back straight and shoulders braced, her expressionless brown face washed by the light on the screen as her fingers speedily and lithely maneuver the keyboard. She only pauses for less than a second to manipulate the small black thing attached to the keyboard on the right, which she constantly clicks. Patsy watches in awe.

"Ah took a course at Medgar Evers College not too long ago," Cicely says. "Marcus say technology g'wan be di way of life in di new millennium."

Patsy cringes at the mention of Marcus. But instead of rolling her eyes like she wants to, she continues to pay close attention to the girl's fingers and the words spreading across the screen. Meanwhile, Cicely is going on and on about how Shamar is good at computers, and how she has to call him into the study plenty of times to show her how to save a document or insert bullet points.

The girl pauses when she gets to the second page of Patsy's application. "I notice that you left your skills blank," she says to Patsy with a questioning look. "Employers will need to know what you're good at to determine whether to hire you. I see here that you're interested in applying for nanny positions? What will make you a good nanny?"

"Is it possible to apply fah ah office job? Ah was a secretary at my old job," Patsy says.

"No company hires undocumented workers as administrative staff," the girl says. "They don't want to be held responsible, especially with U.S. code. It's a federal felony to hire anyone without proper paperwork. Companies shy away from such liability." The girl bites her bottom lip, apologetic and helpless, reminding Patsy of her youth. "Sorry. But perhaps you can apply as a cleaning lady. You wouldn't have to go through HR. The cleaning company takes care of paperwork. Unfortunately, those company positions are full at this time."

"An' if I want to go back to school?" Patsy asks. From beside her she sees Cicely shifting in her chair. She knows she's veering away from their plan by asking this question. Who does she think she is to come to a white man's country, expecting to walk into their positions without crawling first? Patsy knows this is going through her friend's mind just by the frown on her face. The girl doesn't seem to think anything of it. She shrugs. "That's easy. You just have to pay your tuition up front. Schools don't give aid to undocumented students. It doesn't say on your application that you came on a student visa, so you might not be eligible for work-study either. Your best bet is to take what you can get and save every penny to put towards your tuition."

Patsy swallows, reality rushing in like the chilled air inside the office.

It will be impossible to save for tuition and send money home. She has no choice but to *take what she can get*, as the girl puts it.

"So, we're all set with the nanny position?" the girl asks.

Patsy glances at Cicely. It's hard to read the expression on her friend's face at this point.

"Yes," Patsy finally replies, wondering what exactly she can put on a résumé that would make sense for a nanny position. *Is not like me g'wan be expected to perform surgery*, she thinks. All there is to it is making sure the child stays alive, fed, cleaned, and hydrated. At least she'll be getting paid. The girl asks if she has children.

"Yes," Patsy replies. "One."

"That's fantastic! I can put that in your cover letter. *"It brings me great joy to be around children and if it were up to me I could do this forever."*

Patsy reads the letter aloud, furrowing her brows. "What kinda statement is dat?"

"I'm making sure to highlight the thing that will make you an excellent fit for this job."

Cicely, who has been quietly observing, speaks up. "Yuh want dis job or not? You're a mother. There mus' be somet'ing to be said about dat too, isn't there?" When Patsy doesn't answer immediately, Cicely asks again, quietly this time, fixing her with a look of tragic concern. "Is there?"

Something dims in Cicely's eyes as they narrow, questioning.

"I want to be more than just . . ." Patsy pauses as she fishes for the right words. "I want to go back to school," she finally says, emboldened by her frustration to lift her hand toward the computer. "I want to learn how to use a computer. Learn what's inside it. Like how di world can be reached through yuh fingah by clicking one button. How yuh can connect wid other people. How ah can do anyt'ing. Go anywhere. Be someone. Someone else . . ."

But those words sound incriminating—enough to deepen the lines in Cicely's forehead, close her entire face as if the words have rested hot and offensive on her flesh. "What yuh really saying?" she asks.

The girl sits quietly at the computer, her once-busy fingers now resting in her lap. "I'll give you two a moment," she says softly. "I need more coffee anyway." She excuses herself and leaves Patsy and Cicely alone at the cubicle.

All around them there is chatter and the pecking of keyboards. Patsy's lips move to reply to Cicely, but no sound comes. It is apparent that Patsy's personal defect as a woman threatens something sacred for Cicely. Cicely's own mother, Miss Mabley, was the object of perpetual scorn in Pennyfield, the women in town rebuking her wild ways. *"Dat woman g'waan like she nuh 'ave no pickney."* Cicely, as a mother, has become her own mother's opposite. The incredulity and disdain on her face now echoes the judgmental gazes aimed at Miss Mabley.

Patsy understands this history and forgives Cicely her scorn. But what angers Patsy is the things her friend doesn't recall. The sacrifices Patsy made so that Cicely could be where she is now—all because she thought she had no dreams of her own, a future as empty as her insides, scraped clean of yearnings.

Cicely had fallen a grade behind and desperately needed to pass. Patsy took the Caribbean Examinations Council math assessment exam a day before Cicely and gave her all the answers. Cicely hid the cheat sheet in the thick bun she wore to take the exam that day. No one thought to check Cicely's hair. No one dared to think that hair so fine and straight could cover a lie.

That summer Patsy found out that she won a distinction—the highest CXC mathematics score in the whole country. Prestigious schools lined up to accept her into their sixth form. But her excitement was short-lived when her deed was discovered due to the suspiciously similar calculations on both her and Cicely's exams. When the girls were called in for questioning, the principal took one look at Patsy and asked Patsy why she'd copied Cicely's work and didn't have sense to know that she'd get caught. Patsy didn't deny it. She took the blame, which got her disqualified and expelled. Cicely wanted to come forward and tell the truth, but Patsy discouraged her, "*You'll have bettah use fah a good score*," she said. It was only right to listen to her heart and not her head. For she had neither the right nor the permission to think she'd amount to anything other than a secretary. Her place in society was already established by her skin color and wrong address. Had she taken the chance to go to university, they would've handed her a useless piece of paper, promising her advancement as a cruel joke, then would turn around to snatch every penny she would earn. And if she couldn't pay them back, they would publish her photograph in the *Jamaica Gleaner* like they did every week to those poor working-class souls who fell into their trap. Cicely did one year of university, then vanished without a trace until her first letter arrived a couple years later.

Patsy looks at her friend, who is now so accustomed to middle-class life that she no longer has ambition or hunger, a woman who sacrifices her needs for her husband. Aloud Patsy says, "You're a woman wid a mind of yuh own. There mus' be somet'ing to be said about dat too, isn't there?"

Cicely's scowl deepens. "You're di one applying for a job, not me."

"You were always pretty enough, pleasant enough to get exactly what yuh want. Now yuh have a husband wid enough money to mek yuh quit night school an' forget about nursing school jus' to sit at home an' do aerobics. Don't question my ambition when you no longer have any."

Cicely's eyes and mouth go wide with surprise. "How dare you say—"

"You know it's di truth, Cicely. Earlier when ah fainted in di street, ah saw how yuh come alive, doing somet'ing yuh always dreamed of doing. Yuh nurse me back to life. You'd really mek a good nurse one day. Are you really at peace wid yuhself being married to a man wid money without none of yuh own? Living his dreams wid no regard fah yours?

Mabley might not have had di best job in di world opening har legs fah men, but one t'ing she had was hustle."

"Don't bring my mother out di grave fah dis convah-sation," Cicely hisses. "My mother had to literally beg my father on bended knees to give har a room in di big house where his wife had di key. I, on di other hand, am di wife. Di queen ah di castle. In fact, I'm more than a wife. I'm his prize. He takes me to dinners and galas, because him know he'd get more respect wid a beautiful wife who look white, even from di most prejudiced among di white people him call friends. As long as ah don't open my mouth. My mother used to tell me dat my looks can take me nuff places—that it's a pass. A visa through life. Mabley would be proud."

"Is dat yuh only accomplishment? To be di trophy wife?" Patsy asks.

"Sometimes we 'ave to do t'ings we don't like, to get what we want," Cicely says with resolve. "An' besides, ah got a beautiful son out of it. Dat is now my ambition."

Before Patsy can say anything more inside the cold job agency office, the girl returns with coffee in hand and sits. "So have you made up your mind?" she asks Patsy.

"I used to be good at maths," Patsy says to the girl, her eyes on Cicely. Cicely looks away and braces her shoulders.

"Pardon?" The girl swings her chair around, her long legs almost bumping Patsy's.

"When yuh asked me what ah was good at earlier? It was maths. Dey called me a prodigy once—back when ah was in school." Patsy laughs now, disappointment sinking in her gut.

"Uhm . . . that's nice," the girl says with mild interest, clasping her hands around her steaming coffee cup. "As I mentioned earlier, regardless of your background, right now women like yourself are in demand for domestic work. This nanny position would be a great fit."

"Fine," Patsy says.

The girl simply smiles and proceeds with Patsy's job application.

After they are done, the girl offers Patsy and Cicely stationery with the Ray of Hope logo scribbled on it. "Tell your friends about us!" she says, waving them goodbye. Cicely thanks her. At the door, Cicely surprises Patsy by putting a hand on the small of Patsy's back and lets her go first. Something about this gesture tempers Patsy's annoyance. Finally they begin to talk, their pleasant chatter a bit more strained than before.

✦

INSTEAD OF THE RED PEAS SOUP, CHICKEN FOOT SOUP, OR COW foot soup that any Jamaican matriarch worth her salt cooks every Saturday evening, Cicely decides to make pumpkin soup with a touch of cinnamon. *"Marcus's favorite."* The whole house smells of cinnamon. Shamar is upstairs practicing on his violin. Patsy hears the sharp halt of a tune followed by the slow beginning of a new melody. Cicely talks to Patsy over the sound. "Now dat yuh know how to get around Brooklyn, yuh can go to interviews when di time comes." Her voice is cheerful. "You don't have to step one foot into Manhattan."

"Can't wait," Patsy says, her mind still on their exchange at the agency. "Ah want to use yuh phone."

Cicely pauses her food preparation. Slowly, she lowers the dish towel.

"I've been meaning to call Tru," Patsy responds before Cicely says anything.

Cicely nods, though something shades her face as if someone suddenly closed the drapes, blocking the evening sunset flaming above the trees. "I know," Cicely says, her voice placid. She waves off Patsy. "You can use di study, since Marcus isn't here. Close di door."

In the study, Patsy picks up the telephone. She begins to dial the numbers on the calling card Cicely bought her when she first arrived, followed by the 1-876 country code. But she hangs up as soon as she's prompted to dial the other numbers. Resting her elbows on the oblong mahogany desk that still smells like freshly cut wood, she buries her face in her palms. She's not ready. She stares up at the light that comes from the large windows facing the tree-lined street. Marcus's books on real estate are stacked neatly on a small shelf. Though Patsy is uncomfortable sitting here in his study—in his leather chair where he probably leans back, feet propped on the desk, to either admire his wing-tip shoes or smoke those Cuban cigars Cicely says he's crazy about—it's even more uncomfortable sitting with Cicely's words. *"You're a mother. There mus' be somet'ing to be said about dat too, isn't there?"*

Patsy takes a deep breath and picks up the phone again. Methodically she punches the numbers, still holding her breath as if she's about to be submerged underwater as she waits for someone to pick up. It feels like a lifetime waiting. A lifetime of trying to decide whether to hang up on the fifth or sixth ring.

"Hello?" someone finally says. It sounds to Patsy like a child—one of Roy's sons.

"Yes, good evening," Patsy replies. "I'm calling to speak to Tru. Is she around?"

"Who may I ask is calling?" the boy asks in the manner of a well-trained child. Patsy realizes that she has never taught Tru to answer the phone this way. Never had a reason to, since they didn't receive many phone calls. "It's—it's Tru's mother," Patsy says.

There is a long pause after her response, as if the boy himself has been awaiting the call and, finally when he gets it, has nothing to say. Maybe his mother has told him about Patsy. Boys are protective of their mothers.

"He-hello? You there?" Patsy says, guilt shaking her voice.

"Yes, miss," the boy replies. "Tru 'roun di back washing clothes wid Mama."

"Tell har dat har mother want to talk to her."

"Please hold," he says, sounding like a secretary. Patsy cannot help but smile at this.

"Okay, I will," she says, relieved.

What she really wants to say is, *Yes, I will try*. For, as the boy leaves to call Tru, Patsy feels herself losing courage. Hearing Tru's voice will only make it harder, she thinks. *"When yuh coming back?"* Tru will ask—the inevitable question that Patsy has been dreading. Paralyzed with the grief and fear of uttering yet another lie, she realizes this is the question that has kept her from calling until today. *"Soon, soon. I'll be back."* That is all she needs to say. But those words might choke her.

As she waits on Tru, she stares at the high ceiling of the study, feeling small and helpless. Outside, leaves tremble on tree limbs as though fighting to keep a season that has already moved on. The hand holding the telephone shakes. Suddenly there is a burst of sound on the other end. A squeal erupts from a distance, growing louder. When it is close, becoming panting breaths and footsteps, Patsy quickly lowers the phone with a soft click. "I'm sorry," she says aloud, hoping her apology will carry over the dying autumn landscape across the brooding ocean.

W HEN PATSY EXITS THE STUDY, HER THOUGHTS ARE INTER-rupted by the sharp halt of Shamar's instrument. "Wrong key!" Cicely shouts, hurrying to the banister with an empty plate and craning her neck toward the staircase in the foyer so that her son can hear her. "And what did Mr. Ferguson teach you about holding your notes? Start again!"

Cicely only speaks to her son in standard English, never allowing herself to slip into their dialect whenever he's around. From the brief silence that follows Cicely's reprimand comes a beautiful melody. It's as though all Shamar's emotions have left him and entered the playing of his violin.

"You're a mother. There mus' be somet'ing to be said about dat too, isn't there? Is there?" Cicely's question still haunts Patsy and has built a wall between them. With Patsy coming to America, living completely separate lives was never supposed to be their fate. A clear memory comes to Patsy, of a bright day in high school when she and Cicely went

off by themselves to have lunch under the poinciana tree in the school-yard. Cicely often shared her lunch with Patsy, who had no money to buy food. Mama G was out of work and had no intention of finding another job. Cutting her corned-beef sandwich into a perfect line down the middle, Cicely said, "*I want us to always be together. No matter what. We can run away together after graduation, find somewhere to live. Jus' me an' you.*"

Cicely was the one person who had accepted everything about her. But now Patsy senses Cicely's withdrawal, her quiet judgment. Cicely kept her child a secret, but every day she's pouring herself into him. Patsy has left hers on the other side of the ocean.

Patsy stands at the entrance of the kitchen and watches her best friend. Cicely is at the sink, one slipperless foot resting on the inside of the opposite leg, the slipper abandoned next to it. In this moment, she becomes the common girl from Pennyfield who daydreamed constantly, her wistfulness adding sparkle to her eyes that used to flash with turquoise under hooded eyelids. She rolls her narrow shoulders and arches her back as if to rise out of herself, her loosened hair touching the middle of her spine. But just as quickly she hunches again, like a flower unable to blossom. Patsy softens, taking in Cicely's shapely figure, which Cicely jokingly calls "fat," emphasized in the plain blue housedress. Then she thinks of how soft and cool her skin will be despite the heat from the oven. The desire to touch her surges through Patsy. She thinks of the chicken feathers and suddenly there's an ache between her legs. Cicely's politeness around her is more than Patsy can bear. She wants to undress her, massage her rigid body until it loosens, arouse that wild passion they once had, tell her that it's okay now to be free.

When Cicely catches her staring she pauses, startled, flushing pink when she sees in Patsy's eyes what Patsy wants her to see. Her demeanor changes, the peaceful spirit pulling back like receding waves on a shore. Patsy senses her friend fumbling to regain composure, to shut her out. "Ah can use some help," she says, her voice as mellow as Shamar's music.

Patsy moves to wash her hands and assist Cicely with a heavy cast-iron pot she puts inside the oven. Cicely doesn't ask about the phone call. It's as if she already knows not to. She directs Patsy, telling her where to find certain ingredients and kitchenware. In comfortable silence, they sway and hum over their individual tasks—Cicely bending to take a roasted pumpkin from the oven to gut it, and Patsy using a mortar—the one thing Cicely preserved of her Caribbean identity—to pound garlic, raw onions, pepper, and other spices.

Patsy immediately loses herself in the mindless rhythmic thrust of the wooden pestle inside the smooth concave surface of the bowl. She feels useful, assured, for what else is she good at? Or has a firm grasp on in this moment? The flavors run free beneath the curve of Patsy's wet fingers, and the alluring scents rise into her nostrils and bring forth tears. Up and down, around and around, she grinds on the bed of spices as if deepening the sloping bowl with the hard roundness of the pestle. She presses her weight against the edge of the counter, the aroma, the violin music, and the things dredged from her soul swaying her like a willow over her grinding. There's no justification for the way the simple movement carries her, frees her, as the ingredients and her emotions liquefy. A hand grazes her shoulder. Pulls her up against feminine softness. Next thing she knows, Cicely is holding her from behind, her hands clasped below her belly, just under the hidden scar. With a deep guttural moan that sounds as though she has finally pushed life out of a contracting womb, Patsy turns and flings her arms around her friend, burrowing her wet face into the warm oblivion of Cicely's neck.

❦

CICELY, PATSY, AND SHAMAR EAT DINNER TOGETHER. MARCUS called and said he'll be working late. His absence from the dinner table doesn't seem to bother Cicely, though Patsy suspects that a man like that has other women he wines and dines somewhere else. It's just an inkling she has, wondering if Cicely ever questions it too. Shamar talks a lot more when his father isn't around. He engages Patsy about school and music. He loves music, says he wants to be a musician when he grows up. "Like Miles Davis!" he says.

"Who?" Patsy asks.

"Miles Davis. He's a famous jazz musician," he says to Patsy. "He played the trumpet."

"Oh, I see!"

"Shamar wants to play the trumpet," Cicely explains. "But his father thinks the violin is more cultured. He thinks it's important that Shamar reads and plays classical music."

"I hate the violin." The boy pouts. "They never give us popular music."

"Dat nuh sound like fun a'tall," Patsy tells him.

The boy's face cracks into a smile, as if he's glad that a grown-up is finally on his side. When he smiles, he looks exactly like Cicely. Patsy steals glances at her friend as she tells the little boy stories about his mother, their childhood. The little boy laughs, his curious, astonished gaze landing on his mother as she too laughs, bringing her head far back to reveal that sweet spot at the base of her throat, her face flushing pink. How odd her language must sound to him, pouring out of her, loud and free, echoing inside the old house and clashing with its high ceilings with chandeliers, its hushed rooms and champagne-colored drapes. The boy repeats those words—*"Yuh don't say! But yuh see me dying trial! Jeezum!"* as if to commit them to memory like he does Spanish and Mandarin at his private school.

Cicely is miraculously young again with the memory of that other life. Suddenly the child-Cicely boldly sucks her teeth. "Covah yuh ears, Shamar, an' don't listen to dis one!"

Her laughter, to Patsy's delight, is openly vulgar, banging on the dark oak doors and sweeping through each room, boisterous and defiant. A true Pennyfield woman, though more exotic. She hurls herself forward to slap Patsy playfully on the arm. "Stop it! Talk di truth!"

And this spurs Patsy to make her laugh more, tickling her with stories the way she did with those chicken feathers. When Cicely gets up from the dining table for a glass of water (she has been laughing so hard!), she stumbles merrily to the kitchen and pauses at the entrance to catch her breath, her blue satin maxidress emphasizing her full breasts and shapely figure, hugging her quivering frame. The boy's eyes follow his mother, enamored, his smile like rays of sunlight. Even the diamond earrings in her earlobes glint as the boy's eyes seem to retain his mother's laughing face.

A door opens and closes softly.

A shadow crosses Cicely's face. Her hands fall limply at her sides, her bangles clinking softly like chimes in a gentle breeze. Marcus enters from the veil of shadow and Patsy's smile transforms, though not as immediately as Cicely's. No longer is Cicely a woman full of life and ease with herself—a woman who, just seconds ago, threw her head back until it trembled proudly on the stalk of her neck—but a woman reassembling the image in the tall mirror. Cicely's eyes drop to her husband's feet. Shamar excuses himself quietly—so quietly that Patsy doesn't notice until she hears the soft click of his bedroom door. Patsy remains seated at the table, taking slow, measured breaths to calm the rage inside her. It clogs her throat, hardening like phlegm. Cicely tugs at her right earlobe, like a child who knows she's about to be scolded.

10

SHE WAITS BY THE PHONE. HER MOTHER MIGHT CALL AGAIN. SHE sits still, though every cell inside her body is active. *Be a good girl.* Marva puts a wicker chair by the telephone in the hallway and places three thick phone books on it for Tru to sit on so that she can reach the receiver. She's told to use the bathroom if she must, but is determined to hold her pee with all the strength she can muster. She's told she can have a scoop of ice cream after dinner before her brothers devour the whole bucket. She's told she needs to go to bed early for school the next day. She's told a lot of things, but the one thing that matters is the ring that will bring forth the sound of her mother's voice. She listens to her brothers and father in the living room watching kung fu movies.

Marva looks out from the kitchen at Tru. "Yuh all right, dear?"

"Yes, miss," Tru replies.

"Need a cup a wata?" Marva asks.

Tru is thirsty, but her bladder can take no more water. What if she goes to the bathroom and misses the call? She doesn't want anyone talking to her mother first. "No, thank you."

Marva continues to stand there in the faint light that spills into the hallway from the kitchen. Tru refuses to meet her inquisitive gaze, focusing on the mosquito bite on her leg. "If you need anything, let me know," Marva finally says after what seems like a long time standing there. "Is almost yuh bedtime."

11

STANDING ON THE LANDING, CICELY WAITS AND LISTENS FOR sound. "Patsy?" she whispers softly, not wanting to wake Marcus or Shamar.

"Yes?" Patsy responds, her voice climbing up the steps, out of the dark. Had it been a pair of arms, it would have been outstretched, the fingers spread wide for Cicely to pull her close to the source and tighten around her.

"It's me. Cicely. Can I come?" Then, in a whisper that sounds more like a prayer, Cicely says, "I need you."

Patsy gently brushes Cicely's long, lightweight hair down her back. Cicely hugs her knees and closes her eyes. From the way they sit—Patsy wide-legged on the bed, her nightgown hiked and pooled between her legs, Cicely's back to her—they might have been home surrounded by the zinc-roofed houses, the susurrant coconut trees waving in the breeze, and the soft-sloping hills that birth the sun, then swallow it in the evenings. They are two girls again. Two girls surrounded by the walls of what used to be a house on Jackson Lane before it burned to the ground. It was right next door to Cicely's house. Among ashes, away from their own hell, they found their secret hiding place. Weeds had grown inside and crept up the blackened walls toward light, and flowers had sprung from a discarded woman's shoe left by the owner. The past extends itself to the quiet brownstone basement in Brooklyn. In the dim light from the wisteria lamp Patsy observes something openly ripe and languorous creep into Cicely's pose when she lets go of her knees and crosses her legs at the ankles as Patsy brushes her hair. Her hands absently trail the insides of her thighs to warm them.

"Don't know how ah went without dis fah so long," Cicely sighs above the hiss of the steam pipes, and leans back farther so that Patsy can see her face—the slope between her forehead and nose, the graceful rise of her mouth. The present rushes in like darkness racing over the land and crouches in the shadows as Patsy watches Cicely this way, in her inviolate state. How defenseless Cicely seems—has always seemed— as though she were never really fit for the roughness of life. Maybe that's what Marcus is to her. Protection. Comfort. Resentment flows out of Patsy, into her fingers clutching the brush, through the length of Cicely's hair, finally penetrating her skull. "Tek it easy wid me," Cicely chides, opening her eyes. "Unless yuh want pull di hair out me head!"

But Patsy only stares at her, her oil-stained hands in her lap where Cicely's dead hairs have fallen. Patsy silently picks at them and balls them into her fist.

"You should dye it black," she says.

"What?" Cicely asks, turning her head over her left shoulder.

"Yuh hair. Ah prefer it black."

Cicely arches her eyebrows.

"Dis doesn't suit you," Patsy continues. "Marcus doesn't know everyt'ing."

Cicely laughs. "So dat's what dis is about? Marcus?"

"Everyt'ing is about him. Ah can't do dis any longah," Patsy says, closing her legs and pulling down her flowy chiffon nightgown over her knees.

"Can't do what?" Cicely asks, scooting away a little to give Patsy's legs space.

"Intrude on you an' yuh family."

"Who says you're intruding?"

"Marcus nuh hide him feelings well."

"He has no say. You're my friend."

"Cicely, don't humor me."

"Ah mean dat." After a brief pause, Cicely says, "He's jus' not used to guests in di house."

"What is it yuh see in him?" Patsy asks.

Cicely's mouth opens and closes, her eyes wide, incredulous, as if Patsy has struck her. "He's my husband. Ah mean—I married him fah papers, yes. But yuh don't know how hard it is here," Cicely says.

"We could live together. You an' me. Jus' like you said in dat letter—"

"Dat was a long time ago."

"I know yuh not happy."

"A woman can't survive without a man anywhere, Patsy," Cicely says.

"Not even in America. A man like Marcus mek all dis possible." Cicely gestures at the space around them with her hands.

"Is dat all?" Patsy asks. "Is dis di only t'ing he can offer you?"

"How yuh mean? In dis country, yuh can't be too picky, yuh hear? If yuh want to be legal, yuh haffi to marry a man. Yuh can't get around dat."

"How's dat different from being a prostitute?" Patsy asks.

A hush creeps into the basement as Cicely snatches her breath.

"You don't get it," Cicely says after a while.

"What's dere to not get? A man offer you papers instead of money. Same difference. Don't tell me dat neva come wid strings."

"I think we done wid dis convah-sation," Cicely says, struggling to get up.

"What's so hard, Cicely?" Patsy asks, her question like hands reaching to pull Cicely back down. "What's suh hard 'bout considering other possibilities?"

"We too old fah dat kind of t'inking," Cicely says. "What? Yuh expec' to come here an' be girls again?"

"Is not about age," Patsy hisses.

Cicely is quietly rubbing her temples. "Is like yuh living in a dream world. Even today at di job agency when yuh ask di woman 'bout school. Yuh not even set foot good inside di country, an' already yuh t'inking 'bout school? Many of us haffi work hard to be stable before we can t'ink like dat. Is not suh it work. We're women wid families. An' wid dat comes responsibilities, whether yuh like it or not. It's time dat you put t'ings into perspective. At least do it fah yuh dawta."

Cicely's words stamp down on Patsy. She's only half listening as Cicely goes on about sacrifice. How Marcus is such a good example. "He started out wid not'ing a'tall. Spent his whole childhood in foster care. If yuh know what dat's like, you'd undah-stand. Him jus' want di best fah his family, especially his son," she says. "We're giving our son the best education so dat he too can fit into dis white world. And no, it's not called whitewashing his brain. It's called survival. Marcus will tell yuh dat if yuh don't run in di same ring wid white folk, there's no way we can ever get a seat at di table. Now Marcus run him own business. Di best in Brooklyn. Him might even run fah City Council. Because of him, Crown Heights will be the next big real estate dream by di new millennium. Dat mean working late at night if him have to. It doesn't make him a bad husband."

When she's done, Patsy says, "It might be best for me to start looking fah places."

Cicely frowns. "But yuh don't even have a job yet. I owe you dis much . . ."

"You owe me nothing."

There's a loud banging across the room, inside the rusted pipes, which causes Patsy to pause, relieved. She didn't realize that her hands were balled into tight fists until now when she opens them to see the red sickle creases of her nails in the middle of each palm.

"Dis damn old house," Cicely mutters, unaware. Once the noise dies down a little, she continues. "All I'm saying is dat sometimes we haffi sacrifice."

"How much did you sacrifice, Cicely?" Patsy asks. "Tell me."

"Yuh t'ink I'm pitiful," Cicely says.

Patsy pauses, her rage falling away at the memory of them alone in Miss Zelma's house—the shy yet curious way Patsy regarded Cicely, secretly vowing to protect her always. She realizes that her resentment of Cicely stems from Cicely's awareness of her worth—the expectation that she'd always be cared for. Loved. Perhaps that is why Cicely always wanted her around—to brush her hair, rub her down, and soothe her with her words. In the dimness of the basement, Patsy sees it, though she's powerless against it when she hears herself say, "You're far from pitiful." Her mouth is dry all of a sudden.

"Please forgive me," Cicely says.

"What's there to forgive?" Patsy asks.

"Everyt'ing." Cicely's eyes are moist.

Patsy knows what she means by *everything*. It is a balm more bitter than the sinkle bible she rubbed over Cicely's shoulders, its potency mediocre in comparison, considering all that is lost and forgotten in just one word—*everything*. Patsy doesn't want to go down that road again, reopening sutures that had long been sealed.

"Everyt'ing happen fah a reason," Patsy says aloud now, sounding too much like Mama G, who willingly folded herself into the arms of life to be carried by it.

"Does dat mean yuh forgive me?" Cicely asks, breaking Patsy's thoughts.

"Dat's like not forgiving ah onion fah making me cry," Patsy says, thinking of her freedom and how she has Cicely to thank for it. "It's senseless. Is not your fault. Had it not been for you, ah woulda end up worse off."

In the heartbeat of silence that follows, Cicely chuckles, tears on her cheeks. "I'm glad we have each other. An' ah hope yuh not comparing me to no onion."

Patsy lifts her friend's chin with one oiled finger, smudging it with hair grease. "Yuh not pitiful," she says again, half smiling at Cicely. The slow growl of the heater returns with Patsy's thirst. Cicely holds Patsy's hand to her face and closes her eyes, her long lashes creating shadows on the rise of her cheekbones under the glow of the stained-glass wisteria lamp. Patsy watches her face. Then, almost reverentially, she leans to kiss it softly, wets her lips with the tears on each cheek, traces with her finger the outline of her face, smooths her frayed bleached hair. Despite the tenderness, there's a frightening possessiveness she feels for Cicely. Patsy remembers yearning in school to step inside Cicely's skin. For beneath the shimmering gold exterior there lived promise—everything Patsy had ever desired. Each caress declares this, as her lips have not yet learned the shape of the thing with no name that surges in her blood. She stares down, with awe, at the figure in front of her, and finally kisses the scar on Cicely's forehead above her left eyebrow. Cicely's eyes fly open, glazed with something Patsy cannot read, which forces Patsy to pull away, her face warm and burning as though the look had struck her flesh.

"I—I have to go," Cicely says. Carefully she gets up, her dress loose around her as she makes her way out of the basement, up the stairs.

Patsy lowers her head and gingerly touches the marks her nails have made in her palms. For a long while she sits, caressing her loss under the dim light, aware of the familiar darkness crouched just left of her shoulder—the only thing that is hers alone.

ϟ

A T ELEVEN YEARS OLD, PATSY THOUGHT EVERYTHING ABOUT Cicely was contagious. She imagined that Cicely was a neat doll-house on the inside with no clutter, no figurines, no open Bibles, no rosemary oil, no old dusty stereo that played scratchy records for the mind to conjure up the ghosts of two strangers shuffling around the room. She also found it impossible to believe that a girl like Cicely, who was so beautiful and carefree, could have anything to be sad about.

When Cicely first invited Patsy over to her house, it was an event. She followed Cicely home after school that day, excited. On their walk, they picked up sticks and grazed them against fences, delighted to see goats halt at the sound and hear dogs bark. It felt to Patsy like a prelude to something big—she was getting to play with a real life-size doll, having her all to herself. Cicely lived just over the gully, which seemed like a new world to Patsy then. People on both sides went to the same schools and church and utilized the same businesses. But politics divided the terrains, rendering one side orange for the People's National Party and the other side green for the Jamaica Labor Party. Cicely's area was orange and thus had little tolerance for Jamaica Labor Party supporters—"laborites"—coming into their territory. When the

PNP won the election that year, their supporters grabbed their brooms and swept dust from their doorways and walkways into the streets to signify their victory, cleaning out their opponents, *"G'weh! Is we run t'ings!"* However, nothing about Cicely and her neighbors seemed odd or different based on their political affiliations. They waved howdy just the same. The women told them to pull up their slips, fold their socks, and, in Patsy's case, fix her tunic, which was too tight. The men silently appraised their uniform-covered bodies, their lust evident in the way their shaded gazes lingered, hidden in overzealous hospitality and grins. *"Oonuh stay sweet, yuh hear, darlings?"*

Cicely's house smelled sweet. The smell was as alluring as it was pervasive, spread over the small living room with doilies on the center table and fake flowers on the whatnot. There was a small TV with antennas sticking out of it and a sofa with plastic covering. The wooden floorboards were polished to a shine. It didn't look like a prostitute's house, though Patsy had no idea what she thought a prostitute's house would look like. Mama G made it seem as if Miss Mabley were Satan's wife. The other women in the community acted like the woman was lower than a mongrel dog. Maybe because their men's eyes followed her buxom body the way fleas followed the lowly animals.

Cicely's mother was a day woman. Not the type of day woman, like many in Pennyfield, who woke up at the break of dawn to march with baskets on their heads to sell produce at the market downtown or the cheap clothes they got in barrels from Curaçao in their makeshift stalls. Cicely's mother also wasn't one to get caught up in the hype of working at the Free Zone like most of the other women in their community who were in search of something resembling a living wage—women who ruined their eyesight and hands sitting in a factory for hours, hovering over industrial sewing machines to make brand-name clothes for big American companies that hardly paid them. Neither was Cicely's mother the kind of day woman like Mama G, who took taxis to the foot of the hills in Upper St. Andrew to then walk several miles just to drop to their knees and scrub the marble floors of the rich. No. In retrospect, Cicely's mother was a practical woman, a prideful woman, a businesswoman, who used her most valuable asset—her sexuality. Though she was in high demand, she never let that prevent her from sewing all Cicely's school uniforms and dresses, diligently letting out hems and restitching them the taller Cicely grew. She took very good care of Cicely, never letting her want for anything. Because she and Cicely shared the same bed where she conducted business, no customers came at night.

"Har pum-pum tight like gyal pickney own!" a drunk Mas' Jerry once hollered within earshot of his woman, Miss Bernadette, who then smashed a rum bottle on his head at a dance held at Pete's. Miss Mabley apparently skinned out to prove this fact to the woman scorned—her legs as wide as the Martha Brae River running in opposite directions on the boom box to reveal her golden pum-pum to the whole world. *"Seet yah!"* she said to Miss Bernadette, patting her exposed front. *"Ah dis hol' yuh man! Fi yuh singting nuh hol' him. My good-good mek him come back fi more!"* Patsy wasn't there to see it, but the story about Miss Mabley's golden pum-pum spread faster than a racehorse at Caymanas Park. As time went along, people spoke less about it (especially around Miss Bernadette), and some might have even willfully erased it from memory, but the pretty mulatta girl running around with blue-green eyes became the unforgivable thing that could never be forgotten. Because it was one thing for Miss Mabley to reveal her privates at a dance, but it was another thing for her to flaunt its capabilities in the faces of other women—its power to not only lure a white man, but bring forth a child more beautiful than their own children (or any child who had ever been born in Pennyfield).

Cicely turned to Patsy the first time Patsy entered her house and said, *"Shhh. My mother sleeping. Try not to wake har. She like har beauty rest."*

Patsy looked in the direction of the bedroom, shielded by a thin red curtain. She heard the light snores coming from behind it. A pair of men's shoes were parked at the entrance. Between the curtain and the doorframe, she could see a woman's slim ankles dangling seductively from the edge of the bed. Cicely pulled Patsy along. They went to the back of the house to catch the last of the remaining May butterflies inside two jam jars Cicely found under her kitchen cupboard. When they each caught one butterfly, they took it out of the jar and examined it—the velvety yellow wings that colored their fingers with their yellow dust, the worm-like bodies, the small legs, the bright, fire-lit eyes. The soft silky warmth of the wings made Patsy's fingers tingle. "*We should set them free,*" she said. "*See their wings? They were meant to fly.*"

"*Let's play pretend,*" Cicely suggested.

"*Pretend what?*" Patsy asked.

"*Pretend we live together by we self, an' these are our babies.*"

Patsy looked at the two fluttering butterflies trapped inside the jars.

"*We need to free dem,*" Patsy said.

"*No, silly. We could both be their mothers.*"

"*What if ah don't want to be a mother?*"

"*Yuh want to be di father?*"

"*Ah didn't say dat either.*"

"*Yuh want to play or not?*"

Patsy didn't want to disappoint Cicely, so she said, "*Dey don't resemble us at all.*"

"*We adopted dem,*" Cicely said.

"*Adopt?*"

"*Ah wish I was adopted.*"

"*But you have yuh real mother.*"

"*She's not like di other mothers at school. Sometimes ah wish she was different.*"

"*How?*"

A silence passed. Then Cicely asked, "*You neva wish you was adopted too?*"

"*No.*"

"Yuh lie."

"Who would adopt me? I'm not as pretty as you."

B Y THE TIME THE SCHOOL YEAR CAME TO AN END, PATSY AND Cicely had established their ritual, playing hide-and-seek in Cicely's backyard after school, catching butterflies they "adopted" inside jars to co-parent. They searched the bushes every afternoon for fluttering wings, unmindful of flies and other insects. Sometimes they ran along the gully, laughing too loud when they caught grasshoppers. Whenever they got bored, Cicely sat on Patsy's lap or between her legs for Patsy to unlace her long braid of black hair, which fell like a long silk blanket down Cicely's back. Patsy brushed it, happy to play with it like she would a doll's hair. There was a newness to Cicely that she liked—her soft, condensed-milk skin, which smelled just as sweet as it looked.

There was no one to disturb them—at least no one they could see.

𝄇

T HOUGHT YOU'D NEVER COME BACK UPSTAIRS."
Cicely jumps at the sound of Marcus's voice inside the living room. When she turns, she sees him sitting on the white couch, his arms slung over the back, one slippered foot resting on the knee of his other leg. His long burgundy robe is open to reveal his soft belly. His eyes reflect the light of the chandelier, which also creates a sheen on the family photographs on the mantel. When they met, it was his eyes that drew her to him, eyes that reminded her of a stranger she had never met; a stranger her mother kept from her, only telling her that she has his eyes. She had heard them talking. *"She's yuh dawta. Jus' wake har up an' look at her eyes. Blue an' green jus like yours."* But the stranger was never that curious. He stayed inside her mother's bedroom, his

big shoes at the door. They were leather wing-tip shoes—polished and shined. Cicely knew because she crept out of the makeshift bed on the living room sofa where her mother had tucked her in (only when the man came over) and picked one up. She ran her finger along the surface of the shoes. They had no dust on them and the soles looked like they'd never touched ground, though Pennyfield had no paved roads. He came in a nice government vehicle. His blazer, hung on a chair at their small dining table, had gold buttons, intricate stitches, and a J embroidered on the collar. It was wide enough to span the width of his broad shoulders. *"Yuh have to stop wid dat foolishness, Mabley,"* the man hissed from behind the red curtain of Mabley's bedroom. *"Ah have a reputation. A family."* Cicely's mother only cried. *"Ah can't do dis anymore. Not wid another on di way. Ah can't continue to keep dis secret. My children deserve a good life."* A week later her mother was found dead, her naked body decomposing in the Pennyfield dump right by Cicely's primary school, covered with zinc. Cicely was only twelve years old.

Years later, Cicely met her husband on the street one windy afternoon when she was on her way to work. That was when she used to work as a home health aide in Sunset Park to fund her night school courses. Her umbrella blew away into the middle of Fourth Avenue, and he rescued it for her. Even in her pink scrubs, clogs, and braids, which the Africans on Fulton Street pulled tightly into neat boxes, Cicely didn't just accept the man's heavy flirtation, she expected it. She also took one look at his shoes—a pair of wing tips in which she probably could have seen her reflection if she stared hard enough and knew that a man with shoes like that liked beautiful things.

"You'd think with all the cleaning you've been doing that I could eat my next meal from every damn piece of furniture in this house," he says, getting up and straightening with his hands in the pockets of his flannel pajamas. He's walking around now, his burgundy robe like a cape, as he scrutinizes everything with a critical eye. He picks up a butterfly-shaped glass from the coffee table.

"Marcus, what is it?" Cicely asks, her heart beating fast inside her chest.

Marcus seems to grimace at her comment. "A husband can't come downstairs to see what's keeping his wife up at night?"

"Well, here I am," Cicely says, shrugging her shoulders. "You see what I'm up to. I had to put something in the dryer and say good night to my friend." Her eyes dart around the room, searching for words in the shadows crouched in the corners, her guilt immobilizing her.

Marcus stares at her for what seems like a long time, as if watching for something.

"Your friend. Huh."

"Yes." She meets his gaze.

"Well, your *friend* needs to go." He returns his attention to the butterfly-shaped glass in his hand, caresses it with his thumb, hefts it as if trying to discern how much it weighs.

"Go where?" Cicely asks, watching him.

"She needs to find a place."

"But she jus' got here, Marcus. She hasn't even gotten a job interview yet."

"I'm not going to allow her to live off us like a parasite. You know how Jamaicans can get."

"What's dat supposed to mean? You're Jamaican yuhself," Cicely hisses.

"My parents were. They're dead. I was raised by a Jewish family," Marcus says between clenched teeth, his jawbones pulsing like the rage in Cicely's loins, his hands clamped around the glass, threatening to break it.

"It doesn't make you one of them," she hisses.

"What do you know? Unlike certain people, I work for everything I have," he says.

"Certain people?" It's Cicely's turn to grimace. "Have you evah heard yourself speak? Di way how you put down our people as if you're—"

"I'm giving her a day."

"Have you been drinking? A day? What can she find in a day? Yuh know how hard it is to rent a place without papers?"

Marcus looks her squarely in the face and says, "No. I do not know, and neither do I care. Consider this a generous act on my part, because any other man wouldn't have given her another minute."

"What are you talking about?"

"She said so herself. Right? About wanting to move out? Not wanting to intrude on *you and your family*? So how am I a bad person for giving her the opportunity to do so?"

"You were listening!"

"And what is this foolishness about me not having a say about who stays in *my house*?"

"You were listening!" Her hands find their way to the sides of her face, cup her mouth. What else did he hear? Her legs feel like they're about to give.

"My own house!" He slams the glass down hard on the coffee table, which would have cracked had it not been made of solid wood.

"You were listening!" she whispers, lowering herself on the sofa, him towering above her like God Himself.

"And you know what hurts the most?" He's peering deep into her eyes now, the green of his pupils hard marbles. His voice is low, steady. He comes closer, his hand at her throat. "You choosing *her* over me."

"You have no right—" she says, her breath shallow.

"She lied to you, darling," he says, his hand still at her throat. "Just like you lied to me. And just like you lied to her. Because you are pitiful. You're as pitiful as a stray who nibbles at any hand that pets it."

"If I'm pitiful, what does sneaking around your own house make you?" Cicely asks, her composure driven by anger. "If you was half di man you say you are, then you wouldn't—" Before she can finish her sentence, she's searching her mouth for broken teeth. She hardly felt the blow, for when Marcus puts his fist to her face it's almost like it never happened. At least that was how it felt when Cicely was struck by Marcus the first time. She thought it was happening to someone else—an actress in one of those silent movies who dramatically holds her cheek and screams. Meanwhile, Cicely experienced the whole thing floating above the scene, like a woman lying on a couch watching television. It wasn't until she glanced in the mirror the next day, unable to recognize the woman staring back at her, that she realized what had really happened. She wept, trembling all over and turning her head from side to side to study her ugliness. For a woman who had always taken pride in her good looks, this was something new; something to live with.

Cowering under the glittering crystals of the chandelier in anticipation of the next blow, Cicely hears the taunts. The voices of schoolchildren on a playground far, far away: Cicely's primary school mates were unyeilding with their bullying after Mabley's death when they found out what her mother did for a living and how she died. "*There's a brown girl in di ring, tra la la la! There's a brown girl in di ring, traa la la . . .*" Her head now spins from Marcus's blow. The children point, their fingers pinning her in the circle. "*Bull inna pen, cyan come out! Bull inna pen, cyan come out!*"

She doesn't bother to get back up. She knows better. She has lost all the fight in her. She knows that her husband is right. She knows that if she wakes up the next morning and he's not there, then she would have nowhere to go. What can Patsy give her now that he cannot, besides their shared memories and guilt? Infinite responsibilities stretch before her, but she's not prepared to deal with them. She cannot accept the burden of being in America without the advantage of living the dream, regardless of the abuse. Though she has to do things for her weekly allowance, like cook dinner and fuck her husband on a regular basis—even when she's not in the mood—there's still some semblance of stability. So when Patsy appears out of nowhere in her nightgown, pounding Marcus with her fists—"Don't you dare put yuh hands 'pon har, or else me will kill yuh!"—in one quick motion Cicely springs up and shoves her friend hard. Patsy wheels and hits the floor, visibly stunned—too startled to move, her eyes large dark holes punched in the sockets.

"Don't you dare disrespect my husband like dat in his own house!" Cicely hisses. She hopes to communicate her desperation with her eyes. She had wanted to tell her quietly in the basement. But it's too late. Moments later, Patsy scurries out of sight. Cicely only hears her friend's footsteps down the stairs to the basement. Cicely almost runs after her, but Marcus pulls her back with his words.

"I want her out of this house."

He walks past Cicely, who is standing in the middle of the living room wiping blood from her nose with the back of her hand. "I'm going to bed. Don't make me wait too long."

She reaches like a blind person for the nearest thing to hold on to, to steady herself. She touches the surface of the white couch—too hurt to consider the risk of staining it and how much it will cost to hire professionals to clean it. She stumbles, succumbing to uncontrollable sobs as she climbs the staircase toward their bedroom, groping the banister and fumbling with the dress that feels like sandpaper around her. The hurt she saw in Patsy's eyes lashes her—more painful than Marcus's abuse. Regret almost chokes her when she remembers what Patsy did, what she sacrificed, her quiet willingness to suffer on Cicely's behalf. A lifetime of love and friendship lost tonight in Cicely's effort to defend the prison she has built for herself.

12

SIX DAYS. THAT'S HOW LONG TRU HAS COUNTED. SIX DAYS AND NO word from her mother since the missed phone call. The school bell rings, indicating the end of the school day. When the teacher tells the class to clasp their hands and close their eyes for prayer, Tru keeps one eye open.

"Bless us, Father, our ruler, savior, and provider. Grant us with favor and make us worthy in your sight . . ."

She mouths the unfamiliar prayer, sneaking a look over her shoulder toward the door, expecting to see her mother waiting like she used to. But there is no one at the door. Just the blue sky purged of the clouds that look like kings and queens sailing on ships in the clouds.

"Trudy-Ann, are you deaf? I said all eyes closed!" The sound of the teacher's voice pulls her back inside the classroom. She is calling Tru by her full name—just like her father. A name she has to adjust to. A name as foreign to Tru as that of her new school and classmates. Tru is mercilessly plopped in the second grade with children older than her. She knows that she'll be a big girl when she turns six in a few weeks, but Roy, who knows the principal of the new school because she is the wife of another policeman at his precinct, never asked Tru if she was comfortable switching schools, much less skipping first grade. Worse, Tru had to watch Marva fold her old Saints Basic School blue tunic that her mother had specially made by the local seamstress and put it inside a trunk filled with moldy clothes. Tru's new school uniform is bigger on her—passed on to her by Agnus, an older girl who lives next door, and who still sucks her thumb when Marva braids her hair on Sundays. The green tunic makes Tru look like a vegetable, which she hates.

After the class finishes their prayer, rows of chairs screech and voices soar at the sound of the last bell. It's Friday—a day Tru now dreads. Her mother used to treat her to KFC on Fridays after school. Now Fridays mean spending a whole weekend at her father's house doing chores. It also means getting walloped by Mrs. Powell for failing yet another daily quiz—which Tru feels is unfair, since the quizzes are based on knowledge learned in the first grade, which she skipped. She hasn't felt motivated to please this teacher like she felt with Miss Gains. Since her mother left, school hasn't interested Tru much, and it's obvious that this new teacher isn't interested in teaching her. Mrs. Powell grades the quiz on the spot—marking *x* for wrong answers and bold red ticks for the right ones. Tru peers at her answers, knowing that she will get more *x*'s than ticks, and thus a spanking with the sturdy wooden ruler from Mrs. Powell again.

Tru doesn't spring up from her desk like her classmates. She makes a production out of zipping up her schoolbag—the same one she carried to school last year, the one her father tells her he will replace once her mother sends some money. Her hands are moist, her head down. From the sides of her eyes she sees the line formed at Mrs. Powell's desk dwindling. Joseph—whose name Tru knows because, like her, he's the class dunce—is currently bent over, receiving his spanking on his bottom—ten loud ones for each answer he got wrong. Mrs. Powell is hardly tender, even on days when she's in a good mood. She's a big yellow woman with gray hawk eyes, and a mouth that is fixed in a sneer. She beats them until the frayed straps of her brassiere slip below the short puffy sleeves of her blouse and her face turns pinker than the disgusting strawberry-flavored milk Tru is forced to drink at lunchtime in the cafeteria that smells like bleach.

"Next!" Mrs. Powell calls, staring straight at Tru with those hawk eyes. She's last in line.

Tru takes measured steps toward Mrs. Powell's desk. She hands her the exercise book, which has her name and class written on the front, and waits.

"On the roster, it says you're Trudy-Ann," Mrs. Powell says. "Why yuh insist on writing Tru? You dat lazy? In my class I expect you to spell out yuh name, yuh hear?"

"My mother name me Tru," Tru says in a small voice, knowing she will get more lashes on top of what she'll already get.

"Pardon?" Mrs. Powell asks.

"My mother name me Tru," Tru repeats.

"Where is yuh mother now? Is she here? Let her come tell me dat herself. Until then, you're Trudy-Ann. Like it says on yuh records."

Tru nods, defeated. She watches Mrs. Powell's pen, the curve of her mouth as she does the calculations in her head, the fat ringless fingers on her left hand—though she goes by Mrs. not Miss, which Tru learns to call all unmarried women, including Marva. Tru studies those fat fingers that trace the numbers in her exercise book the way she has seen Mr. Lewin, the blind man on Roundtree Road, read his special Bible in church. When Mrs. Powell finishes, she looks up at Tru. "Eight wrong out of ten."

She pauses as if expecting a response from Tru. But Tru, trying hard not to cry, doesn't speak. "What?" Mrs. Powell says. "Yuh don't study? Dey say you were the brightest one at Saints, so how come it seem like yuh 'ave the brain of a gnat inside dis class?"

Mrs. Powell lifts her wooden ruler and gestures for Tru to turn around and bend over. Slowly Tru does as she's told, clutching the edge of the table, tears already filling her eyes. The sound of the first lick on Tru's rump echoes inside the empty classroom. With seven more licks to go, Tru clenches her muscles tight, not wanting to cry out, wishing she could enjoy it like Marva. She hears them at night—her father and Marva—in the room next to hers. When the night is completely still, there is always the low quaking, the heavy breathing, and the clapping sound like an open palm against skin. Tru tries to identify each noise, imagines her father and Marva taking the shape of animals howling at the moon, the way they carry on. One night the sounds pulled Tru out of her bunk and to their bedroom door, where she spied the two crouched figures—Marva naked and sweaty on all fours like she was holding down the floorboards, and Roy kneeling behind her. Marva was crying like she was hurting, although she was telling Roy not to stop. But the quaking slowed, followed by a lurch, and Tru's father yelling, *"Get di hell out!"*

Prickly heat now radiates from Tru's backside to the rest of her body as Mrs. Powell hits her. A flicker of sunlight makes its way through the louvered windows inside the classroom and lies across a table. Tru keeps her eyes focused on it. With each sting of the ruler that Mrs. Powell uses, Tru remembers her father's words, *"She not coming back."* She remembers too his anger that night when she stood paralyzed in the doorway. *"Get di hell out!"* And the buzzing of the dial tone six days before. Those days that are marked off with red *x*'s on the calendar, bright like Mrs. Powell's marks beside wrong answers. Tru doesn't realize the beating has stopped until Mrs. Powell says, "So you jus' g'wan stay there bend over like yuh enjoy it?" But Tru only looks down at her whitened knuckles, still clutching the table, numb.

BOOK III

JOHN-CROW'S CURSE

13

PATSY NOTICES THE PECULIAR SHAPES OF THE TREES, SOME OF which have begun to lose their leaves as Cicely drives her to the place she found for her to live. In the early morning, they have a sorrowful look to them, a dismal charcoal hue, same shade as the black birds that perch on their outstretched limbs. For Patsy has lost her ability to see color. This rain-soaked day, especially, has a mournful air about it. It's hard now for Patsy to think about their sun-washed days together as girls. It's harder for her to trust those memories. Cicely parks the car outside a house on a quiet Brooklyn street. The houses on this street are not brownstones like Cicely's, but squat two-story buildings with decorative bricks on the outside, the roofs slanted, with small square windows looking out of them. They have small front yards with brown grass surrounded by chain-link fences.

Cicely shuts off her car engine and, without looking at Patsy, says, "This is it. I found dis place through a friend of a friend. Di owner seem like a nice woman."

Patsy doesn't say anything. Not even expressing her gratitude to Cicely for convincing Marcus to let her stay six more days until she found something. She goes to open the door on her side, but Cicely places her hand on hers, her lashes darkened by tears and the right side of her face bruised, though she tried to cover it up with makeup. Her apology rushes out in an exhaled breath. "I'm so sorry."

But Patsy cannot bring herself to meet her friend's imploring gaze. She is moved to cry at the sheer insanity, the inner chaos of tangled emotions, which pressed her blind across the ocean to be with a woman who doesn't feel the same way about her. She was certain of what she read in those letters, the true-to-life presence of something she could not explain. They were sitting inside the old house on Jackson Lane, hidden from view, the first time Cicely kissed her. They were fourteen then, gossiping about boys—mostly about the boys who liked Cicely and who she didn't like back—boys who wore jerry curls and called themselves Casanovas. Patsy had sex with all of them. Those were her days of exploring, feeling obligated to please boys she wanted to like her too. The year Mama G started hearing the voice of God, Patsy, only nine years old, had stuffed herself with toilet paper thinking she was bleeding to death. When Mama G found out, she locked Patsy inside the house and prayed with her, anointing Patsy with rosemary oil. *"Keep har temple holy, dear Jesus."* Frightened, Patsy clutched the soiled sheets, smelling a subtle yet overpowering scent coming from between her legs that reminded her of the smell of the sun-drenched zinc she spread clothes on to dry on Sundays. Mama G then told Patsy that her body was a temple, and for a long time, Patsy didn't understand what she meant. She simply existed then, floating near but outside her own body, feeling invincible. Or perhaps *feeling* is not the right word, given that she felt nothing at all. Not until that afternoon when Cicely, who lived vicariously through Patsy's tales of fucking, flushed pink from the indecency of their gossip, put her hand on Patsy's knee.

The touch was so tender that Patsy had to look down at the hand to see if it was really there. Then, without caution or any hint of apprehension, Cicely leaned over and kissed Patsy. Patsy didn't have time to pull back or even process what was happening in that moment. All she knew was that she loved the feel of Cicely's lips on hers. She closed her eyes, breathing evenly as Cicely's lips moved to her ear. *"Show me,"* she whispered to Patsy. And, lying on the grass that sprouted through the cracks in the concrete of the old house amid the debris, both of them still wearing their school uniforms, Patsy placed her arms comfortably around Cicely. They joined, it seemed: their faces close, their mouths opening, their bodies rubbing, and Patsy, who had previously felt she was circling the world on a wind outside herself, came, pouring her soul into Cicely's. Patsy had never felt life bursting inside her like that, hyper-aware of the sun, the earth, the grass beneath them; of herself buried between Cicely's legs, rapt.

After that, their friendship took on a new, ambiguous form. Cicely and Patsy went on dating boys, and reasonably so, for Cicely, like Patsy, knew that what happened inside the old house was not condoned. She observed Cicely's interactions with the boys who hounded her at Roman Phillips Secondary, laughing with her, clowning to get her attention. Patsy's eyes swept on, but they'd inevitably lock with Cicely's with guarded desire. They had no place for this desire besides the old abandoned house, hidden by posts of blue mahoe and palm trees and a fence of weeds, at least six feet tall, that formed a ring around it. Concealed and secured by the lushness and decay around them, on top of a beach towel spread on the ground, the girls attained the fullest freedom.

Then one evening—just months after Cicely started university, commuting from Pennyfield to campus each day—it happened. Patsy's arms were tight around Cicely's waist when she heard the rustling in the bushes, thinking they were mongooses or lizards. Suddenly feet drew near, and before she knew it, a man crept from the bushes and attacked them. Everything exploded like an orange flare, and Patsy's eyes helplessly followed the man's arc toward Cicely. In slow motion, he curved downward, his arms swept out, his whole body lunged in one live motion to scoop her. Patsy remembered seeing his mouth moving, but not hearing anything he said. Everything, it seemed, occurred without sound—the shattering of the rusted mirror that stood nearby,

Cicely's wail as blood gushed from her head, and the man's fall on shards of broken glass.

Now, in the car, Patsy just wants to be alone, to hide her face in her hands and wail or laugh—whichever one will rid her of the bitter taste in her mouth. None of this should ever have happened.

"I still care about you . . ." Cicely is saying.

"Don't," Patsy replies, her voice a choked whisper. "Don't guh there wid me. Ah know why it's difficult fah you. Cicely, we both bled dat day, way back. Dere was no sun in di clouds aftah dat. Me an' Roy neva love like you an' me did love. He knew dat. But Tru came, an' ah thought . . ." Her voice trails. "Ah realized dat wasn't my life. Ah realized dat my life is wid you. When yuh told me ah could come to America, ah left every'ting."

"You left yuh life. Yuh family. Yuh dawta, jus' fah me?"

"Yes."

"Tell me di truth."

"Ah jus' did. Ah wanted to start ovah wid you, Cicely."

"Patsy . . ." Cicely says quietly. "There's no way I'm going back to dat."

"Yuh safe now. No one can hurt you or hurt us no more."

"Dis is my life now, Patsy," Cicely says. "I built a life here wid Marcus. If ah leave he'd neva let me take our son. He would fight fah sole custody if any ah dis ever get out. Ah can't afford to jeopardize what ah have. It was neva my intention to hurt you. Despite what yuh saw dat night wid me an' Marcus, we're happy. An' so is Shamar . . ."

"Coulda fooled me," Patsy says. "We getting out dis car or not? Because I'm done wid dis convah-sation."

As they stand on the steps in front of the house, both damp-faced from the slight drizzle—Patsy with her suitcase next to her and Cicely in her stylish clothes and a purse slung over her shoulder—Patsy tries hard not to look at Cicely, though she senses her silhouette limp with regret. Cicely presses the buzzer again, too slowly. Someone peeps through a white curtain by the front window. There's swift movement behind the door before it opens. A black woman, who looks to be in her forties, appears in a long thick pink robe that swallows her petite frame, with blue and black box braids piled on top of her head. She appears to be wearing a mask at first. She has a wide, screwed face, the face of a person who seems cross with the world—a Jamaican woman, no doubt, whose smiles and laughter are reserved for people she knows well and trusts. But Patsy can hardly imagine her laughing or smiling at all with those expressionless eyes.

"Me neh expec' anyone dis early," the woman says without greeting. Patsy wonders which part of the island she's from, sounding like that. Patsy only made out the word *early*. She realizes that the discoloration she sees on the woman's face is from bleaching creams. The smell of fish hurries toward Patsy and she begins to think it's a mistake, being here at the mercy of a woman who bleaches her skin and cooks fish this early in the morning.

Cicely seems hesitant, as if she's afraid the smell of fish will insinuate itself into her clothes and she would carry it with her all day. She pauses uneasily at the door, her pale hands barely touching the frame, and says, "Uhm—I have to take my son to school. My friend needs this room as soon as possible. If you don't mind showing her around, that would be great. I will pay you security and first month's rent up-front."

Something flickers across the woman's wide face at the sound of Cicely's voice giving her orders. Patsy isn't sure if it's satisfaction or resentment that she sees. The woman's dark eyes size Cicely up, slowly taking in her pale skin, her light eyes, her green cardigan with a gold pin, white button-down shirt, slim-fitting dark jeans, and brown leather loafers, her expensive-looking wedding band with all the diamonds, and her chiming bracelets around her thin wrist as she flashes the white envelope padded with cash. Patsy sees her friend in the eyes of this woman— a woman who is probably from an area like Bull Bay or Old Harbor; a woman who probably went to the toilet in an outhouse and washed at an outside standpipe or a bucket of water with her many siblings; a woman who attended secondary school like Patsy and Cicely, or no school at all, maybe because she had to help her mother sell at the market, forced to cut the prices of their produce in half by the types of people who looked down on them and laughed at their patois.

So it must be with great pleasure and pride that this woman is in this position, hearing a hint of desperation in Cicely's voice. The woman braces her shoulders as if readying herself to say something rigged with irony, a smirk deepening the already deep lines around her mouth. But just as quickly her shoulders curve again and the smirk transforms into a smile that shocks her features when Cicely—making direct eye contact and touching her with ease when she slips her the envelope—addresses her as "ma'am": "Ma'am, I'm so sorry. I know it's early, but she has nowhere else to go."

Any fragments of resentment Patsy imagined on the woman's face die with Cicely's gesture. Addressing Cicely in her best English, complete with the affecting *h*, which working-class Jamaicans use in front of vowels to sound high-class, she says, "Well, h-I was going to straighten h-up a likkle before h-anyone come—ah mean, came. My mother would roll in har grave to know h-I 'ave guests parading through a messy house."

Though she owns a house in America now, with brick exterior and inside plumbing, it's obvious that the woman knows her place, that because of how she was raised, and despite being in a big country like America, she would always think of herself as inferior to the likes of Cicely. So it is with the excitement of a graduate awarded a certificate that the woman takes Cicely's money, tucks it in the pocket of her robe, apologizes profusely for the fish smell and for not having time to clean up, introduces herself as Beverly, and lets Patsy inside.

Patsy presses the tiger's-eye necklace into Cicely's hand. Cicely looks down at it, openmouthed; her brows furrow, but she says nothing. Tears sting Patsy's eyes, an obscure sense of profound loss creeping up on her as she takes her suitcase and follows Beverly inside the house. The front door closes softly behind them.

Patsy looks around her new surroundings, noticing the clutter in the family room—magazines spread out over the coffee table with some of the pages ripped out, a Domino's pizza box, folded clothes piled on a brown sofa, a food tray with cotton balls, nail file, and an open tube of pink nail polish, a wastebasket full of balled-up paper. A group of lazy, rowdy teenagers might be staying here, Patsy thinks.

Cicely's exit seems to have taken with it Beverly's forced politeness. Her voice hardens with an edge when she begins to reel off her dos and don'ts: "No pets, no outside guests, no sex. Dis is not a hotel. Yuh only have access to di bathroom on di second floor. Di family room is exactly what it should remain—a family room. Off-limits to renters. So is di kitchen. If yuh hungry, dere's plenty food places 'pon Sutter Avenue, few blocks from here. Mek sure to clean up aftah yuhself. You buy what yuh break in dis house. If yuh eat my food, yuh buy it back. Or get kicked out. Ah keep a good inventory. Rent is due every Friday, first t'ing. Cash only. Small bills preferred. Jus' put it all in an envelope an' slide it undah my bedroom door down di hall to di right."

When she's through and standing before Patsy with her hands on her narrow hips, she looks much, much older and meaner. "Any questions?" she asks. She waits for less than a second before she says, "Good. Di room is upstairs."

She leads Patsy up the rickety staircase that looks like a ladder, up to the attic. Patsy looks around the small, dusty space that Beverly is charging a hundred and fifty dollars a week for. There's still a mound of junk piled in one corner. There's nowhere to put her clothes. The twin-size bed that Patsy will sleep on is in the center of the room, which gets its light from the small prison-like window that looks out onto the street. Patsy breathes lightly, afraid any sudden movement might upset the unstable floors. Beverly stands at the door, her hand on the knob. "My son, Tyriq, can help carry up yuh suitcase when he gets home from work. If yuh need anyt'ing I'm usually downstairs during di day. I work at nights, so it's important dat ah get my sleep. I only answer to emergencies."

Patsy spends the whole day curled up on her new bed, cycling between sleep and wakefulness. That evening, she sits and stares at the gray sky and the trees. She refuses to go back downstairs, though the house stirs with life below her. As the sun finally emerges from dark gray clouds to make its final bow, she reaches for the tiger's-eye pendant around her neck, out of habit, and finds the area bare. A shadow sweeps the room, and soon darkness spills inside. Patsy doesn't reach for a switch. She doesn't even know where to find one. A liquid trail of disgust floods her chest. The unfairness of her life is the shock she has received upon discovering that a woman can break her heart more than any man—a woman to whom she gave everything and expected nothing in return. It's the *nothing* that gets her—the fact that she was content with the *nothing*. Knowing that she is fully capable of feeling such visceral disgust for herself fills her with purpose, a drive to get on with it, gather the scattered pieces inside herself, and get her life back.

14

IT IS THE LAST WEEK OF SEPTEMBER. IN AUTUMN, NIGHT COMES too soon and seems to linger. Patsy, who thought she knew all about loneliness, is surprised to learn that it exists in a place like America. On television comedies, Americans always seem to have family members or friends who come over unannounced and eat from their refrigerator. Or they have friendly yet inquisitive neighbors who speak to them over their picket fences and wave when picking up the newspaper on green lawns. Always, Americans are surrounded by people in those shows; and always, there's a laugh track over their stress-free lives. Patsy yearns for that America.

Her first thought when she wakes up every morning is, *Will she remember?* Tru must have heard the click on the other end of the phone. Patsy cannot escape what she's done. It's one thing to leave, but it's another thing to call and hang up and keep silent. Patsy has sinned against her daughter. A sin that could be hard to forgive. And the darkness of this sin is like the darkness of the dawn outside. Or the one standing to the left of her, waiting.

IT'S BEEN A WEEK—A WEEK OF JUST LYING ON HER BED, FACEUP, staring at the ceiling, barely able to close her eyes. She listens to the silence. Some mornings she hears Beverly moving about inside the house, muttering to herself. Patsy hears her chatter with her son, the clatter of pots and pans, voices on the radio. She wills herself to get out of bed, wrestling with a familiar heaviness—one that has paralyzed her in the past, smothered her inside its vast darkness. She used to be frightened of it, but now it is a companion, quiet and omnipresent. She fights the urge to give up and surrender to it. Out of sheer will, she uses her right hand to stir her desire for life's simplest pleasure beneath the thick comforter. For to feel absolutely nothing at all is terrifying. At least with a little touching, there is the pleasant anticipation of arriving someplace, rather than merely existing. Usually she is mindful and particular about what she thinks about when she masturbates—the slight rise of a calf muscle, the rhythm of a throat swallowing, a flash of tongue. But now, without notice, slipping through the filters of her mind and rushing into the opening of suspended time, is Cicely. And every time she thinks of Cicely, grief comes over her; its giant hands clasp around her neck so tight that all she can let out is a whimper. What she once regarded as perverse seems fitting now—to let her thoughts and feelings roam about, knock things over, thrash with yearning and then outrage. She cannot bear to feel this loss without having a way of releasing it. Her body stiffens with ache, and she contemplates what it would be like to waste away inside this attic, too small to contain her grief, reeling from pleasure to remorse to pleasure, surrendering to the urges, unable to stop herself, until she drifts, moaning and exhausted, into sleep.

She only comes down from the attic to use the toilet and shower in the bathroom, which has walls the color of Pepto-Bismol. Frilly white curtains decorate the window, which looks over into someone's backyard. She's unable to eat the groceries Cicely brought to Beverly's doorstep one night. Beverly had knocked on Patsy's door and told her that her friend left something for her. *"A bag ah grocery,"* Beverley said. *"Ah tell har yuh not allowed to use di kitchen. She gave me two hundred dollahs extra for you to use it. Be my guest, but only dis once."* But Patsy didn't budge. The groceries stayed on the kitchen counter in the paper bag for a whole week, untouched. When it becomes clear that this is her life now—that she made this decision on her own to come to America and therefore doesn't have the luxury of lying in bed, Patsy at last makes a concerted effort to look for a job.

She used Beverly's phone to leave Cicely a message telling her not to send anything for her; that she is fine on her own. In the act of asserting herself, clusters of metal seem to gather around her heart, forming a protective shield. This machine-mass is ugly, able to stave off emotions—its roar of defensiveness frightening, and its mechanical gestures seemingly controlled by someone merely pushing a button: *"I don't need you,"* she repeated into the receiver, unblinking. And when Patsy hung up, the emotions that welled up inside her like a seething volcano spun without control within the roar of the machine to the point of eruption. Nothing but steam hissed through the twisted pipes of her veins. Fleetingly she saw herself powerless and without any knowledge of her new country, now that the boldness that had brought her here has vanished. But she refuses to become her mother. After Mama G walked off her job as a helper, saying God will provide, Patsy thought her mother had lost her mind. Her panic increased when her mother stopped doing the things she used to—like cook and clean and comb Patsy's hair and shop for groceries and pay the rent. Simple things Patsy used to take for granted. A whole month went by before Patsy, caught in the very teeth of starvation, walked several miles to the cement company where Uncle Curtis worked. The security guard at the front desk stood up from his small kiosk and looked down at Patsy, who was half his height; his face was fixed in a mixture of confusion and panic at the sight of a child in her blue and white uniform tunic that she was surely outgrowing at nine years old, hair braided in a haphazard way she combed herself, navy-blue socks slipping inside a pair of worn black shoes stripped of their faux-leather.

"*What yuh doing here?*" the security guard asked.

"*Ah want to see Mr. Curtis Willoughby, sah.*"

"*Yuh should be at school.*"

"*It's an emergency, sah.*"

The man looked around the big compound and scratched his head under his peaked cap as though he didn't know what to do. He grabbed his walkie-talkie from around his waist and spoke into it. "*Missah Fedrick! Ye-yes—is Tony from front gate. Ah which part Willoughby station again? Ah pickney waiting at di front desk to see him. She seh is an emergency.*" As he talked, he peered at Patsy, his brows raised. She looked down at her feet as she shifted her weight from one leg to the other. Luckily, the hum of machines on the compound was loud enough to camouflage the growl in her gut. Timidly, she stared at the big metal columns and steel pipes against the backdrop of a hill, the hill's grandeur minimized by the larger-than-life machines that produced the country's cement. A gentle touch on her shoulder pulled her gaze back down to earth. She turned and looked up into the kind face of Uncle Curtis. Something about his demeanor—assured and gentle—made her want to cry in his arms.

"Mama not well," she told him when he lowered his yellow hard hat, his face covered in gray dust. His teeth were a startling white against the unnatural charcoal color of his face from the cement. He got down on one knee. *"What happened?"* he asked, his eyes darting over her face like a doctor checking for signs of illness.

"We have no food in di house."

Uncle Curtis shook his head. A cuss word died on his lips when he put his head down. *"How long you been without food?"*

"Since yuh left."

Uncle Curtis had been in and out of their lives. The first time he left on his own. He and Mama G had their quarrels over women he met at the bar, women who sometimes knocked at the gate to ask for him, women Mama G cussed out in the street before she got saved. Uncle Curtis ended up living with his mother in Denham Town. That was around the same time Mama G took another man into their lives—a man she fell on her knees for and prayed to every day for strength, a man whose name Mama G uttered softly, stroking the cross, staring at the world without really seeing it. *"Jesus,"* she whispered to Him like a lover.

"Promise dat you'll come back," Patsy said to Uncle Curtis. *"Mama need you. I need you."*

Uncle Curtis paused. A silence mounted between them as though her request had erected a wall. He became rigid and closed his eyes. This gesture was more charged with sound than the machines. As he opened his mouth to respond, Patsy's belly growled again, this time louder than any of the machines and the breeze that picked up and blew cement in her eyes. Uncle Curtis's shoulder dropped and he stood up. There was a look of tenderness in his eyes and some other emotion she could not identify. He held on to Patsy's hand, and that afternoon he told the security guard to tell his boss that he'd be gone for the day—that his wife (though he and Mama G never married) was gravely ill and his daughter needed him. The fact that he referred to Patsy as his daughter moved Patsy. Her mouth trembled at the sweetness of it. Patsy loved him then.

ę

I T'S FREEZING OUTSIDE WHEN PATSY FINALLY LEAVES THE HOUSE.
Wrapping a thick green scarf around her neck and securing
the zipper on her black winter jacket, which Cicely bought her, Patsy
remembers again the desperation she felt seeing her mother sit around,
detached from everything, clutching the Bible. It comes back to her—
the hunger that made her walk all those miles to find Uncle Curtis.
She takes the first step away from the shame into the autumn sun that
glowed without warmth.

S HE PASSES BY OTHER HOUSES ON THE STREET. THE PORCHES ARE
empty. Two houses have bells that chime in the breeze. Several
houses have pumpkins on their front steps. One house has an oversized
balloon of a black spider, cobwebs, and a white ghost in the front yard,
already in preparation for Halloween, which is at the end of the month.
Patsy remembers what Cicely told her about Halloween—that it is an
event for children to dress up in scary costumes and ask for candies.
Yet when Patsy asked Cicely what's her son's favorite costume, Cicely
somberly told her that they don't partake in Halloween. Marcus hates
it when children ring their doorbell, and would argue that a black boy
needs no costume to be scary in America. But that's not the only date
in October that Patsy commits to memory.

October is her daughter's birth month. Tru turns six this month,
on the eighteenth. Patsy stops just short of the last house on the block,
struck by the realization. But when she remembers the failed phone
call and her cowardice, she continues to walk down the street, weighed
down by her sin.

It feels to Patsy like she's wearing someone else's shoes shuffling the
fallen golden leaves on the ground, someone else's clothes on top of hers;

the jacket and scarf are as foreign to Patsy as the new streets. She stops
at the corner of a busy intersection, watching cars go by. Everything and
everyone seems to be in constant motion. There are two bus stops—one
on each side of the street. She looks left, then right. Yesterday, Beverly
told her that she can catch a bus to downtown Brooklyn where all the
stores and businesses are. With only a hundred dollars left to her name,
Patsy has to find a job as soon as possible. Ray of Hope contacted her
through Cicely, who left a message with Beverly, saying that the nanny
position is no longer available—that the couple wants a nanny with at
least a bachelor's degree. *Americans really serious 'bout dem child care*,
Patsy thinks. Laughter tickles her throat at the absurdity of needing a
bachelor's degree to babysit.

Patsy spots a white woman wearing a fuzzy yellow hat with a pom-
pom on top and a long purple coat, standing at the bus stop. She doesn't
really look like she's from around here, though she stands comfortably,
rocking back and forth on the heels and toes of her laced-up boots, her
hands inside her coat pockets, whistling. She's the only one Patsy can
ask for directions, but Patsy stalls, flipping the question on her tongue,
which feels heavy all of a sudden. In Jamaica she didn't speak to the
white people who wandered into town, adventurous and polite, perpetually flushed. Should she change the way she speaks like Cicely does
whenever she talks to them, or to her son and Marcus? How would they
react to her in their own territory? Cicely mentioned that some white
people can be racist. But how can Patsy tell by just looking at them?
Should she just assume all of them are racist? Cicely said it's in the eyes
and smile—one can tell by their body language and whether or not they
smile like a mannequin or a real person when they talk to you. But how
would Cicely know? As far as Patsy is concerned, Cicely is damn near
white herself. Patsy decides to take her chances and approach the white
woman at the bus stop.

"Guh—good morning," Patsy says in the tone she used with Miss
Clark and other higher-ups at the Ministry.

Good morning is always a safe bet, a sure indication that one has had good home training. But the woman continues to whistle, looking in the direction of the bus she's waiting for, and at the cars creeping behind a big truck sweeping the street with a huge brush. A train roars above their heads as Patsy composes herself and adjusts each word amid the noise rattling the tracks. She clears her throat and speaks louder, since she also learned from Cicely that touching people in America could get you in trouble. In Jamaica, people touch all the time. If you're in line at the bank and didn't hear the teller call you, the person behind you would tap you on the shoulder. If you announce at work that you're not well, the nearest person might put their hand on your back and rub it. In the middle of a conversation, an acquaintance might pause to very gently fold your collar or pop a dangling thread off your blouse. If you're in a bus or taxi and there's no more room, someone might end up on your lap, or you on theirs. Here Patsy raises her voice from a safe distance:

"Excuse me, miss?"

The woman turns. "Hi, there! Can I help you?"

Her wide eyes are cobalt-blue, her face pink. Patsy catches a glimpse of her yellow hair underneath her yellow hat. Patsy is startled by the instant attention she's given. In her best English, Patsy asks, "Is this bus going downtown?"

"It sure is!" the woman replies, her eyes still wide, her voice too loud. Patsy wonders if she always looks so surprised. There's something so bubbly about her, so free. Back home, a grown woman wouldn't be caught dead whistling in the street like that, rocking from toe to heel like a fidgety child. Jamaican girls begin to perform womanhood at eleven, at the latest twelve years old, their childlike wit suspended in the frozen glance of female elders, their youthfulness covered in starched uniforms and slips underneath, their animated curiosities discouraged with the weight of responsibilities like learning how to cook meat so that it's browned properly, learning to clean, scrub stains out of white clothes, raise younger siblings, dodge the invasive lusts of older men. By twenty-five, any hint of animation is drained out of them, the muscles of their faces tightening, downturned mouths fixed in a meanness that mocks any form of gaiety as weary eyes hold in them contempt for those who fail to conform.

Patsy responds coolly, "Thank you."

"Don't hold your breath, though," the woman continues in her loud voice. "The buses are atrocious today." She then looks sideways at Patsy, pauses for a second before she says, "Bad. They're really bad. That's what I meant."

"Ah know what yuh mean," Patsy replies, puzzled as to why the woman would assume she doesn't know what the word *atrocious* means.

The woman raises an eyebrow. "Where are you from?"

"Jamaica."

"Nice!" the woman replies.

Patsy is curious to know if she speaks like this all the time, ending her sentences with an exclamation. That might explain the perpetual startled expression on her face.

"It must be so hard for you, leaving that nice weather for this."

She gestures as if at the chilly air around them. "I always wanted to experience snow," Patsy says. "It look suh nice in storybooks an' movies."

The woman laughs. "Wait till January. You'll see what a headache it can be when it's piled up. I've never been to Jamaica, but I know a lot of Jamaicans."

"You do?" Patsy asks.

"Well, not *know*-know them!" she says in an incredulous tone, as though Patsy had asked her if she knew Diana Ross. "There're just here—in Brooklyn."

"Hm."

She's right. Patsy never went a mile in Crown Heights without seeing a Jamaican flag waving at her. But though Jamaicans lived there, they seemed so far removed, their lives contained within separate spheres moving at the fast pace of American life. Patsy begins to look deliberately at this new neighborhood surrounding her: an overweight mother ambling down the street with four children in tow, leading them inside the Crown Fried Chicken place; the men standing in front of the liquor store, already sipping bottles hidden inside brown paper bags. Her eyes dart to the graffitied brick walls on an old building, the overhead subway station ridden with pigeons, the small group of black teenagers laughing out loud, slaphappy, as they cross the street with their book bags. One of the drunks starts pissing by some parked cars, and the owner of the butcher shop, who is sprinkling salt on the sidewalk, yells at him, *"Hey! Hey! I'ma call the cops if you don't stop!"*

"What neighborhood is dis?" Patsy asks, genuinely curious. Again, it's not anything she saw on television. Not even on *The Cosby Show* or *The Jeffersons*. And those shows had black people.

"East New York," the woman replies. She chuckles to herself and mumbles something incomprehensible about the place being a dump and not knowing how she ended up here. Patsy leaves it alone. She watches as two black men in leather coats leave the bodega outside of which a beggar is huddled, shaking a cup with loose change. They each drop some change inside the man's cup, and he bows his head with gratitude. Both men sip their coffees from steaming Styrofoam cups. One bites into his breakfast sandwich, which is wrapped in foil paper. Their voices float toward Patsy when they get closer. *"Yo! Ain't that some messed-up shit? This nigga on vacation when he owes me."* They're Americans, just like the woman she's talking to. Black Americans. Cicely had warned Patsy against them—said they were lazy and always on welfare. *"Dey don't work hard like us. It's as if dey want t'ings handed to dem."* She found Cicely's dismissal unsettling, knowing it was coming from Marcus. For Cicely is from Pennyfield—a place looked at by the government and other Jamaicans alike as a dump infested with human burdens. She talked as if she had forgotten what it was like to be dismissed by her own country.

There's a sudden movement beside Patsy. The white woman subtly puts her beaten-up leather purse, which no one would want, in front of her. She simultaneously shoots a side glance at the two black men. When the men see Patsy staring at them too, they nod. Patsy smiles at them, her mouth unable to go all the way up, since her facial muscles are stiff from the cold and the shock of being acknowledged. She also cannot get her head to drop like theirs in time.

They simply pass her by.

"I heard it's nice in Jamaica. A paradise," the woman is saying next to her, a bit too loud. Patsy's mind has moved beyond her to the backs of the two black men. Are they upset that she didn't nod back? Is this their way of communicating? To the woman, who finally lets go of her purse, Patsy says, "You should go one day. You'll enjoy it." She's unsure where this is coming from and immediately resents it. She also doesn't know how this white woman, who seems afraid of black men, would fare in a country full of them.

WHEN THE BUS FINALLY COMES, THEY GET ON. PATSY, LEARN-ing from the two black men she saw, nods at the black American woman driver. The bus driver doesn't seem to notice, her hooded eyes glued somewhere else. She smooths her finger waves as she waits for Patsy to dig inside her pocket for the loose change. Patsy takes her sweet time to count her change to put into the slot. She asks the visibly impatient bus driver for a transfer like she has seen Cicely do, then finds a seat near the driver, since she doesn't want to miss her stop. The white woman plops down right next to Patsy. "By the way, I'm DJ!" she all but screams into Patsy's ear, pulling off her mittens with her teeth and digging inside a backpack. She takes out a thermos.

"Like the letters?" Patsy asks, conscious of the others on the bus who turn around to look at the both of them.

"Short for Deborah Jacob."

"I'm Patsy," Patsy replies, not thinking it necessary to give her full name.

"Aren't you cold?" DJ asks. "You're wearing a fall jacket. You need a coat!"

Patsy looks down at the black jacket she has on, with its big flaps at the collar and a stylish zipper in the front, that Cicely found on sale in a store called Filene's Basement. *"Look at you, Miss Foreigner!"* Cicely had said when Patsy modeled the jacket. She didn't mention that the jacket was only for one season. *But isn't it still fall?* "That thing won't hold against a gust of wind," DJ is saying.

"I can't afford a coat right now," Patsy replies. "I have to get a job first."

"Where are you looking?" DJ asks.

Patsy cannot think of anywhere right now. Her plan is to try everywhere. She'll start with applying for anything she can find at the stores at Fulton Mall. Then she will try the restaurants. She has the résumé that the girl at Ray of Hope had typed up for her a couple weeks ago. The résumé doesn't list the two courses in economics that she took at Excelsior Community College. She begins to regret not listing them. Cicely told her that they wouldn't be relevant here. But maybe she would've gotten that nanny job had she not listened to Cicely.

"Do you have an interview?" DJ asks.

"Not yet."

"Try Macy's!" DJ says. "They're always looking for workers at this time of year. My friend Rositsa told me they're hiring like crazy. She's Bulgarian. Would you believe that? The girl could be a Victoria Secret model or something, but she's stuck in bathroom accessories folding towels. She's been working there for so long that she trains people how to fold towels. What's so hard in that? That's how she met her boyfriend, Lenny. Soon after he was hired they were sneaking off into the stockroom. Would you believe that? The stockroom! I started washing every new towel after that. 'Cause you just never know." DJ is shaking her head, her glassy eyes staring straight ahead as if she's visualizing the sexual acrobatics cushioned by stacks of tainted towels. She then glances at Patsy and winks. "My guess is that they wouldn't have to teach you too many tricks in folding towels. You'd be a shoo-in! Don't know much about Jamaica, but I know girls probably learn to fold towels in their sleep."

DJ continues to go on and on about the right detergents, and Patsy tunes her out. She's already excited about the prospect of a job at Macy's. For the rest of the ride, she takes in the view of Brooklyn, the hues of reds, yellows, and browns glistening in the sun. To Patsy, the sights come alive in a different way without Cicely telling her what to look at every other second. The coming winter provides a new canvas on which black and brown people huddle on sidewalks in coats and scarves, brownstones appear endless down the streets, frosted windows of storefronts gleam with the reflection of the blue sky. She begins to feel a part of things—streets become less foreign when she memorizes their names, people less intimidating. Two older women get on the bus. She observes them, eavesdropping on their conversation about the weather. She realizes, like she has with DJ, that Americans like small talk. Things like the weather or the delay of public transportation trigger their banter, bring them together. They're also very loud. DJ reaches above Patsy's head and presses the yellow band.

"My stop is next!" she says, to Patsy's relief. "Good luck with your job search. It was nice chatting withchya."

"Thank you," Patsy replies with a slight wave. Though DJ talked her to death, Patsy is proud of herself. She cannot help but ponder the radical thing that just happened: a comfortable exchange with an American—a white American. For a moment, it feels like her only accomplishment.

❦

FULTON MALL, LIKE FLATBUSH AVENUE, MAKES PATSY FEEL LIKE she's in downtown Kingston. Men with sheets on their heads recite Bible verses to passersby; Indian ladies wearing petticoats shove eyebrow grooming flyers into Patsy's hands; African vendors solicit her to check out the latest bootleg movies; a Muslim man selling incense and oils tells her that she'll smell much better with his concoction, if she can just come a little closer; and black American men call her *sister* and hold up books with library tags on them about Egypt, Africa, and the autobiography of a handsome, stern, bespectacled black man on the cover, staring straight at Patsy with a hand against his chin and a finger near his eye. *Malcolm X* is written in bold letters. People are huddled over tables displaying knitted hats and scarves, sunglasses, jewelry, and watches.

As Patsy walks, she becomes more and more aware of the shortcomings of her jacket. She digs her hands inside her pockets, hoping that will keep her warm. Every store on the strip seems like they're on a mission to compete with each other in who has the best bargain: BIG DEAL. LAST DAY OF SALE. SEE INSIDE STORE. EVERYTHING FOR $5. YOU DON'T HAVE TO WAIT TILL BLACK FRIDAY. There are African men standing outside in heavy coats, ushering pedestrians inside, beckoning them to seasonal displays of shirts and dresses and shoes and hats and jewelry. Headless mannequins stand upright in storefronts, shrouded with fur and leather coats. NEW is written in bold red on bright orange cartridge paper stuck to the jackets with hefty price tags. Patsy decides she might have to freeze until her first paycheck.

"Come try on!" says a man with long dreadlocks wrapped on top of his head like a Russian military hat. She stops. For a second she thinks it's Ras Norbert, bundled in a jacket and scarf, frost curling from his black lips. A sudden warmth wraps itself around her at the glimpse of the familiar face. Her subtle smile almost turns into a laugh-cry that mists her eyes at the sight of *home*.

"I have perfect fur coat for you," the man says.

Patsy blinks. The mist clears. He's not Ras Norbert.

THE MACY'S IS QUIET RELATIVE TO THE COMMOTION OUTSIDE. There's heavy foot traffic here too, but not as much—especially not when the hustlers' bargains seem a lot better. Classical music plays inside the bright, adorned store. It's already decorated with a Christmas tree and dangling snowflakes sprinkled with silver and gold glitter, though it's October. The store smells of newness. She surveys the dignified looks of the store workers, who pay her no mind when she walks into the store. They seem to stand six feet tall above everyone else in their black suits and gold badges. She swallows her nerves and goes up to a well-scrubbed man standing by a glass containing jewelry. The man is dressed in a tailored suit at a cash register. Patsy assumes he must be the manager.

"Excuse me," she says, afraid to speak higher than the faint music in the background. When the man raises his bald head, which matches the tone of his burnt-caramel face, she says, "I'm looking fah work."

The man blinks, his long eyelashes seeming to flutter like a winged insect as if struggling to focus. "Excuse me?"

Patsy repeats herself. "I'm looking fah work."

"If you're looking for HR, ma'am, that's downstairs," the man says. He holds up his right arm like he's directing traffic. "Elevator to the right!"

Patsy wants to tell him that she's not deaf or slow. But there's no use proving this to him. She thanks him and makes her way to the elevator. When she gets there, a middle-aged black woman who would've made a good church usher greets her. She hands Patsy a clipboard and tells her not to leave anything blank. However, when Patsy gets to the section requesting her Social Security number, perspiration pricks her skin. She hands the form to the woman without meeting her gaze and leaves, slipping back out into the cold, spiteful air. It seems to reprimand her, its frigid palms pressed firmly against her back as if to push her out of the country.

15

DAYS PASS AND NO ONE HAS CALLED. EVEN AFTER SHE WENT TO store after store, restaurant after restaurant, five of which were part of the Golden Krust restaurant chain in Brooklyn, where Jamaican women, wearing hairnets, and with closed, bashful looks, take orders from customers behind glass counters, scooping up rice and peas, cabbage and shredded carrots, oxtail stew, curry goat, curry chicken, brown stew chicken, and soups of the day with big spoons. There must be millions of women like Patsy waiting nearby for such jobs, because the managers at the Golden Krusts tell Patsy to come back next week, and when she returns, the positions are already filled.

"Ah can wash dishes, sah," Patsy said to one of the managers, who chewed on a toothpick as she begged him for a job. *"Ah can even clean di floors . . . anyt'ing."*

"Positions full," he boomed.

At a busy intersection, Patsy spots a mother and a daughter waiting for the light to change. The mother is mouthing words of caution to the little girl clad in pink, who is holding her hand. It's hard to look away from them. The air thins and time stands still—a capsule with all the sounds trapped on the outside. *Tru.* Patsy exhales. But the flat-out coldness around her turns her breath to a vapor that curls from her lips, then vanishes. Long after the mother and daughter cross the street toward a row of houses, Patsy remains at the intersection, lost.

S HE IS DOWN TO TWENTY DOLLARS, WHICH SHE PINCHES. SOME-times she goes without food so that she can have bus fare. Other times, when Beverly and her grown son aren't at the house, she pilfers from the refrigerator—slices of cheese, a handful of grapes, an orange, a dash of milk for a cup of Cheerios. Her rent is due, with no prospects of a job anywhere. She's tempted to call Cicely, but decides against it, her pride getting the best of her. She thinks too of Ducky. She had mar-veled at those photographs Ducky sent his mother, Miss Henrietta, who paraded them at church. She showed everyone—even Pastor Kirby—the pictures of her son posing in front of the Bank of America in a suit, his fattened face cheesing, arms folded across a well-fed belly; another photograph was of Ducky posing in front of a Mercedes-Benz; and another in front of a two-story house with a nice green lawn. Mama G had sucked her teeth, *"Dat Henrietta t'ink she bettah than everybody else. Why don't she throw what she claim she got from dat tar-black ugly son of hers in di donation basket?"* Patsy knew it was jealousy deepening her mother's scowl. And she felt she could prove to her mother that she too can go to America and achieve something—finish school, get a job at a bank where she would be in charge of monitoring spreadsheets on computers. But had she known then what she knows now about Amer-ica and its hurdles in place for people without proper visas, she would have done something different. Or would she? There's got to be a way out of this rut.

Patsy puts on every sweater she owns underneath the flimsy jacket and goes back out, determined to find something today.

"I'm looking fah work," she says to the rotund man with a dark, thick unibrow at a furniture store. He's one of those black Indians who Patsy used to see around Kingston, squatted over fruits and vegetables at the market. Her first thought when she saw them was what a waste of good coolie hair, with skin as dark as that. The furniture store is deserted, though it's located on a busy avenue.

"Work?" the black Indian man asks. Patsy notices that his eyes are on her chest and begins to feel uncomfortable asking him. But what if he's the only one who will give her a job?

"Yes, sah. Anything," she says.

"What can you do?"

She pauses. "Sell furniture."

The man laughs, revealing yellow teeth. "No. No. I mean, what are your skills?" He raises his unibrow in a suggestive way. Patsy pretends to ignore it and says, "I can prove it."

The man hesitates for a second. Then he says, "Let's give it a try. You stand outside and get people to buy furniture. For every customer you get to come in, I give you ten dollars. Deal?" He's smirking as if he doesn't believe this will work. But Patsy is so happy that she takes the offer. She agrees to stand in the cold with a sign that reads ROMAN FURNITURE STORE—BEST DEALS ON EARTH. Pride aside, she holds the sign high enough for people to see. If only they knew that her next meal depends on their interest.

"Ma'am, sir, good deal inside!" she says to each passerby. If her coworkers at the Ministry or anyone she knows from home could ever see her now, parading a sign in the street for money, they would laugh. A mix of shame, anger, and sorrow washes over Patsy, but she bites it back, determined.

"Good deal inside! Good deal inside!" she shouts above the street noise.

A Spanish woman with three children smiles politely and walks away. A black man with a cane slows down and then continues walking. The owner watches her from inside the store, his elbows rested on the counter.

"Good deal inside! Good deal inside!"

Every time someone walks away she feels a sting of desperation in her eyes. She blinks away the wet veil, almost uttering the word *Please* at the young couple holding hands. "Perfect fah yuh new home," she says to them, hoping they will agree. A wave of relief hits her when they look at each other, shrug their shoulders, and walk inside the store. Twenty dollars, Patsy tallies inside her head. As if the couple breaks an invisible barrier, two more people walk inside. Forty dollars. The cold seems to clamp down on her bladder, making her want to pee. But she forces herself not to think about it, fearing that if she takes a restroom break she might lose potential customers. A woman pushing a stroller passes by Patsy.

"Good deal inside! We even have furniture fah baby room!"

The woman pauses. "Y'all sell cribs?"

When Patsy tells her yes, she enters the store too. Fifty dollars. When a man in a business suit and tie walks by, Patsy adds, "Office furniture fah cheap, cheap!" She counts sixty dollars when he enters the store.

Four hours later, Patsy tallies a hundred dollars.

"You're a pro," the owner says, counting the money at the end of the day. Patsy counts sixty dollars. She furrows her brows. "Ah thought you said each customer was ten dollars. I made more."

He flashes his stained teeth at her. "I like a smart woman. You should be glad I kept my word and paid you." He's giving her that sly grin again. He puts a twenty-dollar bill on the counter and when she goes to pick it up, his hand lands on hers. "There's more where that came from. You can work for the other twenty and a bonus." He winks. Patsy withdraws her hand with the money. She walks away knowing that she'll never be back.

D AYS LATER WHEN THE MONEY RUNS OUT AND STILL NO PHONE calls, she begins to regret not taking the man up on his offer.

Brushing her teeth for bed, she finds herself wondering how much the bonus would be. She considers his unibrow and his fat round belly, shivering at the thought of fucking him or sucking him off. She spits into the sink and rinses her mouth. Curled in bed, she imagines her soul slipping down around her ankles in the back room of the store, his grimy hands clamped around her hips. But when a bolt of hunger rushes through her, it spreads between her legs, softening the muscles there, and she thinks, *Why not?* She has nothing to lose and everything to gain.

Just then Patsy hears a knock on her door. When she opens it, Beverly is standing there, looking pale, with rollers in her hair. Every time Patsy sees her she looks paler, her lips darker.

"Someone called an' left dis message fah you today," Beverly says. With chestnut-brown hands four shades darker than her salmon-colored face, Beverly gives Patsy a folded piece of paper. Patsy's heart races when she takes the paper, the thought of Cicely flooding her with warmth. Beverly lingers at the door, folding her arms across her chest. "I told you dis place isn't a hotel. I'm nobody's doorman, secretary, or caretaker. I already do dat fah a living, cleaning up aftah old people in Coney Island. But at least it pay me mortgage. Ah didn't expec' to be renting to someone who tek my kindness fah granted, giving out me numbah an' have di nerve not to pay me rent."

Unfolding her arms and putting her hands on her hips, Beverly says, "Where's di rent?"

"Ah promise I'll have it by di end ah di week," Patsy replies, trying her best to sound apologetic.

"I rent fah money, not promises."

"I undah-stand. I'll get it to you by di end of dis week. Please . . . trus' me on dis one."

Beverly looks Patsy up and down and cuts her eyes before she turns and leaves. She doesn't close the door. Patsy closes the door gently and leans on it for a moment, taking a deep breath. She lets out a sigh. Then, slowly, she moves to the bed. She sits with the paper for a while and fingers it. She hopes with all her might that it's Cicely. That she has forgiven her, that she wants to meet somewhere so that they can talk. Slowly, she opens it. *Peta-Gaye* is scribbled above a telephone number. Patsy furrows her brows. *Peta-Gaye? Who is Peta-Gaye?* Then she remembers weeks ago, when she first arrived at Beverly's house, she had seen an ad in the newspaper left on Beverly's front porch. The ad was for a bathroom assistant for a restaurant named Peta-Gaye's in a place called Tribeca. Her eyes had stumbled upon the word *Jamaican*—seeing in it the blue mountains and lush hills; smelling the rum-tinged breath of men playing dominoes in front of Pete's Bar; and hearing again their laughter and banter, which could be as volatile as the ecstatic moans of the sea at night rising and plunging beneath the full moon, and as uproarious as Mr. Belnavis's rooster at dawn, and Ras Norbert chanting, *"Believe me! Believe me not!"* about gold buried in their backyard.

16

T HE RESTAURANT, SHE LEARNS, IS OWNED BY A FRENCH-Canadian white man, Bernie, who thought it a wonderful idea to open a Jamaican restaurant inspired by his one and only trip to the island. With both arms raised behind his head—a matted mass of honey-colored dreadlocks—and an ankle on his knee above the table where Patsy catches a glimpse of his tattered white sneakers, he discloses to Patsy that the restaurant is named after the woman who cooked for him at the villa where he stayed on the north coast. Patsy can't tell his age. He doesn't look like a restaurant owner, but someone belonging on the street, strumming a guitar with his washed-out jeans and black faded V-neck that has lightning striking in the middle of the letters ACDC.

It's lunchtime. The restaurant is not crowded. The bamboo tables are donned with burgundy mats, crystal glasses, silverware placed on the sides, and a candle at the center of each table. Bamboo chairs line the bar that is made to look like a hut on the beach. Reggae music plays in the background. Three waiters rotate from table to table—young college types with forced portly mannerisms, all Americans. Patsy can tell by the casual, friendly cadence of their speech. The bartender, who looks to be the only Jamaican, busies himself wiping glasses and positioning liquor. The two hostesses, who look as if they could be African supermodels—one of whom winks and waves at Bernie—welcome the mostly white patrons, who must have read the newspaper clipping with bold headline "Chef Bernard Newton Makes Jamaican Cuisine Mainstream and Oh So Delicious." Bernie's picture is next to it—him posing in a chef's hat and white tunic, arms folded like Mr. T. Bernie has framed it all and hung it on the front door next to a photo of Bob Marley. Patsy stares at the newspaper clipping. "Don't you just love him?" Bernie asks. He must have thought she was staring at the photo of Bob Marley, with his long dreadlocks that look like dreadlocks and not the wet puss tails on Bernie's head.

"He took reggae where I'm taking Jamaican food," Bernie continues.

Patsy doesn't answer immediately. She doesn't have the heart to question Bernie about what he knows about Jamaican cuisine, much less how he plans to influence it. Neither does she have the heart to disappoint him by telling him that she's not into Bob Marley; that Bob Marley was forbidden in her household; that she'd rather listen to Peter Tosh, since Uncle Curtis told her he wrote most of Bob's lyrics anyway. She still thinks it's unfair that Peter is the lesser known of the two. Maybe that's how it is—maybe life favors certain people and relegates the rest to living in their shadows.

Patsy adjusts her face into a smile and nods. They are seated at the

back of the restaurant next to the kitchen, where Patsy can see the Mexican cooks. Bernie must have thought it brilliant to hire Mexican cooks
to re-create Peta-Gaye's recipes. (None of which was written down,
Patsy is sure, since most Jamaicans don't measure ingredients. Who
needs to measure when you can taste the food in your hand-middle
to see how much more salt, pepper, flour, or what have you it needs to
taste right?)

She listens as he describes the job of a bathroom lady.

"Your job is to treat patrons the way Peta-Gaye treated me and my
family when we were at that villa—with great care, attentiveness, and
always with a smile. You make sure that the place is tidy and welcoming.
People say food and service make a good restaurant, but I say the bathroom
is the dealmaker—customers like a good bathroom. If they think they can
eat off the floor inside a stall, then they'll trust our hygiene in the kitchen."

Patsy nods and nods, though she cringes internally at the visuals of
eating off a bathroom floor—tidy or not.

"This is one of the best Jamaican restaurants you'll find in the tri-
state area," Bernie says, flashing unusually white teeth and tucking a
stray puss-tail behind his ear; his two platinum bracelets catch the natural light coming between the bamboo plants. His hazel eyes shine with
pride when he says, "We've been open for two years. The mayor and his
wife come here a lot. When you have customers like that, you make sure
to give them top-notch luxury."

He stares at Patsy as if expecting her to speak. That's when she says,
in patois to this man who seems hungry to hear it, "Making people
comfah-table is my passion, sah."

A smile spreads across Bernie's face. "You remind me so much of
Peta-Gaye," he says. "The way you sound, your look, your mannerisms.
I think you'll be perfect. Welcome to our family, Patsy."

He extends his hand across the table. Patsy stares at the hand before
shaking it. It's her first time shaking someone's hand. Who knew her

first handshake would be with a white man who swears he knows more about Jamaican food than actual Jamaicans? She stores the irony for Cicely, wishing she could tell her everything. About the free food Bernie gave her to sample—curry salmon (which she has never heard of) and oxtail wallowing in a stew with no butter beans in it (unheard-of). She ended up spitting out the rubbery oxtail meat inside a napkin, and the curry salmon gave her a bad case of diarrhea. *Poor souls have no clue that Bernie is a fraud*, Patsy thinks. And poor Peta-Gaye, who will never know that her name has gone abroad to sell mediocre food—a fate that would surely make her granny roll in her grave.

17

THE JOB TAKES SOME GETTING USED TO. THE FIRST NIGHT PATSY was left alone to clean the toilets, she stared at the tiled floors and stained bowls, water dripping in the sink, unable to believe that this is her life now. Worse, the stalls have no trash bins. And though there is a sign that reads PLEASE DO NOT THROW PAPER TOWELS OR FEMININE PRODUCTS IN THE TOILET, the toilets keep getting clogged with sanitary napkins. Patsy almost cried the first night when she could still see the red of the blood on the pads and tampons she was expected to get rid of. She thought of the beautiful women she observed applying lipstick and powdering their noses in front of the mirror, unable to believe they could do such a thing. Patsy had to plunge several times before pulling out the almost disintegrated pads, each more grotesque than the one before.

In Jamaica, this is the lowest job one could get. She wonders how many other Jamaicans come here and end up doing this. Patsy cannot recall anyone writing relatives in Pennyfield saying they found a job cleaning toilets and handing out paper towels.

But it's either this or having sex with the furniture store man. The manager, Alan, is black. He might be black American, but Patsy isn't sure, since he has no accent. He's very chummy with Bernie and only speaks to the hostesses, waiters, and bartenders, but never to the lower staff like the dishwashers, busboys, and bathroom assistants—unless he's giving orders. He made this known to Patsy on her first day when she greeted him with a hearty "Good evening!" and he snubbed her, letting her greeting fall on deaf ears. Patsy decided right there and then that she didn't need to be friends with Alan's high donkey behind anyway. When he stands, his bottom juts from the curve of his back, erect in those bright suits he wears, feet pointed outward. It also swings when he walks. But what's more tragic than a man with a woman's behind is her pay. When Alan hands Patsy her first weekly pay in cash, she notices that it is significantly smaller than what she expected.

"Ah t'ink there's a mistake," Patsy says to Alan, assuming he, more than anyone else, would understand her concern.

"Excuse me?" Alan asks, furrowing his meticulously plucked eyebrows, which he might have gotten done by one of the Indian ladies who wave flyers at people at Fulton Mall. Instantly he assumes the air of a person who has not known struggle. His question appears genuine, the whites of his eyes a stark, almost brilliant contrast to his onyx pupils that seem to gleam with childlike curiosity. But what more can she expect from a man with long, effeminate fingers, which display shiny buffed nails and soft pink flesh underneath like they have never been dirtied?

"Dis is two dollars and fifty-eight cents below what Bernie say I'll get," Patsy says.

Alan seems a bit surprised by her calculations, which reminds her of the principal who could not believe that she scored perfect points on her CXC mathematics exam. Leaning over just slightly to peer at the few twenty-dollar bills in her hand, he shrugs and says, "You may want to take that up with Bernie. I'm certain it's not a mistake. It's different when we're paying you under the table. At least it's something."

She takes what she gets. And although she resents him for his apathy, the way he simply shrugged her off, she knows that he is right—that it's better than nothing. It becomes clear to Patsy that she needs another job to supplement this one, and clearer still that she needs papers if she wants to survive in America.

S HE QUICKLY MASTERS THE ART OF BEING INVISIBLE, STAYING IN her corner and observing women examining their faces in the mirror as they wash their hands. Patsy listens to their chatter and bathroom laughter filling the air like bleach. She learns intimate details about these well-dressed white women who don't bother to whisper, talking to each other from separate stalls. Most of them, she learns, think they're fat. This might explain the kale-ackee wrap—another unique entrée Patsy has never heard of and is absolutely sure that the real Peta-Gaye had never cooked—being the most popular item on the menu. Even the stick-thin women who look like they could use a whole plate of oxtail stick their fingers down their throats over the toilets, thinking Patsy can't hear them or not caring if she does. She doesn't know for certain if they're vomiting to stay skinny or if they're doing it because the food is disgusting.

Some only seem at ease with themselves after they powder and repowder their nose. A few of them end up breaking the ice, sometimes asking Patsy to help them zip, tuck, button, or dab spots out of clothes. Some confess things to Patsy that she doesn't think are any of her business—like the woman with long dark hair parted in the middle like Cher's, who told her that she was on a blind date with a man her cousin set her up with: *I hope he doesn't think I'm too old or less attractive than what my cousin described.*

Another woman broke down in tears and told Patsy that her husband just asked for a divorce over dinner. *"Hush,"* Patsy told her above her sniffles, handing her a paper towel for her to blow her nose. *"It g'wan be all right,"* she said. *"Everyt'ing will be all right."* That night, Bob Marley's music was playing in the restaurant, and Patsy wondered if she said that to the woman because she was expected to, or if she really meant it. She wished that she had someone to comfort her this way.

Patsy watches these women, mesmerized always by their primping, yet strangely envious and respectful. For, somehow, even though she's cleaning up after them and pumping their soap and hand lotion and egos, there is no question that they are truly women; they can so easily prove it by flipping their long hair, putting on the fanciest dresses that show as much of their fair skin as possible—skin that is never looked at as less than, skin that can grant them a place anywhere in the world, skin that makes men open doors and give up seats, and hair that makes Patsy recall those dolls Mama G couldn't afford to get her for Christmas. They're like the dolls that reminded Patsy of the uptown children Mama G looked after, smiling broadly every time she talked about them, dolls that were passed on to Patsy secondhand from those uptown children who had outgrown them. How she treasured them! How she loved and cared for them. Until she met Cicely.

*

Fionna, the other bathroom lady, who works with Patsy during her weekend shifts, is the only one Patsy can talk to. Fionna is a small-boned Trinidadian woman in her late twenties like Patsy, with a short haircut that frames her peanut-colored cheeks. She's so polite that she says thank you even when the women don't tip her.

"All di women here want to be skinny," Patsy muses as she rolls the warm hand towels and stocks them on the marble counter by the green eucalyptus plant inside the gold-plated ceramic pot. Scented candles glow underneath the two oblong mirrors above the wide sink, which has two brass faucets with jaunty tubular shapes and a slanted spout. Patsy and Fionna pull the single levers down for the women each time they wash their hands, and give them the warm folded white towels.

"Is so American women stay, m'dear. Dying to be thin." Fionna laughs from her side of the sink. "Mek dem g'waan waste away."

"But dey got all dis food." Patsy shakes her head, unable to fathom all the waste. "How dey starve themselves, wid all dis food?" One thing about America that Patsy loves is the ability to overindulge in foods like pizza, hamburgers, and all-you-can-eat buffets for cheap—foods that you can get for a dollar ninety-nine, foods that would've been considered foreign delicacies back home, foods that the people on the hills eat. Here, she can't get enough of them.

"Dat's because men like dem women skinny here," Fionna says as she lights the scented candles by her mirror and dims the overhead light a little, which deepens the emerald green bamboo wallpaper. "Di more yuh look like a beanpole, di more attractive you are to American men. Dem not into meat a'tall, a'tall. Jus' bare bone."

"But what kinda man like a woman dat can break?" Patsy asks.

Fionna puts her hands on her hips. "Excuse me, but I'm tiny and I can't break. In fact, di more hung him is, di bettah."

Fionna covers her mouth, slightly flushed by her own indecency. Patsy laughs at her coworker's sudden shyness, liking her even more for her underlying brashness. When she sobers, Patsy says, "Everyone is suh nice, though."

"Be careful wid dat," Fionna replies. "Dey smile in we face. But dem same one would go behind we back an' stab we. I used to work as a bathroom lady at another restaurant before dis one. Yuh know what happened? I got fired. One day, out of di blue, my manager pull me to di side an' tell me dat a woman complain dat she wasn't happy wid me service. When me check it out, it was one of the women who I thought was the nicest to me. She would tip me well, compliment my hair, an' everyt'ing. Di woman couldn't even tell me she was unhappy to my face. She had to go report it to di manager. Dat's why yuh can't be too comfortable wid Americans. I ain' saying yuh can't talk up-talk-up wid people. All I'm saying is dat Americans funny. Keep yuh business to yuhself an' mek dem do all di talking."

"An' dat Alan, what's his deal?" Patsy asks.

"Yuh mean Alana?" Fionna laughs.

Patsy laughs too. "Why him suh uptight?"

"Chile, dat's what happen when people forget themselves."

"What yuh mean?"

"Yuh don't notice?"

"Notice what?"

"Dat him is Jamaican?"

"Jamaican? Alan?" Patsy asks. "Yuh lie!"

"Chile, ask where him come from."

"Him don't talk to me like dat."

"Jus' compliment *she* outfit an' *she* favor yuh."

They both laugh again, this time unable to control themselves. However, their laughter snaps into silence when an older woman with red hair enters the restroom.

P ATSY AND FIONNA FALL INTO A QUICK AND EASY FRIENDSHIP, splitting the tips from the jar at the end of the night. Sometimes they use the money to buy dinner at the cheap diner up the street where the tables smell of the wet rag they were wiped down with; where lipstick stains remain on glasses and mugs; where the utensils are stained, blackened by oxidation and where the food drips with grease. Patsy and Fionna love to order tea to rid any gas from their stomachs from long hours working without eating. It's hard to take breaks when the restaurant is busy. Patsy notices that Fionna also likes to sweeten her tea with extra sugar, since there's no condensed milk. Patsy feels somewhat restored sitting across from Fionna, their commonalities fortifying their bond. At the diner, they talk about home. Patsy doesn't mention Tru and the crime she committed against her. She decides that some things are better left unsaid, though it continues to haunt her—some days more than others. Since she started working at the restaurant, she realizes that most of the money she earns goes to rent. Even if she had the intention of sending money to Tru, it wouldn't have been possible with Beverly raising the rent.

Fionna likes to talk about her childhood in a town in Trinidad called Laventille, where she grew up watching an aunt sew carnival costumes and her uncles preparing for band competitions—all of them dancing down a hill with their neighbors on carnival day into the Savannah. Each time Fionna talks about it, her eyes mist. She moves the greasy food around on her plate before she pushes it away. "I just need to work harder," she says. "I want to send my family lots of nice things. I want to put my sisters through school, send my mother money to build a new house in Cascade, one ah di nicer areas in Trinidad, and pay fah my uncle's eye surgery. All dis I want to do when I make enough money. Jus' di other day, I did four double shifts to send my mother an' sisters something to help wid expenses. Ah couldn't tell dem dat ah don't mek much at all. Jus' so dey can say dat I made it."

"An' where does dat leave you?" Patsy asks, stirring her tea with a stained spoon.

"Nowhere," Fionna replies, her light brown eyes looking tired. "Nowhere," she says again, her voice distant, drowned in the chatter around them inside the diner.

18

O NE NIGHT THE FLOORBOARD LOOSENS IN BEVERLY'S ATTIC AND caves in. Patsy isn't home when it happens. She had just gotten off her shift at the restaurant and arrived home when she noticed the hallway taped off with red tape, and her one suitcase already resting near the entrance. Beverly allows her to stay the night on the couch, but gives her only a day to find another place to live.

Fionna offers to take Patsy in, sharing a bed with her inside her cramped studio in Brownsville. The studio is so small that only one bed can fit. It might have been a walk-in-closet, which the owner turned into a single room, sealing off access to the bedroom it once belonged to and blowing out a wall to make a door on the opposite side. On the first night, Patsy couldn't sleep, having never slept with a woman in the same bed before. They sleep side by side, not touching. Though not the most comfortable arrangement, especially since Fionna snores and jabs Patsy with her knees from time to time, they continue to share a bed.

Gradually, after the first month of living together, Patsy notices how it has begun to feel natural. At the Western Beef Supermarket where Fionna shops, they scour the coupons for sales together, making sure to pick up family-size cornflakes, tea biscuits, frozen meats, and frozen vegetables—since fresh vegetables are more expensive and go bad too quickly. Patsy learns that American supermarkets can be deceiving; it's tempting to buy down the whole place when you see "sale" written in bold underneath, before realizing that everything adds up. Also, as undocumented, they aren't eligible for food stamps or any government assistance. Because of that, Patsy and Fionna ration the little money they have for food, being mindful of what they're spending by making lists of what they need for the house. They also rinsed a jam jar, which they now use to store loose change for the laundromat across the street where they take their clothes—something they did separately in the beginning until one morning Patsy found Fionna's clothes with hers and washed them anyway. They split the rent—paying the landlord in cash—which allows for small pleasures like catching a movie together, ordering a cup of cappuccino at the diner next to their job, or combing through the aisles of Goodwill for cheap secondhand clothes, something else that Patsy never thought she'd ever do. In Jamaica, not even poor people would be caught dead wearing secondhand clothes. They'd rather forgo food and rent, and in some extreme cases their children's school fee, to buy a nice dress or suit for church or a dance session—like the women across the gully by the tenement yards on Garrick's Lane and Cooper Lane. These women took pride donning the most resplendent costumes for dances while their half-naked, runny-nose children ran around pulling on their unruly, uncombed hair. At the Goodwill, Patsy is surprised to find clothes in good condition, holding up shirts with all the buttons still on them, polyester skirts that haven't been pressed to a shine from overwearing, and shoes that still have their soles.

"American people love t'row weh good t'ings, eeh!" she muses.

Days later, Fionna walks through the door with a small round chrome Formica table. "Look what ah found!" Fionna says. "Americans really like to waste t'ings fi true!" She tells Patsy she had found their mattress in the same way too, leaned up on a tree, spotless.

FIONNA HAS A BOYFRIEND, ALRICK, WHO GREW UP WITH FIONNA in Laventille. One came after the other, since they couldn't stand to be apart. Because Fionna is Catholic, they cannot live together until they get married—at least that is what Fionna maintains. Alrick works as a mechanic and lives in a basement in Sunset Park with four other men. He's careful not to bring Fionna around his roommates—not with all those men crammed in one space. Patsy knew about him from her conversations with Fionna, but one day when Patsy was listening to the radio in bed, Fionna came home from working at her other job, with Alrick following at her heels. Since then he has been dropping by frequently. He has the body of a weight lifter and the smile of a cartoon villain.

Fionna doesn't seem to mind his constant presence. Sometimes the three of them order Chinese food and watch movies Alrick buys on 125th Street from the peddlers near his job in Harlem. They watch movies like *Fight Club, Sleepy Hallow,* and *The Sixth Sense*—movies that make Fionna curl up next to Alrick on the bed and bury her face in his chest. Patsy looks up sometimes and catches Alrick's gaze, even when he has his arms around Fionna. Occasionally Fionna and Alrick share a ganja spliff, which Patsy declines, excusing herself to take a walk, trying not to think of the crack pipes and needles on the sidewalks. Or sometimes she browses the aisles of the bodega downstairs where the cat rubs its tail on her legs. She knows to give the couple their privacy. And when she returns to the studio, Alrick is usually smiling, the whole studio smelling like sex. Patsy often waits for Alrick to leave so that she can go to bed and wake up early for another day of job searching before work at the restaurant.

On this particular night, Alrick doesn't leave. Fionna gives him a blanket, and he lies on the floor, half of him under the bed. At one point during the night, Patsy wakes up to find him standing over her, panting, a musky smell rising from him. She inhales sharply, frozen as though the thing he has in his hand is a gun pointed at her. At first she thinks he might be sleepwalking. So, it's all right. He's just standing there, not really doing anything. Just holding it and panting. Patsy pretends to be asleep, not knowing how to move her limbs to cover herself with the comforter or nudge Fionna awake. She no longer knows how to breathe until Alrick's rapid breaths and the warm liquid on her right thigh fill her with instant knowing and dread. She lies still, a bad taste in her mouth—rage mixed with saliva. And yet, her body doesn't do the thing it ought to do. It doesn't sit upright or let out a scream to express its shock and outrage. Absent is the urgency to do something, say something, feel something. She recalls another time and place on a night like this when she was frozen in the same way. She was ten years old when she first felt the mysterious weight bear down on her in the dark, and something forcefully slipping into her and bringing forth the most visceral pain. How hard it was then to shriek. Something prevented her from doing so, clamping her mouth; and she wasn't sure if it was real. She was already familiar with the dark menacing thing in her periphery that no one else can see besides her; it always existed, even then, waiting. That night, as a child, the only thing certain to Patsy was Diana Ross's voice crooning "Do you Know Where You're Going To" from the old stereo, which had begun to collect dust inside the living room since Mama G no longer listened to the records that she and Uncle Curtis loved. Patsy let the incident—which might have been a bad dream—pass unrecorded, untold, a bad taste remaining in her mouth well after. It tasted like death itself—a death that numbed her body of its despair when she saw the bright red spot on the sheet. She was unable to place the unidentifiable loss of something that made all other losses bearable and all other invasions welcomed.

Inside the studio, she waits impatiently for Alrick to zip himself up and settle under his blanket on the floor. Light disgust drips in the back of Patsy's throat as the wet skim of Alrick's pleasure hardens on her leg. Eventually she snuggles closer to Fionna and puts her arm around Fionna's waist, her face pressed into the nape of Fionna's neck. But Fionna, groggy with sleep, stirs and moves away, leaving Patsy to decipher in the dark whose back faces her: That of her roommate? Or of her mother?

19

Tonight, as Patsy cleans the bathroom mirror, Fionna talks freely about finally getting to visit Trinidad if all goes well. It's a slow night. The tip jar is almost empty. She tells Patsy that she's almost done saving to pay an American gentleman to marry her so that she can get her papers. Patsy's movement slows as she wipes water from around the sink. It's the first Patsy is hearing about this gentleman. "Yuh serious?" she asks her roommate.

Fionna pauses too, her eyes widening as she realizes that she's said too much. Fionna looks over both shoulders to make sure no one enters the restroom before she says, "I didn't want to mention it before I knew it would be possible. Him charging me only three thousand."

"Only?" Patsy gasps.

"Some people pay more than dat," Fionna replies. Then, lowering her voice, she says, "I pay in installments. Before yuh know it, I'll have me papers."

Patsy frowns. "Dat's a lot of money. An' what about Alrick?"

Fionna shrugs. "Di marriage is a business one. Alrick will be fine. He's really supportive. He knows dat if I get my papers, then he will get his too. Eventually. It might tek a few years for me to get my citizenship, but once ah get it, I marry him an' he can get his green card."

She's reapplying bright red lipstick in the mirror and using one hand to brush down her hair. She's meeting Alrick to go dancing after her shift is over. He hasn't been over much since the incident the other night. Maybe it's guilt keeping him away. Patsy is grateful, because with no money, she has nowhere else to go. However, the incident has bolstered her job-searching efforts so that she can afford her own apartment.

"As soon as di papers come in di mail, I'll file for a divorce," Fionna is saying. "We got it all figured out."

"Yuh don't have a problem wid dat?" Patsy asks.

"If you want to stay here, yuh gotta do what yuh gotta do," Fionna replies with a faint American accent. She purses her lips. "Maybe you should start looking for an American gentleman to marry too."

"What if I don't want to do dat?" Patsy asks.

"Then you'll always be illegal, genius."

There's that word again that Patsy hates—*illegal*. She's no longer a person, but an illegal. An alien. She can't understand why she's deemed a criminal for wanting more, for being in a place where she can live out her dreams—even if it might take a while to achieve them.

"You have to get rid of dat pride of yours," Fionna tells her.

"It's not pride, it's caution," Patsy replies. "What if di man take advantage? What if him demand more money? Or worse, sex? What would you tell Alrick then? Whatever happen to marrying fah love?"

Fionna throws her head back and laughs. This time she laughs so hard that spit flies from her mouth and sprays the bathroom mirror. She cleans it with the ammonia in the bottle she carries. "Love?" She continues to chuckle. When she sobers, she says, "We can't afford to love in dis country. We not at dat place yet as immigrants where we can choose love. Like everyt'ing else, we tek what we can get—grab on to any lifeboat so we don't drown in dis place call America. Love? Love won't get we papers."

"Yuh saying yuh don't love Alrick?"

"Yuh not getting what I'm saying," Fionna says, lowering the ammonia bottle. "People die to get into dis country. Yuh t'ink we have di luxury of choosing how to stay? So what if it's a sham marriage dat might require sex? A likkle sex don't compare to di shame of getting sent home wid jus' we two long hands. Alrick knows dat. He knows we have to protect we self, an' love small. 'Cause if we delude we self into thinking we got a choice, then we end up wid nothing. We end up wid broken hearts an' hungry families. We only cotching here. One mistake an' we gone. Dis is not our country, an' immigration will do everyt'ing dey can to remind us of dat. We have neither di right nor permission to enjoy human things like Americans—vacation, rest, strolling in di park, di sunset. Who are we to do dat when we taking up space, taxes, an' air, according to dem? Dey have all di power to punish us fah stealing from dem—fah daring to t'ink we can dream, much less love."

Patsy continues to wipe and wipe, even when there's nothing left to clean. She remembers sleeping with Vincent during all those years of uncertainty, America on her mind. She did it with the ease of knowing she was getting something grand out of it. But to come to America—the place she expected to find freedom—only to go back to the bargains of the past is impossible. Fionna is now humming a song on the other side of the sink. Patsy knows that she hums when she's sad about something. Patsy thinks about Fionna's final words. Quietly she mourns, realizing that she must mutilate the very thing that sprang inside her, unearthing itself, reaching and reaching toward sunlight. She has only dealt with it alone, her neck bent over Cicely's letters like they were roses that drew her face to them. It demanded solitude, this thing she nurtured. But Jamaican soil was bad for it. Certain plants can't grow there, don't belong there. American soil, she thought, would be better. But it's best to bury it now. Cicely is right after all—that night in the basement when she told Patsy that she needed Marcus, yet could not admit to loving him. Patsy looks down at her pruned hands, stripping from the strong chemicals in the cleaning products. If she marries an American man for a green card, she wouldn't have to do this for long. Mama G was right. For to enter into, and remain in, any promised land—be it Heaven or America—one has to conform. Or, in her own words, *"Yuh mus' suck salt if yuh want to succeed."* Yet Patsy cannot see herself going down that road. She might never be free.

❧

ONE NIGHT, PATSY HEARS FIONNA CRYING INTO HER PILLOW. Patsy had gone to bed early and never heard when Fionna came in from meeting the American gentleman for dinner. Fionna must have been extra-careful to not wake Patsy like she often did when she lifted the covers and lay down next to her in the bed. The digital clock on the microwave reads eleven forty-five p.m.

"What's wrong?" Patsy asks, rubbing sleep from her eyes.

Fionna smells like cologne—not the invasive musk Alrick wears, but a subtler scent that reminds Patsy of aromatic tobacco. She doesn't respond to Patsy's inquiry. Neither does Fionna turn toward her. Patsy refrains from questioning her any further. Instead, she spoons a sobbing Fionna, holding her tight until her sniffles die down; until the stars vanish and the sun shines through the thin white curtains.

20

HER FIRST CHRISTMAS IN AMERICA IS SPENT WORKING AT THE restaurant. Alan said she could get time-and-a-half by working the least popular shift. Privately, Patsy is grateful that not everyone in America celebrates Christmas. She can still walk into a bodega and pick up milk, turn on the television and see regular programming, catch a bus to work, and make extra cash. Even when she's splitting rent with Fionna, she's still living from paycheck to paycheck, unable to save money to send home to Tru. Patsy wanted to at least send something for Tru to buy herself a Christmas gift. She wonders if it's still worth it to send all she has in order to give the impression that she's doing well, when in truth she isn't. She wants to be alone, wanting nothing of the pretense, the charade.

On her way home from work, it starts to snow. Struck by the presence of snow—actual snow—she stops and tilts her head toward the sky, allowing the flakes to melt on her face. It looks to Patsy like shredded paper flung from the sky. It's not as magical as the glittered snow she and Tru spent hours shaking just to see whirls of it fill the glass sphere. None of the emotions she expected to feel seeing snow for the first time are there. She thought this, like all her other firsts, would've been experienced with Cicely.

Despite Patsy's protest, Fionna decorates the studio with a fake table-size Christmas tree that she puts on a folding chair by the window. "Stop being a Grinch!"

Christmas carols play from the radio on top of the microwave. Two Domino's pizza boxes with just the uneaten crusts inside them and a large half-empty Sprite bottle sit on the small round Formica table that Fionna found on the street.

"Cheers!" Fionna says to Patsy, holding up a glass of eggnog she bought at the bodega. The eggnog reeks of the rum she spiked it with. "What's a good eggnog without liquor?" she asks Patsy when Patsy wrinkles her face. Fionna is sitting cross-legged on the floor, wearing a backless sparkly red blouse she donned for the occasion with tight black jeans. Patsy, who has on her long johns, reaches from the bed, aggravating the squealing springs, as she clinks her glass with her roommate's.

"I got somet'ing for you." Fionna springs up and bounces to her purse. She pulls out a small gift-wrapped box. "Now yuh can't say dat all Trinis hate Jamaicans," she jokes.

"Well, it depend on di gift."

"Open it," Fionna chides. Her cheeks are reddened with rouge, same color as her lips, and her newly cut bangs are feathered just the way Halle Berry does hers in the *Essence* magazine Fionna bought just weeks ago.

"Yuh didn't have to," Patsy says. She feels bad that she didn't get Fionna anything.

With more coaxing from Fionna, Patsy tears the gift paper and pries open the box. She pulls out a Statue of Liberty snow globe.

"I saw it in Time Square when I was coming home from work and thought of you. I notice you have a thing fah snow globes."

"How did you . . ."

"Caught you looking at dem at dat Dollar Tree store we went to buy curtains," Fionna replies, reading her mind. "Since we in New York City, ah figure ah could get you a Statue of Liberty one."

Patsy stares at it. Turns it in her hands. Watches the snow fall on the green statue holding its torch. Tru's face surfaces in the gleam of the glass.

"Yuh all right?" Fionna asks Patsy after a while.

Patsy puts on a smile and gestures with her free hand. "No, no—ah mean, yes! T'ank you. Ah really appreciate dis gift."

"Don't seem like it."

"Honestly," Patsy replies. "Ah couldn't have ask fah a bettah gift."

But she feels alone in her struggle to try and balance herself, her emotions—at least to keep her past at bay. She's beginning to get used to the notion of a future without Tru, her silence in this moment a scissor's blade dragged along the ribbon of her past until it curls into a neat bow. She's determined to be a new woman in America. Her gift to herself. This means she must do the work to separate her past from her present. Some days are better than others. Always, in the quiet of her thoughts, she wonders how Tru is faring without her. Is she angry? *It's fah di bettah*, Patsy reminds herself, applying the thought like a soothing balm on a cut. *Once ah start to save up money to send, she'll know ah still care.* Later, she goes to bed, lying next to Fionna on this silent night, restless at the sounds of children—*imagined or real?* she can't tell—crying for their mothers.

≱

THE NEXT DAY, BOXING DAY, SHE SITS IN AN ALL-YOU-CAN-EAT Caribbean restaurant on Rockaway Avenue by herself and listens to other people's laughter and chatter swirling around her. Fionna had invited her as her plus-one at a party thrown by one of the hostesses she met and hit it off with at her second job at Applebee's, but Patsy declined. She wanted to be alone. She chews large chunks of macaroni and cheese, ham, and soggy string beans, and drinks a glass of watered-down sorrel, focusing on the white plate, silver utensils, and the blank Christmas card for Tru in front of her. She might start with, *Merry Christmas*, though by the time the card gets to Tru it will be way too late. She needs to communicate something other than a greeting. She wipes her hands in a napkin and writes:

It's snowing a lot in New York. The streets and sidewalks are white. I know you would have appreciated all this snow. I hope you're being a good girl. I think of you often and will send you a gift as soon as I can.

She considers adding an apology or something like: *Sometimes when you love someone deeply, you sacrifice a lot for that person. It's more selfish when you don't consider what's best for the person you love. One day you will understand.* But Patsy thinks against this. She signs off with, *Your mother, Patsy, with love.*

≱

AND STILL, THREE DAYS INTO THE NEW YEAR PATSY IS RESTLESS. There's an opening inside her that she can't close. It's this feeling of yearning that makes her go to Cicely's place. She rides the number three train from Rockaway Avenue all the way to Crown Heights, the night egging her on. She could never do this in the daytime. She turns onto the quiet street. The night is starless and without a moon.

There are no light posts on this street, just the arcade of bare trees casting dark shadows like elongated human fingers, broken and distorted. The lit windows of the austere brownstones are like embers of warmth where life stirs, where families gather below the high ceilings. Enveloped by the night, Patsy positions herself on the side of Brower Park facing Cicely's brownstone. The lights are on in the living room, the chandelier glistening above the dining table. Though it is three days into the new year, the Christmas tree is still in a corner near the window, lavishly decorated with elaborate bows and glass ornaments. Patsy imagines the place still smelling like cinnamon, and the gifts are still piled around the tree inside big boxes, the wrappings undone.

Yesterday she stood in front of a clothing boutique, attracted to the display of jewelry on fake tree branches—big, gaudy rhinestone earrings, some looking like chandeliers, with matching bracelets; twinkling gemstone pendants. The window was decorated with white frost and a sloppy drawing of a waving snowman. A dancing Santa Claus wiggled near the display singing, "Ho! Ho! Ho!" Patsy had spotted a nice pair of ruby earrings inside a box. Staring at them, she found herself thinking of Cicely, though the small ruby earrings were nothing compared to the swanky jewelry Marcus buys her. Patsy was suddenly annoyed with herself; annoyed because Cicely still has that effect on her. Of all the people that she could get gifts for, she thought only of Cicely.

Many years ago, Patsy gave Cicely gifts she bought from Woolworth in downtown Kingston that she could afford—scented powder with a soft puff, a compact with various shades of eye shadow, a smooth river stone painted blue, a cup with a rose on it.

"*Why yuh doing dis?*" Cicely asked her the last Christmas they saw each other before she left.

"*Doing what?*" Patsy asked.

Cicely held up the box with the cup inside it, a smirk on her face.

Patsy shrugged. "*Because ah t'ink it's nice.*"

"Yuh know yuh don't like Christmas. Yet you've been giving me presents all these years. Who yuh fooling?"

"Consider dem tokens of appreciation for our friendship," Patsy replied.

Cicely laughed her low, sweet, baby-girl laugh.

The wind lifts suddenly and forces Patsy back to the present. Just as she tightens her scarf, about to turn away from Cicely's living room window, Cicely comes into view. It's as though Patsy willed her to do so, or she knows that Patsy is out there in the dark. Patsy admires her old friend's effortless beauty in a long silk robe—how she pulls her hair up into a loose bun, revealing the soft profile of her face under the glow of the lamp by the mantel. A mixture of guilt and shame comes over Patsy, spying on Cicely this way. Like the rich white people in the city, Cicely and Marcus seem content to leave their curtains open and display evidence of their status—though Patsy gets the feeling that the white people, unlike Cicely and Marcus, display their things because it may have never entered their minds not to. In their world of haves, the have-nots don't exist, and could not possibly materialize to steal from them.

Music floats from the upstairs window. Shamar's violin plays a beautiful melody. Downstairs, Cicely is drawn to the mantel. Patsy watches her friend pick up the photographs, dust them, put them back. Then in walks Marcus like an actor in a stage performance. Patsy didn't see him waiting in the wings. He's wearing a robe too, much thicker than Cicely's, over his pajamas. He holds Cicely from behind and pulls her to him. He bends and kisses her neck. She edges away a little, her eyes still on the mantel. Her fingers touch his arms lightly. He turns her gently and kisses her, not like a man who would hit his wife, but like a man who knows his woman belongs to him and only him. From a distance, it appears that Cicely is kissing back with passion, her neck bent too far backward. Marcus pauses to look down into her face. He uses one finger to blot something from her lips, maybe crumbs or a wine stain from the glass she pours herself with dinner. They don't move. They simply stare into each other's faces.

Patsy feels herself crumbling inside. *She loves him after all.* She looks away from the scene. She makes her way back to the subway station and boards the train. In the darkened window of the train, her face is a mask, all the emotion seemingly drained from it. She has never felt so lonely. She notices that the people on the train are Jamaicans, most looking like they're heading home from jobs this late at night, exhausted; two women talk animatedly in patois, recounting their day—*"Lawd, me tyad suh till! Suppose yuh see how di pickney dem spoil. Jes'as Christ, me neva see pickney suh bad an' hard-ears in me life! American children got no discipline, an' yuh can't even spank dem!"*

A man in construction gear stares at Patsy from the seat opposite hers. He too looks Jamaican. He smiles a gentle smile, one Patsy imagines as pity. She remembers Vincent and how he stared at her at the bank. How being with him had been a good distraction, a way to delay what was waiting for her at the end of the day—the slow-moving darkness that could knock her down and slip its sadness deep inside her. A sudden wave of sexual urge comes over her. When she gets to the studio, she sees Alrick waiting outside, leaning against the door with his arms folded across his chest, his gym bag slung over his shoulder. Fionna is working a late shift tonight at the Applebee's, where she also cleans, and won't be off until midnight.

"Ah t'ink she's avoiding me," Alrick tells Patsy. "She don't answer my calls."

"You can come inside and wait," Patsy says to him, swallowing the resentment she has been harboring toward him.

Patsy knows that Alrick has already looked her up and down as he always does, his eyes, without Fionna there, liberally sliding over her body, which is getting chubbier with her steady diet of McDonald's fries, hamburgers, and chicken nuggets. When Alrick follows her inside, she offers him a glass of water. He looks at her over the rim as he drinks. Lust wells inside her. Not the usual lust to nibble on Cicely's creamy earlobes and leave a crimson mark on her neck while tasting the sweetness of her flesh, but something primal, animalistic—an urge she hasn't satiated in the months since arriving in America, one that grips her now at the sight of Alrick's Adam's apple moving up and down, and his tongue licking his full lips. She wants to fuck.

She doesn't ask permission, nor does she apologize when she drops to her knees and begins to unbuckle Alrick's belt. A bit of laughter sounding like a gasp erupts from his throat. Her aggressiveness excites him, giving length to his penis. He doesn't protest when she takes him into her mouth.

Patsy, wanting desperately to feel anything but grief, pants as he fucks her from behind, his fingers digging into her hips. She stares dead in the eyes of sorrow as her body relieves itself with each thrust. As the creeping chaos stirs in her hips, she slips a hand between her legs, her fingers rabidly trying to free her from Cicely's grasp—the life she imagined with her, the life she now has. But it's a hopeless, stubborn struggle, which impels her to cry, "Harder!"

The enormous thrust Alrick makes causes her to let out a deep, ear-shattering howl, letting go and giving in to the hurricane force of plea-sure that annihilates—for a quivering few seconds—everything else. Her loneliness resumes when he pulls out, the sexual desire falling away, leaving in its place only guilt. Patsy is conscious now of their naked lower halves, their wet, mingling scents, the Statue of Liberty globe on the table. She turns away, waiting impatiently for Alrick to slip off the condom, zip himself, and leave. She sobs then.

21

THE CARD WITH A GLITTERY SILVER SNOWFLAKE AGAINST A bright red background is confirmation for Tru that her mother still thinks of her. When the card came, the last of the Christmas ham had already been used up in the ackee and salt fish and callaloo; the fourth pint of sorrel Marva made for the season was gone; the rum cake devoured; the doll Tru received as a gift from Marva and Roy abandoned; and the pepper-lights that Roy had strung around the veranda grille and the mango tree in the front yard taken down and put inside a box. Yet it feels to Tru like Christmas has finally come. She sits on the highest limb of the ackee tree she likes to climb up to be by herself in the backyard and presses the card to her nose. She inhales it to see if she can smell her mother—the flowery fragrance she used to wear. But all she smells is the bland, factory scent of the card. She's kept it safe and sound inside her drawer, only pulling it out once each day to look at it.

She stares at the words. Allows them to form sandcastles in her mind—ones the sea and time cannot destroy. *Your mother, Patsy, with love.*

It's late Saturday morning. Roy is inside sleeping and Marva is moving furniture around, mopping the floors. Instead of hair grease and dry heat, the whole house smells like Pine-Sol and floor polish. Tru and her brothers aren't allowed inside until she's done, and mostly because Roy must not be disturbed. Tru and her brothers are slapped when they disturb him. He's the man of the house and is treated as such—with respect and attention. His opinions are regarded with importance and his needs are met immediately, even if Marva has to drop whatever she's doing. Mornings and nights, she brings him his dinner and massages his shoulders with one of the oils she concocts herself. Sometimes she massages his feet, bending and stretching his big toes. Roy responds well to these massages. Only his voice, his groans of pleasure, fill up the house.

The washerwoman Marva hired is mutely scrubbing clothes between her fists in the backyard. Her name is Iris. She doesn't talk much. She's a young girl from the country, about seventeen or eighteen years old, who just came up to stay with her aunt, Miss Burgess. Miss Burgess sells fruits out by the taxi stands on the main road. All Tru knows is that the girl has a troubled past and has come to Kingston to turn her life around (whatever that means). Though Miss Burgess is responsible for Iris, she cannot afford to feed Iris. So Marva took the girl in, gave her a cot to sleep on inside the shed in the backyard and food to eat. In return, Iris washes clothes for the family and sometimes cleans the house now that Marva is pregnant. Tru is Iris's responsibility too. When Marva tires of running after Tru now with her big belly, it's Iris who chases Tru with the speed of a sprinter. Usually the chase happens when it's time for Marva to comb Tru's hair—a thick mass of kinks that breaks all the combs. But today everything is calm. Even the two mongrel dogs are napping, oblivious to the roosters high-stepping in front of them. Tru is holding her mother's Christmas card and staring up at the sky, where heat and sun give the illusion of a haze. She likes to imagine her mother reaching toward her out of the sky, her hand, her fingers, poking out of the clouds to touch her. If this were to really happen, Tru would be prepared to hold on to the hand, pull on it like she would a kite string, and snatch her mother out of the clouds. Tru often gazes at the sky for a sign, and whenever she's busy doing something, like putting her head down on the desk like the teacher asks, or concentrating on schoolwork, she worries that she misses the sign. It makes her fidgety—a constant distraction in class. She gets walloped by Mrs. Powell—*"Keep yuh eyes on the board!"*—though she has begun to come first again in class, surpassing Dwight Evans, who is the smartest boy in her grade.

Looking down into the yard, the Christmas card in her hand, Tru quietly accepts the world down there for what it is—a temporary arrangement until her mother comes back for her. The card doesn't say so, but the gesture of it does. Tru doesn't need words to fill this blank space. She can feel the coming of her mother in the breeze that rustles the leaves.

She climbs down to the lowest branch and leaps boldly onto the dusty ground, landing flat on her feet. She still has a Band-Aid on her right knee, which she cut open the last time she jumped. Jumping out of trees has become a favorite pastime for Tru, since she loves to climb them. She can climb the highest coconut tree all the way to the top—an ability that has won her the respect of boys at school and in the neighborhood. Nothing beats the sensation of leaping boldly off a branch, high above everything, caught in the brief stillness of suspension. In the air, she feels free, away from Marva's surveillance, Roy's sternness, her brothers' farting odors even after they bathe, and Iris's sad eyes.

Iris doesn't stir from her intense scrubbing to look Tru's way when she lands. Tru runs toward the house, suddenly thirsty. She pauses at the entrance, scratching an itchy ankle with the toe of the other foot. She listens to her father's loud snores coming from the bedroom. Her hands trail the walls, then the doorframe. She can barely make out the slap-slap of Marva's house slippers. It might be safe to enter, she thinks. For a second, the house seems to cease breathing. The palm trees outside do all the thrashing in the easy breeze. This is a silence that occurs in between her father's grunts. As Tru makes her first step into the house, she feels a strong pull on her blouse. When she turns, Kenny is standing behind her, his arms folded across his chest.

"What yuh did dat for?" Tru asks her brother.

"Mama said not to go inside di house while Papa sleep," Kenny replies. He's a combination of various unfortunate physical characteristics. He's very thin, with big ears, and a big head that is shaped like an egg. He plays in the house, spending his time drawing or making trains and cars and buses with empty cartons and cans. Jermaine and Daval pay him no mind. Thirteen and fifteen respectively, Jermaine and Daval have taken on the mannerisms of grown men. They guzzle water from big glasses with handles, they wipe their mouths with the backs of their hands, they chew on toothpicks and play with blades from pencil sharpeners under their tongue, they talk to the television during soccer or cricket games. Every Saturday, if they're not at the shooting range with Roy, they're helping Marva carry heavy grocery bags from the market, and every Sunday they uproot weeds from the fences with bare hands and wield cutlasses over their heads as they chop grass or whack overgrown tree limbs. Jermaine shaves the two scrawny hairs from under his chin in the bathroom mirror like Roy, and Daval sprays a can of deodorant under his armpits every morning before school. Kenny is an enigma in this family of rough-and-tough boys.

Tru puts her hands on her narrow hips. "Let me be," she says.

"Yuh disobeying Mama's rules. Yuh heard what she said. Papa need him rest."

"And I need wata."

"Yuh can drink it outside by di standpipe."

She glares at her brother. Though they are the same age, he's shorter. If Tru were to fight him, he'd be defenseless against her. Kenny is not rough like a boy should be. Roy says so too. He and Marva argue all the time about how Marva raises Kenny under her frock. Knowing how much their father's criticism hurts Kenny, Tru bares her teeth and says the word that will shut him up for sure: "Sissy!"

A shadow crosses Kenny's face, his downturned mouth quivering at the attack. In a second, Tru and Kenny are on the ground, wrestling each other. They roll around on the dirty concrete path near the back entrance, overturning potted plants and waking up the sleeping mongrels, which start to bark. Kenny is warm on top of Tru, the heat of his anger matching the blood heat of his body. "Who yuh calling a sissy, yuh ugly troll?"

Tru pushes him off her and straddles him. That's when Kenny, lying on the ground, his head dirtied and eyes dark with malice, says, "Dat's why yuh mother don't want you. Dat's why she hang up when she call. I answered di phone an' dat's what she tell me! She tell me you was a ugly baby! Dat yuh favor duppy! Dat you's a blood-sucking vampire!"

Fury clogs Tru's throat. For Kenny still has that over her—the fact that he answered the call, which she was denied. Kenny wouldn't have known how important this call was to Tru had she not badgered him for weeks after it happened. At night, lying in the dark on the bed inside the room they share, Tru would ask, "*What did she soun' like? Did she soun' American? Could you hear anyt'ing in di background? Did she say she was in snow? Did she say how cold it was? Did she . . . did she . . . did she?*" Kenny eventually discerned Tru's weakness and taunted her, pretending to hold back facts or divulge fabricated stories. Out of the blue he might say something like, "*She mention working as a clown at Disney World.*"

Instead of pinning Kenny's head against the ground or jabbing his sides with her knees like she wants to, Tru hacks and spits in his face. A whimper comes from beneath her as the spit lands between Kenny's eyes and runs down his cheek. He stiffens.

"Get off me!" he yells. Tru sits on top of him, staring at his agony, his disgust. She laughs. "Serve yuh right for calling me a ugly troll."

But she's not comforted by Kenny's defeat. Tru remembers her mother's card, and her parting words—"*Be a good, obedient girl an' I promise I'll be back fah you*"—and stops. She snatches up the card, which had fallen out of her hand during their scuffle.

Just then Marva steps outside and sees Kenny lying on the dusty ground, his face wet, both him and Tru dirtied. She looks from Kenny to Tru. "Is what kinda foolishness oonuh going on wid?" she asks.

"Him call me a ugly troll," Tru replies.

"You started it!" Kenny retorts. "You called me a sissy!"

Marva throws up her hands, her big breasts, and her newly forming belly on top of the one she already had, lifting with them. Because of her stature, Marva's pregnancy wasn't apparent to Tru at first. Not until she began to lose customers. Usually on Saturdays the kitchen area is filled with a handful of neighborhood women who come to

Marva to do their hair. From early Saturday mornings to evenings, women would be bent over the kitchen sink or sitting underneath dryers, the high soprano of their laughter and chatter filling the house and carrying a feel of merriment that sets Tru at ease. But all that stopped suddenly. Many of the customers believe that it's bad luck for a pregnant woman to do their hair. *"Mek dem g'weh!"* Marva told Iris one morning when Miss Paula, one of the women who had been getting her hair done by Marva for years, called to cancel last minute. Tru hid in the tree and eavesdropped on the conversation between Marva and Iris. *"All ah dem backwards-like!"* Marva said. *"Yuh know what di woman tell me? Dat she not comfortable wid me doing har hair in my current state. Dat she t'ink har edges falling out because of me! Me! Dat woman had no edges to begin wid! An' di other one, Miss Yasmine, going around telling people I ruin har good hair. Good hair? Dat woman born wid pickey-pickey head! She favor peel-head johncrow! Which good hair me ruin? She shoulda thank me fah having di patience wid dat course bush of hers!"*

Now Marva unleashes her frustration on Tru and Kenny. "Listen! Oonuh behave oonuh self, yuh hear? Yuh see yuh father sleeping peaceful inside. Oonuh coulda wake him, carrying on like hooligans out here. What yuh have to say fah yuhself?"

Kenny begins to cry. One thing he hates even more than Roy's criticisms is his mother's admonishment. "She push me dung 'pon di groun' an' start to fight me. Then she spit in me face."

"It nuh give you di right to fight back!" Marva says. "She's a girl. Yuh shouldn't hit girls."

"Why yuh always defending her?" Kenny cries. "Is like she can do nuttin wrong!"

Roy, who must have woken up to the commotion, comes outside in time to see what's going on. His tall, dark frame fills the entrance. He appears well rested, his eyes no longer red like they were last night when he came home and went straight to his bedroom to lie down in his policeman uniform. He comes outside just in time to hear Kenny say Tru pushed him. Tru is sure she will get in trouble now, but when she looks up at her father, he's smiling down at her, something hidden under his smile. To Kenny he says, "Yuh mother know best. Yuh shouldn't be fighting girls, especially yuh sistah, when yuh can't handle it."

From her father's smile and the way he winks at her, Tru knows she has somehow appealed to him. Meanwhile, something darkens in Marva's eyes and Tru feels a strange uneasiness in this moment. Marva turns away without saying anything more, and walks back inside the house, the slap-slap of her slippers echoing with each step. Roy follows her, his laughter hurtling through the house. He stops only to catch his breath. "Ah tell you. Dat boy is somet'ing else. Is where yuh get him from? Might as well yuh did give me a girl."

The strange uneasiness remains, prompting Tru to turn to Kenny, who is quiet, his eyes fallen to the shadow at his feet.

"You're not a sissy," she says to him. "I only said it because ah was upset."

But anger flashes in Kenny's eyes with bloody depth.

"I wish you didn't come here. I wish you'd jus' go back to where yuh come from," Kenny says to Tru, burrowing his face in his hands.

22

THERE ARE TWO TYPES OF DEVIL'S COLD—ONE IN WHICH YOU cannot bring yourself to leave the room, much less the bed, to do the simplest things, and the other in which you go through the motions in a constant stupor. Patsy lies in bed, turned away from the dark heavy thing that has returned, its shadow dimming the room. With the cover over her head, she closes her eyes, not wanting to see it. God knows how long she's gone without eating. She could die, she knows. Though death doesn't seem that scary after all. Not as scary as the dark thing. Here in America, there are no bush teas for it. No bitter mix of Ramgoat roses, rosemary, lemongrass, bissy, and other herbs. No pastor to come with a bottle of sanctified olive oil. No neighbor from the country who can wring the neck of a goat and sever it with a machete for you to bathe in its blood. No time to lie down and let it run its course. She's powerless against it.

"Di real hell is allowing dis place to eat you alive," Fionna says to Patsy when she notices that she has been lying in the same spot on the bed inside their studio from sunup till sundown. How many rotations has the sun gone through since Patsy climbed in the bed that night after seeing Cicely? She slips in and out of sleep. She wakes to Fionna shaking her.

"Patsy. Patsy? Patsy!"

It reminds Patsy of her daughter's voice—how it would pull Patsy from the lips of a deep sleep. Here she is in the midst of it, hating it, terrified of it, and yet her only thought is of Tru. During those years, it was the anticipation of going to America to see Cicely that had kept Patsy alive. But what is keeping her alive now? Where will she find the strength that would protect her from the spells? How can she live, knowing that she lost Cicely to her American dream? It's then that what Fionna had said about not having the luxury of choosing love makes sense to Patsy. That's what it all comes down to—choice. When has she ever been given a choice? Never. She was never given the choice to say no the first time her legs were pried open, never given a choice to rid her body of the grievance she had to carry for nine months, never given a choice to look at another woman and allow herself to be carried by the feeling without blood, bright red on glistening glass, sticking to her like shadow. And now. Now the promise of life comes with accepting the fact that she will never have a choice.

"Come . . . let's go," Fionna says. "Ah told Alan you was coming in tonight . . . dat you was running a high fever, but dat yuh all right now. Yuh want to get fired?"

"I can't," Patsy tells her.

"What yuh mean, yuh can't?" Fionna sits on the bed, her weight pressing down on the mattress. She puts her arms around Patsy. "You've been like dis for a week. Dis is not a place to feel sorry fah yuhself, yuh hear?"

"Ah can't take dis . . ."

"Can't take what? Come. You mus' push through whatevah going on wid you. We in dis together. I'm sure yuh didn't come to dis country to die."

There's a difference between wanting to die and not wanting to live. She doubts she can explain this to anyone. She's tired of dealing with the dark thing mocking her as a nameless, faceless interloper on foreign soil. Before, it had mocked her as a helpless secretary trapped inside a cubicle, an unwilling mother with no way out but inside her dreams. Patsy cannot afford to go back to that either. She wishes to confide this to Fionna. But it would be one less hassle if she can make Fionna go away and leave her alone. So, when Fionna tugs the sheet from Patsy, Patsy delivers the blow. "Ah had sex wid Alrick."

A hush falls inside the room when Fionna steps back. As she glances up at Fionna, she sees the vulnerability there in her eyes, the exposed vein in her neck. All that is preventing Patsy now from pulling the blade with her tongue—telling Fionna how Alrick had pressed her up against the wall, right there where she stands looking down on her, and fucked her good and hard—is the pity she sees on Fionna's face. Patsy expects her to lash out, hit her, tell her to leave, but she doesn't. Then, quietly, shamefully, Patsy says, "I'm sorry."

Fionna only laughs, clasping her hands together to cup her mouth. It sounds genuine, like that of a woman who has known every secret there is to know and has pitied the person thinking she could be so naïve. Patsy stares at her, puzzled at the sight of the tearful gratitude her confession has brought to her roommate. The dark cluster breaks and falls apart in her panic.

"Girl, please," Fionna says. "Is dat why yuh down on yuhself? Dat man would screw anyt'ing in a dress. Dat's jus' how dey are, especially Caribbean men. Don't you know dat? Your men, especially. Chile, please."

"So you knew?" Patsy asks.

"No. But I know his dick an' what it's capable of."

"An' yuh okay wid it?"

"Look here . . . ah judge di penis different from di man. Why hate a man for his faults? Who he loves and who he fucks are separate. We've been friends for longah than we been lovers. Dat's di only thing keeping us together. Comfort. I'm glad you told me. Ah consider you a friend too. I know dis might soun' foolish, but him weakness don't mek him a bad person. Neither does yours. When yuh fall in love wid yuh best friend, it's different. You accept everyt'ing 'bout dem. Di good, di bad, an' di downright ugly." Sitting back down on the bed, Fionna strokes Patsy's arm. "Maybe yuh should talk to somebody."

"Somebody like who?"

Fionna shrugs. "Someone yuh can confide in. Someone who can help you. Like a professional. 'Cause rather than watch you do such a piss-poor job at slowly killing yuhself, I'd rather kill yuh myself," she jokes.

"I jus' . . ." Patsy's voice trails.

"Who hasn't thought about giving up?" Fionna asks, reading her mind. "Dis place don't make it easy for us. Is like walking 'pon hot coal. At least in sleep, we can dream. But di weirdest t'ing 'bout life is dat it's only understood backward. Yuh neva know what's at di end ah dis tunnel waiting fah you, sweetheart. Now come get dressed. We got life to live an' rent to pay."

❦

Patsy arrives extra-early, just after the dwindling lunch-hour crowd and a little before happy hour and the arrival of patrons coming for dinner. She's there to apologize to Bernie for missing so many days at the restaurant. The place is bustling as usual. A loud voice bellows from the kitchen when Patsy passes by on her way to Bernie's office. "What's di mattah wid oonuh? Dis is a Dutch pot! How oonuh call oonuh self cooks if oonuh nuh know dat? Blasted dunce-bats!" The patois is spoken loudly, as though it never entered the speaker's mind to be ashamed of it in America with all these white people around overhearing it. It must be the new chef that Fionna told Patsy about. Ever since he was hired, there had been shouts and fights in the kitchen. Serge is his name. Bernie's first real Jamaican chef after a searing review in the *New York Post* by a Jamaican columnist about Peta-Gaye's lack of authenticity. Bernie must have jetted to Kingston, snatched Serge from the trenches of Delacree Road, Denham Town, or even Pennyfield, for all Patsy knows, brushed him off, and hired him.

Alan scoots out of Serge's way when he emerges, a tall, dark, sturdy man in a white apron. "Spices! Ah need real spices!"

"Arrogant son of a bitch," Alan quips under his breath, rolling his eyes as Serge approaches him. "Bernie wants American-friendly foods on the menu," Alan says to the angry chef.

"An' oonuh call dis a Jamaican restaurant? Kiss me ass," Serge barks. Alan bristles.

Serge bold-steps his way behind Alan, who hightails it toward Bernie's office. Serge slows when he sees Patsy. "How are you, beautiful lady? Pardon my behavior."

The anger that sparked his voice earlier instantly cools. She smiles, heartened by his friendliness. She greets him, feeling herself blush, aware of his widening grin.

"Hello," she replies, almost forgetting why she's standing at Bernie's door.

"Another Jamaican, I see!" Serge extends his hand and Patsy shakes it. He's such a gentleman, she thinks, not at all what she pictured after Fionna's description of what he said to her last week: *"How yuh feel 'bout mek'ing me baby, sweetness?"* Fionna told Patsy that had he not been the chef, she probably would've slapped him. Patsy didn't say to Fionna then that she knew just the type of Jamaican man she assumed Serge to be—the type who would openly flirt with any woman, from the Queen of England to a toothless homeless lady, expecting their adoration. His arrogance would draw him from the kitchen to greet the customers as they eat his food, laughing haughtily as they praise his curried goat, rice and peas, oxtail stew, and ackee and saltfish, and with wicked mischief say something like, *"Jus' wait till ah open me own. Dere's more weh dat come from."* Now he simply bows to Patsy like he was trained at Buckingham Palace and says, "Aftah you, madam wid di cute dimples. Can I call you Dimples?"

"My name is Patsy."

"I like Patsy too. All right, then, Miss Patsy Dimples. Aftah you . . ."

She cannot help but smile as she steps past him while he holds the door for her.

"Wait, wait, what are you doing?" Alan asks from behind Serge. "We need to settle this once and for—"

Serge turns to him sharply and says, "Shut yuh raas mouth! Yuh got no respec'? Ladies first! An' when me seh *ladies*, me nuh mean you!" Leaning in slightly while holding the doorknob, he says to Bernie, "We will talk when yuh done."

Patsy thanks Serge and closes the door behind her. Bernie's office is a box with collages of reggae and rock bands, which reminds Patsy of the insides of a teenage boy's room on American television sitcoms, complete with an oversized poster of a beautiful woman. In this case it's the famous photograph Patsy has seen on every Jamaica Tourist Board billboard back home of the coolie model who resembles Cicely, emerging from a river, hair slicked back, wearing a wet see-through T-shirt with JAMAICA spread across her breasts. Patsy looks away from it and focuses on Bernie, who is leaned back in his chair with his feet on his desk.

"I'm surprised those two knuckleheads didn't run you over in the hallway," he says, bristling with sarcasm and annoyance. There's nowhere for Patsy to sit, so she remains standing. "Someone finally decides to show up for work," he continues.

"I was sick."

"Fionna told me. Do you have a doctor's note?"

"Ah don't have one, sah," Patsy says quietly. "Is not somet'ing doctors can treat."

Bernie sighs and takes his feet down. "What were you sick with, Patsy?"

"I—I was haunted."

"What?" he asks, his face a mesh of questions. In just moments it transforms from concern to unease to suspicion. Perhaps for the first time, he's regretting his decision to hire real Jamaicans. *These people are crazy!* she can almost hear him thinking.

"Haunted?" Bernie asks. "By what?"

Patsy knows better than to trust him, but she's used up all her energy in just getting here. She doesn't have the strength to lie. So she tells him.

"Devil's cold," he says when she tells him the name Mama G has referred to it as. "Is it contagious?"

"No."

"What are the symptoms of this . . . uh . . . Devil's cold?"

She discloses her experiences with the dark thing that haunts her. How it comes so close sometimes that she can feel its cold breath breathing down her neck; how, like gas in the belly, a sore throat, or arthritis pain, one has to let it run its course.

"That must be something. How can you prevent it from happening again?" he asks, leaning back in his chair and folding his arms across his chest. She gets the sense that he's humoring her, his mouth twisted to the side as though he's trying to suppress a laugh.

"Ah can't prevent it. Is in we blood."

"Oh, really. So, it happens anytime it wants, huh?"

"Yes."

Narrowing his eyes, his displeasure more apparent, he delivers the blow. "Then you're fired. See Alan for your final pay. If you'll excuse me," he says, getting up and heading toward the door behind her, "I have a business to run. A real one."

Patsy retreats, an unsheathed sword jabbed in her chest. She stumbles forward after him to explain further when he opens the door, but stops herself when she realizes there is nothing more she can say. It's too late, her defeat certain.

She opens the door and pushes past Serge and Alan going at it in the narrow pathway near the kitchen—Serge calling Alan a battyman and Alan calling Serge a poor excuse for an ape and that he should go back to whatever jungle he came from, Bernie in the middle, preventing them from killing each other. *"You're both animals!"* he yells, red-faced. None of them see Patsy pass them by. None of them see her disappear.

23

ONE EVENING TRU COMES HOME FROM SCHOOL TO SEE MARVA stunned and colorless inside the living room, her oblique eyes staring out at nothing in particular. She's wearing one of those big shapeless dresses she's taken to wearing, her hands on her belly. Roy is there at her side, rubbing her shoulders. Shadows invade the room, moving up Marva's limp body and slanting across Roy's eyes as he whispers, "Maybe it's fah di best. God know we can't afford another mouth to feed." His words seem to desecrate something fragile, which unleashes Marva's hysteria.

"She wasn't jus' another mouth. She was ours!" she cries softly.

WEEKS LATER, THREE WOMEN COME TO THE HOUSE. THEY'RE Marva's sisters. Women with strong backs and broad shoulders like Marva. Women who wear head-wraps and long skirts, smelling of herbs and ripened fruit. Women who squat in the backyard to dig a hole and murmur something to the earth. They took the country bus all the way from Saint Mary. Their presence breaks the disquiet inside the house. One of them—the older one with the eagle-eye and ash-gray skin, whom Tru's brothers call Aunt Cherry—is especially scary to Tru. Marva doesn't come out of the room as often, and when she does, she appears lost, walking around in her nightgown glossy-eyed and dazed. The women talk in hushed tones as though their voices were metal and Marva were glass. Tru presses her ear to Marva's bedroom door to listen.

"Hush. Nuh cry, Marva."

"He—him seh him nuh want another one."

"No. No. Let him know what yuh want."

"He don't—"

"Him only talking a bag ah t'ings. Him will come aroun'."

"Him neva even care dat we lose di baby . . ."

"Of course him care. But him is a man. Man nuh show feelings like dat."

"But our baby . . ."

"It nuh mean yuh can't try again."

Marva says something inaudible and Tru has to press harder against the door to hear.

"How yuh mean what if yuh can't 'ave another one? Stop talk like dat, Marva. Is not di end ah di world. Jus' be grateful fah di t'ree boys yuh already 'ave."

"But a girl . . ."

"Yuh can try again."

"Ah don't know. Him 'ave him dawta here. To him, dat's enough."

"Hush yuh mouth an' don't talk like dat. What you give him should be enough too."

"I can't figure out why him would . . ."

"Talk, baby. Francine, get har another piece ah tissue."

Marva blows her nose and continues, her voice tremulous with anger. "Ah can't figure out why him would do such a t'ing. Bring har here without my consent, then tell me ah can't 'ave one of my own."

"Well, what can I say? Dat woman know what she was doing when she put crosses 'pon yuh. Why else would she leave a child like dat?"

"Don't get me wrong. Di likkle girl is sweet. But she's not . . ."

Marva starts to cry again.

"Hush, baby."

"Sure, di likkle girl is sweet. Di Devil is also sweet before yuh find out seh him is di Devil. Har mother leave har here for a reason. What ah want you to do is protect yuhself."

"From who?"

"Dat girl's mother."

Dread seeps into Tru's blood. Tru imagines that it's the older sister with the eagle-eye doing all the talking, poised at Marva's bedside like a john-crow hovering over death on a coconut tree in her black clothes.

"Dis will help wid di evil dat girl's mother will bring."

"Stop talk foolishness, Cherry," Marva hisses.

"Remembah wah Mama used to say? Tek time mash ants an' yuh fin' him belly. Here—dis mixture will get rid ah any Obeah spell. Rub it all ovah yuhself morning, noon, an' night. Pray wid it too. Put a likkle in yuh tea in di morning. An' in his tea too. Don't rest it anywhere. It mus' be 'gainst yuh body at all time. Only carry it 'roun yuh waist. Don't put it anywhere close to yuh heart 'cause it could backfire an' yuh unborn child might become di unlucky one. In di meantime, ah g'wan pray fah you." They pray, rebuking the Devil in the same way Mama G does, casting out spirits and dousing every sentence with the blood of Jesus. "Father God, we covah dis house in di precious blood of Jesus. We covah our sistah, Marva, in di precious blood of Jesus an' smite Satan an' him army. Holy Jesus, sen' down yuh angels in dis bakkle field. Cast out di evil in dis house. Let our sistah Marva know dat evil shall not claim victory ovah us, even when it come as sheep."

These words spoken by the women become living things to Tru. They charge the air with an unrelenting force that seems directed at her. The unceasing assault sends Tru running out the door—disturbing the sleeping mongrel dogs and squawking fowl. The words chase her up the ackee tree, sharp-edged wings flapping down, growing louder and louder. And as she sits there, struck silent, the day changes. Beyond the leaves, the sun bleeds across the evening sky.

24

PATSY ARRIVES AT THE ADDRESS SHE SAW IN THE *VILLAGE VOICE*. Magic Maid had an opening. She eagerly scribbled the Bushwick Avenue address on a piece of paper. Fionna frowned when Patsy told her about the interview.

"*Ah heard bad things about dem*," Fionna said while filing her nails in bed.

"*Like what?*" Patsy asked, watching her.

"*Dey pay chump change an' only hire Spanish women. One of the waitresses at Applebee's used to work fah dem. She quit aftah one week.*"

Patsy takes her chances, showing up at the old brick building, noticing the broken window on the ground floor where a thin red curtain flaps out, then in; the rusted fire escape with a pair of old sneakers hanging from it; and a yelping noise that sounds like a tiny dog or a young baby or both. People are speaking Spanish above the noise. On the ground, snow has turned to gray sludge. Patsy steps over the mound and enters the building. She hurries up the dark steps and down a narrow hall toward the drab-looking door with a peephole and 5A plastered on it, the A slightly peeling off. As she lifts her hand to knock, she notices that the door is already cracked open. A woman's voice comes through the crack; the rapidness of it all, flung against the door and along the orange walls of the narrow hallway, gives Patsy pause.

"I'm so sorry, ma'am. Ma'am, will you listen to me? Ana is well trained—she took care of her brothers and sisters in the Dominican Republic since she was little. I swear my niece has never pulled this before. Ma'am, I understand you're upset, but I promise she has been nothing but a good employee. I'm trying my best to see what I can do. I am very sorry, but we have a no-refund policy. I'd be happy to send someone else over as soon as— Hello? Ma'am? Ma'am, are you there? Fuck!"

Patsy raises her right hand to knock again, but decides against it. *What me getting me self into?* Lowering her hand, she almost turns to walk away before deciding that this is her only chance. She takes a breath to steady her nerves and pushes the door open. A big-boned woman with unnaturally black hair and olive skin is behind a desk in a studio apartment, which is made to look like an office. A curtainless window with child-safety guards sits above a loud heater with caged metal bars that blows hot air into the space. Patsy has to take off her jacket to feel comfortable. Photographs of women, mostly Spanish, with aprons and dusters, decorate the cream-colored walls with the Magic Maid logo of a woman in a maid uniform flying on a broom, her head bent backward in an ecstatic laugh, stars trailing behind her.

The telephone rings off the hook. The woman behind the desk is leaning over it, her fat, ringed fingers resting on the receiver like she's waiting to feel a pulse, but she doesn't pick up. For a moment Patsy thinks the woman is frozen, her body poised solemnly in her chair, her hollowed face creased, the hair at her temples graying.

"I'm getting too old for this," the woman finally says. "That's what I get for hiring family members. Give them an opportunity and they blow it and drag you down with 'em."

"Uhm . . . good aftah-noon," Patsy says lightly. "Are you Minerva?"

"Who's asking?"

"My name is Patsy. I'm here fah di housecleaning job," Patsy says.

Minerva gazes up at Patsy as if suddenly aware of her presence, her eyes tired, though seemingly buoyant almost, above a pair of sagging bags beneath them. Had it not been for the faint mustache and drawn-on eyebrows, she would've been beautiful. She pauses with her hand still on the receiver. With her gaze steady on Patsy, she says, "How soon can you start?"

"I can start as soon as possible, ma'am," Patsy says. She fumbles inside her purse for the résumé the agency helped her type up months ago. It's creased at the edges, but she hasn't gotten a chance to return to the agency and have them print another one.

Minerva stops Patsy before she can give her the paper. "Well, consider yourself hired."

"Ma'am?"

"You're hired."

It's Patsy's turn to pause, excitement skipping through her veins. She watches Minerva dab perspiration from above her lips with a piece of tissue. Patsy has forgotten that she's standing until Minerva motions with her fat, ringed fingers for her to sit on the chair in front of her. "You look like a nice girl. Let me guess, twenty-five?"

"Twenty-eight," Patsy says.

"Still young. But I'm giving you a chance. All you need to know is that when you enter these homes, you're representing Magic Maid. Me and my husband worked hard to build this business from the ground up. We make sure that our workers are decent and hardworking people. With the exception of my good-for-nothing niece. I don't expect any stealing or delinquent behaviors from you. But just in case that happens, I will not only terminate you, but report it to authorities. Now, you and I both know that getting arrested isn't exactly ideal. You walk a straight line, understood?"

Patsy's mouth opens and closes before she says, "Understood."

"Good. We pay minimum wage. Five dollars fifteen cents per hour." The words hang in the air. *Five dollars fifteen cents per hour? Wha me aggo do wid dat?* The pay is barely higher than what the restaurant paid. Something on Patsy's face must have given away her disappointment, because Minerva adds, "The more jobs you do, the better. It all adds up. We also provide you with cleaning supplies. Do you own a car?"

"No."

"You might need one."

"But I'm not—ah can't get—ah don't 'ave—"

"Papers? Not a problem. Many drivers in this city don't have papers. It's easier to drive to jobs, especially with all those cleaning supplies you will carry."

"I can manage," Patsy says.

Minerva raises a drawn-on eyebrow before she shrugs and says, "All right. Suit yourself. What size are you, dear?"

"Uhm . . ." Patsy thinks. Lately she has been wearing two sizes bigger than what she normally wears. To be safe, she tells Minerva extra-large. Minerva reaches into a box next to her feet and hands Patsy a black T-shirt. Patsy holds it up to the light. The Magic Maid logo is printed in yellow on the upper left.

"You must wear our shirt with our logo at all times," Minerva instructs. "That way clients know you're one of us. People here don't open doors for black faces unless you're the delivery guy or a worker. Also, wear comfortable shoes and clothes you wouldn't mind getting dirty."

H ER FIRST CLEANING JOB IS IN BROOKLYN HEIGHTS. THE STREET reminds her of Cicely's with its endless colonnades of handsome brownstones. She lugs her cleaning supplies, inside a heavy bucket with a handle, up the wide concrete steps of the brownstone with its cast-iron railing. Patsy pauses to catch her breath at the bright red door with the brass handle, unable to decide whether to knock or press the doorbell above the last name BRADFORD. She presses the doorbell. There's no answer. Patsy stands on the top step, feeling silly. She tries to peer inside the house, where she can see an oil painting of a naked reclining woman on the wall, a bookshelf crammed with books, a marble sculpture on the mantel, and bare wooden floors. As with the other houses on the street, there are no curtains. On her way, Patsy could see huge displays of artwork on the walls, chandeliers hanging from high ceilings, grand arches of doorways leading to other rooms, winding staircases leading to other floors, mantels displaying exotic vases and fireplaces. Like Cicely and Marcus, these people are begging to be robbed, Patsy thinks, suddenly resentful of Cicely for having become the type of woman to take pride in the flagrant display of her assets this way.

The optimism she felt earlier, knowing that she'll walk away with extra money from this job, dissolves in doubt when she rings the bell again and no one answers. Maybe the person canceled the appointment and the agency forgot to tell her. Just as she's about to walk away, she sees a woman coming toward the building with bags of groceries. "Hello, there!" she says to Patsy in an easy-breezy tone. "You must be the new cleaning lady!"

She's tall, about five feet eleven inches, looking like one of those Scandinavian models in the *Vogue* magazines that Fionna likes to look at (sometimes with a flashlight at night when Patsy tells her to turn out the lights so that she can sleep). "*These are real American women. Look how skinny they are! Look how fair! Look how soft their hair and skin! What would it take to look like dat? Do you t'ink we would be cleaning toilets if we look like dat?"*

"Yes, I'm Patsy," Patsy tells the woman, whom she can't stop staring at, though she's dressed like a homeless person in baggy cargo pants, an oversized orange coat she probably made herself with patches, and a New York Yankees cap turned backward. She's just the type of woman that the American magazines tell you to look at, save for the brown hair instead of the preferred yellow ponytail, secured in a rubber band like an afterthought. No one else could get away with this type of shabbiness. But there's an air to this white woman different from that of the other white woman Patsy met at the bus stop, whose name she has forgotten. This woman gives the impression of understated elegance—someone used to the best of everything and who doesn't have to try too hard to impress. With high cheekbones, an angular face with a handful of carefully positioned freckles around her nose, and a wide mouth, she has a commanding look that announces itself and demands full attention. Patsy automatically moves out of the way for the woman to open the door. She watches as the woman digs inside her baggy cargo pants for the house keys, feeling awkward just standing there with her hands at her sides, the bucket at her feet.

"Uh—yuh need help?" Patsy finally asks.

"Oh, no, no. I'm fine. I do this all the time."

Patsy watches her fumble with the two heavy grocery bags and the keys. As soon as the door swings open, a dog leaps toward the woman and begins licking her face as she lowers the bags on the hardwood floor.

"Hey, Chi-Chi! Have you been a good girl? Mama is back, and she has company! A new cleaning lady!" Patsy wonders if she has forgotten her name already.

The dog, which doesn't look like a dog at all but a toy, jumps up on Patsy too and she yelps. She's immediately embarrassed by her reaction to the dog, hoping that she didn't lose any points for almost kicking it.

"This is Chi-Chi," the woman says to Patsy, picking up the dog and holding it to her chest like a mother nursing her baby. "Don't worry, she's friendly, even if she can be a bit much. It just means that she likes you."

Patsy's guard comes down once the dog is out the way, and she finds herself grudgingly charmed by this woman. She glimpses herself in the foyer and smooths her hair and Magic Maid T-shirt after taking off her jacket, but suddenly feels foolish for such grooming when she remembers that she's only here to clean this woman's house, and that a dog liking her is not a compliment.

The woman, who still hasn't introduced herself, leads Patsy to the kitchen, where there are copper skillets and different-colored pots hanging above an island counter. Ceramic plates are stacked neatly inside wooden cabinets, along with books about vegetarianism, how to do the right cleanse, and easy steps to making your insides "as clean as a whistle." The woman reaches into her grocery bag for an apple and bites into it without washing it. She lets the dog lick the fruit before she puts it down. Patsy stares at the barking thing wagging its tail, unable to believe the woman would let the dog lick the same fruit she'd eat. Finally, she introduces herself as Esther—as if this is an afterthought too, like her ponytail. Patsy wishes she and Cicely were on speaking terms. She would've told Cicely how she was right—that Americans treat their dogs like family members, and some even introduce the dogs by their names before introducing themselves, as if the dogs are more important. She and Cicely would've had a good laugh.

Esther begins to show Patsy around her apartment, which occupies two floors—the garden and the first floor, which has windows that swallow a whole wall. Chi-Chi is running behind them, sniffing at Patsy's feet as Esther breezes ahead. Patsy tries to ignore the furry animal.

The bedroom is larger than the studio Patsy and Fionna share. There are things covering the night table by the bed, clothes everywhere. The bright living room with peach-colored walls looks like something out of a magazine, with a teal sofa, a rustic coffee table with an ivory vase, and even the cramped bookshelf with books about yoga, travel magazines displaying people meditating in exotic places, a bronze Buddha statue, and hardcover novels. Above the mantel is the oil painting of the reclining naked woman Patsy spotted from outside, who she assumes is Esther. The come-hither smile is as haunting as it is unnecessary. Patsy imagines Esther's guests looking up at their hostess's crotch or pale nipples as she serves them sandwiches, expecting them to speak intelligently or at length about anything other than the obvious. Esther lives alone and tells Patsy how much she loves having her own freedom, which is why she never has roommates.

"It's such a New York thing, you know," Esther says, biting hungrily into her apple. "People assume that because I'm a young, single, female that I should have a roommate. I can't see how anyone can live with roommates," she says. "Even when I go to Europe in the summers for yoga retreats I stay in flats owned by friends of my parents'. I always have them to myself. I need my independence. You know what I mean?"

Patsy nods and smiles as though she knows exactly what Esther means and shares the same woes. She also hears Fionna's warning in her head: *"Americans funny. Keep yuh business to yuhself an' mek dem do all di talking."* She looks away, feeling bad for having those thoughts. Politely, she assesses the beautiful mess around her. Each room seems to have an item of clothing—T-shirts and yoga pants hung on doors, a slip left on the wooden floor, unwashed laundry, including dirty underwear piled in a hamper. It baffles Patsy that the dirty panties aren't washed by hand as soon as they're taken off, and hung to dry like Patsy was taught to do as a girl. The bathroom has toothpaste splattered against the mirror, unemptied trash, and toiletries spread out on the counter. Though the place is obviously messy, it's still picturesque. It's as though each misplaced item of clothing, shoes, handbag, were strategically placed there to add character, an unkept charm.

"My other cleaning lady vanished on me," Esther tells Patsy in a tone indicating a crisis. She shows Patsy a raggedy mop inside a closet without further instructions, as if Patsy is supposed to automatically pick up where the other cleaning lady left off.

When left alone, Patsy looks around the place, wondering if she had made a mistake saying to the agency that she's willing to do housekeeping. What does she know about good housekeeping? Mama G did this for a living, back when she used to work. Patsy remembered her buying bleaching creams to lighten her knees and elbows blackened from scrubbing floors inside houses she cleaned on the hills, or coming home and soaking her feet in hot water while complaining about the day's work, and about the rich people—how they swooshed by her without a good morning or good afternoon, how they spilled their coffee or tea and simply rang a bell for her to clean up, how they made her serve them food without ever offering her any, how she had to wash their dishes and clean their tables before they let her go home, how one woman followed her around like she was a child and barked at her if she didn't do something properly. Patsy was with Mama G one day at the market downtown when Mama G spotted one of her employers and waved in clear view of the woman. However, the woman walked by Mama G like she didn't recognize her outside her helper's uniform. *"Dey treat people like dawg if yuh nuh 'ave money like dem,"* Mama G said to a very young Patsy, pulling her along. And when Patsy tripped and fell from the sudden force, Mama G shouted at her. *"Why yuh suh clumsy? Yuh have two left foot, gyal? You is nothing but a disgrace! Yuh mek me shame! Get up an' don't mek me have to drag yuh 'cross dis market!"*

The scene dissolves in the bright glare inside Esther's lilac bathroom. Once she slips on her rubber gloves, Patsy drops to her knees with the bucket of cleaning supplies. The uncertainty and discomfort of cleaning someone else's house is tempered by the relief of income after getting fired from the restaurant. It takes Patsy a while to dust, mop, scrub the bathroom tiles, vacuum the two mats in the kitchen and inside the foyer, and spread new sheets over the queen-size bed. She avoids the painting at all costs, her eyes dutifully trained on the mantel she dusts beneath it. She puts the dirty laundry in the hamper where it belongs, including thongs, which she holds up like the tails of dead mice, their strings so thin she could floss with them. As Patsy cleans, Esther lounges on the teal couch, her legs dangling from the armrest. She reads a book the whole time, Chi-Chi napping next to her.

"This looks great!" Esther says when Patsy finishes three hours later.

Patsy smiles, her pride oddly inflated by the compliment. But then she remembers again what Fionna told her about the woman who smiled, tipped well, complimented her, then got her fired. This is what prompts Patsy to say, "Yuh laundry."

"What about it?" Esther asks, rubbing Chi-Chi's head.

"I can do those too, if yuh like," Patsy replies.

And just like that Patsy goes from cleaning lady to washerwoman. She spends an extra two and a half hours doing Esther's laundry, glad that she learned how to operate a washing machine. Just a few months ago Patsy had never conceived of the idea of washing clothes without a basin and cake soap. She had quickly realized that Americans use only machines to wash clothes, that in America there are places dedicated to washing clothes. Patsy spent the first twenty minutes one Sunday afternoon at the laundromat around the corner from Beverly's house in East New York learning how to operate the machines and pour detergent and something called a fabric softener into a small hole. The laundromat attendant—a fat black American woman who chain-smoked in the restroom and hacked into a handkerchief—was patient with Patsy. She even supplied Patsy with extra quarters. After a few of her sweaters and blouses shrank to sizes that could fit the dolls she used to buy Tru, Patsy began to pay attention to the tags on each item of clothing to see whether to adjust the machine to hot or cold, delicate or regular; and, depending on the load, heavy, medium, or light. She still chooses to wash her underwear in the shower and hang it to dry on the shower rod.

When Esther's clothes dry, Patsy folds what needs to be folded and hangs what needs to be hung. With Esther's careful instruction, she takes the more expensive clothes to the dry cleaner's around the corner. The short, bald Chinney man reminds Patsy of the Mr. Chin at the wholesale on Princess Street in downtown Kingston where she used to shop. She feels an instant connection to him. There are many Mr. Chins who own wholesales back home, but the Mr. Chin on Princess Street had better sales. She remembers those hot Saturday afternoons crammed in lines, shouting out the items on her grocery list through the mesh partition at the wholesale so that Mr. Chin, as slow as he was, could fetch them. He shouted back in patois, *"Me nuh deaf, yuh nuh! One at ah time or else me g'wan lack up di shop! Mek me see wha oonuh aggo do, to rhaatid."* Sometimes Mr. Chin's three teenage children, dressed in their Catholic school uniforms on a weekday—the two boys in their khaki and St. George's boys' school crest on the pockets and the girl in her white Immaculate Conception High tunic—would help out, harried, running back and forth to meet the demands of customers. Other times it was Mr. Chin's double-chinned wife, who never smiled at anyone except Joe-Joe the haggler on Orange Street, who used to bring her guineps and pink hibiscuses from somebody's yard. She and the children were never the friendliest, sick of being called "Chin" like every Chinese person in Jamaica. *"Beg yuh a pound ah flour, Missah Chin! Beg yuh two-pound ah cornmeal, Missah Chin! Missah Chin, gimme a bag ah rice, a pack ah Shirley biscuit, two cake soap, four tin ah mackerel!"*

It's quiet inside the dry cleaning place, except for the radio tuned to an American news station. The Mr. Chin at the dry cleaner's is laid-back, with a friendly round face. He eases out of his chair, where he sat with a newspaper, to greet Patsy. He adjusts his glasses on his nose and takes the clothes without question. There is no mesh partition between them. Neither is there any of the bulletproof glass that Patsy notices in the Chinese restaurants in her neighborhood in Brownsville. Just a wooden counter. A porcelain cat figurine sits on it. Numerous clothes are hung inside plastic on racks behind the man. Patsy is surprised by his personable manner.

"How are you today?" he asks.

"I'm fine, thank you," Patsy replies, watching him sort the clothes with short, stubby fingers, one of which has a Band-Aid wrapped around it. He takes Esther's information and hands Patsy a piece of paper with the price and the day Esther can come back for them and pay. "Have a good day," he tells her. She says goodbye, almost bumping into the door on her way out, still unable to believe that in this neighborhood she is seen by a Chinney man as a person, and not just as an outstretched black palm.

OTHER HOUSEKEEPING POSITIONS OPEN UP AND PATSY TAKES them. She realizes that she learns faster about Americans by being in their most intimate spaces. Some are cautious at first, seeing a black woman show up at their door wearing a Magic Maid T-shirt. But then she speaks, and they hear her accent—which seems to lower their shoulders and melt their faces into smiles. *"Oh, yes, yes! Please come in."* Patsy discerns recollections of palm trees, sunshine, and white-sand beaches which they often eventually bring up, asking her if she knows this hotel or that beach somewhere in Negril, Ocho Rios, or Montego Bay where they once spent an anniversary, birthday, honeymoon, vacation.

One of them got so comfortable that she told Patsy that she likes hiring immigrants, because they work harder. Said her parents hired American blacks back in Georgia, but then they began to ask for "too much." Patsy didn't ask what that meant, but somehow that "too much" stayed with her, incited her to go above and beyond—even staying later than usual to scrub crayon stains off a whole wall inside a grandmother's apartment. She didn't tip Patsy. And Patsy knew better than to ask.

She prefers when clients leave her alone inside their apartments to go jogging, grocery shopping, to brunch, or wherever they go to give her some space. She examines bookcases, runs her hands across the surface of expensive-looking furniture, peers at family photographs, sifts through closets, tinkers with keys on pianos, studies the names on bottles of wine, perfumes, soaps, shampoos, and lotion. She moves from room to room, dusting and cleaning, cleaning and dusting. Sometimes she sifts through trash in a study. She doesn't know what she's looking for, but likes to find handwritten notes or to-do lists. There's something personal about them, human. Other times she sits at desks, or at the head of tables, imagining them hers.

25

TRU LEARNS TO DISCERN SILENCES. THERE'S HUSHED SILENCE— the silence that feels like the whole world has ceased breathing— one that accompanies Marva and forces Roy into seclusion. There's still unresolved tension inside the house. It behaves as though it were a newborn that grew into a toddler: rambunctious and moody. Roy only buries himself in work, coming home later and later every night. Yet Tru is often awakened by the quaking noises in Roy and Marva's bedroom. Recognizable to Tru are the sounds Roy and Marva make without having to speak.

On Sundays when Roy is home, he turns the television up to a high volume or buries his face deeper in the Sunday *Gleaner*, his sudden bursts filling some kind of hopelessness: "No child deserve to be born in dis godforsaken world. Dis country wid its senseless murders an' corruption is going to di dawgs."

In these instances when Roy mentions the word *child*, Marva, reeking of the garlic she has taken to carrying in a pouch around her waist, turns from her cooking by the stove and glares at Roy in his armchair, her nostrils wide, her smooth black skin glistening as her facial bones seem to harden with her eyes. Roy only ruffles the newspaper louder above Marva's stirring.

THIS SILENCE FOLLOWS TRU TOO. OR PERHAPS SHE IMAGINES IT, when she visits Mama G in Pennyfield and greets her old neighbors, whose demeanors change, their gazes pitching on the faded dresses they've surely seen her in before, with their frayed collars and loosened hems. It's as if they're searching for something—a sign, perhaps, that her mother *really* left for America; that it's not a lie covering the fact that she's cooped up in the countryside somewhere like Albino Ricky's father, who is rumored to be living in Clarendon, penniless and barefoot among cows and pigs, thinking he's one of them. The children at school laugh about it, because everyone knows that Albino Ricky's father is a madman, though the boy swears his father emigrated to England.

The hush-hush becomes more apparent to Tru when Roy allows her to accompany Mama G to Pennyfield Church of God Assembly for the Righteous on Easter Sunday. Everyone is dressed in their Sunday best except Tru, whose pink church dress with the bow in the back has gotten smaller since last summer when she last wore it to the airport to bid her mother farewell. The shoes are smaller too, squeezing Tru's big toes. "Yuh growing like ah stalk," Mama G says, patting Tru's head of pressed curls. There's a slight tinge of resentment in her grandmother's voice, as if she didn't expect Tru to grow so quickly, her knobby knees exposing the fact that her mother hasn't done so much as write, much less send anything. "Dat good-fah-nuttin' father of yours don't got no money fi buy yuh new church dresses?" Mama G asks, though something in the way she looks away makes it known to Tru that she means her mother.

Tru hangs her head, unable to tell Mama G that Roy and Marva don't go to church. She senses the hum of questions underneath the gaze of the church folk. It gets worse when Pastor Kirby, who looks like a shriveled chocho with his green robe sweeping the floor, uses Mama G as an example of an exceptional servant of God. "When we put God first, all di blessings will come down," he says. "Look at Sistah Gloria. She could have chosen to hold on to her pension like some stingy souls in here, buying new frock an' hat an' shoes fah Easter, an' not give to di church. She could've even chosen to give up hope aftah har dawta guh farrin' with not even a word if she alive or dead—" Tru feels the warmth of the sudden attention, a pulse throbbing like a fever at the side of her neck, and something—she cannot pinpoint what—shifting like sand beneath her. Pastor Kirby continues, "Sistah Gloria coulda rely on Pope like all those lazy, godless people in our community who line up to eat outta him dirty hand middle like those dirty politicians. Sistah Gloria could've decided to lay dung in har bed an' lock harself inside di house, heartbroken an' discouraged, aftah all she did fah dat girl." Tru almost looks around. *What girl?* Surely Pastor Kirby couldn't be talking about her. She's right here. *Can't he see me? Can't he see me sitting here? I'm right here!*

"But no, Sistah Gloria comes to church faithfully every day ah di week, knowing dat dere's someone more important than earthly possessions an' disappointments. *God!* How many of you have chosen God as yuh soul mate? How many of you hypocrites love yuh husband, wife, children, money, or even Pope, more than yuh love God who gi we Him only son?"

People shout, "Amen!" and "Hallelujah!" Mama G sits quietly, her chin up, hands folded in her lap. Her lips are parted, and eyes remind Tru of the black gold of the sun—their pride, joy, or both. Suddenly she rises from her seat, her head flung back, hands in the air, her mouth moving as she speaks in a foreign tongue Tru cannot understand.

When Pastor Kirby instructs people to bow their heads to pray away the dark, sinful ways of the selfish, Miss Belnavis doesn't close her eyes.

Instead, she keeps looking down at Tru with a tender gaze. And even when Tru mistakenly steps on Miss Richardson's toes in an attempt to escape to the bathroom, Miss Richardson doesn't cuss her out like she does the schoolboys who steal mangoes off the tree in her yard. Instead, she says, "Is all right, baby. It g'wan be all right."

Mama G's eyes are shut so tight in prayer that she doesn't notice when Tru returns and sits back down to hide from the talking eyes. It's exactly how the teachers at school looked at Olivia Moore when her mother died of cancer. How their heads bow slightly in her presence and their chatter quieted. Here, in the atypical silence of the church, and in spite of Mama G's status as a martyr, Tru begins to perceive her woeful existence as a motherless child.

THE SILENCE PERSISTS. JUST LAST WEEK MARVA BROUGHT TRU and her brothers with her to the supermarket. She ran into an old friend. *"Yuh looking good, Marva! Last time ah saw you was graduation at HEART! How yuh do?"* The boys went off to the snack aisle, leaving Tru. The woman, who reminded Tru of one of the ladies at Mama G's church with roving eyes masked with too wide of a smile, looked from Marva to Tru. *"She's so adorable. Ah didn't know yuh have a dawta. She look jus' like you!"* But before Marva could speak, Tru responded with, *"She's not my mother. My real mother is in America."* An awkward silence fell between the two women. Marva didn't say another word to Tru, even in the taxi home, and even when they returned to the house and she pulled out bags of onions to season the meats she bought. Marva chopped up so many onions that night, the knife banging and banging on the cutting board, that tears streamed down her face and into the food.

❧

M OST TIMES, TRU FINDS HERSELF ALONE WITH THE LONG, everlasting silence of her mother. A silence that hums like the light poles in the evenings, resonant and consistent.

It is during one of these heightened silences that the sounds from next door waft up toward Tru on the ackee tree branch where she sits. She hears the laughter and shouts of boys playing soccer in the open lot next door. They're a little older than Tru. On that branch, hidden from view, she watches them play with a makeshift soccer ball. They bounce it from knees to toes and kick it between two long bamboo sticks they use as goalposts. Their feet are dirty from kicking up dust, their faces sweaty and scorched by the sun. When they take a break, they pour water from a bottle over their heads and take off their shirts to wipe their brown faces. They play for hours. They high-five each other and jump on each other's backs, their kinship apparent and walled off from Tru. As she peers at them through the tarnished light of dusk, jealousy thicker than mucus fills Tru's mouth. She wants to play with them. But more than that, the quiet desire that rises up above all desires in the soundlessness—she wants to be them.

_

O NE DAY, WHILE SITTING IN HER HIDING PLACE HIGH ABOVE everything, Tru spots the makeshift soccer ball hidden between the rusted zinc fence and a moss-green tree trunk. It had rained the whole week. The limbs of trees are bowed with the weight of water from the heavy rain showers. Forlorn hibiscuses hang their heads, oblivious of the glittery sunshine that now peeks its head out—a golden apology for floods that destroyed some people's homes in nearby Windfield and in the countryside. The yard turns a deep shade of green with all the weeds sprung, and running Marys wind themselves around tree trunks and fling themselves across flower beds. The mongrel dogs lick water from newly formed potholes in the street. And there, in the thick grass in the open lot by the fence, is the abandoned ball.

Easily Tru leaps from the lowest branch over the fence, landing in mud. She gets up and brushes herself off, too excited to care that her shorts and T-shirt now look like she rolled around in a pile of dog mess. There is no one here to claim the ball. The other house is across the lot, its windows closed and its back door boarded up. There is a shed storing the materials and tools that will be used to build a new house on the open lot. Tru overheard Marva talking to Miss Ellis, their neighbor, about the old man who will be returning to Jamaica from London after living there for several years. His wife just died and he's moving back home. But no one appears to be inside. The crickets are screaming and the birds are chirping in the thick wet grass. A glistening diamond cobweb stands in Tru's path and she knocks it down, crunching sticks with her house slippers to get closer to the ball. Bending into the overgrown shrubs, she grabs it.

Up close, there is nothing spectacular about the ball. It's made from a Juciful juice carton, the color faded. The mud gives it an earthbrown color, and the inside is filled with scraps of paper, cloth, and some sand. But in Tru's hands it feels powerful, the mud-brown no different from a wild red burst of color. In her fingers, she can feel her pulse—a faint jumping under her skin when she caresses the ball. She holds it as if it's a gift. Something still and small. She looks at it in her hands, suddenly feeling the urge to kick it full-range. The first kick is a weak one, barely making it past the two bamboo sticks, which are still in place. She does it again, this time with a deliberate force that sends the ball flying through the air, a slanting brown arc, plowing into a wild, overgrown garden. A bullfrog leaps out of the bushes when the ball lands and a few lizards disperse, darting through the leaf-strewn field toward the nearest tree. Tru kicks the ball again and again, sending it sailing through the air each time. She remembers all the moves from watching the Reggae Boyz on TV, keeping the ball off the ground without touching it and doing the wiggle dance the athletes do every time they score a goal. She spends the whole day amusing herself with the ball. When she kicks it once more, she hears, "You have good force. But yuh need a target."

Tru stiffens at the sound of her father's voice, convinced he has come to reprimand her for not being at the dinner table on time. Marva likes to share Sunday dinner early and prefers everyone to be at the table.

However, Roy doesn't seem angry. His face isn't set in stone like it has been since he brought her to his house, and he doesn't chastise her for being muddy or for playing with something that isn't hers on the abandoned lot. Instead, something else softens Roy's rigid cheeks, extends the circumference of his pupils. He's standing there dressed as he would to go jogging at the break of dawn, in a T-shirt, gray sweatpants, and a pair of sneakers. Slowly, Tru's fear recedes.

"Give me," he says gently. He extends his arms, the scar on his right hand visible. Tru tosses him the ball. "Now watch," he says. He balances the makeshift soccer ball from toe to toe. She watches him kick it squarely between the bamboo sticks. He makes it look easy.

"Try dat," he says gently.

Tru tries again, but misses.

"Focus on where yuh want di ball to land," Roy coaxes. He puts his hands on Tru's shoulder. "See dat right dere?" He points at the posts. "Jus' shoot. Imagine it's somet'ing yuh really, really want. Imagine dat yuh whole life depend on it. Dat di only way yuh g'wan get it is to kick dat ball wid all yuh might between dem poles. Give it yuh best shot."

This time, Tru assesses the distance between the ball at her feet and the bamboo sticks. She thinks about the thing she really wants—the only thing she ever wanted besides the other thing that has taken shape in her heart. She can feel her father's eyes on her back, warm like the sun that fully surfaces from the clouds before it thins, leaving lovely ribbons of fuchsia and violet. She feels herself being pulled into view, examined for the first time with interest. Her fear dissolves, and from it emerges a faint confidence imbued inside her like tea from a tea bag. When she kicks the ball, she floats near but outside her own body, the intense force carrying her away from gravity. The ball shoots like a bullet between the bamboo sticks. She hears only the loud bang of the zinc fence it hits before it lands. It startles her. More assuring is the pride that comes over her when Roy applauds from behind. "Dat's my champ!"

Tru looks back at her father, who seems to stretch into infinity in the last light, a radiant sepia halo surrounding his head.

She wants to tell him about Marva's sisters and what they said about her mother. But he's smiling so bright at her. She doesn't want words about Marva to crush this fragile thing between them. So instead she says, "Yuh want to know what ah wish for?"

"What yuh wish for?" he asks.

"I wish for Mama to come back. She'll be back soon, right?"

Roy's smile dims. After a long pause, he says, "It's time to go. Dinner will be ready soon. Drop dat ball an' wash yuh hands." He sounds like his old, hardened self again. Then quickly he turns, taking long strides toward the house. Tru follows behind him, confused and searching the backs of her father's mud-crusted heels for the faded light.

26

PATSY HASN'T GOTTEN USED TO DOMESTIC WORK. HOWEVER, domestic work, like the cold, is something she has to tolerate. Just for the time being, until she can save up enough to send money home to Tru and get her own place. She's gotten so good at it. Clients depend on her to show up and clean their houses, appreciating how she knows exactly where and at what angle to place their favorite slippers, how to vacuum the folds of their drapes where dust gathers and wipe down furniture until it looks brand-new. Clients leave her alone in their homes with bank statements in full view on top of kitchen counters or desks and expensive-looking jewelry on vanities.

At this point, Patsy has done everything—cook, clean, wash, stand on shaky ladders to feed birds, walk dogs, empty cat litter, supervise visiting elderly parents—all but feed and wipe a baby. Until Esther gives birth in the bathtub to an eight-pound sixteen-ounce baby girl, whom she names Sky. Patsy had cleaned the tub to prepare for the event. The midwife handled the rest. The baby's father was also there. Patsy has only met him once—a man who introduced himself as Christof when Patsy came to clean one day and found him sprawled on Esther's bed in the middle of the day with no clothes on. He's a thin man, as lithe as Esther, with nice hair that he wears in a bun on top of his head. He looks like Jesus when he wears it down, which might explain Patsy's instant dislike for him. He owns the yoga studio where Esther teaches. Christof and Esther didn't marry like white people tend to do when a baby comes unexpected. Instead, they decide to "cohabitate"—a word Esther uses constantly when friends and family ask her whether or not she's engaged. "*We don't believe in marriage.*" Christof now lives in the brownstone that Esther's parents bought.

One day, Christof wasn't around and Esther was stuck with the crying baby. Patsy had come to clean and found Esther disheveled on the couch in her robe, crying. Her hair looked unwashed and messy, and gone from her face was the healthy glow she carried during her pregnancy.

"She doesn't want my milk," a tearful Esther said to Patsy.

Patsy looked into Esther's large brown eyes, wide and bloodshot from lack of sleep. She didn't know what Esther wanted her to do about it. Patsy had hoped that the new mother would figure it out by the time she was done cleaning, but she didn't. The baby cried and cried and an exasperated Esther put the baby in Patsy's arms, sobbing. "I'm so bad at this."

Patsy blinked, her outstretched arms suddenly weighted with the squealing infant.

"Please—" Esther said, holding herself. "You gotta help me. Please, Patsy."

Patsy looked from the crying infant to the weeping mother, then back to the infant. How did she wind up being responsible for another life? The baby started to wiggle in Patsy's hands. It was clear that the infant was losing patience. Esther, who must have picked up on Patsy's immobility, said something. "What did you do when yours cried like that?"

"Pardon?"

"You have children. Right?"

"Why?"

"Because—I dunno—" Esther shrugged and wiped each flushed cheek with the palm of her hands. "I—I just assumed. You strike me as a mother, like most Caribbean women I meet here—"

Patsy shook her head and quickly handed the baby back to Esther. "I'm not *most Caribbean women.*"

"I'm sorry . . . I didn't mean to say that. I—I don't know what I mean! Please, I don't want to be alone with her," Esther cried.

Patsy wasn't sure what exactly had made her pause right then. Perhaps it was the way Esther was standing there looking like defeat itself, with slumped shoulders, rings underneath her eyes, and wild hair—a far cry from the confident, glamorous woman Patsy had first met. Or maybe it was the terror that she saw in Esther's eyes, the same terror she once felt as a new mother. The moment gave Patsy an opportunity she barely understood as it was happening, a realization that she had a power that she thought she lacked and that she could use this to redeem herself. She took the baby and walked calmly to the kitchen, where she had seen formula line the cupboard. She bounced the baby against one shoulder and used the other hand to mix the formula, settling into a chair to offer the furious baby her bottle. After what seemed like hours of crying, the baby, bright-eyed and satisfied, quieted in Patsy's arms. From that day on, Patsy cared for Sky, providing her with food, daily baths, and, though Patsy didn't want to admit this to herself at first, love.

*

PATSY BEGINS TO WORK AS A LIVE-IN NANNY FOR ESTHER. ESTHER offers her extra to take care of the baby in addition to her house-cleaning work, and Patsy gladly accepts the job for what it is—a job. The thought of facing Tru ever again after caring for a newborn baby in America made Patsy lose a lot of sleep during her first few weeks of being a nanny. But the money is a lot better than what she used to make, and she still doesn't have many other options without a visa. Also, now she has a room of her own with her own bed. Sometimes, when it gets too quiet, she misses Fionna's nighttime chatter and contagious laughter. But most nights Patsy snuggles in her new bed with a smile, thinking how much her life has changed in just a few months.

Esther gives her instructions and she follows them, feeding the baby every two hours. Esther doesn't appear as distressed with Patsy around. Patsy is the one who wakes to feed the baby at night—something she doesn't mind, since she's been finding it harder and harder to fall asleep anyway. She's also the first to wake up to check on the baby inside the nursery, which used to be the room where Esther once stored clothes and shoes. Patsy walks around the brownstone singing Jamaican folk songs with the baby to her chest. *"Carry me ackee guh ah Linstead Market not a quati would sell."* The baby gurgles when Patsy sings to her. Sometimes Patsy accompanies Esther to the yoga studio. Patsy holds the baby up to the glass so that she can see her mother bending and twisting every which way, and her father bustling about, putting up schedules for new classes.

Patsy bathes the baby and dries her in clean, fluffy towels that she washes in the machine, then douses her with baby powder. Sometimes she takes her on strolls to the Brooklyn Promenade, delighting in seeing the water and the sunset above the skyscrapers through her eyes. The Twin Towers look resplendent in sunlight.

"Mama . . ." Sky says when she first starts to talk.

Patsy doesn't correct her.

When her brother, Blue, is born a year and a few months later in the spring of 2001 with the same bright eyes, Patsy is delighted. Esther is not as frightened of the boy as she was at first with Sky. He nurses easily and cries less. When he cries, it's only to be with Esther. Patsy had to work a lot harder to win him over, carrying him on daily walks to the Brooklyn Promenade too when he refuses to lie quietly in the stroller. Somehow, this baby likes sunsets. Maybe because he was born on a Wednesday evening in Esther's bathtub, which gets a lot more sunlight in the evenings. But when the planes hit the towers that fall, Patsy had stopped going to the Brooklyn Promenade for a while.

It's been a year now since 9/11. It's odd to look at the skyline without the Twin Towers there. It's even harder to look out and not remember that horrendous day when the city was engulfed in smoke. Patsy had never felt such dread and panic, thinking that the country she had fled to for freedom was under attack. She had hugged Fionna, who had visited her in Brooklyn Heights, hoping she was all right, and cried. She also had never felt more a part of her new country, conversing with strangers on the street about the tragedy. It was as though the smoke had erased any barriers between them. For a while, at least. Because of Baby Blue, Patsy has learned to live without the towers, just like the rest of New York City.

The words Patsy could never say to Tru at that age flow from a small opening inside her at the sight of these children who aren't hers. All the love she has never known pours out of her now. At night she gathers the babies in her arms and rocks them till they fall asleep. No Jesus figurines peer down on her, judging. No smell of rosemary oil stifles her. No familiar dark eyes gaze up at her, convicting her of everything she's done and everything she has failed to do.

27

T HOUGH THE NEWNESS OF TRU'S ARRIVAL HAS DIMINISHED, IT IS not forgotten that her needs can shift the whole house like Marva's belly, which looms large again.

"Dis child g'wan run us to di poorhouse!" Marva cries if Tru leaves food on her plate, busts open her forehead jumping out of trees, catches a bad cold, or comes home with a teacher's note about a class trip or extra lessons that may cost money. Tru cannot do anything without a price tag associated with it—everything is tallied. With the new baby on the way, Marva works hard to ease the worry of bad mind and ill will. She walks around with garlic and crushed coal tied in a knot around her waist to protect the baby against evil.

Shortly after Tru's tenth birthday the dark flow of blood put a stain on everything. That year, Tru's newly developing breasts raised a shade of suspicion in Marva's eyes: *"You's no more a likkle girl, but a woman. Look how yuh filling out."* Her breasts made Roy a bit uncomfortable when they first appeared; he locked his eyes on his tools to build another room in the back of the house so that Tru could be away from her brothers. In private Tru constantly rubbed her breasts until pain coursed through her body. Though they were no bigger than the round oranges she spied on Iris's chest when she saw Iris naked in the outdoor shower, they had begun to assume the weight of unfair misery. It was around then too that her hips started to widen, the coarse hairs appeared underneath her arms and between her legs. A shadow began to spread across her face, deepening her complexion and sculpting her features, and the hair on her head grew thicker. Marva saw fit to straighten Tru's hair. She washed it and anointed it with a chemical that smelled like roach spray. She lovingly combed through Tru's hair with a fine-toothed comb, admiring its length. When Tru's head started to feel like it was on fire, Marva rinsed out the chemical with eucalyptus leaves. Now Tru's hair shines like the sea in morning light, flat against her head in great abundance. The sight of her changing self frightens her.

Marva buys packs of Stayfree pads and shows Tru how to use them and how to move and sit with the bulkiness between her legs. She takes care, filling the hot red water bottle for Tru to alleviate her cramps. She acts as though she has spent her whole life preparing for this moment, pleased to have taken on this new role. She knows exactly what to do. She dutifully soaks Tru's soiled sheets and even cleaned the mattress when Tru bled through to it. Eventually, she sits on Tru's bed. In a confessional tone she says, "Yuh can't be jumping out of trees or tumbling 'roun wid boys no more. Yuh must close yuh legs. Cross dem at di ankles like so." She shows Tru. "Try to walk like a lady too. Boys don't respect yuh when yuh g'long like a hooligan. Yuh must be a lady in di streets at all times. An' besides, yuh soon sit yuh GSAT exams to get into high school. So is good dat yuh get a head start wid how to behave," Marva says. Since Tru has skipped a grade, she's already in grade six, set to take the Grade Six Assessment Test to begin the transition into high school. She hasn't even begun to think about the high school she wants to attend. Marva continues, "At home, yuh g'wan have to help out more. You's no longah a likkle girl. Dis is di age yuh learn fi be a woman." But Tru turns her back to it, her heart refusing to beat.

Gone is Tru's time playing soccer with her friends or climbing trees. The pain of her immediate isolation is as sharp as the one inside her womb. It's as though someone has taken a knife and is wedging it along the inside of her lower belly like a coconut being gutted. Her mother's old Christmas card calms her. The glitter has long rubbed off, the color faded, but she keeps it close to her on the bed where she lies. She stares through the curtains, which bellow in the breeze, at the sliver of blue sky and the stream of sunlight. Her toes curl underneath the sheets, her back pressed against the cool, hard surface of the wall each time the unspeakable ache splits her in half.

*

ONE DAY, SHORTLY AFTER HER CONVERSATION WITH MARVA about becoming a woman, Tru spots a group of Wilhampton girls while sitting on the sunny side of the veranda by herself, shelling gungo peas for Marva. Tru's school had let out early for Easter holiday and Marva needed her help with dinner. Her eyes follow them. She wonders what they're doing in Rochester, given that it is rumored that only rich girls go to Wilhampton—ones that live up in the hills of Upper St. Andrew. Girls in Rochester and neighboring Pennyfield tend to go to Roman Phillips Secondary. Even if they pass exams for other high schools in Kingston, Roman Phillips is more convenient, affordable, and sensitive to any violent upheaval that sometimes prevents students living in Pennyfield—like Tru's best friends Sore-Foot Marlon and Albino Ricky—from going to school. Pennyfield has become a name that Kingston schools and employers alike shy away from, denying applicants with that address. Nobody wants to deal with extended absences and the sob stories. No principal wants to be bothered with looking into the eyes of children who have seen sad stuff, bad stuff, the things-that-are-better-watched-on-the-news stuff. Tru decides that the four Wilhampton girls are probably taking a shortcut. Two workmen, cotching on cement blocks being used to build the house next door, whistle at them. But the girls don't give the men the satisfaction of an exchange when they throw recycled come-ons at their heels: "Pssst. Come yah, baby. Oonuh sweet like angel. Beg yuh a wuk off yuh good body, nuh?"

They are beautiful girls who walk like the world belongs to them; their performed aloofness is as captivating to Tru as the way they float down the street, their books pressed to their chests. They create their own breeze, their blue uniforms fluttering between their legs, the back hems trailing. Just then the sun peers brighter through the branches, the light adorning the landscape. Tru stares long after the girls round the corner, licking her lip sweat. In that moment, Tru, with the blood bursting inside her, her breasts forming, painful and private, and the heat bearing down on her like the weight of Marva's words—*"Dis is di age yuh learn fi be a woman"*—decides that the quiet desire, which rose up above all desires in the soundlessness that day when she sat in the ackee tree watching the boys play, isn't as easy as a wish.

Months later, when Tru, only ten years old, sits the nationwide Grade Six Achievement Test for high school and passes for Wilhampton Girls', Marva scans the *Jamaica Gleaner*, which prints all the names of successful students, and stumbles upon Tru's name. "Well, dis is nice," she says. "Wilhampton. An' where's yuh mother to pay fah dis?"

BOOK IV

JANE DOE (2008)

28

Patsy counts years in seasons, something she never had to do in Jamaica, since there is only one season year-round—well, except for the cold fronts in December and January that give Jamaicans a chance to wear sweaters displaying foreign logos on them; or spark excitement from women selling in the arcades downtown, who claim the cool blast of air from abroad gives them the fair, "air-conditioned" complexion foreigners have, which no bleaching cream can achieve. Patsy has yet to see her complexion change from brown to beige in America, though she has experienced ten winters. And even if her complexion were to change from brown to beige, she has learned that every black person in America is looked at in the same way by white people. Just like she has learned that each season has its own unique color, sweeping whole months and landscapes with warm amber, which fades into brown, then gray, and then a bold green dotted with pink blossoms before the full bloom of sunflowers. Patsy imagines them as four women drifting through the sky. They make their rounds, their skirt tails blowing in the wind, heavy baskets on their heads to pour sunrays, rain, or snow.

A total of ten years have whisked by in America like the hairs fallen out of Patsy's head, so thin and light that they go unnoticed until masses of them gather around Patsy's feet or on her pillow, dead. Once she struck the match to burn them their burnt smell hovered, and continues to hover, with the dark cloud, the weight of the sky. Patsy's visa situation has draped itself like a thin gauze throughout the years and she is caught in its mesh. For the most part, she has learned what to avoid. She knows, for example, to never mention her visa status to anyone—not even to a priest; how to only rent rooms from landlords that take cash; that she should scream for help in crowded areas to avoid calling the police herself and risk deportation; that it's best to go to the emergency room when she's sick, since it costs way more to see a regular doctor without health insurance; how to store the money she's been saving for Tru—finally able to put aside a little bit—in a Danish butter cookies tin, which she keeps inside her closet since she doesn't have a bank account, too afraid to open one without the right documentation. When she can, bit by bit, she stores away a few dollars. It's something.

Now she sits in the emergency room at Wykoff Hospital in Bushwick on a Saturday morning, among the wounded and suffering. Her right leg shakes as she waits to be seen by one of the overworked residents darting in and out of sight in green scrubs. This, she cannot do on a weekday, since the wait could be an entire day, depending on the severity of the case. When the receptionist asked her what she's there for, Patsy told her cancer, hoping she'd get seen immediately. But she has been here for three hours. She should've told the woman chest pains, though her initial response isn't far from what she suspects is the truth. Why else would her hair be falling out if it isn't cancer?

It's already three-thirty. Half her free day is gone. Saturdays are the only days Patsy has to herself to run errands. She doesn't get many days off with the Rhinebecks—the family she currently works for, babysitting their three-year-old son. Patsy has worked as a nanny for toddlers for nine, going on ten years. She stops working for the families as soon as the child turns five—an arrangement that has been agreed upon in advance with each family. Most mothers want her to stay since she's so good with their children, but it's too painful for Patsy to see the children grow past age five—the age Tru was when Patsy left her.

Just as she's about to gather her things to interrogate the receptionists—both of whom take too many pauses between being rude to patients and gossiping about this, that, and the other—Patsy hears her name.

A young Indian doctor who looks like he's still in high school greets her. "Miss Reynolds?"

"Yes."

"It says here that you think you may have cancer?" He's looking at the information that the receptionist handed him, his eyes fatigued and glazed. "What are your symptoms?"

Patsy tells him about her hair falling out. She unwraps the purple scarf—a scarf similar to what her mother began wearing after she cut off all her permed hair when she was baptized. Though Patsy has taken to wearing headscarves for a completely different reason, she hates looking like her mother at thirty-eight. She shows the young doctor what's left on her head. He slaps on a latex glove as though her scalp is contagious and examines it. When he's done he says, "You might have alopecia."

"Alopecia?" Patsy asks.

"Yes, ma'am," he says. "Scientific word, Alopecia areata."

Patsy blinks, not at the strange diagnosis, but the doctor calling her ma'am. *When did she become ma'am?*

"It's an autoimmune disease where the immune system attacks the hair follicles and—"

"Dat can't be right. Could it jus' be stress?"

"I would suggest that you go to your primary care doctor, who can run some tests."

"If I had one, I wouldn't be here, sah," Patsy says.

The young doctor rubs his eyes and yawns. He appears shrunken with weariness. "Arighty, then, my suggestion is to wait a few months to see if your hair grows back."

"How long is a few months?"

"Give it six months."

She looks at his head full of healthy dark hair, envy drying her mouth. "So what yuh expect me to do without hair?"

He shrugs, dismissive. "For a start, you can try wearing a wig."

Patsy wants to hurl a bad word or two at him, unable to believe the audacity of this Indian man with his head full of wavy hair to tell her to wear someone else's hair over her own. It could be his mother, sister, or niece's hair from India, for all she knows, propped on those mannequins in the beauty stores on Flatbush Avenue.

He checks the watch on his wrist. "Any more questions, ma'am?"

"It's Patsy."

"Right. Patsy. Do you have any more questions?"

"No," she says quietly. And even if she does, she decides that she can always go to the library in her area, where they started a free computer class, to google autoimmune diseases and then alopecia areata.

"Great!" the doctor says. "Enjoy the rest of your day."

And just like that, he's gone.

As she waits for the bus outside the hospital, the J train roaring above her head on Broadway, Patsy blames her ailment on fate. She has taken into her life the grimness of this city. And all the stress and illnesses that come with it. She exists in a colorless world now. In her mind, Pennyfield has faded like an old photograph the shade of rust—the fruit trees, the houses, the people, the sun, the bountiful hills. Everything and everyone the same as they were the day she left to chase dreams that have since dissolved.

❦

A T HOME IN HER RENTED ROOM, PATSY SITS ON THE SUNKEN twin-size mattress, her feet flat on the cold linoleum floor, eyes fixed on the peeling wall paint. She can hear the sounds of pigeons nesting and sirens going back and forth on Albany Avenue. To Patsy, who hasn't dreamed in years, America is a coffin. The window looks out into a vacant lot entangled with weeds and trash, surrounded by red-brown brick buildings, her own room a squalor in a boardinghouse full of other immigrants packed like sardines above a fish market. The raw, pervasive smell of fish permeates the walls, attracting large black flies that Patsy sprays constantly.

She gets up to shower in the shared bathroom down the hall, hoping to wash off the smells of sickness from being in the emergency room all day. If only she can get there before the revolving cast of shady characters whose arses warm the same toilet seat as hers and whose dead skin and dirt she avoids by wearing flip-flops in the shower. She's relieved to find the bathroom empty. When she's done showering, she avoids the mirror while drying off. The bathroom is small and bright. She's aware that people can barge in at any time, so she hurries up, donning the bathrobe that Fionna had given her. They talk every day since Fionna's move to Connecticut, sometimes twice in one day. Patsy calls her on the cheap Nokia phone she got from Mrs. Rhinebeck for emergencies and often complains to Fionna about the landlord, Mr. Fagan, the older Jamaican man who hasn't bothered to put locks on the bathroom door.

"Di man stingy like star-apple," she vented over the telephone to a laughing Fionna, who talks to her between breaks cleaning rooms at a Marriott Hotel in New Haven. *"Him don't fix nuttin' a'tall, Fionna. Yet him have di nerve fi charge people three hundred a month. Yuh ever see me dying trial? Three hundred fah dis dump!"*

"Sound like my husband. Cheap like ah don't know what. Ah haven't seen a dime from all dat money him making driving taxis." After the first marriage arrangement fell through with the American gentleman, Fionna found her new play-husband through a friend of a friend who knew a former lawyer that specialized in matching citizens with green card hopefuls. *"Is like Match.com fah illegals!"* she told Patsy when she tried to convince her to enroll. But Patsy refused.

Fionna still intends to marry Alrick once her divorce is finalized in a year or two. Patsy no longer questions the specifics of Fionna's agreement with her husband—be it sexual or otherwise. All she knows is that he's Liberian and drives a taxi.

"When yuh coming to visit?" Patsy keeps asking Fionna.

"Soon, soon," Fionna always says. But soon hasn't come yet. They haven't seen each other in three years. *"When yuh moving out here to Connecticut?"* Fionna says in return, pronouncing Connecticut as *Can-addic-ate* like the Americans and not *Connect-e-cut* like it should sound. *"Dey got lots of us here too. Plus, di houses are biggah, so more families hire live-in nannies."*

"New York is it for me," Patsy then replies, still determined to fashion a relationship to this city of her sojourn.

Patsy turns away from the stained oval mirror above the rusted sink as she dries her body, avoiding too the ugly branch underneath her navel. Her face she doesn't have to see at all, its visage often maliciously thrown at her in reflections in the dark windows of subway cars, fleeting, transfigured. What would Tru, Mama G, and Roy think if they should see her now? What would Cicely say about the short black wig shaped like a bob with bangs that she bought at the beauty shop on her way home? Patsy doesn't recognize herself. But she hasn't recognized herself for years, buried under this weight, which she wears like armor— seventy-five pounds of extra flesh, her hulk-like shadows spanning the width of walls and sidewalks. All she does for comfort these days is eat. She cannot remember the taste of food after she swallows. The fat softens her, swallows her up inside its folds to make her nonthreatening, invisible—yet visible in a way that makes it difficult for people to walk right through her on the street, or sit on top of her on the subway.

"Aye, Fluffy!" Jamaican men, who have not too long ago come from home, whisper just above the incessant hum of the city, their lingering gazes aimed right at her. It doesn't happen often, but when it does, Patsy can tell that her body is just a place where their eyes stop and their erec-

tions point, while their minds move back to the milk-scented bosoms of their mothers that nursed them into adulthood. She'd be the epitome of good health and contentment back home. But it doesn't matter. She's never going back home.

29

EVEN WHEN HER FORMER NEIGHBORS IN PENNYFIELD SAY SHE resembles her mother, Tru secretly prefers what she has in common with her father. It's hard to see much of Roy these days. He has become scarcer with his intense hours at the police station. Saturdays are the only days Tru can get herself to wake up and catch him before his early morning jogs. It's five o'clock when Roy pushes open the front door in a white T-shirt and a pair of black jogging pants. Marva and Kenny are still asleep, though Tru hears a sound in Kenny's room and the soft click of a door closing.

"Roy, wait up!" Tru calls after him, jogging to catch up. She's wearing her T-shirt and a similar pair of jogging pants. From afar, those awake early enough to see them might think they're a father and son, since Tru is now tall, slender, and deliberately flat-chested, her hair cut short like her father's.

"If yuh call yuhself a champion baller, then yuh mus' can run fast," Roy replies, not slowing down for her. He continues to move forward, his head straight. The relationship between Tru and her father has improved enormously after Tru began to prove herself stronger and more athletic than her brothers. Roy is never the one to inquire about her homework or exams. He doesn't know about the afternoons she plays soccer after school with Sore Foot Marlon, Albino Ricky, and their friends in that abandoned lot behind Roman Phillips Secondary School in Pennyfield. But he knows how much she loves soccer and how good she is at it. He affectionately calls her "Champ."

Tru eventually catches up with him, their shadows elongated as the stars slip away. The only other people awake at this time are the women marching themselves to the market to sell. The sky is a brilliant navy blue with just the half-moon still shining bright. Tru is aware of their breath syncing and the sound of their light footsteps hitting the pavement. The velocity aggravates the hibiscus and bougainvillea bushes hanging over fences, wet with dew. Together they run through the sleeping lanes of the Rochester housing scheme. Dogs behind the gates and fences raise their heads and start barking at the sound of their shoes on gravel. They're jogging in the direction of Sackston, a neighboring community where the houses—from the vantage point of the surrounding hills—look like reflections of each other, joined together with their zinc roofs, beige walls, white louvered windows and doors. Yet, upon close inspection, and depending on the lane, each house has something distinctively its own—bright pink and green and purple walls, concrete balconies on added stories, French windows, sliding doors, slab roofs, gardens with bright red hibiscuses, iron grilles with elaborate designs to keep out thieves. Here, marble lions rest on gateposts while next door elephants join together. The imagination of the homeowners, mostly higher-paid civil servants, is limitless, the designs a triumph amid the working-class clutter.

Tru is panting, wiping the beads of sweat running down her face. Meanwhile, Roy seems like he could run around the world and back hardly breaking a sweat.

"How yuh doing back there, Champ?" he asks when Tru begins to slow down.

She swallows a gulp of air and replies, "I'm all right."

"Good. Race me up dat hill." Roy begins to speed up, and Tru has no choice but to meet his challenge up the incline. It's worth the time with him, she reminds herself. She runs and runs, beating her father to the top of the hill. When she looks back and realizes her victory, she holds up both hands and screams.

"Yuh t'ink dat's somet'ing?" Roy asks when he joins her, breathing hard.

"I beat you," she says, full of glee.

"Well, let me ask you somet'ing. You ever stood on top of a hill where yuh can look down on all of Jamaica, feeling jus' for a second dat yuh own it?"

Tru looks at her father, confused. "No?"

He stares at her a moment longer before he says, "Turn around."

When she does, Kingston is a sea of sparking lights before her. One by one they flicker off as the sun rises over the wharf. Tru nearly stumbles backward, awed by the beauty. Roy laughs softly from behind her. "You can't only t'ink 'bout winning, an' when yuh get there, can't turn around to see what brought yuh there in di first place. Look at all dis. We tek a lot fah granted."

Tru is unable to look away. Seeing the sky this close, she cannot help but utter, "We're closer to God." She turns to Roy. "Dat's what she promised me before she left. Dat she'd move us to a house on the hill."

"Who? Yuh mother?"

"Yes," Tru says quietly.

"Come over here," Roy says.

Tru obeys and stands next to him. He rubs the back of her neck with his hand. She hears him breathing softly.

"Why doesn't she call?" Tru asks.

"Who knows?"

She's never heard her father mince his words. She knows how he feels about her mother. She hears him and Marva arguing still about her, about money. Tru imagines America as a huge, demanding machine her mother deftly tends to. In her dreams, she cries out, "Mama!" as the machine feeds and feeds, its mouth opening to bite off her mother's head. On those nights, Tru wakes up crying, angry at the machine, which could not see that she needs her mother. Could not spare her. "I'm sure they have telephones in a place like dat."

"Dey got a black man running fah president now, too. Don't mean it g'wan be easier fah black people if him win. In dis life, what you see is what yuh get," Roy says. "Yuh see dat?" He points to where the sun rises like a newly cracked egg yolk. "Dat's a certainty. As long as you're alive, yuh know yuh can depend on seeing it every day. Yuh can't place hopes on no one else, because everyone g'wan disappoint you. It's life. Get dat right, or else yuh g'wan end up mad an' angry fah di rest of yuh life. Yuh not g'wan have everyt'ing handed to you like dat. Yuh neva g'wan have a mansion or a nice car or a servant serving yuh ice-cold lemonade if yuh jus' sit there expecting people to feel sorry fah you. No one will ever be sorry. No one owe you anyt'ing. Not even happiness. Nope. Neva. Yuh g'wan have to harden yuhself. Toughen up like coconut to survive in dis world. You's not no delicate woman. So neva mek me see yuh cry like one, expecting people to do fah you. Compared to some children, you have a family. Me an' Marva are yuh family. A family dat can provide an' send you to a good school. Dat's sweet. Real sweet. But yuh know what you'll always have no mattah how tough or educated you be? A broken heart. Welcome aboard."

"Marva cries all di time," Tru says quietly.

"What yuh hear when we argue, is convah-sation between two grown people . . . two people who only tolerating each other."

Tru lifts her face in time to catch a glint of something shading his eyes. "You don't love her anymore?"

"When you get to be my age, you'll see how complicated relationships can be. Fairy tales aren't fah people like us, Champ. Yuh father is no prince. Ah made plenty mistakes. What me an' Marva had disappeared a long, long time ago. It ended di day ah chose yuh mother's needs ovah hers."

"Is it because of me?" Tru asks.

"No. You got nuttin' to do wid it."

"Sounds like it."

He turns to her. "It started way before you. Ah met yuh mother when she was sixteen. Thought she was a pretty girl, wid those dark eyes yuh can fall into." He looks out at the sunrays spreading across Kingston City. "Ah could tell dat she was always searching fah somet'ing biggah. But ah neva concern me self wid dat, still. When yuh young an' in love, yuh don't care 'bout much. She was my first love. She neva stopped being dat."

Tru blushes. She's never heard him talk like this.

He looks at Tru again. "Ah know yuh didn't follow me all di way up here to hear all dat. What is it yuh want to tell me? Yuh 'ave a boyfriend?" he asks.

Tru's face flushes hotter as she peers at the ground—at the earthworms wiggling small holes in which she wishes to crawl with such a question thrown at her by her father. She thinks of Sore-Foot Marlon, who is no longer *Sore-Foot*. How she felt when he slung one arm around her shoulder like he does with the other guys, his breath a warm gust on her cheek. She tries not to think about how close and comfortable they are with each other. And even if she does, so what? He'll always be Sore-Foot Marlon. She listens to him and Albino Ricky brag all the time about stripping girls of their creamy innocence, their egos as loud and pungent as the jet of urine from their stout, fleshy cocks—one dark and one pale—which they unleash anywhere to piss. Seeing their cocks doesn't make Tru giddy, but envious. Unlike the girls at her school, who wonder about each other's virginity, shyly and discreetly asking the most womanish one among them, who claims to know everything from the mysterious flow of periods to the taste of cum, "*What's it like? Does it hurt? Which is bettah . . . to do it standing up or lying down? Do you feel different? Is it true dat it mek yuh belly flat an' yuh bottom biggah?*"—curiosities Tru chooses to ignore altogether. Not that she doesn't feel the urge, or has never allowed herself to wonder what it'd be like. She overhears her father and Marva going at it at night and even remembers walking in on them when she was younger. More than once she has tried to conjure the image of what it'd be like to be pulled in like quicksand, feeling the rush and simultaneous terror of falling into an abyss with another person. In those fantasies, she's a completely different person. She envisions being somebody like David Beckham or Ronaldinho for the fantasy to work. For to picture herself the way she is would seem wrong. Her mind can never move past the how and the who, settling instead for just the pleasurable sensation whenever her hand travels to the moist spot between her legs, which makes her muffle her gasps with her pillow. It's all too complicated, she thinks. Aloud, she says. "I have no time fah t'ings like dat."

Roy visibly sighs with relief.

"Good," he utters solemnly. But then his jawline firms, and his thick eyebrows form into a quizzical arch. Before his mouth forms the question Tru senses coming her way like a fastball, she says, "I can find a job to help. Ah know you an' Marva struggling . . ." Her voice trails.

"Yuh have no business worrying 'bout money like dat at dis age," Roy replies with a slight chuckle. "Focus on yuh schoolwork. Dat's what's going to get you far. Ah try my best to do what ah can. Dat fancy school yuh going to? Yuh making yuh mother very proud. She always used to tell me dat she wanted you to get di best education. Dat's one t'ing she used to stress. An' now look at you . . ." He smiles. "A Wilhampton girl. Not many girls in dis country get such an opportunity."

Tru looks down at her feet, feeling guilty. For the first time in her life, she regrets the wish her heart formed years ago, now straining her mind to shape her parents' dreams for her. *"Be a good, obedient girl,"* her mother had said, though in the dark recesses of her mind she knows there's no place for her there, at that school. Or anywhere, it seems. She knows that her mother wanted her to be at that school. She knows she might be potentially ruining what's supposed to be so simple, so easy, if she drops out. *"Be a good, obedient girl."* When she first started there, wearing her knee-length blue tunic and white blouse, her gait was unsteady, awkward, as if she had just mastered the ability to use her feet. She knew this uniform had great significance to the larger Jamaican population and worked hard to carry this torch of perfection. Her gestures were not natural to her either. But she made herself into the girl her mother wanted her to be, her uniform a costume for the performance of her mother's desires. She wore it so long that it almost became impossible to remove. Until recently, when she has begun to accept that her mother does not love her. In a way, that grief seems to mysteriously give her the honesty and courage of a drunk too numb to care. She is the only one in her cohort who had to repeat fifth form this year after failing the CXCs in June. She took nine subjects and failed all but math. Roy begged the headmistress to allow her to repeat the grade to take the exam over. It was either that or she leaves school to learn a vocation like most students who fail the CXC exams, unable to advance to sixth form. Once upon a time, Tru used to be the brightest and the youngest in her class. This is the first time that Tru has ever been the same age as her classmates. Now, almost two months into the new school year, when Tru walks through campus the girls part to let her through. Not only is she a repeat, but a freak. She's nothing like them—the way they sit in their groups, backs straight, legs crossed, skirts down to their calves, hands resting lifelessly on textbooks whose contents they merely regurgitate. How her mother used to admire Wilhampton girls as ladies-in-the-making; and how Tru, lanced with guilt, knows she has never felt at home in her body to be molded as such. Where is her place, if not with them? The question forms like a small welt on her mind, inciting a slight throbbing at her temples.

"I know it's not easy to bounce back from failure, but a true champ neva stay down aftah di first blow. A true champ try even harder," her father is saying. "Even if it means ah have to take out another loan fah our mortgage or work more shifts at di police station to pay fah dis extra school year an' yuh CXC subjects. I'm up fah promotion anyway. So, believe you me, it g'wan work out."

For a long time, there is silence. The chirping birds make the only sounds. Tru averts her eyes. When she looks at him again, he's looking at her. He hasn't examined her this way since that day he showed her how to kick a soccer ball. A cooling breeze rustles the trees around them. Finally, Roy looks at his watch. Tru swallows her courage to tell him that she wants to transfer schools—even after all the trouble Roy went through to keep her enrolled at Wilhampton; and even though there is a high probability that it's too late, since it's October and the next CXC exams are a term away in June. Maybe if she speaks up now, she can re-take the exam at Roman Phillips. She feels insane trying to fit in at Wilhampton Girls High and cannot see herself getting through another school year. There's also the shame of seeing her former classmates—the ones who sat the CXCs with her and passed—now in sixth form as prefects, giving detentions and demerits. What's the use of continuing to wear a Wilhampton uniform when her mother will never see her in it?

"Race me back down to di house?" Roy says.

Tru doesn't move.

"What?" Roy asks.

"Did she . . ." She searches for the right words. "Did Mama ever love me?"

Roy sighs. "Yes, she did. Don't evah doubt dat."

"I want to hear more. About Mama."

He blinks.

"What is it yuh want to know?"

Tru shrugs.

Roy sighs. His chary glance leaps from the hill toward the peak of the Blue Mountains behind them. "She was . . ." he begins, then pauses. For the first time Tru notices that his eyebrows are slicked with sweat.

"There is no one word to describe yuh mother. She always used to seh death will come fast. Before we know it. She wanted to be free. To fly . . ." He chuckles. "Ah always used to tease har an' call har Birdie. Because she neva belong in a cage."

Tru pictures the woman in the faded photos in that dusty album she found in Mama G's whatnot. Tru kept the photo of the woman whose smile never touched her eyes. Even in the one photograph where she is holding a baby girl, whom Tru recognizes as herself, the young woman's smile is tentative, unsure, her arms positioned the way one might pose with a stack of textbooks.

"Di only one who did know Birdie bettah than anyone else was—" He stops himself, scowling deeply as though he's suddenly sick from the memory.

"Who?" Tru asks.

Shaking his head, he wipes sweat from his upper lip and spits in the dirt as if to curse the land.

"No one," he says, looking down at his right hand clenched in a fist— the one with the ugly scar Tru had been afraid of when she was little. How it seems to slither across the back of his hand, shiny. When she was younger, she once asked her father if he ever killed anyone. Roy had looked at her, a bit startled. Then his face dimmed as though his own soul had left him to wander the vaults of memory. *"Do you know what it's like to risk yuh life every day?"* he asked, answering her question with a question.

"Before me an' yuh mother break up she told me, *'Ah can't promise yuh love. Ah can't promise yuh me.'* Those were her exact words . . ." His voice trails and he squeezes Tru's right shoulder with his other hand. "But she gave me you."

30

PATSY PUSHES BABY TOWARD THE PARK, THOUGH HE'S OLD enough to walk. Baby's real name is Thomas, but Patsy prefers her nickname for him. He loves to look up at the trees along the path, branches stretched above their heads, crooked limbs pointing toward the sky. He also likes to look at yellow cabs sailing in traffic along Central Park West. It's the vibrant yellow that he likes, squealing at them while Patsy pushes him. "Mommy! Mommy!" They must remind him of the rubber ducks he bathes with—the ones his mother meticulously lines around his basin. Regina likes order. Sweaters, dresses, suits, and shoes are color-coordinated and neatly organized inside the Rhinebecks' walk-in closet. Dishes and crystal glasses are stored behind glass cabinets. Books are alphabetized on the large oakwood bookshelf in the home study where Regina works for hours at a stretch.

"Mommy is at work," Patsy reminds Baby in her best American English. "She's not in the cars."

"Yes, she is!"

"Okay, if you say so."

"Can I wave?"

"Be my guest."

Patsy stops pushing and allows the redheaded boy to wave at the passing taxis while she stands next to him.

"Wave with me! So she can see us!"

Patsy glances sideways over her shoulder before raising her right hand. Of course, this wouldn't signal a taxi to stop. Definitely not for her. When Baby grows tired of waving, Patsy resumes her stroll, taking an alternate route down Columbus Avenue by the boutiques and jewelry stores that stretch before her like smug faces with glass eyes. She doesn't look at them. They seem in league with one another to make her feel like an outsider, a landless wanderer.

Yet, here she is on the Upper West Side, pushing a stroller like it's her baby inside it, and as if she belongs in this kind of neighborhood where there is a store that sells gluten-free pastries and yogurt and a market that only carries organic fruits and vegetables. If Cicely could see her now. One time Patsy tried to shop at the market and had to drop the bag of apples like she had seen worms crawling inside when she saw the price. "*Organic me r'ass. People really pay ten dollah fi two likkle dry-up apple?*" She wished she had Cicely around to ask this. Cicely might have shrugged and suggested Patsy try one and see. "*White people eat healthy. That's why dem live so long enough. Look how many ah dem in nursing homes,*" she might have said. And Patsy chuckled inside the market, drawing the stares of the workers and customers.

These imagined conversations with Cicely are more real to her than the details she sees about her friend's life on television or in the local newspaper as wife of Republican Councilman Marcus Salters, for the Thirty-fifth District of the New York City Council, which includes Fort Greene, Clinton Hill, Prospect Heights, portions of Bedford-Stuyvesant, downtown Brooklyn, the Brooklyn Navy Yard, and Vinegar Hill— almost the entire borough of Brooklyn. After 9/11, Marcus's business boomed. His real estate ads were all over the place, it seemed. He made a mint, then ran for New York City Council and won.

The borough is now dealing with more foreclosures than the market has seen since the Great Depression. To Patsy it seems like a plague, the foreclosures moving like a dark cloud over the borough, taking with them families that have lived inside these brownstones for generations and leaving behind empty houses, the windows and doors sealed with wooden planks. Marcus Salters's New York City Council platform is to enact legislation to help landlords evict squatters and allow eligible landlords to apply for loans to help them with foreclosure and repair in order to attract the right kind of tenants, which for Marcus Salters means wealthy, and usually white. For Patsy, it means that her days living in Brooklyn are numbered. She fears that this project, which Marcus Salters calls the New Brooklyn, could attract the majority of landlords, especially in Crown Heights, like Mr. Fagan, who are immigrants themselves, and who have opened their homes to undocumented immigrants. Although this is a long way down the road, Patsy hates to think the day might come when she'd get priced out.

The ads are everywhere. The first time Patsy saw one, she stopped in an intersection and looked up at Marcus watching her from the huge billboard on the side of a building on Bedford Avenue, which read WELCOME TO THE NEW BROOKLYN. MARCUS SALTERS, YOUR FAVORITE NEW YORK CITY COUNCIL MEMBER. Patsy looked away from Marcus's seemingly omniscient, mocking gaze, feeling as naked beneath it as the day he saw her in the basement. Patsy stood still, unable to move until angry drivers beeped their horns.

Yuh did good, Cicely. Yuh did good. Ah jus' hope yuh happy now.

P ATSY CROSSES THE STREET WITH BABY TO THE SIDE WITH LESS snow, perhaps looking like a big scandal bag floating over the sidewalk. The only thing missing on the back of her bubble jacket is a smiley face like on the scandal bags she gets from the Chinney restaurant in her neighborhood. It was a rare find at Goodwill, with fur on the hood and cuffs. She wears it even when it's supposed to be sixty degrees. Ten years in America hasn't made her any less resistant to winter weather. To Patsy, cold is cold.

New York got some snow last week and again this week. Not even November yet, and the limbs of the trees hang dangerously low with leaves still on them. *"Global warming,"* Regina had said to Patsy. It was the only explanation for this crazy weather. Last week a woman died when a branch fell on her. Instead of cutting down dangerously leaning branches, the mayor's only solution was to warn people to be careful.

The man wouldn't have gotten Patsy's vote, if she could vote. Patsy sucks her teeth when she has to take the stroller into the street to avoid any leaning branches. It's midday, so there's more room on the sidewalk for strollers than at rush hour, when she's forever maneuvering between women with briefcases, wearing tailored suits and high heels with red soles, even in the snow. Privately, Patsy admires them—the high heels with devilish red soles and the women wearing them.

Often she finds herself stopping in her tracks or dodging well-dressed pedestrians to avoid an accident with the massive stroller. Regina told her to guard it with her life, because she spent almost two thousand dollars for the thing that doesn't even fold properly. Two thousand dollars to push a boy who can walk. She surely doesn't budget this much for Patsy's paycheck.

Regina is somewhat of a recluse, staying in her study all day, directing all her maternal instincts to the people inside her head—some of whom she mentions to Patsy, following Patsy from room to room as Patsy dusts, sweeps the floors, washes the dishes, cooks, or tends to Baby. Sorting and matching his socks, collecting his scattered board books, scrubbing remnants of Cheerios from the soles of his shoes, Patsy goes about the business of raising a child while his mother watches, unseeing, rambling through intricate plots that only exist in her head. "*So, what do you think?*" And Patsy would say it's a good idea, though she only half listens. The stories have managed to win Regina awards, which she rests on the bookshelves inside the house. They outnumber the family photos. Meanwhile, Mr. Rhinebeck gets paid to stare inside people's mouths and convince them to give him loads of money for things like invisible braces and veneers. Patsy remembers how he bragged about an old woman who got veneers at ninety years old and wondered why a woman that age, who had lived her whole life just as she was, would spend so much money on appearance when she only has her casket to look forward to.

Now, just as Patsy makes her way into the street, a bike messenger comes out of nowhere. He swerves around Patsy and nearly collides with a yellow taxi. The taxi driver presses on his brakes and his horn. "Why don't you move out the way, fatso!" the bike messenger, a scrawny man with heavily gelled hair, yells at Patsy over the roof of the taxi. "I could've gotten killed!"

"Yuh riding 'pon di wrong side!" Patsy says, gesturing at the sign on the bike lane that indicates that he should be riding on the other side. "*You* nearly kill *me!*"

The bike messenger flips his middle finger at Patsy. "Black rhino!"

He pedals away on the wrong side of the street. Patsy fumes, feeling warmth spread from her neck to her face. If it weren't for Baby she would've had a few choice words for the man. For the rest of her stroll she's preoccupied with what she should have said. *Who yuh calling black rhino, yuh scrawny yellow mongrel?* It's lunchtime, but her appetite is gone. No longer does she want to sit at the regular pizza place to rest. Worse, Baby, who witnessed the whole thing, extends his legs—which he does when he wants to walk—revealing tiny white Velcro sneakers. "Miss Patsy, why did that man call you a black rhino? You're not black, you're brown!"

Patsy doesn't answer him right away. She pushes the stroller for two more blocks, feeling her stockings ride up and her thighs rub together. She slows her pace once she gets to the playground and stands by the marble benches and tables facing the swings. The snow hasn't stopped children from being children. At least there are distractions, Patsy thinks.

The park is divided: housewives versus nannies. The housewives stick to themselves; they quietly monitor each other's choice of snack, leggings, preschool. If they do acknowledge the nannies, they do so smugly, their eyes roving over the children foisted by their mothers onto strangers. It's different from the looks Patsy gets from young black women on the street who glance at her stroller and see Baby inside it, their faces darkening as though their heads bumped on something that swung out of nowhere into their path.

The nannies are divided among themselves too, each group a faction of the United Nations. They sit in their respective circles to swap gossip, recipes, information on bargains, immigration lawyers, and the latest news from home. On any given day, a nanny can be heard pondering in her native tongue the state of corruption in her country while pushing toddlers on swings or helping them down the slides.

Patsy hopes she won't see Beatrice, Judene, and Shirley, members of her posse, today. If left alone she can buy a salted pretzel from the vendor who parks his cart nearby and eat in peace, dipping the pretzel in extra mustard—a taste Patsy has come to like while being in America. In Jamaica she only ate mustard on frankfurters on trips to Hope Zoo.

Patsy helps Baby out of his stroller. She bends and pulls his hat over his ears before he bolts toward the monkey bars. He waddles on the beams, awkward in the bulky coat Patsy bundled him into earlier. Patsy buys a pretzel and eats while she observes Baby and the people at the park. Dog walkers stand still outside the fence, patiently waiting for their shaggy animals to urinate or shit on the curb; midday joggers, covered from head to toe, are huffing and puffing air that visibly curls from their mouths. She spots an older woman with hair as white as the snow-covered pavement and skin as dark as the ice-slicked roads. Beatrice pushes her stroller into the park, her nose in the air. Beatrice spots her and waves. Patsy only smiles with her lips, showing no teeth.

Beatrice is the first to speak. "Wha g'wan, Patsy? How yuh look suh?"

"How me look?"

"Like s'maddy wid di weight ah di world 'pon har head. An' why yuh wearing dat terrible wig?"

Patsy sucks her teeth and wipes mustard off her fingers with a napkin.

"Not every day we can wear a smile. Some of us don't 'ave di luxury of a vacation in America, you know," Patsy says, eyeballing Beatrice.

"Where all dis coming from? Yuh soun' a likkle salty."

Patsy remembers when she first met Beatrice and the other nannies she hangs around. Their dark eyes, sunken and tired, had stared—as though basing their self-importance on the children they push around—scanning her face to see if she was worth speaking to. Patsy, on the other hand, was glad to see other Caribbean women pushing white babies—all except Beatrice, whose baby was darker than the others on the playground. Patsy had taken one look at the child and said, *"Oh, him adopted?"* The other women were silent, a resounding hum resonating from their throats. Patsy suddenly had the feeling that she had said something wrong. Her first day in the park and already she had offended someone.

"Why yuh say that?" Beatrice asked Patsy. She was wearing a turban on her head that hid her snow-white hair. But her high cheekbones gained more prominence.

"A lot ah rich white people adopt black babies from other countries like Africa," Patsy said. *"Can't even comb dem hair."* The first time Patsy saw a black baby with a white family, she thought it might have been one of Miss Foster's children—the ones Miss Foster sold to the mysterious visitors who parked their nice rental cars at her gate in Pennyfield at night. However, in America Patsy had seen more black babies from third world countries with white people than with black parents. It's as if they graduated from colonizing countries to adopting babies from those places, training them to be like them.

"I'm not working for nobody," Beatrice finally said. Judene and Shirley swapped glances. *"This is my grandson,"* Beatrice told her.

"Oh."

Judene and Shirley looked down into their strollers, where tiny white fists were tightly clenched, pumping the air as if demonstrating their own silent protests.

"Ah neva mean to offen'," Patsy said to Beatrice. *"Is jus' dat me hardly see people like us around here who . . ."* Patsy's voice trailed. There was nothing else she could say that would help the situation she had gotten herself into. But Beatrice, not one to let an opportunity pass by to brag, was generous with an explanation. *"It's my daughter's baby. She's a tenured professor at Barnard who lives four blocks that way."* She pointed

to the handsome row of brownstones that led to Central Park. Patsy looked at the baby—his wild curly hair, his pale eyes, and his dark skin. Patsy knew then that she didn't like Beatrice but simply tolerated her because her options for friendships weren't many. A child, however beloved, is not good company.

But Beatrice, though from the same country, is from a different world than Patsy. While Patsy and the other nannies have to watch the babies like hawks on the playground—fidgety when they believe they have been talking too long in their circle, looking like a Caribbean Association meeting—Beatrice simply takes her time. Beatrice can leave anytime she desires and talk as long as she wants. Though she works for free, she's the most rewarded, having the opportunity to live in her daughter's house and care for a child who is a part of her, a baby who she will see grow and who will know her as Grandma.

Patsy is reminded every day, both by Beatrice and by the children Patsy has been caring for over the years, of what she's missing out on by not raising Tru. *"Girls. Dey stay with you forever,"* Beatrice would muse. Patsy only listened, too ashamed to say she hasn't even seen the development of her own daughter. She's present, always, to see the first steps and hear the first words uttered by the children she has babysat, but has missed the most important firsts for Tru—her first period, her first crush, her first day of high school.

Patsy has not reached out to Tru since she sent her that Christmas card ten years ago. With much force, she severed all communication with her daughter, thinking it easier this way for both of them to move on. The absence of a mother is more dignified than the presence of a distant one. By now, Mama G or Roy might have convinced Tru that she had not come into the world through normal circumstances; had not floated for nine months inside a warm, liquid place, nourished by a tube connected to another human being. Once Patsy severed this lifeline, it shriveled and disappeared, leaving no trace of its existence.

It's not like she didn't try. During the first few years of babysitting,

Patsy stood in line at the Western Union multiple times, willing herself to send something. But then, what good would it be without the explanation? The pages of apology? The promise of visiting soon, knowing that it would never be possible without papers? As time passed, it became harder and harder to justify. Though her courage disintegrated, she began to work overtime to save up money in that rusted cookie tin in her closet. An aspiration to send a barrel of gifts and money for Tru flourishes and thrives, more than the promise of reconciliation.

But lately Patsy has been plagued by guilt and regret more than usual. She's spent nearly a decade taking care of other people's children— children who won't remember her when they become adults with their own families. She watches the other nannies break into smiles when they hear their children's voices on the phone from across the ocean, then at home after work she eats a whole cake from the bakery on Church Avenue by herself, stuffing and stuffing, but still empty.

Beatrice stands beside her now, sighing. "Arthritis getting worse, an' dis weather not helping."

"Is dat yuh only worries?" Patsy asks her, shifting slightly to create more distance between them.

"Is a big worry, yes. A pain in di you-know-what."

"Yuh taking anyt'ing fah it? There's medicine fah everyt'ing here. Even medicine fah happiness," Patsy says, remembering the commercial she saw with the happy, skipping couple who got that way because of a drug named Prozac. Patsy googled it before her free computer class at the library and read: *"Medication improves your mood, sleep, appetite, and energy level and may help restore your interest in daily living."* Patsy went to the Rite Aid to ask for it and was told by the pharmacist that she couldn't get it just like that without a prescription. She thought of the Indian doctor again and his nonchalance about her wearing a wig.

Beatrice sucks her teeth and rubs her leg. "Me nuh believe inna dem t'ings. Yuh know me is from di country." It annoys Patsy that Beatrice chooses to speak patois with her. Though the woman is clearly from upper

St. Andrew, a woman with means and status, she likes to speak patois to flaunt her country origins with the nannies she assumes are below her.

"Try some guinea bush," Patsy says.

"Weh me aggo get dat from up here?" Beatrice asks.

"Dem sell dem on Flatbush Avenue, right on Caton. At dat market . . ." Patsy's voice trails when she sees the look on Beatrice's face. Beatrice wiggles her nose as if she smells something foul in the air. "You'd neva catch me in Brooklyn, m'dear."

"What's wrong wid Brooklyn?" Patsy asks, taking offense as though Brooklyn is her home. Her real home. Beatrice refuses to let go of the class thing from back home. In defense, Patsy wants to blurt out something smart, but cannot think of anything.

"Grandma, play!" the curly-headed boy says from his stroller, reminding Beatrice to let him out. Beatrice undoes the stroller and lifts the boy out. "Yes, boss man. There you go. Be careful!" she says after the running toddler.

"Vikter grow big, eh?" Patsy says, looking after Beatrice's pretty grandson, the ice melting inside her. "Him g'wan be popular wid di ladies."

"Yes, m'dear. Him already is. Dem grow so fast. Him is four going on forty."

"Same wid Baby," Patsy says, hating that she's bragging about her employer's child. "Three, going on thirty."

The two women chuckle. "Ah remember when Michaela was dat age," Beatrice says, her eyes blinking rapidly to rid themselves of the laughing tears. "Oh, she was a big one! Mouthy too! Every day me get a call from ah teacher. Dat was before—" A shadow comes over Beatrice's face. Patsy stares at her, partly because she's amazed at the sudden transformation in the woman's face, and partly because Beatrice hardly talks about her daughter, much less mentions her name. She mostly focuses on her grandson, the way she now focuses on her hands clasped in front of her.

"Before what?"

Beatrice looks at Patsy as though surprised to see her standing there listening. "Nothing." She sighs and straightens her shoulders. Patsy begins to gather her things, picking up a discarded snack cup and waving Baby down from the jungle gym. She's grateful for the excuse of having to get Baby back home before his mother exits her study like Jesus resurrecting from the dead.

"Carry some guinea bush fah me," Beatrice says, opening the pouch she carries around her neck. "Here is ten dollah. If it come to more, me will pay yuh di difference."

Patsy takes the money, suppressing the urge to tell her to haul her fancy arse to Brooklyn to get it herself. "Yuh know yuh can always go to a real doctor fah di pain," Patsy says instead. "You got di money fah dat."

"No doctor in di world can relieve my pain," Beatrice says, her melancholy reminding Patsy of Mama G and those older self-righteous women in the Pentecostal church, always in their long skirts, and always wearing pained expressions, taking pride in their suffering for Jesus. "But ah good bush tea can mek me forget it's there," Beatrice finishes.

"All right, we will talk tomorrow," Patsy says, glad that at least she can still move about without physical pain. That much she has over Beatrice.

31

THE SUN IS SLOWLY SETTING BEHIND THE TREES IN CENTRAL Park when Patsy walks out of Regina's apartment building, bidding good night to Ransel, the Jamaican doorman who tips his hat goodbye as if everyone in the building is the governor general. Tired and still irritable, she walks down Central Park West to the subway station. As she passes people on the street, she barely glances up at their silhouettes. It's not like when she first arrived in America, when it was fun to people-watch with Cicely. They would laugh like they did as little girls, trying not to point at someone dressed like a clown. "*Is suh American people stay,*" Cicely would muse. "*Dey jus' don't care.*" And it's true. Patsy has seen some people wearing pajamas outside with curlers in their hair to go to the corner store or walk their dogs. They even wear jeans to work. Americans love jeans. Regina owns a pair of faded high-waisted ones that she wears every day with a poncho to work in her study.

Patsy makes her way into the subway station, her head weighted down by the gathering darkness above it, and she doesn't expect to almost trip over a soul. When the person materializes in her periphery in a green robe and a crown, sitting on a subway bench, Patsy is not sure at all if she's imagining things. The man is above-average height. She can tell from his knees, which stick out too much from the bench. She regards his dark, narrow face—the type one might see in old photographs of smiling uncles before chubbiness and a full beard set in—fixed in apology. His brown skin is the shade of cassava against the green robe.

"I'm sorry," he says. "Ah was jus' stretching my legs. Ah didn't see anyone coming."

"Typical," Patsy replies. "No one ever see me coming."

"What dat supposed to mean?" the man asks. He cocks his head sideways, peering at her.

Patsy sees something in his eyes so powerful that it halts her. Any other time, she would have shrugged the person off and walked farther down the subway platform. But this time she stays, not wanting to go much farther. The man might be slightly demented, for all she knows. That might explain why he would be dressed in a Liberty Taxes costume when tax season doesn't begin until January. It could be for Halloween, she reasons. But that is two weeks away. She has seen him before, she thinks. Or it could be someone else. They all look the same in that costume, parading all day long down city sidewalks January through April, Mondays through Saturdays, dressed as the Statue of Liberty. They work hard for their commission, since it's off the books. Patsy wonders if they're really successful in getting customers off the streets. In New York City, working off the books is as common as bodegas and dollar stores. People like Regina and Patsy's other employers, who make their money the conventional way, seem to prefer filing their taxes in their own time rather than be coerced by a heavily accented immigrant in a Statue of Liberty costume.

The man is smiling at Patsy, raising one side of his mouth. "Yuh look like ah angel, wid dat face of yours."

Patsy cannot help but smile, her annoyance evaporating. "Yuh mus' be seeing t'ings. I'm far from it."

"An' dem dimples. You know what my granny used to seh about dimples? Dat they're a mother's lasting kiss."

"Well, dat's di biggest lie yuh granny evah tell, because my mother nuh know nuttin' 'bout kisses 'less is Jesus' foot."

"She also used to seh dat they're kisses from angels."

"Yuh don't have any other pickup line?"

"Who says I'm picking you up?" he asks.

Patsy's face burns. Of course he's not trying to pick her up. Why would she think such a thing? How many men have tripped over themselves in the last ten years to fuck her without remorse? Things have changed since living in America. Here, besides her daily touching in the mornings before getting out of bed, sex is an infrequent, transient occurrence— anonymous and dehumanizing, save for its ability to give her what she's looking for—to feel whole in this place, invincible, less alone, though for only a few minutes. Under such circumstances, she can walk into a dimly lit seedy reggae club on Clarendon Road telling herself that she's there for the music. (Try as she might, Patsy could never get herself to go near the lesbian club on Fourth Avenue with graffiti on the outside and a steel door where a tall, stocky white butch woman with spiky purple hair smokes a cigarette from the side of her mouth as she checks IDs.) After downing enough drinks, she looks up and sex is there, smiling at her across the club or ogling her backside out the door before bending her over in a cluttered room on Avenue D with her clothes still on, sparing her the embarrassment of a full glance. Afterward, when they disengage, they turn away in slight disgust, secretly relieved that they wouldn't have to call or see each other again.

The man fiddles with a small gold crucifix pendant around his neck, looking down on his free hand as if his pride has already been trampled. He laughs, though his dark eyes are weary. "I'm sure yuh have plenty men trying to be wid yuh already," he says.

"What yuh doing out here in dat costume?" Patsy asks him, changing the subject, for she knows he's being kind.

He shrugs. "Is fah a performance."

"You're an actor?"

"You can call it dat. Isn't dat what life is about? Pretending?"

The truth in the man's words saddens Patsy. "It's hard to pretend an' not worry 'bout getting caught," she says to the man.

He laughs. "Ah hear a beautiful accent. Yuh from yard?"

"Yes."

"Where 'bout?"

"Pennyfield."

The man's eyebrows rise. "Oh?"

"What?"

"Ghetto girl." He says this in the sweetest tone, reminding Patsy of the beginning of a calypso song. She notices a steel-pan player setting up his drum in the middle of the subway platform to play.

Patsy sucks her teeth. "It nuh mean nuttin' up 'ere."

"Nuh true?"

Patsy smiles, blushing in a way she hasn't blushed with any other man but Roy. "Whatevah."

"Really, though. Pennyfield is a dangerous area. Laborite territory."

"Maybe to outsiders," Patsy says in defense.

"I'm from Tivoli Gardens," he replies.

"Oh. So is di pot calling di kettle black."

"Touché." He laughs. Patsy laughs too.

After a long pause, the man says, "Wish ah met you earlier."

"Why is dat?" Patsy asks.

The man is staring at her, his gaze examining her face, caressing her skin, which warms under it. Something about the way this man looks at Patsy makes her think of Cicely—how she was able to look at her that way too and make her forget herself.

"Tell me yuh name," he says. It's a demand that is gentle in delivery.

"Patsy."

"What is dat short for? Patricia?"

"Dat's right."

"Ah like Patsy."

He smiles at this as if the sheer loveliness of the sound of her abridged name touches him. A light to behold.

"And what's yours?" she asks.

"Barrington. Some call me Barry fah short."

"I like Barrington bettah," Patsy says.

He laughs. "My mother thought it sounded like a distinguished name. Like me was g'wan be somebody big wid a name like Barrington. Maybe di next prime minister of Jamaica or somet'ing." He shrugs his shoulders, already rounded with defeat. A shadow lances his face. "She woulda roll in har grave to see me now, har only son, being a wutless brute."

"Don't say dat," Patsy says.

"Ah came here back in '92. Still have nothing to me name." He turns to Patsy, his eyes moist with frustration. "Nothing a'tall. An' now it's too late, 'cause ah can't work no more. Ah used to do construction." He tells Patsy of his fall from a building on Madison Avenue. He fell fifteen feet and landed on his back while helping with the demolition of a building. His final task was the removal of a chandelier in the lobby when the marble bannister gave way and collapsed. "Can you imagine? Di one time ah ever get to hold somet'ing of any value." He shakes his head. "Ah had to covah my own medical bills since ah don't have any papers. Can't even get a disability check. An' yuh know di hurtful part? Ah can't go back home. Can't even sen' money fi me nine children dem. Everybody know seh me is a failure."

"Ah know what yuh mean," Patsy says. "Ah can't go back either. Ah don't want to give my mother di satisfaction of calling me a failure to my face—to tell me dat is God's punishment fah coveting all dat I t'ink can be mine too. Everyt'ing is about God to her. An' if you's not God, you's Satan." Patsy shrugs. "All I wanted to do was take back my life and . . ."

"And what?"

"Hope dat my daughter become a bettah woman. She's bettah off being raised away from me, by har father."

"Dat's big of you to admit dat," Barrington says. "Ah don't get one bad vibe from you, but whatevah it is, don't be suh hard on yuhself."

"What's di point of raising up a child in a world I couldn't change?" Patsy chuckles. "Maybe dis is fate."

As if on cue, the steel-pan man starts to play "Amazing Grace" on his drum. The Caribbean women waiting for the train hum and sway with their eyes closed, their rounded bodies like black birds perched on electric lines. They are probably on their way to a second job from a first job of cleaning, washing, cooking, ironing, wiping, or feeding. Barrington looks at Patsy as though he has already accepted her decisions. Not once does he blink or turn, even as the chilly breeze races across the platform. "How is it fate if yuh have control ovah it?" he asks.

"Pardon?"

He shrugs. "Soun' like yuh dun give up already."

Patsy looks down at the train tracks, the garbage, the cackling rats, the gutter. She lifts her eyes to Barrington's face and sees Cicely's. How Cicely with her bright skin, blue-green eyes, and long hair had chosen *her* when no one else did. *You're my home in this world.* How she floated outside her own body, selfless in her desire to crawl under Cicely's skin. All she ever wanted, and still wants—as insane as it sounds to admit this, shamefully, to herself—is Cicely.

The green light flashes, signaling the arrival of another train into the station. The echo of the train arriving on its cold nerve of iron makes her teeth hurt. How many trains have gone by? Patsy hasn't noticed. She likes talking to Barrington. She doesn't know why those things tumble out of her mouth so easily with him. She watches as Barrington struggles to get up from the bench, using both hands to push himself up.

"Don't want to hold you up any longah," he says.

Patsy panics, wondering if she said too much. "You all right? Ah didn't mean to tell yuh all dat," she says, watching Barrington struggle to get up. She offers to help him, but he waves her off gently. "I can manage."

"Ah like talking to you," Patsy says.

"Same. But it's time fah me to go," he says. He winces in pain when he stands. "Had been like dis since di accident," he explains. Every pinch of his nerve—he says—from his neck down, reminds him of that fall. He walks with a limp.

"I'm half of a man. What would anyone want wid half of a man?"

He looks at Patsy with those dark, pleading, weary eyes as if daring her to answer his question. They remind her of Uncle Curtis before she tasted the swig of rum on his breath. "You'll be all right," Patsy tells him. Because it's the only thing she thinks to say in this moment.

"No. You will be all right," he says. "We all mek mistakes. Yuh mus' forgive yuhself."

The steel-pan player switches to "How Great Thou Art." Barrington seems mesmerized by the song. He looks like he's about to cry, his sadness and pain fully visible to Patsy. She can't make up her mind whether to keep her gaze on Barrington's beautiful face, creased in exquisite pain, or to retrieve a piece of paper inside her purse that she can use to write her contact information. She rips a piece of paper from an envelope in her purse and scribbles her number with a pen. It would be the first time she'd ever been so bold with a stranger who hasn't really shown sexual interest. And even if he had and she made herself available, he doesn't seem like one to not call again. Suddenly she's hopeful again in this city, deaf to the persistent car horns and sirens. Blind to the somberness of falling leaves in preparation for the coming winter, which would freeze over parks and rivers, turning everything still like glass.

In this moment, failure doesn't frighten her at all. Especially not with the tender, forgiving gaze of the man with skin the shade of cassava in the green Statue of Liberty robe on the platform. The steel-pan player continues to play. The velocity of the coming train scatters a group of pigeons, lifts the coattails of the humming day women, and snatches the paper from Patsy's light grasp. The paper blows, sailing down the platform in the opposite direction. Patsy runs after it. She fetches it and turns in time to see Barrington leaping in front of the train—so graceful is his leap, his arms stretched out like falcon wings as he shoots forward in front of the oncoming train. It's the first Patsy has ever seen anyone fly.

32

O N HER BIRTHDAY, TRU PICKS UP THE CARD HER MOTHER SENT her almost ten years before. The glitter has long rubbed off, but the words are still there: *Your mother, Patsy, with love.* For the first time since receiving the card, Tru wonders if this was a reminder for her mother too. She tries to see her mother's face in those words—lines outlining her mouth, her eyes—but cannot make them out in the empty spaces. Tru folds the card carefully and places it inside her underwear drawer. She sits on the edge of her bed with her face lost in the shadow of the evening's gloom. She can hear water gushing from a standpipe, the cackle of washerwomen, the crying of babies, young children playing, and the mongrel dogs barking at their laughter. Through the soot-blurred window of her room, she makes out Marva putting a pot of something on coals, though she is pregnant again. All the babies had died at birth so far. This is her third pregnancy in ten years—with twins this time. She should be on bed rest. Tru also makes out the mango trees weighted down by dusk and the hills above them where her mother once promised her a castle close to Heaven.

She stares now at the dresses lying on the bed—the ones Marva gets made for her. The same seamstress makes all of Tru's school uniforms too, smiling each time Tru gets measured and taking the liberty to touch her breasts. *"Yuh getting to be a fully developed woman!"*

All the dresses the woman makes looks like they belong on doll babies, as bright and frilly and puffy as they are. Tru has to wear one to her grandmother's house. *"Don't come 'roun here looking like no ragga-ragga. Is yuh birthday. We g'wan celebrate properly,"* Mama G had said over the telephone. Every year Mama G bakes her a cake. Sighing, Tru peels her faded red T-shirt that reads PELÉ in bright yellow over her head and pulls down her knee-length soccer shorts, ignoring the scars, crisscrossed like nets, on her upper-right thigh. She draws up each leg on the stool by her bed to take off her shin guards, socks, and sneakers. With her right hand, she undoes the two safety pins under her left armpit to adjust the Ace bandage covering her breasts, loosening it just a little, catching a whiff of the musky scent of sweat. Her relieved sigh is muted by the sounds in the backyard. Each day she wraps the lengthy bandage that athletes use for chest-muscle strain slowly and reverentially around herself, the way the ancient Egyptians—according to Miss Frasier's history lessons—might have buried their dead. She has done away with sports bras because of their inability to fully disguise the shape and size of her breasts. Tru wraps herself, knowing that she cannot endure the day without playing ball after school with the boys, kicking it with a mighty force over some lame goalie's shoulders. However, such victory is often short-lived, since she knows that the next day she must return to her all-girls high school, to the pettiness of teenage girls, to the loneliness of feeling different from them, and to the curious faces of her teachers.

She has acquired movements and habits that seem boyish to others, but are natural to her. Like crossing her legs with an ankle over a knee, or spreading them outright, since she's always wearing soccer shorts anyway. *"Close your legs, Miss Beckford. This is not a fish market,"* her teachers at school often chastise. And the girls in the class titter; a few more than others, lighting up in ways she has seen women do for her father. But Tru pays them no attention at all.

She considers herself one of the boys. Not that she feels being a girl is a handicap. That's mostly in the minds of other boys—boys she plays with who might not know she's a girl, even after several games. She wears her hair short in a low fade and sports her father's shirts and her brother's pants outside of school. Women and girls pause in restrooms when she enters. She doesn't apologize or explain. She simply stares back at anyone who stares—an act that incites people to loudly suck their teeth and cuss her under their breath. *"Ah wha dat?"*—it's a question that rarely offends Tru. She likes this ambiguity, feels secretly affirmed by it.

Tru knows that while neighbors might talk, everyone is terrified to do or say anything to her, given that she's Sergeant Beckford's daughter.

S HE FOLDS THE FADED RED T-SHIRT AND SHORTS TO WASH LATER, douses her chest area with lavender-scented talcum powder since she has no time to bathe, then puts on the yellow dress her grandmother insists she wears. Standing in her dress in front of the mirror, she feels like she does not belong to herself, imprisoned by the lace sleeves, the thin bow in the front, and the sewn-in petticoat that swirls about her, especially in the backside. *You can do this*, she reminds herself, as she does every morning before school in her blue tunic, white socks, and black oxfords.

Inside the kitchen, she grabs a tangerine. Kenny is in the living room, his technical drawing homework spread out before him on the tile floor. He raises his head when he sees her. "What yuh doing in a dress?" he asks, his mouth fixing into a grin, one she wants to slap off his face. At sixteen, he has grown into a lanky boy, his limbs longer than his midsection, his head small, his features lacking coherence as though each part belongs to someone else. He looks like a boy always cowering, always waiting on his father to deliver a cuff to the head. Most of the beatings and shaming Kenny gets from Roy have to do with the fact that he's not as fast or as strong as Jermaine, Daval, or even Tru.

"Borrowed one from yuh closet," Tru replies to her brother. "Tell Marva I'll be back before dinner."

Kenny stares at her, his face creasing into a meanness usually reserved for his bullies and Roy. Had his pupils been lighter she would've seen a hint of green in them—as green as his Calabar High School necktie. "Why yuh don't tell har yuhself?"

"Tell har what?" Marva is standing in the entrance to the hallway, looking like the living room sofa itself in a cream floral dress, her arms akimbo on her wide body, always big with babies inside it.

"I'll be back before dinner," Tru says to Marva, who is wiping sweat from her upper lip. "Jus' going to see Mama G." The same shadow that crossed Kenny's face falls over Marva's too, transforming it.

"I see," Marva says, regarding Tru's dress, her eyes briefly appraising it before dimming again. "Thank God fah dat grandmother of yours. Only she can talk some sense in you, mek yuh stop dressing like those straggly boys yuh keep company wid."

"They're my friends."

"Ah don't care what dey are."

Since Jermaine and Daval moved out—Jermaine finding work as a desk clerk in one of the hotel resorts on the North Coast, and Daval finding work as a store manager at a Digicel store in Hanover where his girlfriend lives—Marva has been focusing all her energy on policing Tru and Kenny. She has always been protective of Tru, mindful of everything she does. It's as though she has fully taken on the role of mother without Tru's consent. Things fell apart between them when Tru started to rebel. She stopped listening to Marva's instructions—whether to wash dishes, help her prepare dinner, go with her to the market, or iron her father's shirts. The more Tru spent her energy trying to convince Marva that she was wasting her time using Tru to act out her fantasy of having a daughter, the more Marva showed Tru love and compassion. But Marva didn't have unlimited patience. And the more Tru questioned and pushed, the more tangled her emotions grew inside. It spread, tainting her responses to Marva with vitriol. Soon Marva's gentleness became swift outbursts of frustration that seeped into all of their interactions.

"Mama G waiting. She doing somet'ing nice fah my birthday," Tru says in a quiet voice.

Marva raises her eyebrows, her surprise obvious. Either she has forgotten Tru's birthday, or is shocked that Mama G has organized something special for Tru. Roy didn't say anything to Tru either on his way out of the house this morning. Usually Tru's birthdays come and go like any other day. She stopped celebrating birthdays the year her mother left. So when Mama G called, telling her to come on this day for a treat, Tru remembered again how special this day should feel.

"Well, happy birthday," Marva says, her words like gravel. "At least you got something."

"I didn't say—"

"Nobody ever give to Marva. Everybody jus' take, take, take! I guess I'm jus' a nobody expected to raise other people children an' get nothing in return. What am I supposed to be running here? A foster home? A charity?"

In all these years, Marva has never referred to Tru's mother by her name. Marva believes wholeheartedly that Mama G is getting something from Tru's mother, which isn't true at all. As Marva talks, Tru senses Kenny's silent agreement, though he's looking down at his homework intently. Or maybe he's ashamed of the insults—so used to fending them off himself. Tru takes it, since she knows Marva would rather say this to her than to Roy.

" . . . As if ah don't have enough trouble trying to feed my own. Now ah got two more coming. Well, dis time it g'wan be different. Yuh hear? Oonuh not g'wan kill off me next babies dis time! Me not putting up wid people an' dem indiscretion anymore. I'm not about to lose my babies worried 'bout how some people could be so cold an' heartless—jus' dump dem pickney off on you an' g'wan 'bout dem business. No, sah. Dat not g'wan continue. Dat trifling woman don't even call to see if har own child alive or dead. What kinda somet'ing dat?"

When Marva gets around to talking about Tru's mother and Roy's other women, Tru knows it's time to go. She pushes past Marva toward the front door that opens to the veranda as the sun readies itself to slip between the sloping hills. It casts a dust-yellow haze over Pennyfield.

"Where yuh t'ink yuh going?" Marva says, following her outside with a wobble. "Me nuh done wid yuh yet! You an' yuh father cut from di same cloth. Both ah oonuh ungrateful like . . ."

But Tru doesn't stop. Not that there will be any repercussions. Marva doesn't love her enough to discipline. Tru decides that Marva is too deeply involved with the changes taking place in her body, giving herself up to them, perhaps finding perverse gratification from the perpetual sacrifice and attention to care. So when Marva says, "Is who you t'ink you is?" Tru snaps, "I'm not *him*."

T RU CROSSES OVER THE GULLY TO WHERE THE HOUSES LOOK
more like shacks with zinc fences. Ras Norbert is sitting under the
lignum vitae tree on Walker Lane, chanting, *"Believe me! Believe me
not!"* He's by himself, with his brooms surrounding him like an inan-
imate audience, their shadows stretched to infinity. *"All di riches yuh
can only dream . . ."*

Tru waves at him, "Evening, Ras Norbert!"

His eyes, pale blue with cataracts, dart in search for her, his pupils
only making out her shadow. "Evening, bless-ed," he says, returning his
gaze toward the swollen violet clouds in the sky as the last remnant of
sunset fades. "Walk good."

"Yes, sir."

Miss Maxine and Miss Foster are talking to each other, Miss Foster
leaning against Miss Maxine's gate. They stop talking when they see Tru.

"Barrel come yet?" Miss Maxine says, giving Tru a toothy grin.
Miss Maxine breeds fowl for cockfighting, which happens every Saturday evening. A crowd gathers right by the big tree where Ras Norbert usually sits. The roosters, egged on by spectators hungry to see
blood, begin moving their feet, raising dust from the dry earth, their
beaks open like sharp scissors ready to snatch the other's jugular. The
people watching laugh and clap, slap their knees and stomp their feet,
shouting, "Kill 'im! Kill 'im! Kill 'im!" For deep down—under the shrill
cries, under their weary eyelids, under the frayed clothes, under the
tension of black skin and muscles and veins, under the tongues where
saliva pools to stir up the taste of victory—Tru, who sneaks out sometimes to watch the fights, senses pain and frustration at the monu-
mental indifference of the surrounding hills. It's that thing she cannot
see, but senses in the shadow of their flared nostrils, their curved

mouths, their carved, lean faces, and eyes with no light in them, just two cleanly bored holes.

One win could mean not waiting for handouts from Pope, who also takes care of their women and children, or from the politicians that come around, not bothering to ask their names, much less offer them jobs. One win could recover their manhood. When a bet goes wrong, men draw knives at each other. Any man—be it his father, brother, cousin, neighbor, or best friend—in the way of a win is a dead man. Last time when such a fight happened, Miss Maxine had kicked off her house slippers, stood on the D&G crate under the tree, and shouted above the chaos: "*If me see one ounce ah human blood inna dis place tonight, me swear 'pon me granny grave ah Dovecot dat me g'wan stop cook fi all ah 'oonuh ole hungry neaggar! Oonuh g'long an' kill each other an' see if me joking!*" The men instantly lowered their knives and the crowd dispersed.

"What yuh mother sen' come besides dat nice frock yuh wearing?" Miss Maxine asks Tru in a mocking voice.

Tru smiles, despite her annoyance. "She didn't send anything."

"*She didn't send anything,*" Miss Maxine mimics. "See what me talkin' 'bout, Foster? Is dat good school making she soun' suh proper."

Tru bows her head. The last thing she wants to do is offend her elders with her speech. But she can't help it. Her headmistress, Mrs. Rosedyl, and the teachers at school have gotten into her brain. Every time Tru slips into patois, she hears, "*Ladies! Where are your manners?*" Tru swallows and corrects herself for Miss Maxine. "Ah mean Mama neva sen' nuttin' come, ma'am."

"Yuh too lie," Miss Maxine says, pushing up her mouth and sneaking a look at Miss Foster, who nudges her. "Not even ah piece ah frock she can sen' come fah me?" Miss Maxine prods. "Me used to be har friend."

"Maybe next time," Tru says, making her way inside Mama G's yard. Tru makes a mental note never to wear anything new around here again. No one ever made a peep about her mother in all these years. The fact that her mother is on their mind as soon as they think she sent Tru something infuriates Tru.

"Patsy reach America an' treat us like strangers. Nuh true, Foster?" Miss Maxine says, scratching her arm as if her grudge has festered into mosquito bites.

Miss Foster nods, her mouth returning to its usual upside-down U. "Same suh. She g'long like she neva know we. She mus' be up dere living life."

Tru wants to scream at the women. How dare they pretend to know more about her mother than she does? Had she been their age, she would've told them about themselves—Miss Maxine, who never knows how to keep her head full of Bantu knots out of people's business; and Miss Foster, who keeps all those children locked up inside her house like a zoo where strangers can come and gawk at them—opening their mouths, squeezing their cheeks, prodding their bellies.

"Talk di truth," Miss Maxine is saying to Miss Foster.

"Yes, m'dear."

"So when she g'wan send fah you?" Miss Maxine turns to Tru.

Tru shrugs.

The women say nothing to this, their silence loud.

"You have a good evening," Tru finally says to the women, filling the awkward pause.

"M-hmm. You too, dear," Miss Maxine says.

Tru is relieved that light flickers on inside the house now that the sun has gone down. Mama G shuffles out and opens the veranda grille. She's still in her housedress.

"What yuh doing talking to dat Maxine?" she asks Tru. "She faas like ah don't know what. Always in people business." Mama G sucks her teeth.

"I didn't tell her anything."

"Good."

She ushers Tru inside the house and shuts the door. Mama G's

Jesus music on Love FM serenades Tru. The house smells like rosemary and menthol, the latter from the cream Mama G rubs on her joints for arthritis pain. For the first time Tru realizes how cluttered the house looks with all the Jesus figurines and scriptures framed on the walls.

"Yuh look nice in dat dress," Mama G says, looking Tru up and down. "Is a pity yuh don't grow yuh hair out. Di Bible seh dat hair is a woman's glory."

"Grandma, how many times ah have to tell you dat I like my hair dis way?" Tru moves away from her grandmother's hand, which is reaching toward her fade. When Tru decided to cut off all her hair, she did so in mourning. It was the day after she went on Facebook to see if her mother had a profile. There were so many Patricia Reynoldses. Tru spent the whole day on the home computer, clicking on all the profiles, coming up with nothing. The next day she sat in the barber Lester's chair—the same barber her father goes to on King Street—unmoved by Lester's brief hesitation. *"Yuh sure Chief would agree to dis?"* Lester asked, his voice shaking as though he was about to commit a crime. He did it anyway, and Marva nearly fainted when Tru came home, her prized hair—the one thing about her that Marva loved—gone.

"YUH STUBBORN LIKE YUH MOTHER. HAVE A SEAT," MAMA G SAYS, removing an old phone book and pushing some envelopes off the chair. Tru would've said something about the clutter, but she reconsiders, given that Mama G might suggest she help her clean up. She sees the cake her grandmother baked for her sitting on the dining table, hoisted on a plastic container turned upside down inside a bowl of water to prevent ants from crawling into it. It's the same dining table where her mother used to sit to read those letters. As Tru stands there before the cake, a knob turns in her mind and opens a door to a dark room, forcing her memory's eye to adjust to an image—her mother looking peaceful, beautiful, caged in the glow of the lamp as she reads a letter, her index finger trailing each line on the ruled paper the way it would a raised bump from a mosquito bite on Tru's arm. *"Mama, what it say?"* This single outburst startled her mother. She looked at Tru like she did whenever Tru interrupted her while she was speaking to another grown-up or listening to the news. *"What yuh doing up? Guh back to bed!"* Tru never knew who sent those letters or why they affected her mother so. By the time Tru lost the snow globe at school when she loaned it to a girl named Trisha whom she wanted to impress, she had gotten used to seeing her mother's back hunched over the dining table like that. Sometimes her mother would be in bed with the curtains drawn and the sheet over her head. *"Is suh Satan strong,"* Mama G explained. *"Di war between God an' di Devil is not fah us to undah-stand."* She squeezed Tru's shoulder then.

"Happy Birthday," Mama G says when Tru finally sits.

"Thanks, Grandma."

There are no candles or prompts for Tru to make a wish.

"Grandma? What was wrong wid Mama?"

"What yuh mean?"

"When she used to get sad aftah reading those letters . . ."

Mama G's face looks stricken, her eyes flashing. "Nuttin' dat God couldn't solve, dear. Nuttin' dat God couldn't solve."

"Who was it dat wrote to her?" Tru asks.

"Yuh not g'wan eat a piece?" Mama G says, changing the subject.

"Not yet, Grandma," Tru says. "I can bring dis home an' eat aftah dinner."

"Suit yuhself," Mama G says.

Tru looks down at the table, wanting to ask her grandmother more questions that have been bothering her—questions her father avoids. Like how come her mother hasn't written or called? *Be a good, obedient girl.* What does that even mean now? She's been trying to be a good girl her whole life, hoping for her mother's return. The sadness Tru has been feeling lately catches up with her, especially on a day like this one—her birthday—easing its way around the table in the dimming light. Mama G must have sensed this when she catches Tru staring at the cake and guessed it has something to do with her mother. Because she mumbles something about forgiveness and disappears into the room to get ready for tonight's revival at her church, leaving Tru alone at the table to stare at the elevated cake and the ants lining up around it.

❧

WHEN TRU GETS HOME, SHE TAKES OFF THE DRESS, THROWS IT onto the floor, and makes yet another opening on the skin of her upper right thigh, breaking the surface with the razor she uses to carve a space for herself. A sanctuary. She watches the red bulb rise and rise like a lung inflated with a sudden intake of air.

Later that night Tru wakes up, thirsty for a glass of water, and finds Roy sitting by himself at the dining table. It reminds her of the times she caught her mother doing the same thing in the wee hours of the night, reading those letters she kept locked away in an attaché.

Alone, without his gun and uniform, Roy is just a man slumped at the table. It's like the world is resting on his shoulders. He's shaking his head, his hand—the one with the scar—trembling slightly as he reads what's on the piece of paper he holds. Tru watches him through the beaded curtains. She watches knowing that every line in his dark face has something to do with her, even though he says it isn't so. As Marva's belly grows and grows yet again, the shadow persists inside the house like the coming of a storm, a plague, death. She tries to push away these feelings but fails each time she sees her father bent over the table this way, shaking his head. As if he senses her, he lifts his head and straightens his back.

"What yuh doing hiding back dere, Champ?" Roy asks with a strain in his voice.

"Jus' coming fah some wata," she replies. "What yuh looking at on dat paper?"

Roy peers down at the paper in his hand and crumples it. "Nothing."

He gets up to pour himself a glass of the dark liquor he keeps in the cabinet on the top shelf. Tru knows that her father drinks sometimes, but he never does it in front of her. There are just certain things he doesn't do in her presence.

He throws his head back with the drink, as if simply swallowing it won't be as effective. Tru watches his face crease. He puts the glass down and stares, turning and turning it. "When ah became a policeman, ah used to t'ink ah could mek a difference," he says to the empty glass. "Ah used to t'ink ah could catch criminals an' lock dem up so dat we can live in a real paradise. Now I jus' want to quit."

Tru waits on him to explain. She's never heard her father use the word *quit*. Something about hearing him utter that word frightens her. Tru looks off into the shadows that creep into the room, refusing to watch her father surrender. As if he knows her thoughts, he says, "Dey denied my promotion again. Dey told me ah haven't earned it yet. Now, you tell me what else ah need to do. How many more years me haffi wait? How many more quota me haffi fill? I've been giving dat police force almost fifteen years of my sweat an' blood." He clenches his fist around the crumpled paper in his hand. "Fifteen years. Now dey telling me dey can't give me di one t'ing me want. What more dem need?"

He looks at Tru now as if she has all the answers. At the sight of his troubled face, her own anxiety surfaces. Suddenly Roy seems more like the child and she, Tru, the parent. "Did you ask dem why dey didn't give it you?" she asks him carefully.

He shakes his head. "What ah got to ask dem for? I already know why dey didn't give it to me. Dey know I'm not like dem. Yuh t'ink ah want to spend my life tiptoeing an' biting my tongue jus' because arresting certain criminals could get me in more trouble than letting dem get weh? I'm committed to upholding the law ovah anyt'ing else. Yuh t'ink because I grew up wid half ah dese clowns who get deported and start calling themselves dons, dat I can't put dem in prison where dem belong? Dem sadly mistaken. When those bad man see me coming, dem know who is in charge. But half a dese big man connected to di same crooks. Those pompous john-crow Devils living in dem big houses on di hills feeding dem self wid our carcass. See how wealthy they are? Is we back dem feeding off. An' look at me. Blood money. Dat's what's pulsing in di vein of high society."

He pours himself another drink and swallows again. Perspiration rolls like bright tears down his face. "I coulda been rich long time ago," he says. His eyes narrow as his thoughts form. "But ah couldn't bring myself to accept bribe. You know how much policeman ah know who do dat? Everyone know seh di police force is corrupt. Money run t'ings in dis country. Dat's how nuff policeman get ahead in dis goddamn country. But I was always more committed to working fah di law than fah myself. Maybe me is di fool in all ah dis. People might be laughing when dey see me. Dem might be sayin' to themselves or to each other: '*Look! Cuh di fool-fool Beckford! See him deh wid di big dunce hat 'pon him head!*' His wry smile becomes a sudden suck of air. "Maybe is me alone in dis whole wide world who t'ink abiding by di rules g'wan benefit me. Look where it got me. I'm almost a pauper, depending on handouts from America dat will neva come," Roy says. He looks at Tru. "What kinda man does dat make me?"

33

PATSY WAKES UP SHIVERING IN THE DARK, THINKING ABOUT HIM. She still cannot believe what she saw. Was it a bird with silvered wings, kissed at the tips by the glare of the train lights? It's hard to relive it. The frightened looks of the hysterical crowd; the squeal of the engines on the tracks that will forever echo in Patsy's ears; the flash in his eyes just before his departure; the veil that slipped from them, which revealed to Patsy that he was already gone before the leap—a mere gesture of smoke, in comparison to what he had already suffered.

Still, in the hard light of morning she searches for his face, his forgiving eyes, in crowds during her commute to work, struck by the commuters' apathy as they shuffle like cattle. She scans the deep scowls on each of their faces for him. Sometimes she thinks she hears him say her name in the roar of a train engine, the way he laughed as if her name coated his tongue with sweetness. When she gets off the trains, sometimes she pauses at the sight of a bum on a bench, a rat gnawing at garbage on the side of a trash can, the shadow of a naked tree branch on the sidewalk, each looking at first like Barrington until she blinks.

There was quick cleanup after the incident. There is nothing left, not even a stain of him. Business goes on as usual. It's how the city works. After big parades, bending figures pick up the garbage, hunched in duty. It has always been a mystery to Patsy, who has never woken up to messy streets after a parade. She decides that New York City Transit workers are like scavengers, sifting, plucking, snatching, and stuffing things inside trash bags—dead things, empty things, lost things.

AT HOME, INSIDE THE CAGE OF HER ROOM, PATSY SITS UNBLINKing on her too-narrow bed, her fingers spread on her kneecaps. Her head is cocked to the side, her mind flying through the window, over the abandoned lot full of weeds, and skidding on the edges of the red-brown buildings darkened by cloud shadows. The reporters had carelessly printed the address in their article as they accosted neighbors in search of an idea of who this man was and if they had suspected that he would do such a thing. To them, he was just a John Doe. But to Patsy, he's Barrington, who she learned lived in a basement just ten blocks from her place—closer to the cemetery.

When she finds herself at his door, the landlord—a shifty-looking pudgy man with a unibrow and tufts of white hair coming from his ears—doesn't think it odd. He allows her to see the room, though, closing the door behind him, he asks in a Trinidadian accent, "You is not one ah dem journalist, are you?" When Patsy says no, he gives her a crooked smile.

"Is two-fifty a month," he says, sniffing and rubbing his broad nose. "You want?"

He never even bothered to throw out Barrington's things before showing the place. Patsy looks around the room, saddened by the mess—a twin mattress, similar to hers, lying flat in the middle of the room on stained parquet floors, the two ends touching the stripping walls painted baby-blue; a mini-television with antennae hoisted on two crates; and a mound of clothes and shoes piled in one corner looking like a smaller version of the Riverton City Dump in Kingston. The room has a musty smell that could be attributed to many things—either the lack of windows, the pairs of socks lying like limp tongues outside the sneakers, or the clothes themselves, moldy with sweat and body odor inside two trash bags. No one has come to take his things. Not even to burn them. No family. No friends. No girlfriends. What a tragedy to die alone, Patsy thinks. She spies his Jamaican passport. In this country, it's useless. People like Patsy and Barrington are invisible here. If it were Patsy who had jumped, she probably would've been Jane Doe. She knows Barrington's passport is stamped with a long-expired visiting visa—once thought to be a ticket to freedom. But maybe he's freer now.

"So, what yuh t'ink? You want it?" the landlord asks Patsy.

"Why yuh didn't get rid of his t'ings?" Patsy replies.

The man shrugs, rubbing his nose again. "Didn't have time. Don't worry. It'll be all gone before yuh move in."

Before she answers, his phone goes off, and he puts a chubby finger up to Patsy, indicating for her to wait for him to take the call, and walks out of the room. "Sonofabitch, weh me money?" he shouts at the person on the other end of the line.

Patsy takes this as her cue to leave. She has no business being here. She should have known better. Her heart punches her rib cage as if to punish her. She turns to leave, but the punching grows stronger and stronger, louder and louder inside her ears. A pounding she has not heard in a while, indicating the rush of blood through her veins. Every day, she goes through the motions in a colorless city without feeling. Until now, as her blood surges red-hot through her—wild, like life in the raw. Patsy grabs what she can, stuffing one of Barrington's striped shirts inside her big leather handbag. It seems as though it offered itself to her hand. She would have taken more if it could all fit. And the fact that the landlord trusts her enough to leave her alone, inside this room with the dead man's things, only increases her desire to take more. When the landlord returns in the doorway, Patsy thanks him and leaves.

Later, inside her room, she glances up at Barrington's shirt swaying on the wire hanger from the curtain rod by the window as though a body fills it, its muted sighs and shifting form making the night more bearable. It's a beautiful shirt—the blue and green stripes vibrant against the off-white color, though it's a common design. That night Patsy decides to lie with the shirt in the hush of her room. She takes the shirt with the shyness and caution of being with a new lover. There's something sweetly forbidden about the act. Yet it fills Patsy with something she hasn't felt since Uncle Curtis put his index finger coated with honey to her lips and kept it there. It was their special game. She thinks of him now, with his lazy eyes and slow smile. He slept in the living room each night after he emptied his bottle of rum. Mama G drove him to drink, Patsy knew, for every time they argued he would leave the house and come back limping, his fingers deftly fumbling with the notch on the stereo, his eyes shiny red, and his eyelids a pair of heavy drapes. At nine years old, Patsy would sit on the cushion next to him inside the living room and wait until he stirred awake. His face would come alive when he saw her, a hint of recognition, warm and gentle. *"What yuh doing up, eh?"* With Mama G closed off to the world, excluding him and Patsy, Uncle Curtis's smile was real, the only thing Patsy believed in. *"Yuh too beautiful not to be sleeping,"* he'd say. *"Ah g'wan start to call you me likkle vampire."* He would stroke her face with his finger. She appreciated her face back then. She even considered it beautiful, because he said so.

"I couldn't sleep till yuh come back," she'd tell him, hoping they would dance to his sad songs, she on his toes as they moved around the room together. They were already joined by their own feelings of inadequacy. Patsy lived to hear the words, *"Come mek we dance."* And while they danced, he'd say to her under the spell of rum, *"Remembah dis one, Gloria? Remembah how we used to love when it come on?"*

Patsy would close her eyes to remember a time she knew nothing about but forced her imagination to recall. She imagined him and Mama G in their Sunday best, two-stepping to the old hits from Marvin Gaye, the Temptations, and the Supremes. She became Gloria, driven by her imagination of a woman she hardly knew. She prompted Uncle Curtis to tell her more. Then she'd ask him to show her their dance moves. She loved when he spun her around, her nightgown twirling about her as if the hems were lifted by birds. He would then dip her so low that she felt she had to cling to him for dear life, giggling.

"Do it again," she'd say.

"We might wake yuh mother."

"Jus' one more time."

Their nightly ritual was secretive, born out of the mischief of disobeying a rule behind God's back—be it playing ungodly music inside the house, staying up late to dance, or in Uncle Curtis's case, drinking rum and smoking cigarettes. By the time he offered Patsy a swig of rum when she was ten, she knew how to keep secrets that bound herself and Uncle Curtis inside their own intimate circle. *"Yuh like di taste, don't it?"* His voice was always playful and teasing. Patsy rested her head on his chest, her neck suddenly too weak to hold it up. She felt him inhale.

Although her eyes were closed, she knew his gaze was on her face, and an image of what she must have looked like to him set in her mind's eye. There was never reprimand coming from his gaze when she looked up at him, the rum warming her blood, even as he said, *"Time fah you to go to bed. Yuh mother might say somet'ing."* It was gentle, patient. Had she been asleep longer on his chest, she knew he would've continued to watch her under his lashes; watch her stir into the woman he still loved and mourned. A woman who had left him for a man neither of them had ever seen. Though the thought of Mama G intruded on their peaceful moment, Uncle Curtis's soft gaze put Patsy at ease. She sensed his restlessness, his desire to move on, and wanted him to stay.

On one such night, she saw his Adam's apple rising at his neckline, and felt him tense. He turned suspiciously to the door locked between them and Mama G. Something sad lanced his eyes and he took another sip of rum. Then drained the whole bottle without giving her any. When he looked at Patsy again, she saw something else in his eyes—something stronger, more urgent. It reached out to claim her, confessed that despite their age, despite their sneaking around at nights to make their own joy, despite him wanting to leave since the love between him and Mama G was already gone, they would always be joined by secrecy. He beckoned Patsy close that night, sank to his knees and held her. When he put his arms around her, she felt something that she had never felt before— love. Genuine, unconditional love that thrust sharp from his trousers. It made her cry out before he put a honeyed finger to her lips and kissed them softly. *"It only hurt di first time. Ah promise,"* he said, his own tears—or were they hers?—wet against her cheeks.

WHEN SHE WAKES UP THE NEXT MORNING, DAYLIGHT POURING through the curtainless window at half past eight, Barrington's shirt is twisted around her neck. Any tighter, and it would have choked her.

34

IT'S NINE-THIRTY WHEN SHE FINALLY GETS TO WORK. RANSEL, THE doorman, gives her his usual mock salute. "Look like yuh wake 'pon di wrong side dis mawnin'!" In the three years she has been working for Regina, Patsy has never been late.

"Yuh see har from mawnin?" Patsy asks him in a near-whisper, not having to say Regina's name, since Ransel knows every nanny by the people they work for. She hates making him, of all people, an accomplice. "Ah forgot to set me alarm clock."

"Tell dat to she." Ransel looks over his shoulders both ways, his voice as low as Patsy's. He waves to a white man with silver hair walking his Dalmatian that's as big as a pony. "Good day, Missah Jacob!" He grins at the man, revealing all thirty-two teeth in his mouth. The people in the building—who are all white except for the one or two black people who act like Patsy doesn't exist when she rides the elevator with them—greet Ransel with the same stiff, thin-lipped smiles: fences of white teeth that seem to keep him at a distance, discourage small talk. When the man waves back and disappears outside, Ransel spins around to Patsy, lowering his voice again. "As far as me know, di husband left from last night wid a big suitcase," he says, hurrying Patsy to the last of the four shiny bronze elevators in the remodeled building. Their feet slap across the checkered marble tiles.

"What?" Patsy asks. "Yuh sure 'bout dat?"

"Cross me heart an' hope fi die," Ransel replies, signing himself.

Patsy shakes her head, flashes of Barrington leaping in front of the train coming back. "Yuh all right?" Ransel asks, his dark face creasing with concern.

"Please don't seh dat. Ah can't deal wid another death right now . . ." Her voice trails.

"Yuh know is jus' a figure of speech." Ransel laughs. "Yuh know is what ole-time people used to seh . . ."

"Fah-get wha ole-time people used to seh. Me nuh waan hear it!" Patsy quickly presses the button to the fifth floor, relieved when the door closes on Ransel and his grin.

She run-walks down the long hallway. When Regina opens the door, Patsy can tell she's upset. "Good mawnin', ma'am." Regina bristles at Patsy's greeting. If Regina weren't so polite, she'd probably have a few choice words for Patsy. At first Patsy never understood how the woman could be home all day yet still needed a babysitter. It didn't make any sense. Back home, people would call a woman like that *good-fah-nuttin'* and lazy. But while Patsy had profound distrust of the other woman's ability to lock herself inside her study the whole time while she's there, inaccessible behind the high wall of silence, her mind in another place, Patsy envies her freedom. Regina's only complaints are about deadlines. Her next book, about the adventures of a Nigerian doula, needs to be finished and she's having a hard time with it. As one can imagine, being that she's a white woman from California. But then again, maybe Africans can't write their own stories—at least not the starving ones Patsy has seen on TV with big bellies and straw limbs with flies pitching all over their oversized heads.

"Where were you?" she asks Patsy. "You didn't call. I was worried. And Paul just up and—" She shakes her head full of red curls, her pale face flushed pink and her large hazel eyes red like she had been crying. Patsy knows not to ask questions about the personal lives of her employers unless they volunteer the information.

"Never mind," Regina says. "You're here now. Thomas is playing in the living room. I gave him his favorite toys."

Regina hurries to the coffee maker brewing on the island counter before it's done dripping and pours herself a cup of that special coffee she gets from Indonesia whose beans were eaten and defecated by cats. It's a gift—the pounds of cat-shit coffee beans stacked in the cupboards. Patsy knows it's from her friend—the man who goes off to these exotic places to write poetry; the Japanese man Patsy thought was gay, because he wears his hair long and silk chiffon scarves around his neck like a woman; the man Regina threw a party for because he won some big poetry prize, and continues to invite over when her husband is away on business trips. *"Akio makes me laugh,"* she said to Patsy once in passing after returning from one of her writing residencies in the middle of nowhere, blushed pink, girlish.

Without another word to Patsy, she disappears down the hallway and into her study. Patsy does the usual—hangs her coat inside the coat closet, removes her boots, washes her hands in the guest bathroom from palms to elbows with organic antibiotic soap—a technique suggested by Regina, who gets paranoid about germs. Patsy then heads straight for the kitchen to prepare breakfast for Baby. He likes his first meal around this time. The kitchen is newly renovated, so there are things Patsy has to search for— like Baby's special spoon that he likes to eat cereal with. He has been eating regular food like a grown-up since he was fourteen months, forgoing his baby seat for the dining table. Maybe because his mother is up in age. Regina waited till she was forty to have him—her first and only child. In Jamaica, forty is considered way too old to have a baby, and if the woman were to get pregnant at forty, the baby would be a wash belly baby—the last child out of how many children she's had before.

Baby also potty-trained early. One thing his mother did was teach him how to use the bathroom so that she didn't have to go through the trouble to change him—something Patsy doesn't remember doing with Tru. One day she noticed that her daughter crawled—or did she walk? *couldn't be!*—to the toilet and sat there. Just sat there. Her daughter must have sensed Patsy's urgency for her to grow up, because she also began walking to school by herself at the age of five, needing no help to cross the street or ignore strangers. (Granted, the school was not that far.) Miss Gains, her basic school teacher—*whatevah happen' to dat woman?*—had marveled at this too, saying Tru was grown for her age.

Patsy pours whole-grain Cheerios into Baby's green cereal bowl, and a cup of almond milk from a box. He's looking at her with those old-man eyes while sucking on his bottom lip. He's sitting in the middle of the living room with its floor-to-ceiling bookshelves, his toys spread around him like a hurricane has swept through. Regina must have given him all his toys at once to keep him occupied.

"Yuh ready to eat?" Patsy asks him, searching for his crayons and coloring book from the mess. Baby loves to color. Patsy likes to sit with him and help him decide what crayons to choose. He likes to color hills purple, the sky yellow, the sun green, and the sea red—colors Patsy once thought jarring and out of touch with reality, but has come to appreciate. However, today Baby sits slouched in the middle of his room, his eyes lowered as he fiddles with a red stuffed animal that he likes to play with.

"What's di mattah?" Patsy asks, squatting before him. "Yuh not g'wan eat nothing?"

Baby shrugs with his small shoulders.

"Yuh feeling sick?" She presses the back of her hand to his neck, her brown hand contrasting with his pink flesh.

He doesn't respond, focusing intently on his stuffed toy. Patsy wants to take it away from him to get his attention. She has never seen him this way. She comes down on her knees, feeling a sharp pain from something hard, which makes her yelp and fall backward. Baby doesn't laugh at this like he does whenever she trips or bumps into furniture around the house. The culprit is a toy soldier. She tosses it into the pile of toys already on the floor.

"How much time yuh mother mus' tell you to put away yuh toys after yuh play wid dem? Talk to me," she says to Baby. "What troubling you?"

"I want my mommy," Baby whispers. His voice is soft and wispy.

"Mommy left fah work." Patsy gestures toward the short hall where Regina's study is located. "She don't like when nobody disturb har."

"She said she was going to play with me if you didn't come."

Patsy pauses before she says, "Well, I'm here now."

"You're not her."

"I know."

He takes her hand anyway and allows her to help him onto his chair. He eats his cereal quietly, still clinging to the stuffed animal with his free hand. Just then Patsy hears the door to Regina's study open and Regina's footsteps on the hardwood floors. "Mommy! Mommy!" Baby squeals, kicking his legs and banging the table with his spoon, nearly spilling his cereal.

"Yes, dear. Mommy is working, but she just needs to ask Patsy a question," Regina says, referring to herself in the third person. Patsy catches herself before she rolls her eyes, knowing what sort of thing Regina is about to ask. She braces herself by holding on to the edge of the table. "I've been thinking . . ." Regina begins. "Ifeoma comes across a ten-year-old pregnant girl on her journey and delivers the girl's baby? Wouldn't she die? Is it realistic if she lives?"

"Uhm . . ." Patsy tries to think of something to say.

Regina continues, "I mean . . . gosh! How tragic is that? I want this to be a feel-good book, you know—an Ifeoma-saves-the-day kinda book. But I imagine, in places like Africa where things like that happen—all the rapes and incest . . . girls die, right?"

Patsy squeezes the edges of the table. It must be a luxury, she thinks, for Regina to make up stories without ever coming out of her study and out of her head. Regina is looking at her with an expectant look on her face.

"Ah wouldn't know what dey do in Africa," Patsy says.

Regina pours herself more coffee. She takes a sip, then lowers her cup, wheeling from the counter to the middle of the room, where she paces barefoot on the hardwood floors that Patsy mopped and shined two days ago. Baby's eyes follow his mother like green ping-pong balls. "Africa is beautiful. Just like Jamaica is beautiful. Right? I've never been, but I've seen pictures. It would be terrible for me to put such tragedy in the book when my intention is to take people on a fucking safari—if you catch my drift!" Patsy glances at Baby, hoping he didn't just hear his mother curse.

"Then don't write it," Patsy finally says, turning back to Regina, her voice steady, cautious. Any softer and it would've been a lullaby. "It's unrealistic," Patsy tells her, mercifully sparing the woman the disgrace of truth. Even Mama G herself had to justify such a thing as the Devil's work. So why now should Patsy let anyone else believe otherwise?

"Unrealistic that it could happen to someone so young? Or that she lives?" Regina asks.

"Dat she live . . ." Patsy confesses, turning away from Regina's furrowing brow to pretend to clean crumbs off the already pristine table.

"That's it!" Regina says, laughter ringing in her voice. "I knew I was way off with that story! I don't want anyone dying in my book. I'll make her older." She ruffles Baby's hair and kisses him on the forehead before she disappears again in her study and slams the door. Baby looks as though he's about to cry. Patsy waits a heartbeat after Regina closes the door before she apologetically touches Baby's hand clenched around his stuffed animal. "Come. Let's take a likkle stroll."

"I want my mommy!" Baby says into the bowl in front of him.

Try as she might in this moment, Patsy can no longer calm him. His voice rises like the sea during a hurricane, commanding and inevitable, everything buried, dredging from its oceanic floor.

As clear as day, Patsy sees Miss Mabley's beautiful bronze face, smells her perfume, and remembers the pain that ruthlessly cracked her open like the shell of a pomegranate smashed on concrete. *"Jus' breathe. Yuh g'wan be all right. You'll see."* Patsy and Cicely were playing in Cicely's backyard that day, when Patsy felt the rush of water between her legs and the debilitating cramp in her belly. Cicely ran to get help, and out of nowhere Miss Mabley appeared in just a slip and a pair of house slippers. She rushed Patsy to the hospital, cradling Patsy like her own child: *"Dis child need help! Someone please help har!"* Patsy wailed against the pain, thinking she was going to die. *"We're seeing di last days,"* Mama G had said at the hospital, her voice low, laced with triumph as though her prophecy had come to pass. And just like that, Patsy let go. Her spirit gave way to the exhaustion she could no longer resist. It was better that way—better to exist numb, a mere husk that could float even on the most treacherous seas, than to feel pain.

When she woke up, it was over. The doctors never bothered to sew her up properly, since Patsy was from Pennyfield, and people thought of Pennyfield residents as animals fit for nothing but birthing way too many babies, blocking roads to get what they wanted from indifferent politicians, and killing each other the way *ole neaggars* did. The incision became infected. When it healed, it grew into a pinkish red branch under her belly. She was twelve. She'd never even known she was pregnant. She never saw the baby's body. She was told she would never have children again.

"I want my mommy I want my mommy I want my mommy!" Baby continues to cry, knocking over his cereal bowl and spilling milk on the table. It drips onto the floor. Patsy distractedly watches each droplet, the spread of white liquid on the mahogany surface where echoes of footsteps seem far, far away. She doesn't bend to clean up the mess.

&

W HEN SHE REACHES BROOKLYN, SHE SCURRIES PAST THE BANKS and salons and shops and churches and WELCOME TO THE NEW BROOKLYN signs on Flatbush Avenue. Each time she passes a glass storefront she catches a glimpse of her face, a black streak blurring into nothingness. Patsy's dark, shapeless thing hovers close by amid the fes-

tive mood. It's the evening of the election, polls are still open, and people are bursting into song and some into prayer that Obama will win. It
reminds Patsy of the Reggae Boyz representing Jamaica in France at the
World Cup ten years ago—how Jamaicans from every walk of life joined
hands, sang, and cheered for their victory. For the first time in the years
that Patsy has been in America, black people are overjoyed. Obama's
amicable face smiles from calendars, posters, mugs, T-shirts—anything
you can find on Flatbush Avenue with the words YES WE CAN scrawled
across them.

On her corner, Patsy bumps into a middle-aged woman bundled in
a dark coat with just long johns underneath and a pair of Timberland
boots, her hair like wires sticking out her head.

"Yuh 'ave one breadfruit me can roast tonight, ma'am?"

"No," Patsy says, walking by her, not bothering to tell her that this
is not Jamaica. And that one cannot roast breadfruit on a sidewalk in
Brooklyn. In the cold.

"Me children hungry!" she calls after Patsy.

Patsy stops. She turns and looks into the woman's glassy eyes. She
sees herself peering through the crazed eyes of this stranger. She knows
that the woman is not in Brooklyn, standing on Flatbush Avenue, but
home. She went crazy in America, her mind halting in the loneliness,
anxiety, and the soundlessness of things falling apart: a sweet surrender.
What a relief it must be, Patsy thinks, to stare into the eyes of sorrow
and break without the pretense of holding it together.

Patsy digs inside her pocket and gives the woman some loose
change—a few pennies and a dime. It's all she has to give. The woman
thanks her like Patsy has given her gold, before limping away, singing a
Jamaican folk song Patsy knew when she was a girl, but no more.

Once inside her room, Patsy sinks to the floor, pressing to her chest
the shirt of the dead man she will never get to know. What she has
kept inside for years, balled up in a steeled fist, explodes as a scream,
her throat releasing everything she has kept, every wrong done to her.

Someone knocks at her door. A woman asking if she's all right in there. But she doesn't respond. She weeps finally, finally with the rage of a woman touching an earlobe for the feel of an heirloom earring and discovering it gone, not knowing when and where it fell, and powerless at this point to find it. Her castaway innocence has long been drowned by the sea, and Patsy weeps for the girl who died with it. The lifelong pain twists her into a fetal position on the floor until the sun slips from the sky and leaves it black. Worn, stripped, and hoarse, Patsy's cries taper, and something else emerges: A voice. Barrington's voice. *"How is it fate if yuh have control ovah it?"*

BOOK V

BARREL OF LOVE

35

AT SCHOOL, TRU EATS LUNCH BY HERSELF. HER GAZE STRETCHES across the lawn, where other girls are eating their lunches undisturbed by the white-hot sun in the empty sky hovering close, toward the fence that divides the girls' school from the boys' school Sore-Foot Marlon once attended. The lunchtime chatter floats up into the branches of the mango trees and swirls with the gentle breeze across the schoolyard. In comparison, Wilhampton Boys' School—hidden next door behind the high hedges and barbed-wire fences—is quiet, a hush that makes Tru imagine their bowed heads inside classrooms, their brows drawn close as they try to concentrate. They are never at lunch at the same time as the girls' school—these boys who are groomed to be the next prime ministers, attorney generals, and businessmen. Both the girls' and boys' schools were founded by a British couple, Joseph and Martha Wilhampton, whose families owned plantations on the island. They bequeathed a good amount of their estate to building a school that would train the best and brightest, boys and girls, to lead the country. It was decided that the girls' and boys' schools would be separate, with different leadership.

Most of the Wilhampton Girls' campus is shaded with oaks and chestnuts and lignum vitae trees. Blue and white British-style uniforms decorate the old high school campus—one of the most prestigious in the country—with its colonial buildings so white that they appear to glow in sunlight. The hallways in the main building are lined with decorated plaques awarded to the school for excellence since 1845. There are also photos of fair-skinned beauty queens smiling with jeweled crowns on their heads under the alumni achievement board. Generous funds have been allotted to the landscaping, expanding the library and auditorium, repainting and remodeling the stripped and faded buildings that have been around since the 1800s. Men in khaki uniforms work the compound to keep it looking pristine, and women in hairnets mutely serve food in the canteen or scrub menstrual bloodstains off the toilets in the restrooms.

A group of three girls—Nadine Rodriques, Jamela Coudron, and Saskia Rawlins—gather nearby on the wooden benches that circle a tree. Tru ignores them, though they talk loudly about what they'll wear to the school fete in December, biting into crunchy apples they get in their barrels sent from America. They call themselves the Branded, but everyone else calls them Barrel Children—a name that could get the speaker punched in the face. Though it is true that these girls are raised by barrels sent from America or wherever their parents reside, Branded is a name they claim for the expensive brand-name clothes they wear to school fetes and parties—outfits that not many teenagers can afford unless if they're wealthy like the Uptowns.

The difference between the Branded and the Uptowns is that the Uptowns are wealthy high-colored girls admitted to schools like this one because generations of their families went there and continue to donate money. The population of the Uptowns dwindled when the school started admitting black girls—not the kind mixed with the milk-honey shade of the Lebanese or Indian, nor the café au lait hue of white and Chinese. But black-black from the bottom of Kingston's melting pot. After what usually seems like long absences, the Uptowns are spotted around Kingston wearing uniforms of private schools their parents whisked them off to in a frenzy of panic. Some transfer to safer, uptown-friendly schools like Campion College. While the more moneyed ones flock to boarding schools abroad. Rumor has it that their departure halted repairs to the school's library and auditorium—a dilemma that sent a stern message to Mrs. Rosedyl, the headmistress.

The rumor became true when messages started appearing all over the newly painted walls—*"Wilhampton is nothing but a kennel since that hag, Mrs. Rosedyl, let the dogs in."* Since then the school fee mysteriously quadrupled. A joke. Since girls like the Branded, funded by money sent by parents working overseas, still populate the campus—girls who have more in common with Tru, though she doesn't share their bragging rights. In fact, Tru is envious of them. Girls who at least receive things from their parents, even if it's only that. *Things.* Could she, Tru, if given the chance, be so forgiving?

"I dunno," Nadine Rodriques is saying in response to something. She's resting her head of curls on Jamela Coudron's lap under the tree, fully covered in a pink sweatshirt over her uniform, though it's hot outside. "I haven't yet told Daddy what to send for the fete. But whatever it is has to be bettah than Genevieve Sinclair's, since I know she'll be bringing Marlon. He's so cute!" she says.

"He is!" the other girls squeal in unison like a chorus of robins.

Tru would've rolled her eyes had she not been pretending to be deaf to their conversation.

"I want a boy like that too," Jamela swoons.

"Plus, he can get into any concert for free," Nadine adds. "His uncle is a producer. He knows all di dancehall artists."

Tru almost chokes on her chicken bone, since Sir Charles only deejays at dancehall sessions in Pennyfield.

"Have you seen dat gap in Genevieve's teeth?" Nadine asks, her cat eyes narrowing into a near-perfect horizontal line of disdain. "You'd think an Uptown girl could afford to get braces."

"But she's stylish, though," Jamela replies. Jamela has a perpetually amused look on her face as though everything she sees is a wonder. She wears her straightened hair parted down the middle, pigtails on both sides of her head as if she's still five.

"Don't mattah. She has bad teeth," Nadine retorts, bursting Jamela's bubble of awe.

"Bad teeth, but good hair and nice skin," Jamela replies, her vacuous stare reaching upward, through the tree branches, toward the clouds. "That's why boys like Uptown girls."

"Sounds like you're the one with a crush."

"Eww, dat's nasty! But let's be real. Genevieve can do no wrong."

"Anybody can buy weave and bleach their skin for a likkle high-color like dat, you idiot." Nadine snaps in patois—a forbidden language on campus, though the girls speak it in secret. They glance over their shoulders to make sure there are no teachers in sight to hear them.

"Money can buy everything but good genes," Saskia Rawlins, who has been quiet the whole time, interjects. "I asked my mother to send me a leather dress. Now it's winter where she is in England, so it should be easy."

Tru sneaks a glance at Saskia, since she has never heard anyone else talk about their mothers being away. She mostly hears of fathers leaving for jobs overseas. Through her lashes she observes the girl, looking for a crack of anger, a tiny dot of resentment, a blemish revealing some form of hurt, which will ease the growing pressure inside Tru. She remembers the first Mother's Day without her mother. Her teacher had the class make cards for their mothers—pouring out numerous crayons, Sharpies, vials of glitter, and glue sticks to paste red hearts with I LOVE YOU MOMMY scrawled on top. Tru had made a card that year. But she didn't know where to send it.

Next to Tru, a girl named Olivia Moore was excused from the assignment—the girl whose mother had died from cancer. Miss Powell allowed Olivia to read a Regina Rhinebeck novel from the pile of dog-eared books donated by the Peace Corps people from America, who came to the school. The rest of the class worked on their cards. Tru couldn't ignore the pang in her gut, nor the knee-jerk impulse to grab the book out of Olivia's hands and rip each yellowed, dog-eared page. Just to see her cry the tears Tru could not cry. Though death was the ultimate betrayal, Olivia, unlike Tru, was pitied, cuddled, for not having her mother present.

But here, in the schoolyard underneath the shade of the tree, Tru observes nothing indicating Saskia Rawlins's true feelings. She is well hidden behind the high slanted facial bones, small nose, and wide mouth, her sparkly dark eyes and deep brown skin completing the mystery. Tru snatches her gaze away when Saskia looks in her direction.

"Leather?" Nadine asks, frowning. "In dis heat?"

"If you can wear a sweatshirt to prevent the sun from messing with your bleaching creams, then why can't I wear leather?" Saskia retorts, flipping her relaxed hair over one shoulder.

Nadine rolls her eyes. "There you go again wid yuh self-righteous talk."

"I'll wear dat purple strapless party dress I wore for my Sweet Sixteen party to the fete," Jamela says, gazing dreamlike toward the flagpole at the roundabout where the Jamaican flag flaps freely in the breeze.

Nadine sighs. Finally she says, "Dat dress is really cute. But people already saw you in it."

Jamela pauses to contemplate Nadine's statement. "That's true," she replies too quickly.

"What about you, Tru?" Tru looks up, surprised to see Saskia Rawlins smiling at her. "What are you wearing to the fete?" The other girls are quiet. *"What yuh asking her for?"* Nadine mumbles to Saskia under her breath. The whole fifth form knows that Tru is the designated freak, with her short hair and boyish ways, yet Saskia Rawlins insists on smiling at Tru. Sometimes she does it in passing, lingering just a few steps behind her friends. They barely speak at all, aside from brief encounters in morning devotions when each class in the upper school is lined next to the others in the large auditorium, or in the locker room after Tru's class finishes PE and the net-ball team, which Saskia plays on, enters to gear up for after-school practice.

"I'm not going," Tru says, rising from the bench.

❧

T RU PREFERS TO WAIT UNTIL THE LOCKER ROOM CLEARS. SHE doesn't have to wait long, because as soon as she enters, the girls cover themselves with their towels or whatever they can find, their eyes sliding toward her, then down. They dress themselves in record speed, scurrying out of the locker room, giggling freely outside as if they have just narrowly escaped death. Once there's nothing but the sound of water dripping from the showerhead, Tru hurries up to change out of her uniform and into her soccer gear. She pulls a white polo shirt over her head. She examines herself in the long mirror to make sure there're no bumps on her chest. But she still sees them. No matter how tight she does the bandage, she never feels secure. For good measure, she lifts her T-shirt and undoes the bandage, slowly releasing her breath before she adjusts it once again. A light sheen of sweat breaks out on her forehead. She sucks air, grits her teeth, and pulls, bearing the slight pain. She starts to sweat in the heat and her breath pales as a sob compresses her lungs. It comes out as a gasp.

"Does it take you a while wid dat?"

Tru freezes at the sound of the voice. When she turns, Saskia Rawlins is standing behind her. She's already dressed in her net-ball gear—a white polo shirt with the school's name written on it, a short pleated blue skirt that shows her knobby kneecaps and long legs with a pair of shiny shinbones, and a pair of white sneakers that look extra white next to her brown skin.

"Yuh not flat-chested after all," she says to Tru, taking a few steps toward her.

"Why yuh not at practice?" Tru asks, suppressing her heavy breathing and quickly wiping away sweat and the tears of frustration that had fallen down her cheeks.

"I was late," Saskia says. "Coach bench me."

Tru knows that Saskia saw her. She waits for the questions written on Saskia's face. Up close, it resembles a rich dark brown cut of velvet. Tru looks away.

"So, is it true?" Saskia asks. "Girls are talking all ovah school."

"Dat is none of their business," Tru says too quickly.

"Dat's what I tell dem too," Saskia says.

Tru grabs her things. "I have to go."

"It's okay. I won't tell."

"What's there for you to tell?" Tru asks, slinging her book bag over one shoulder.

Saskia shrugs. "It looks painful."

"Not as painful as having breasts."

"I don't know 'bout you, but I like breasts."

"Good for you," Tru says.

"I meant to say—"

"I didn't take it any way," Tru says. She can't help but smile.

"Wow, I never expected to see dat," Saskia tells her.

"What?"

"You smiling. Yuh always so serious."

"There's not much to smile about."

"Dat's too bad."

The 3:25 freeze bell goes off outside—a call for abrupt silence on campus where all the students, teachers, and staff are expected to stop what they're doing for a full minute of reflection—a tradition adopted from their British founders. Tru is stuck here with Saskia in the quiet, which sweeps through the empty locker room. She struggles under the blanket of stillness, feeling herself falling into a rare spell of shyness, fidgeting beneath the merciless hand on the clock and Saskia's knowing gaze. This moment seems to last longer than a minute; longer, perhaps than anything Tru has ever endured in her whole life. When the bell rings again to end the freeze, Saskia is the first to speak. "Is someone coming for you afterwards?"

"No."

"Do you want to walk to di bus stop in Half-Way Tree?"

"You'd risk dat?"

"Risk what?"

"They might say you're tainted."

Saskia puts her hands on her narrow hips. "I dare them."

"Maybe another time," Tru says, smiling.

Saskia nods and bites her bottom lip as she digs inside her book bag and fishes a pen. "Here . . ." Opening Tru's palm, she scribbles a number in the middle. Tru's hand shakes a little. Saskia doesn't seem to notice. When she's done, she looks up at Tru. Before she says anything, her teammates enter the locker room and she discreetly lets go of Tru's hand. But her touch echoes all over Tru's skin. The girls' laughter and chatter fill the space. They greet Saskia, surrounding her with their babble about how unfair Coach was today. Tru uses the opportunity to slip out.

*

BY THE TIME TRU GETS TO THE PLAYING FIELD AFTER SCHOOL, Albino Ricky and Sore-Foot Marlon are in the middle of a game, playing with other boys Tru had grown up with in Pennyfield. They were playmates at Pennyfield Primary, running around with fake guns made of sticks and rubber bands as cowboys and Indians. Albino Ricky had the advantage as a cowboy, since he had access to real guns. Tru had access to real guns too, but was terrified of them. Roy never hides his guns. He keeps one in his sock drawer, one in the nightstand by his bed next to a King James Bible, and one he carries around for work, which he also sleeps with under his pillow. *"Yuh jus' neva know when a man need him gun."* Once Kenny took the gun from Roy's sock drawer to play a game of police and bad man. He pointed it at Ray-Ray, a snotty-nosed boy down the road. Luckily the gun was unloaded. Ray-Ray ran home to tell his mother, who told Marva. That night Roy beat Kenny so badly that he walked with a limp for days. *"Me not raising no bad man in dis house!"* Roy bellowed as he beat Kenny, who tried to tell him he was playing a policeman, like him. Most of the guns Albino Ricky carried around—even now—were new, and the barrels empty. He got them from his Cousin Bentley, who got the name because he was often spotted coming out of or going into a nice car. He's one of Pope's boys. Albino Ricky never talks about his role in hiding weapons for his cousin, and Tru and Sore-Foot Marlon know better than to question him.

Tru watches their graceful dance with the soccer ball. The ball seems so light, bobbing up and down on each boy's head, knees, and chest before they kick it. Though they're a small street team made up of ten, they play well, like a real team. There are boys on the sidelines dressed in their khaki school uniforms or regular clothes watching them and cheering. How joyous they look on this bald patch of land, sweat glistening on their brown faces, grinning from ear to ear with hands raised in the air. "Goaaaaaaaaaal!" they shout. There's a burst of hoots and hollers around her as the boys give each other high fives. Once again, their happy, carefree dance seems to exclude her.

"Whoa! Look who decide fi show up! Tru Juice!" Albino Ricky says as the group of boys clear out and it's just the teammates standing around, guzzling water from Igloos or wiping their faces with towel-size rags that they put over their heads. Sore-Foot Marlon and the other boys turn around as Tru approaches. She high-fives each of them. When she gets to Sore-Foot Marlon, he swiftly catches her hand and holds on to it. She doesn't pull her hand away. At least not immediately. She smiles at him, aware of the sun warming her flesh. Tru's nickname for Sore-Foot Marlon no longer suits him, since his once-malnourished body has developed into an athletic one with long, toned limbs that are no longer ridden with eczema and sores that ripped open with the stones she and Albino Ricky aimed at him when they were little. It's as if the sores of Marlon's childhood had swelled and burst and scabbed to reveal a smooth brown finish that has become a twinkle in every girl's eye.

"Pope was here earlier. Him was looking fah you," Sore-Foot Marlon says.

Tru looks at him, confused. "Pope? Why?"

Albino Ricky speaks up. "Ah told him yuh can play. Ah didn't mention you're a girl, though."

"Why would you do dat?"

"How yuh mean?" Albino Ricky asks, pulling another cigarette from out of his pocket. He sticks it in the side of his mouth to light it. His skin, like his hair, which is cut closely to his head, glows reddish in the sun. Albino Ricky gets a lot of girls too, because he's the closest thing to light-near-white they'll ever find in a place like Pennyfield. Plus, he's a Casanova, coolly blowing smoke from a Craven A every chance he gets. He continues to talk with smoke coming out of his mouth. "You're our best player, an' Pope want us to represent Pennyfield. Yuh t'ink ah was g'wan ruin it by telling him our forward is a girl? We could be di next stars of di east like Harbor View, Tivoli, an' dem places wid good players."

Tru is shaking her head, unable to believe what she's hearing, unable to believe he would do such a thing without her permission. "But ah don't live in Pennyfield anymore."

"You're still one of us," Albino Ricky replies. His tawny eyebrows, as fine as corn silk on his freckled face, are drawn; and his dark eyes that seem to burn away his lashes are locked with Tru's.

"Pope believe dat we can win a trophy fah Pennyfield," Albino Ricky is saying. "We can give we community a good name. Plus, we need di money."

"Money?" Tru asks. "How much?"

"Twenty-five thousand in cash," Albino Ricky says. "American dollahs. Not no so-suh Jamaican money."

Tru glances at Sore-Foot Marlon, who doesn't seem troubled by what Albino Ricky is saying. "Pope's money, or ours?" she asks.

"Ours!" Albino Ricky says. "All twenty-five thousand of it!"

"So, yuh in or what?" Asafa, the squat, soft-spoken goalie, who has been watching and listening the whole time, asks Tru. Asafa is not one to make small talk, so when he speaks, people pay attention. Tru never liked him. Sore-Foot Marlon and Albino Ricky invited him one day to play soccer since he goes to Roman Phillips with them, and he stuck around. Tru only speaks to him when she has to, like to tell him to pass the ball. She can't answer his question now. She knows that her father would kill her if he finds out that she's playing for Pope.

Pope is a constant but unobtrusive presence in Pennyfield, as quiet as he is dangerous. Although people in Pennyfield know he's capable of doing crazy things, they're mostly grateful that he does good by them and that he only uses his power to bend the laws in their favor. Because of him, little children go to school and eat regular meals. Pope hands out rice, flour, cornmeal, and canned food every Tuesday. No one knows for sure where he gets it from and how he gets it. There are many rumors about the trinity brothers and how they run their business. Rumor has it that Pope owns cargo at the wharf, and that his brothers Bishop and Cardinal are big drug lords in America. But that's all it seems to be, rumor. Tru is almost certain that Pennyfield residents like Miss Richardson and Miss Belnavis—Mama G's church sisters—wouldn't line up on Tuesdays at the modest seaweed-green house on Cherry Lane to receive their loaves of bread and staple goods if the man was a deadly crook. On those days, Pope's posse take breaks from playing dominoes, smoking ganja, or tilting their heads back to throw rum over their tongues at Pete's Bar, to help out with the distribution of food. Meanwhile, behind those lighted windows inside the green house, Pope sits hidden, watchful, maybe even pleased.

So what exactly does Roy have a problem with? Tru wonders now. It's the police who give Pope the final label—badman. They are the ones who say he's guilty of some unforgivable thing. *But what?* Illegally exporting marijuana, which happens to be the country's natural and most lucrative resource? Wouldn't that make the poor farmers wealthy? And wouldn't that help pay off the country's massive debt? Tru tried asking Roy once and he just told her: *"Mek sure yuh stay far away from dat man."*

When Tru doesn't respond right away to her teammate, Asafa gives the final verdict. "Ah know she was g'wan be a wuss 'bout it."

"Wait," Tru says. "Yuh didn't give me any time to think. You know my father wouldn't—"

"Maybe she can sit dis one out, Ricky," Sore-Foot Marlon says in Tru's defense. "I know Chief. Him won't agree wid dis. Maybe it was a bad idea . . ."

"Suh is now yuh t'ink to say dat, my yute?" Albino Ricky asks, his voice sparked by anger. He drops the remaining cigarette butt on the ground and crushes it with one foot. "Why yuh neva bring dat up when Pope was here?"

"Yo!" Asafa shouts, jumping in. "We can always get s'maddy else who can play forward."

"But Tru is di best forward we 'ave! She play bettah than all ah oonuh combine," Albino Ricky says. He turns to Tru. "Tru, we need you. Yuh acting like yuh don't want people like Pope to tek notice ah yuh skills. Or like yuh don't want di money. Is not everybody 'ave ah mother who can sen' dem money from foreign."

"You know dat's not true," she says in a low hiss.

"Maybe yuh jus' telling us dat," Albino Ricky says.

The other boys look Tru up and down with steady eyes. Tru knows that they're thinking the same thing; they don't have to say anything. She glances at Sore-Foot Marlon, who is also unable to meet her gaze. Albino Ricky continues, "Do it fah all ah we," he says.

"Oonuh pussy-whip to rhaatid." Asafa sucks his teeth and whispers this under his breath as he toys with one of the dreadlock twists on his head. "Is a whole heap ah money we playing fah. Yuh t'ink ah g'wan mek har ruin it fah us? Why we need har? She's jus' a girl anyway."

"Say dat again an' yuh see who pussy-whip!" Tru says, her fists clenched.

"Cool it," Sore-Foot Marlon says to her, touching her lightly on the arm. "Him nuh worth yuh energy."

"Fine," Tru says, pulling away from Sore-Foot Marlon's touch. She walks away from the group and Sore-Foot Marlon follows behind her. "Tru . . ."

"Leave me alone."

"Jus' wait a likkle!" He catches up with her and she increases her pace, walking farther into Pennyfield toward her grandmother's house as opposed to home in Rochester. She's not in the mood to deal with Marva and Kenny's silent malice.

"Ricky mean no harm. Yuh know dat."

"Dat's your best friend, not mine. Not anymore."

"Tru." Sore-Foot Marlon holds on to her hand and slows her down until she stops. His face confesses his mild annoyance, though his light brown eyes appear to be where the last of the sunlight went. "Jus' calm down," he says. "It'll be all right."

"You talkin' like yuh don't know who my father is," she says.

"Look, yuh don't have to do what yuh don't want to do," he says.

"You also didn't correct dem," Tru says.

"Correct dem 'bout what?"

"My mother sending me t'ings."

"Because it's not my place."

Sore-Foot Marlon drops his head and digs into his faded blue Jansport book bag slung over his shoulder and fishes out a box. "Before I forget . . ." He slips something poorly wrapped in brown paper into Tru's hand. Tru takes it. "What's dis?"

"Happy belated birthday," he says.

She opens the box and pulls out a mix CD with various dancehall artists. She tries to hide her surprise. "You didn't have to . . ."

"I wanted to." He's massaging the back of his neck and looking over his shoulder. "I know how much yuh like these."

"Ah don't know what else to say."

"Thought ah could be original," he says, showing a flash of white teeth.

"Does Genevieve Sinclair fall fah dat?" she asks him with a smirk.

Sore-Foot Marlon tugs at his left earlobe. "Jus' accept di gift."

Sore-Foot Marlon and Genevieve aren't really an item, but he likes to woo her with gifts. They met when he was at Wilhampton Boys'—before he had to drop out when his scholarship ran out and his mother, a street haggler, could no longer afford it. But he acknowledges that a girl like Genevieve Sinclair, with her own driver, is out of his league. He'd need way more than the little lunch money he gets, which can only buy a beef patty and a cocoa-bread at Tastees.

"Ah coulda bought myself a CD," Tru jokes.

"Really, Tru Juice? Yuh know how much trouble Uncle Charles had to guh through fi burn it?"

"Dis is tacky." She laughs, though flattered. His Uncle Charles is the most popular deejay in Pennyfield. He goes by the name Sir Charles and wears a patch over one eye like a pirate. He barely looks up as he mutely spins old and new hits every Saturday night after Miss Maxine's cock-fights. Albino Ricky told Tru that he heard the patch might be a disguise since it is rumored that Sir Charles once killed a man in his hometown in Montego Bay in a dispute over a woman, and is still a fugitive, now protected by Pope. Every youth in Pennyfield who dreams of becoming dancehall artists begs him to play their demos at dances.

She looks down at her palm and closes it, Saskia Rawlins's number, still hot, in her fist. "Thank you," Tru says to Sore-Foot Marlon.

She puts the CD into her frayed book bag with its spoiled zipper, still agitated.

"It still doesn't make sense."

"What?"

"Why after all these years Ricky would attack me like dat about my mother."

"Does it mattah?" Sore-Foot Marlon asks with a shrug. "If yuh know it's not true, then don't let it bother you."

"I guess," Tru says, lowering her head.

She thinks of her father; how he too seems frustrated, yet oddly protective of her mother. Even in his arguments with Marva over the cost of sending Tru to Wilhampton, which was her mother's dream for her. A fierce surge of purpose wells in her. She knows suddenly that she is responsible for carrying half the financial responsibility. Twenty-five thousand U.S. dollars seems attractive now. The fear that gripped Tru earlier releases her into the optimism of her burgeoning plan. "I'm in," she says.

"What's dat?" Sore-Foot Marlon asks, giving her a quizzical look, his eyebrows arched.

"I said I'm in," she repeats.

A slow smile spreads across Sore-Foot Marlon's face. This sudden transformation, revealing some kind of relief (or disbelief), makes his face terribly affecting in this moment.

"Now, dat's tacky," Tru says.

"What?"

"Dat smile."

He waves her off. She jogs a little to catch up with him and pushes him lightly. "You know yuh heard me." In response, he puts an arm around her shoulder and they continue their walk like that across the dusty gully toward St. George Furnace.

A group of men by Pete's bar pause their drinking and chatting as Tru and Sore-Foot Marlon pass them by. They see two teenagers— boys—walking with their arms around each other. Callused hands clasp around rum bottles, knuckles cracking, appearing to press through blackened skin. The quiet that falls over the men stirs like a malicious wind. "*Wha dem batty bwoy a do 'bout yah?*" When the boys draw closer, the men's shoulders go up. But realization brings the shoulders back down like the Walls of Jericho when the men see that one of the boys is really Mama G's granddaughter and the other one is Miss Olive's eldest boy from Garrick's Lane. The men nod their greetings to the teenagers, swiftly hiding blades of wrath under their tongues to mumble pleasantries. But the hum of their questioning resumes, about the girl—her manner, her clothes. They rub their flies, the taste of salt at the back of their throats. Every one of the faces of the men turns to look at her.

Tru and Sore-Foot Marlon walk on, unbothered. They laugh out loud, the laughter following them on their walk home together, passing Ras Norbert smiling up at the final bow of the setting sun, thick and red-orange at the bottom of the sky, which casts their shadows stretched to infinity.

36

THE FOUR-FOOT-TALL CYLINDRICAL BLUE BARRELS LINE THE Church Avenue sidewalk in front of a place called Little Jamaica— not too far from where Patsy lives. It's a small place that is crowded with Jamaicans, waiting to send things home to relatives. They wait impatiently in the long lines. More urgent than the need to get to their American jobs on time or run errands is their one opportunity for the month, maybe for a whole year, to stuff all their love into barrels. Patsy decides to go with a barrel because of its size—it's more efficient and economical to ship a vast number of items. She remembers watching people back home receive barrels from relatives abroad, lanced with envy since it looked like they could open up their own store.

Despite the fact that the space is small and stuffy and smells like cheese, Patsy has gone in there a few times and waited in line before getting cold feet and leaving. Truth be told, nothing she sends for Tru will ever be enough. However, after she heard Barrington's voice speak to her inside her room, she stood up frightened, afraid that she had let too much time pass by. She decided she cannot go on forever feeling sorry for herself and making Tru pay for it.

She also stands in line for selfish reasons, mostly for the interaction with other Jamaicans—Jamaicans who remind her of the ones she knew back home. She feeds off this experience, feels refreshed by it. Most times she goes for weeks, sometimes months without it, feeling alone, displaced among the crowded streets and tall buildings. Since Fionna moved away, she hasn't had much opportunity outside of work to talk to people, so she actively searches for these interactions—park benches where she sees the women pushing white babies, Golden Krust restaurants where the men in hard hats, orange vests, and Timberland boots stuff their faces with boiled yams, callaloo, and cornmeal porridge for a long day's work constructing buildings they can never afford to live in. She also seeks these interactions in the Chinney grocery stores along Flatbush Avenue where she buys goods she misses from home; or at the market on Caton where she buys creams. And here, now, in Little Jamaica, where Patsy stands and waits in line, willing herself once more to buy a barrel.

"Good morning," Patsy says to the voluptuous woman behind the counter, who has a deep bronze color and reddish brown dreadlocks that touch her shoulders. Over the last few weeks that Patsy has been coming, she's never made it to the front of the line.

"Did you jus' say morning?" the woman asks Patsy, putting her hands on her wide hips. There's a twinkle of mischief in her large expressive eyes as she waits on Patsy to acknowledge her error. "Oh!" she says, slightly embarrassed. "I mean aftah-noon."

"Late aftah-noon," the woman corrects, pursing her lips together. "Somebody's been partying all night long, ah see."

Patsy has always noticed this clerk's jovial personality and suspects that people like coming to Little Jamaica during her shift, because not only does she make pleasant small talk, but she also makes every customer feel special—women walk away feeling like they had just met up with a longtime friend, and men walk away feeling they could conquer the world. She makes no demands for people to form neat lines. Neither does she hurry them along or let anyone feel small for not having the right change or being short a penny or two. This is probably why Little Jamaica gets the largest crowd during her shift.

She smiles at Patsy as if she's already familiar with her. Her name tag says CLAUDETTE. Patsy notices the can of Red Bull next to Claudette and says, "You might be talking 'bout yuhself wid dat drink. Yuh know how much caffeine in dat t'ing?"

"It's di only way ah know how to function," Claudette says, shaking her head.

"You know bettah than dat," Patsy says, smiling, surprising herself with the easy familiarity she already feels with Claudette.

"Why yuh assume dat?" Claudette asks with a smirk.

Patsy shrugs. "You strike me as one of those naturalist sistrens. A Rasta woman."

Claudette laughs. "Don't let di dreadlocks fool you."

"They're nice," Patsy says, admiring Claudette's long, neatly twisted dreadlocks, and suddenly feeling old and tired at thirty-eight with a bad wig.

"Thank you. By the way, I was jus' joking with you earlier." Claudette smiles, her dimples pronounced like Patsy's. That's what they have in common so far, dimples, Patsy thinks. She remembers the boys she used to allow to lift her skirt behind the church or school building as a girl. How it was their individual idiosyncrasies that she found endearing—a scar, a mold, a birthmark, an extra finger, a pimple. None except a boy named Paul had dimples. She sneaks a glance at Claudette's deepening ones, wondering what else they have in common.

"It happens all di time," Claudette is saying, shaking her head of locs. Patsy's gaze moves to her lips. "People tell me all sorta t'ings—mawnin', evening, night. Some ah dem all seh happy Monday! Dat's when me panic. T''ink seh is me wake up 'pon di wrong side ah time. You know how much trouble I would be in if it was really Monday mawnin' an' I'm not at dat godforsaken job of mine at dat nursery home? Dog woulda nyam me supper."

Patsy throws her head back and laughs. She hasn't laughed like this in a good while.

"So, what can I do for you today?" Claudette asks.

"I'd like to buy one ah those." Patsy points outside to the large seventy-seven-gallon cylindrical barrels on the sidewalk. She wonders how she'd bring one home without a ride, and where it would fit inside her small room.

"Dat will be fifty dollars," Claudette says.

Patsy hesitates.

"What is it?" Claudette asks.

"Do you know when it would get there? To Jamaica, I mean . . ."

Claudette shrugs. "It depends on how fast you can fill it wid items an' get it back to us. Normally it takes 'bout two weeks. But Christmas is di worse. Have you started buying t'ings to put in di barrel?"

"No. I've been saving up."

"Yuh might want to start buying t'ings. Dat's what a lot of people do. Dey buy stuff likkle by likkle to fill up the barrel ovah a period of . . ." She pauses. "A year?"

"A year?"

"Well, at least six months."

"I—I don't know . . ."

"Don't worry. Tek yuh time. Yuh don't have to rush," Claudette says as if she read Patsy's mind. There's something sweet and soft in Claudette's eyes.

"It's my first time . . ," Patsy confesses.

"There's always a first time fah everyt'ing."

Before Patsy hands over the money for the barrel—it can't hurt to get one—the FedEx man arrives. Claudette waves a handful of cash at him. "Wh'appen, Dexter? Sadiq in di back," she says, then yells for Sadiq to assist the man as she takes care of Patsy and her change. When Sadiq doesn't respond, she cusses him under her breath and tells Patsy to wait a minute. Dexter makes no move to help her while she bends to lift a crate of packages to give to him. He simply stands there, rubbing the dark hairs under his chin as he checks out her backside bent over in her tight jeans. Her shirt lifts a little, revealing the chains of colorful glass beads that snake around the brown flesh of her waist.

Dexter gives her a toothy, lopsided grin as he takes the crate. Claudette sees the look and gives him a talking eye. "Yuh don't got no time to stand dere grinning like a jackass," she says. "Yuh got deliveries to make."

"Ah can tek time off jus' fah you," he says.

"Yuh jus' got yuh job six months ago. Yuh bettah work to keep it."

She fans him off playfully and he blows her a kiss.

"Jamaican men t'ink dem is God's gift to women," Claudette says to Patsy, shaking her head and smiling, marking off something in a notebook she uses to keep track of pickup and deliveries. "I'd guh wid a woman before me date another Jamaican man. Dem is crosses." Before Patsy can say anything to that, Claudette asks, "Do you have a ride fah dat barrel?"

Patsy's face flushes hot. She has waited seconds too long to respond to what seems like a perfectly normal question, her eyes fastened on Claudette's wide mouth.

"Uh—uhm—no. I was going to take a taxi."

"Where yuh live?"

"Albany an' Church."

"Oh! Not too far. Why would you spend eight dollahs just to go down di road? Ah can lend you a hand trolley if yuh promise me you'll be back wid it."

Patsy smiles. "You don't have to do all dat," she says to Claudette. "Really . . ." But Claudette is undeterred by Patsy's mild protest, carefully wheeling the large red trolley around the counter. "There's a few more ah dese in di back, so it's not an inconvenience at all." She is gentle and attentive as if no one else is in the store besides the two of them.

"Thank you," Patsy says when she's done.

"No problem," Claudette replies.

Patsy waits for her change, not knowing how to politely remind Claudette that she hasn't given it back to her, and wanting to remain in this warm exchange between them.

"I'm losing my mind," Claudette says after a while, hitting her forehead with her open palm. "Ah forgot to give you back yuh change." She reopens the cash register.

"No worries," Patsy tells her. She catches a flash of Claudette's tongue as she licks her thumb to count the money. Patsy looks away as if she's witnessed a private act. She gives a nervous laugh, unsure how to behave in the face of such kindness and patience. "Dese people g'wan kill me." Her voice is light, playful, to camouflage her discomfort. Already she hears the searing sound of air drawn sharply between the molars of the screwed-faced Jamaicans in the line behind her. "*Hurry up, man!*" The sucking of teeth only gets louder. "*Yuh nuh see seh people 'ave places fi go an' t'ings fi do? Cho, man!*"

Their hands touch briefly when Claudette gives Patsy her change. Patsy fumbles with putting it inside her purse. She doesn't bother to count it. *When did she become the type of person who doesn't think about numbers?* Claudette puts an empty barrel on the trolley and Patsy pushes it outside, maneuvering between the queue of visibly annoyed people inside the store, who are glaring at her with their arms folded across their chests.

"Walk good an' come back soon!" Claudette calls after her.

Patsy lives to hear those words.

37

ROY'S GRAND ENTRANCE THAT EVENING LIGHTENS THE MOOD inside the house as if light has been switched on after a long power outage. With a loud, booming voice he announces his presence—something that hasn't happened in a long time. "Evening, evening!" His jubilant tone is followed by Marva's probing questions. "Where yuh been all night? While yuh out dere gallivanting in di streets, me deh here min'ing yuh children!"

"Jus' ease off me, woman. Me not even step foot good through di door yet. 'Low me, mek me show yuh where ah been."

Tru has taught herself not to listen to or get involved in Marva and Roy's quarrels, so she stays inside her room and listens to music on her headphones. But something is different in the quarreling tone tonight between Roy and Marva. There's laughter in her father's voice when he says, "I got somet'ing nice fah you an' di twins." Tru overhears Marva's sharp gasp followed by a, "Lawd Jesus, Roy! How yuh afford all ah dat?"

Marva's outburst moves Tru to the door. She peers out of her bedroom through the beaded curtain that partitions the living room from the hallway. Her father is standing in the living room, looking resplendent in his decorated sergeant's uniform and black peaked cap—a stark difference from the man who was slumped at the table drinking liquor a week ago. He's holding a bassinet that can fit two babies. The bassinet still has the flashy Courts furniture store tag on it. At his feet are big bags marked *Little Lees.* "Look, look inside them!" he tells Marva. Like a child on Christmas morning, Marva digs inside one of the bags, and when she sees what's inside, she drops it and covers her mouth with both hands.

"Is wha 'appen to you?" Roy asks, smiling.

"Roy—"

"An' there's lots more where dat came from. Dis is jus' a taste of what g'wan happen when me get promoted to inspector!"

"Did you?" Marva asks. "Dem finally promote you?"

"Not yet, but it g'wan happen soon. Operation Kingfish will do it."

"Operation who?"

"Our superintendent jus' tell us 'bout Operation Kingfish. Is di biggest crime unit evah."

"Dey took you off di narcotics team?"

"Yuh nuh hear one t'ing me say, woman? Kingfish is di biggest crime-busting team in di whole country! Even di FBI an' CIA involve. It g'wan be big. Dese criminals who t'ink dem badder than we g'wan get a taste ah dem own medicine. Hear me? It's di right case dat will show Sergeant Beckford as a force to contend wid." He's gloating as he says this. "Right now me want you to feel like a queen. Open up di gift dem nuh," he coaxes. When she hesitates, shy all of a sudden, he says, "All right, let me." He pulls out gift after gift—baby clothes and toys and Pampers. So many baby things that it looks to Tru like he raided the store. Marva stands next to him, gasping at each gift he pulls out. "But jeezum! Wha' wrong wid dis man, eh?" She asks this of no one in particular, her voice filled with affection and laughter.

"If yuh g'wan have twins we haffi prepare, nuh true?" Roy winks at her. "You say ah neva do anyt'ing fah you." He brings her close, and she doesn't resist him as she often does. She allows herself to be teased and pinched playfully. She rubs her belly like someone who has just eaten a big meal and is now very satisfied, her eyes shrouded. It softens her plump face. They stop their teasing when they notice Tru.

Roy smiles uneasily. "Wh'appen, Champ? Here, ah have somet'ing fah you too." He picks up one of the bags and hands it to her.

Tru takes the bag and looks inside. She pulls out a World Cup jersey with all the countries' flags on it, which sits on top of a shoe box. Inside the box is a brand-new pair of Puma sneakers with spikes. It's her turn to gasp and cup her mouth with a hand.

"Only she one yuh have gifts for? Yuh act like she's yuh only child. We have a son here dat neva get one penny from yuh." Marva gestures toward Kenny, who is standing just a few steps behind Tru. Tru lowers the bag.

"Marva, why yuh g'wan be like dat?" Roy asks, frowning. "It was di likkle girl birthday last week."

"Likkle girl?" Marva laughs. "Which part di girl deh? Tell me! All me see is a boy, a young man, a—"

"Marva—" Roy holds up his hand—the one with the scar—and Marva backs down.

"Here," Tru says to her father, looking down. "Take it back. She's right. I—I don't need it."

Truth is, she had seen these shoes on display at the mall. Had been saving up money so that she could buy them.

"It's a special gift for you," Her father says with a wink. "Yuh t'ink me did forget about yuh birthday, don't?" he asks her.

Tru says nothing. She knew he had forgotten her birthday a few weeks ago and is now overcompensating. She's too embarrassed to admit that now, as she meets his apologetic gaze. Marva sucks her teeth loudly, the sharp sound deflating the mood. "An' what about yuh son? Where is fi him gift? His birthday was last month."

"Jesus Christ, woman!" Roy digs deeply inside his pocket, crumples a few bills, and flings them in Kenny's direction like rocks. "Here, tek dis! Tek everyt'ing! Dat's five hundred dollahs right dere. Guh buy some backbone wid it." Then to Marva he says, "Yuh happy now?" Kenny doesn't move from the shadows to take the money. Tru swallows, unable to look at Kenny.

"Roy, is where yuh get all dis money from?" Marva asks.

"Don't worry 'bout dat," he replies.

"Jus' be honest. Dey don't pay sergeants dis much."

"Well, if yuh mus' know, ah throw partner an' got my draw."

"Partner? How many times ah tell yuh not to pool yuh money wid those crooks Johnny and Raymond?"

"Cool it, Marva. I'm in good standing wid all ah dem. Today was a good day."

"Nothing good ever come out ah gambling."

"Is not gambling, Marva."

"What yuh call placing bets 'pon horses then throwing yuh money? I know what a partner is, Roy. Gambling 'pon horses is not it. You is no bettah than those ghetto youth yuh complain 'bout all di time, who bet 'pon cockfight t'inking it g'wan solve dem woes."

Roy sucks his teeth. "Did I evah mek yuh starve?"

"Dat's not di point, Roy."

"If you so concern where di money coming from, then gimme back di gift dem. I try to tell yuh dat di money is mine when ah win it."

"How much yuh had to put in?"

He doesn't answer. He takes off his hat and rubs one hand over his closely shaved head.

"Roy?"

"A couple hundred U.S."

"Have mercy!"

"What yuh mean have mercy? I won, didn't I?" He turns to Tru. "Is wha' do har? She nuh see most ah di money right here? Di rest went to all di bills. Who yuh t'ink pay those?"

Marva puts her hands on her head. "Is not about winning," she says through her teeth. "Yuh don't get it! What if yuh evah lose? Dat coulda been money down di drain!"

"Yuh evah see me lose? Listen to how yuh talk. Everyt'ing is about what coulda happen. Yuh soun' like one ah dem negative people who can't celebrate nuttin' good. No mattah what ah do, to you it's still short of murder."

"Dis is murder, Roy. Dis is we life savings, bills, di children tuition, an' everyt'ing if yuh don't pull out now—" She shakes her head. A streak of malice flashes in her eyes. "An' what kinda man you is, gambling an' taking money dat don't belongst to you? You should be ashamed, shoving it in yuh pocket like you is a damn gigolo!"

He steps back. A dark shadow falls across his face, transforming it into something cruel. But just as quickly it disappears, remnants of it settling into the dark pits of his pupils. "Ah done arguing. What is done is done. Ah tek care of what needed to be taken care of. Wid me own money. Yuh either accept di gift dem or ah tek dem back to di store."

"Tek dem back. Every single one ah dem."

After a long pause, he puts his hat back on and grabs up the bags. "Fine."

Tru's eyes move in a swift arc from Roy to Marva.

"Ah taking all di gifts an' giving dem to someone who deserve dem."

"Someone like who?" Marva asks, her voice low, cautious, as though skirting along a dangerous edge.

"Nuttin' yuh don't already know," Roy replies.

She comes close and lifts her face to his in a beautiful pose as if she's about to kiss him. It's not hard for Tru to picture them in the privacy of their room, crouched in positions of love—his rough hands closed around her, his face to her breasts, her moans accompanying the fierce shake of her head. She reaches for him, a tremor passing from her hand to his face, the loud slap bursting like fireworks inside the dim space. Her passion breaks with every hit of her fists against his chest as though begging him for something, perhaps a reaction—something that would assuage the rage deep inside her. Remorse flits across his face and finally he pulls her to him and holds her. She fights him off. Between clenched teeth, she cries, "You's nuttin' but a worthless piece ah shit parading in a man's uniform. You is a lowdown dirty dawg!" Marva spits. "How yuh g'wan do dat to me again? How yuh g'wan have another pickney on di way same time? Yuh is a terrible man! You!"

He turns his back to her and picks up each bag. Tru holds on to her gift, afraid he might take it back too. Something cold runs through her veins as she watches her father empty the living room of its light. Kenny peels himself away from the shadows and walks over to his mother, his long, skinny frame almost invisible next to her big, heaving one. "G'long!" Marva shouts to Roy's back. Then she murmurs at the sound of Roy's car engine revving up. "See if I care 'bout who yuh have out dere. She can have you, an' all di long-mouth pickney dem fi feed, 'cause me done!"

"Is okay, Mama," Kenny says, holding his mother, a darkness shading his face. He appears years older all of a sudden, something fierce creeping into his attitude. No longer is he a boy submitting to his mother's rage and his father's condescension, but a man standing next to his mother, holding her up.

"Oh, God. . . . how! How can a man be suh coldhearted?" Marva cries.

"He doesn't mean it," Kenny says quietly.

But Marva only shakes her head. She stares down at the tiles as if she sees something vile slithering across them. She looks so vulnerable standing there in her floral dress. Her lifeless eyes scan the room. "What a man live by g'wan kill him," she says. "Mark my word."

Kenny takes her to her bedroom as she continues to murmur to herself. The bedroom door closes and Marva's cries are subdued into hollow whimpers. Tru gazes around the living room, the quiet unnerving. She stands in the same place she's been standing since the exchange between her father and Marva. She strokes the sneakers—the rubber soles, the sturdy spikes, the asymmetrical green laces—knowing they will never give her the comfort she needs.

38

THE LARGE CYLINDRICAL BARREL NOW STANDS FIRMLY IN ONE corner of her room, a checkpoint, a mooring, a visual that reminds Patsy that she did, in fact, make a decision to buy one. She never enters or leaves the room without looking at the barrel. Even when she's standing next to the barrel, it always feels to her as though she's looking up at it.

Still, she has nothing to put inside it, so she waits, going to work each day, then coming back home. She closes her eyes to erase the image of the homeless woman, and of Barrington leaping in front of the train, and of the dark waiting thing just above her left shoulder, unmoved.

She finally gets the chance to bring the trolley back to Claudette the following week . Last thing she wants is for Claudette to think that she stole it. Little Jamaica is packed as usual. Patsy makes it just before closing; she is the last one in line. When she gets to the front, Claudette says, "Finally!" She gives Patsy a welcoming smile as Patsy rolls the trolley toward her. "So, you waited forty-five minutes in line jus' to drop off dis degeh-degeh trolley?" Claudette asks jokingly.

Patsy laughs. "Pretty much."

She wants to say to Claudette that seeing her breaks the monotony of loneliness. How her voice, like molasses, soothes her with a simple greeting. Never, not since Barrington looked at her with his tender, forgiving gaze, has anyone in this country made her feel seen. Really seen beyond her role as caretaker, soother, mother.

"Ah don't mind . . ." Claudette is saying. "Good company is good company. Time fly quicker dat way."

Patsy quietly agrees.

"Is there anyt'ing else dat I can do for you?" Claudette asks.

The other Patsy—the one who would have abruptly turned and walk away, expecting to be swallowed inside a cave of doom—must have kept walking. For this Patsy stays and acts on her instincts. *"How is it fate if yuh have control ovah it?"*

"Do you want to go out somewhere? Maybe get food or somet'ing to drink?"

Claudette smiles. "Sure. Ah have to lock up first, though, if yuh don't mind waiting."

Patsy suppresses a sigh of relief. "No problem a'tall."

When Claudette is ready, they walk several blocks toward Avenue K and East Flatbush to a restaurant named Sammuel's Den. Claudette swears by the food and says it's owned by a cousin of hers. It literally looks like a lion's den, with lions in various states of repose painted on the green walls. A framed picture of a smiling President Barak Obama is mounted on the wall near the door. A yellow, green, and red Rastafarian flag hangs by the hostess stand. There's no one inside the restaurant besides the two cooks dressed in all white, sipping water around one of the back tables. Patsy and Claudette find a table and sit. A young Rasta man with a full beard and locs neatly twisted in a bun comes out to greet them from the kitchen. He looks like he could be Claudette's brother, but she introduces him as Sammuel, her baby cousin.

"Ah knew him since him was dis big," she says, lowering herself so that her palm almost touches the floor. It's hard for Patsy to imagine Sammuel, who is well over six feet tall and built like one of those American football players, as a tiny baby crawling on the ground.

"Ah g'wan mek sure seh oonuh well taken care of," Sammuel says, smiling, before he disappears into the kitchen. Soon after he's out of earshot, Patsy asks, "Did he play ball?"

"Yes! He was a linebacker at Hofstra before him hurt himself. Yuh into football?"

"Not American football. Jamaican football. Or ah should say 'soccer,' as di Americans call it."

"Look at you! So you were one ah those Reggae Boyz fanatics?"

"No. My . . ." Patsy's voice trails.

A waiter appears out of nowhere and pours Claudette and Patsy water and hands them a menu. Patsy is grateful for his presence. He takes his time telling them about the special, which is a vegetarian oxtail stew made of fake meat. Patsy wonders what's the use of people being vegetarian if they still have to eat fake meat to feel satisfied. Doesn't it defeat the purpose? She orders the fake oxtail anyway, since it's the only thing that makes sense on the menu. She quietly laments the fact that it seems virtually impossible to get a good plate of real oxtail stew in America. Claudette orders Sammuel's vegan Ital special that includes stir-fried edamame noodles, roasted asparagus, broccoli, almonds, and some type of leaf Patsy doesn't bother to ask about.

"I was right about you," Patsy jokes after the waiter leaves.

"How so?"

"You being vegetarian."

Claudette laughs out loud. "I plead di fifth."

"Hm."

"I cheat sometimes."

"Really."

"Shh . . . don't tell anyone."

Patsy laughs. "Don't worry. Yuh secret safe wid me."

Easily, they slip into conversation about Jamaica and homesickness and the crosses employers they work for here in America, and the obligation to send things back home to family. Patsy learns that Claudette has no children of her own, but helps to raise her sister's two children, a boy and a girl. "We're a tight-knit family," she says, playing with the rim of her water glass. "Dey love me—those two. Ah visit dem in New Jersey every chance ah get. Ah was hoping to see dem on Thanksgiving dis coming week, but dey going to my brother-in-law's family in Atlanta. Ah try to get my sister to move to Brooklyn, but she like it bettah over there. Plus, Jersey have bettah public schools."

"How old are di children?" Patsy asks.

"Di boy is eleven. Di girl is nine," Claudette says.

"Nice," Patsy replies.

"What about you?" Claudette asks. "Do you have children?"

Patsy dabs the sides of her mouth with a napkin. Silence falls across the table as Claudette awaits a response. Two men clad in heavy black coats walk into the restaurant and wait to be seated. Patsy moves around her water glass. "Ah have a dawta," she finally says.

"How old?"

"Sixteen."

"Is she di one yuh sending di barrel for?"

Patsy nods.

"We ship an average of one hundred and forty barrels a day. Most of dem parents shipping to children back home."

"Dat's a lot . . ."

"Who yuh telling?" Claudette laughs. "Keeps me employed."

"Do you get a lot of mothers?"

"Yes."

"Hm."

"Have you started filling up di barrel you bought?"

"Ah wish ah knew how . . ."

"Like ah said, it takes time. Sixteen is a tough age. It's when hormones start churning. My mind tell me dat yuh dawta might like makeup. Now dat she might have a likkle boyfriend. Teenagers are funny. Di more yuh shelter dem, di worse dey rebel. My poor mother didn't know what to do wid me an' my sistah at dat age. Dat woman had enough strength fah two men. Bent us in shape real quick, though."

The thought of Tru as a teenager singes Patsy in a way she hasn't prepared for: daunted by the inevitable—the gate of adulthood being opened; the stealthy but sure footsteps of infatuation; the stillness of deception under the cover of night; an uprooting of something dormant and precious, primed for devouring. Patsy closes that gate behind her and secures the bolt. "Is yuh mother still in Jamaica?" she asks Claudette.

"No. She's here now. She lives wid my sistah in Jersey."

"Does she stay wid you too?"

"No. I live by myself." Claudette shrugs. She stares down at the table in front of her. "I guess my sistah is di lucky one. Married, wid children. Her husband is American." Claudette laughs and Patsy laughs with her, for the sake of easing the sadness. "My mother treats my baby sistah like she's di eldest. She get more respec' as a married woman an' a mother. Plus, she was di one who filed fah my mother. Me? I'm still dat likkle girl my mother pester about marriage an' babies. Mind you, I'm forty." Claudette laughs a little again—Patsy realizes that it's a habit of hers, to deflect. Claudette's eyes hold in them a distant look. But the mood evaporates with a quickness that makes Patsy blink. "I like di peace an' quiet, anyway. And I'm hardly home." Claudette shifts her weight on her chair. "Between di senior home an' Likkle Jamaica, I'm always gone. You, on the other hand, seem like a homebody."

"Ah thought ah struck you as a party animal." Patsy laughs. "Isn't dat what yuh said when we first met?"

"You will neva let me off di hook wid dat." Claudette glances down at the table again and smiles, her dimples a chasm where Patsy's lust stirs. "Yuh seem like an interesting person I'd like to get to know."

"Di feeling is mutual," Patsy replies. She immediately regrets that she has to be at work tomorrow. Regina had intended to leave home for a cabin deep in the woods, with no cell phone reception, to finish her book. But when Baby's grandmother couldn't come, the plans fell through. "Thanks fah agreeing to dis," Patsy says to Claudette.

"No need to thank me." Claudette is still looking down at the table as if she cannot think of anything else to say. "I'm free most Saturday nights. In case yuh evah want to do somet'ing . . . maybe even stop by my house. God knows ah love Sammuel's food, an' ah might have been raised vegetarian, but no one can cook oxtail bettah than me."

39

THEY MEET AROUND THE CORNER AFTER SCHOOL, NOT FAR FROM the school gate. Tru skipped out on last period to change out of her uniform into comfortable clothes—her new Puma sneakers and Nike tracksuit—black with white stripes down the legs—before the sixth-form prefects noticed. Not that she's afraid of these sixth-form prefects—girls like Kimesha Gregory and Althea Phaliso, who don't care that Tru and them started first form together. Now they turn their noses up at her. Last time they caught her out of her uniform, they wrote her up for a demerit. The tracksuit was her father's, but it shrank to her size when Marva put it in the dryer, which Roy bought from Courts last Christmas. Marva stopped asking him how he gets the money and who he has to pay back; she just accepts the gifts as they come.

"You look nice," Saskia says to Tru with a shy smile.

"Thanks." Tru stuffs her hands deep inside her pockets.

At first Tru and Saskia walk in silence, neither seeming to know what to say. Saskia squints in the late afternoon sunshine peering through the palm leaves. With one hand, she attempts to smooth over the straightened hairs that have lifted from her bun, looking like fine Anansi legs reaching out and upward into the blue sky. Tru stares at them, feeling a queer urge to reach over to help her. But she has never put her hands in another girl's hair. She fingers the straps of her book bag instead, suddenly feeling restless.

"Did you see what Mrs. Rosedyl was wearing at assembly today?" Tru asks, though she rarely cares.

But it makes Saskia come alive, catching a guffaw with her hands. "It was hideous! She reminded me of Big Bird in all dat yellow."

Tru laughs too, grateful to have broken the ice. They talk easily after that about teachers, grades, their upcoming CXC mock exams. They talk all the way to Half-Way Tree and realize that they catch the same bus. Saskia doesn't live too far from Tru. She lives in Sackston, one town over, where Marva takes Tru to get her school uniforms made. When Saskia reaches her stop, she suggests that Tru come over and watch *106 & Park* with her. She seems lonely, though she's constantly flocked by her friends and teammates at school. She has a satellite dish that has over a hundred American channels, she says.

Once they reach Saskia's neighborhood, a group of gangly teenage boys in khaki uniforms make catcalls at Saskia. "Psssst. Hey, Wilhampton girl! Stop, let we talk nuh." She ignores them. They remind Tru of how she is with her friends. How they laugh and talk badly in the streets, because together they are carefree and fearless. She has never minded her friends' roughness or their crass jokes, whistling just as loudly with them at beautiful girls, and laughing so hard that the soft parts of her quiver when the girls flip them the bird or full-out ignore them. But these boys are not Sore-Foot Marlon and Albino Ricky. These boys don't take rejection well. These boys take their rejection out on Tru. "Is dat yuh man?" they jeer at Saskia. "Ah see is *him* satisfying you at nights wid him fake cock."

Tru's face warms.

"Some big dick yuh mus' have, eh?" says one to Tru. "Yuh carry it around in yuh knapsack?"

"Nah, maybe she strap it on," another boy bellows.

"Dat's hard to believe. How she g'wan tek a piss wid a fake cock or really feel what ah pussy feel like?"

"Is so dem do it in blue movie."

Tru and Saskia move quickly past the boys, pretending to be deaf to the taunts. But the boys' voices only get louder.

"Yuh know what ah can't undah-stand wid sodomites . . ," another boy answers. "How come dem not satisfied wid dem own. Pussy ah di same everyweh."

"Maybe theirs different."

"How different?"

"Big an' ugly."

"Naw. Dem probaby 'ave teeny-tiny hole since dem neva get stick."

"Wilhampton look like she 'ave a tight pum-pum ready fah di stick-ing," the loudest one hoots. He smacks his lips. "Come mek me save yuh, Wilhampton!"

Saskia turns to hurl an insult at them and Tru stops her. "Jus' ignore them. Yuh only giving dem what dey want if you say something." This is more patois than she has ever spoken to Saskia. They walk away, their backs braced against the boys' howls.

When they reach Saskia's home—a compact house painted bright yellow, with a shingle roof and a large, breezy veranda with white grilles around it—Saskia introduces Tru to her grandmother, who looks Tru up and down and says nothing. Saskia seems to ignore this and takes Tru to her bedroom. "We'll have more privacy there." It's as though Saskia lives with no rules, the barrel her mother sends from England inside the room poised like a distant parent. Marva doesn't let Tru and Kenny have friends over; and before Jermaine and Daval moved out, they weren't allowed to have friends over either. She's distrustful like that. *"Friends will tek yuh business an' carry it go road."* Even when she had hairdressing customers, they only sat in the back of the house, close to the kitchen. Saskia's grandmother proceeds to clean nearby as the girls watch television in Saskia's room. She hums and hums the same tune. Tru has caught the woman's eyes several times peering at her from the top of her spectacles. Her eyes communicate some suspicion, condemning eyes sharpened by disgust. "Yuh sure I'm welcomed here?" Tru asks Saskia.

"Don't mind her," Saskia whispers, cutting her eyes at her grandmother's back and closing the door. "She's harmless. Also, sorry 'bout earlier. I've never seen those boys before."

"What yuh apologizing for? I'm used to it," Tru says.

"Dat's why ah rate yuh. Yuh so brave."

"Brave?"

Saskia shrugs. "Jus' how yuh dress an' carry yuhself. Yuh not afraid?"

"Ah can't be scared to be me. Ah wouldn't call dat brave."

"What yuh call it, then?"

"Existing?"

"Yuh t'ink yuh can exist here?"

It's Tru's time to shrug. "Ah have been doing it so far. So . . ." Her voice trails.

Saskia stares at Tru, her arms folded across her chest like she's examining her again. After a while she says, "Ah can't wait to leave dis place. I'm going to live with my mother in Brixton next year aftah graduation."

"Yuh talk to yuh mother a lot?" Tru asks.

"Every day," Saskia replies.

Tru imagines Saskia and her mother exchanging stories about their day like girlfriends. Suddenly she's lanced with envy. But the emotion dissolves when Saskia turns on the television. They watch music video after music video, switching back and forth from BET to MTV. Saskia turns up the volume when Beyoncé's new song "Single Ladies" comes on. She gets up and begins to sing and twerk. Tru watches her with delight, taken by her dance moves. "Where yuh learn to dance like dat?" she asks.

"Ah watch a lot of music videos," Saskia replies. "I'm an only child, so ah find things to occupy myself. Come, let me show you." Saskia reaches out her hands for Tru to join her. Tru does a two-step inside the spacious bedroom, watching Saskia do a hand wave with her other hand on her narrow hip, turning like Beyoncé. She stops to twirl Tru like they're on a ballroom floor. Tru stubs her toes on the chair at Saskia's homework desk, and in an effort to break her fall brings Saskia down with her. They collapse onto the carpeted floor in a fit of giggles. The quiet that comes over them this time is a comfortable one, though Tru is aware of their sudden closeness. Saskia toys with a strand of her hair, which has come undone. This time, Tru boldy reaches over to put it behind Saskia's ear. They exchange a glance. Tru acknowledges the thing that unlocked deep inside her the moment Saskia wrote her number in her palm. Like a bad nerve, it jumps—a belly-jump so great that Tru moves away a little and wheels her gaze elsewhere before she does something stupid. She catches a glimpse of a Hello Kitty sweater hung on the wardrobe. "Yuh wearing dat to sweater day tomorrow?" she asks, trying hard to sound casual.

Saskia shrugs. "My friends want to make sure di whole school see us together in our sweatshirts."

"Do you like dat?"

"What?"

"Doing everyt'ing because dey tell you to."

Saskia shrugs. "No. But they're my only friends at school, so . . ."

Saskia looks down at the small space between them on the plush beige carpet. Tru does the same. "Maybe aftah school we can do dis more often," Tru hears herself say.

Saskia raises her head. "Sure. I'd love dat."

Her breath is a warm gust of air against Tru's face. Just then, Saskia's grandmother's reproachful voice sails under the door. "Is six 'clock. You children finish wid whatevah oonuh doing inside dere? Is what oonuh doing in dere locked up like dat?"

Saskia rolls her eyes. "Seriously, Grandma?"

"It's late. Tell yuh friend goodbye."

As Saskia ushers Tru to the veranda, Tru gives the shrewd-eyed woman one of her radiant smiles. "You get home safely, young lady," Saskia's grandmother says, emphasizing *young lady* like a reminder.

40

PATSY SPENDS THE WHOLE WEEK THINKING OF CLAUDETTE. THE following Saturday, she rings Claudette's doorbell to be buzzed into the building. Claudette lives in an apartment building on Ocean Avenue, a fourth-floor walk-up. Once inside the building, Patsy takes off her coat. She is dressed in a burgundy suede skirt, with leggings and a plunging black blouse to reveal some cleavage, both of which she bought at Goodwill for special occasions. "You look beautiful," Claudette says when she opens the door, smelling like the spices Patsy grew up with.

"Thank you." Patsy smiles, blushing. "T'ings smell good in 'ere."

"Mek yuhself comfah-table," Claudette says, running back to the stove. "I'll consider dis a late Thanksgiving meal—Jamaican style—since ah cooked nothing on Thursday. What did you do fah Thanksgiving?"

Patsy shrugs as she looks around the studio. "Ordered Chinese food, watched di Macy's parade on TV, an' sleep."

Claudette chuckles. "Sounds exactly like my Thanksgiving, except I ordered pizza."

They both laugh. Their laughter is followed by an awkward pause before Claudette says, "Here, let me tek yuh jacket."

Claudette's studio is neat, partitioned by beads to separate the living/dining area from the sleeping area. Patsy purposefully avoids glancing in the direction of the low bed on a box spring flat on the floor, decorated with colorful pillows, which is shielded by the beads. She's more intrigued by the fact that Claudette has a studio all to herself. "Di lease is in my cousin's name. Ah pay him rent," Claudette explains, as she hangs Patsy's coat. Below the smell of spices there's a scent similar to the spirit oils Patsy's psychic Belizean neighbor burns inside the building. Patsy attempts to sit on the beanbag propped in front of a small television next to the bookshelf, but when she almost topples over, she gets up and makes her way to the kitchen area, where Claudette is now busy preparing the food. "You need any help?" Patsy asks.

"Not at all. Jus' sit an' mek yuhself comfah-table," she repeats.

Patsy looks around the studio some more, occupying herself with the miniature bookshelf, stocked with mostly paperback novels with shirtless men embracing women on the cover. Patsy kneels and reads the spines. She doesn't recognize any of the books. They're certainly not the type Regina reads. Regina only selects books for inspirational value—volumes of anthologies. Oversized hardcover books with personal notes on the inside, signed by the author. A few times, while waiting in the pharmacy with Regina for prescription medicine or in line at the supermarket (since Regina hates shopping with Baby by herself, resenting his tantrums when she refuses to buy him something he wants), Patsy has seen her wiggle her nose at the kind of books on Claudette's shelf.

One slim volume stands out among the romance novels: a book of poetry with *Emily Dickinson* written on the green spine.

"Emily Dickinson!" Patsy says aloud. "Yuh read har poetry?"

"Yuh know who she is?" Claudette asks.

"Saw her poetry on di subway years ago. Di one about hope."

"A woman at di nursing home gave it to me before she died last year," Claudette says, still stirring the pot and tasting the food. The book is badly dog-eared but in otherwise good condition. Patsy runs her finger along the hard spine. "Keep it," Claudette says from the stove. When Patsy glances up at her to see if she's joking, Claudette says, "It's my gift to you."

"Thank you."

Patsy clutches the book to her chest and walks with it to the framed photographs on the walls. There are lots of baby pictures, mostly of a girl and a boy at various stages, whom Patsy assumes are Claudette's niece and nephew. In the center of the wall is a photo of Claudette dressed in a leotard accentuating her ample curves, wrapped in a pink and purple boa, her bright red dreadlocks fanned around it. She's laughing, perhaps at a joke told by someone who isn't in the picture or at herself dressed in a ridiculous costume, her head tilted back, her dark brown face radiant, her teeth a perfect white arch as you can see the roof of her mouth and her squinted eyes. In a few photos, a younger and much thinner Claudette wears a bone-straight bob, grinning ear to ear on a beach. Claudette's black one-piece bathing suit reads PALM STAR RESORT.

"You worked fah Palm Star Resort?"

"Yes. Many, many moons ago."

"Ah heard yuh got to be a certain shade to work dere. How did you—" She stops herself from saying any more, afraid she might offend Claudette.

"Is all right," Claudette says. "Yuh can ask. How did I get to work dere?" Claudette shrugs by the stove without turning to face her. "What can I say? I was lucky."

Patsy laughs. "I'm sure."

Claudette's movement slows. "I was a masseuse."

"What was dat like?"

"Ah met so many people. I was dis country girl from Westmoreland. Raised in a closed community of Rastafarians. So it was like a dream to move to Montego Bay an' be around all those tourists—people from all walks of life. Ah got so much exposure. Dat's di biggest perks wid working in di hotels."

Patsy watches Claudette's back, sees her shoulders move, aware of the involuntary spasm of the muscle between her legs that gives way to a trickle of moistness as she imagines Claudette over a body on a bed, dutifully kneading the flesh below like wet flour.

"People come to Jamaica to escape," Claudette continues. "So ah made sure dey got di best escape possible."

"You—you knew 'bout di prostitution bust?" Patsy asks.

"I left a year before all dat happen."

"So yuh knew about it."

"Let's jus' say dey arrested di wrong people. Those girls were young an' poor. Dey had nothing. Yet, is dem g'wan spend time in prison. Fah what? Trying to survive? Di real masterminds behind it still eating bettah than we eating now. Ah can guarantee dat." Claudette reaches for a glass spice jar and sprinkles some of the contents into the pot.

"Dat's how it always work back home." Patsy turns to look at the photos again. "Di biggest crooks nyam di best steak. Dey said di general manager knew about it, but fled di country immediately without ah trace."

Suddenly the glass jar falls and breaks. Patsy jumps, frightened by the sound; the image of the man hovered over her and Cicely comes back and almost knocks her over. Shards of glass and blood everywhere. She doesn't realize that she's crouched with her hands clamped to her ears until Claudette runs over to her and puts a hand on Patsy's shoulder. "Yuh all right?"

Patsy drops her hands from her ears and slowly eases back into the present, Claudette smiling ever so gently at her. "Yes," Patsy says, almost breathless. "I'm fine now."

CLAUDETTE SERVES THE FOOD, POURS THEM EACH A GLASS OF red wine, and blesses the dinner.

"You ever think about opening up yuh own restaurant? Dis is delicious!" Patsy says between bites of her oxtail, butter beans, and rice. "Yuh put the restaurant where ah used to work to shame. Seriously. Ah haven't tasted good oxtail since ah left home."

Claudette laughs. "Glad you enjoying it. Ah neva like di headache of a restaurant. But my dream is to open a massage parlor or a courier boutique. I'm saving to put down 'pon a likkle space on Flatbush Avenue. If ah do di courier boutique, I know Sadiq customers will follow me there."

"You'll be so good at it."

"Thanks," Claudette says, blushing a little.

"You know what will mek it even bettah?" Patsy asks.

"What?"

"A computer. I notice yuh log everyt'ing in one book."

Claudette sucks her teeth. "Dat's because Sadiq too old-fashion. But believe me, I'll be outta dat place in due time. What about you?"

"What about me?"

"What do you want?"

"Want?"

"Yes, want."

"No one has ever asked me dat before," Patsy says.

"I am now."

"I always wanted to go back to school an' study computers," Patsy says. "Not like what dey teach you at di free computer class down at di library, but more technical t'ings . . . like programming."

"Why don't you?"

Patsy shrugs. "No time or money."

"It's not too late."

Patsy lowers her fork. "It is for certain things."

"Are you at peace wid it?" Claudette asks.

"No."

"Then there's your answer," Claudette says after a while. "Follow yuh heart. It's di least yuh can do. I know it's easier said than done."

Patsy nods in agreement. She drains the last of her wine and asks for more.

41

"WHOSE DI MYSTERY PERSON?" FIONNA ASKS THROUGH THE receiver as Patsy pushes Baby in Central Park. "You haven't called or answered yuh phone in God knows when."

"Stop wid yuh exaggerating, Fionna." Patsy talks into her headpiece, imagining Fionna going from room to room, spreading beds, fluffing pillows, and emptying trash at the hotel where she works. It's nice having someone to talk to about Claudette. "Ah called last week an' got no answer. Figured yuh was out wining an' dining wid yuh new man."

"Wining an' dining which part? Di man don't know what dat is!" Patsy laughs.

"Seriously, though, Patsy. Who got you so busy dese days?"

"Someone ah met when ah was buying a barrel."

"Him 'ave papers?"

"No."

"How yuh mean, no? What's di use of picking up wid ah man at a barrel shop of all places without papers? Yuh know yuh family g'wan t'ink yuh wealthy when dat thing arrive. Yuh might as well get a green card out of it."

"Fionna, yuh know ah don't care 'bout getting it like dat."

"Let's see if you'll be saying di same t'ing when Immigration show up. Dem worse than di NYPD. Yuh see what happen to Abner Louima?"

"What does Immigration have to do wid Abner Louima?"

"Yuh want to know what's worse than being rammed in di yuh you-know-what wid a baton? Deportation."

"Fionna, stop wid dat nonsense."

"Don't *Fionna* me. Dis mus' be one special man if him have yuh so sprung dat yuh forget we in America an' need papers."

"Well . . ."

"I knew it!"

Patsy pauses with the stroller. Baby is asleep inside it. She looks up at the bare tree branches. Patsy remembers the gay parade she came across by accident years ago in the Village. None of those gay people marching through the streets half naked, wrapped in rainbow flags, looking so self-assured and flagrant, looked like her.

"I really like him," she says, swallowing the guilt.

"Do whatevah makes you happy," Fionna replies.

Patsy slows. "Don't pretend like yuh mean dat."

"Ah don't. But you're not a child. You grown."

"Thank you very much fah acknowledging dat."

"Patsy . . ." Fionna's voice trails. There is a serious tone to it. "Jus' promise me one t'ing. Promise me dat you'll be careful. Think about what ah said. Ah have to go. Call you lata." She sucks air through her teeth into the receiver. "Kisses!" Patsy does the same and ends the call. She thinks about the way Claudette looks at her and how she said, "*Are you at peace wid it?*" It's the way she said it. Not in a dismissive, judgmental way, but in a way that reminds Patsy of the rush she once felt as a teenager when she put her hand over a candlelight flame confirming that she was real, alive; that the burning she felt somewhere inside was as absolute as the one out there, burning her skin.

She pushes Baby in the park, surprised to see Judene. It's a quarter past one, which is earlier than when Judene usually enters the park. Her eyes aren't glued to her baby, but are gazing into distance, staring past the trees and the sea of cars on Central Park West and Eighty-sixth Street.

"Is what do you?" Patsy asks. She sits next to Judene.

"Delroy."

A siren passes just at that moment and Patsy has to pause before she can ask. "Is what happen?" Judene begins to cry, her shoulders jerking with all the weight that has rounded her spine. Baby stirs awake in the stroller, so Patsy lets him out to play. Then she puts her hand on Judene's shoulder.

Judene sniffles. "Delroy dead."

"What? Delroy? How?"

"Dey rob him store, an tek all di money. He didn't want to pay di extortion fee dat him owe those criminals. Ah told him if him evah need more money, him mus' jus' ask me. Ah told him dat him shouldn't tek di law in him own hand, 'bout him need to tek a stand. Him wouldn't listen. Him was too stubborn. Dat money woulda save him life . . ."

Patsy pulls Judene to her. She knows how much Judene loves her twin brother. Judene sends money to him and his family every chance she gets—enough to help him open up his clothing store in downtown Kingston. Only God knows how she gets the money to help her brother set up shop. But then again, she's a live-in nanny who doesn't have to pay rent, the disadvantage to that being that she's expected to be on call 24/7 and therefore has no autonomy or life of her own. Judene continues. "Police should catch every one ah dem criminals an' hang dem! Dey kill me only brother. Him was all ah 'ave . . ." She sobs quietly, unable to bellow in the bright park filled with children. Beatrice enters the park and spots them.

"Is what going on?"

Judene wipes her face.

"Tell har what happen," Patsy gently coaxes. When Judene shrugs, Patsy says to Beatrice, "Judene brother gone. Dey rob him store downtown an' kill him. He owed extortion money . . ." Her voice trails, because she knows that's how dons like Pope operate. She knows there is definitely some filthy connection and it does not matter at all to Patsy whether it might be a different don from a different community. They are all the same.

"Have mercy!" Beatrice puts her hands on her head. "Is what do dem? Why dem had to take di lives of innocent people? I'm so sorry to hear, dah'ling."

Judene begins to cry again. Patsy looks off into the playground and spots Judene's baby crawling around, picking up dirt to put into his mouth. "No, no, no!" She hurries over to scoop him up and put him in his stroller near Judene, hoping that none of the housewives saw. The last thing Judene needs now is trouble with her boss.

"Why yuh come into work today?" Beatrice asks Judene as soon as the toddler is secured in his stroller, sucking the pacifier Patsy gives him from Judene's baby bag. "Yuh should be mourning an' planning yuh trip fah di funeral," she says.

"I can't," Judene says. "I don't get time off. An' if I go, I can't come back here."

"It's your twin brother," Beatrice says. "You should go."

"How?" Judene asks. "I have no papers. My visa expired long time. If I go, I'll have to stay in Jamaica fah di rest of me life."

"She's right, Beatrice," Patsy says. "Yuh can't expect her to give up everyt'ing like dat."

"Nonsense. Not even fah har own brother?"

"What do you know?" Patsy says to Beatrice. "Yuh have a visa and the ability to travel back an' forth. Heck, yuh 'ave di ability to take all di time off in di world an' fly to France or Italy whenevah yuh please. How yuh g'wan tell a person wid no such privilege what dey should do?"

Patsy and Beatrice stare each other down. Then Beatrice says, "Only a selfish, heartless person would say something like dat."

"Is not heartless. I'm being practical."

"All right, then. Since I'm not di right person to ask, then let me ask you something, Patsy. If yuh mother died tomorrow, yuh telling me dat you wouldn't go to har funeral?"

"My mother died long ago," Patsy says. "Di day she gave har life to Jesus, she took her own."

"What about yuh children? I'm sure a woman like you have plenty back home."

"What's dat supposed to mean?"

"Isn't dat what you people do? Have children oonuh can't take care of?"

Patsy pauses, the words bundled in her belly, as lifeless as a stillborn. "Don't you dare make assumptions about me an' my life." Her voice is a low hiss.

"See? You can't answer my question," Beatrice says, adjusting her turban. "That's what ah don't understand wid you people."

"You people?" Patsy asks.

"Yes, you people! There's plenty t'ings to do at home."

"Only you can say dat, Beatrice, wid yuh high-an'-mighty self," Patsy says, trying hard not to let her voice shake. "You, who nuh know struggle. You, who neva feel di heavy load of responsibility when yuh don't even know where help will come from. You, who live up in those hills wid enough money fi send yuh daughter to a school like Columbia. Some white people can't even afford to sen' dem children to dat school—"

"Michaela had an academic scholarship."

"A scholarship? From yuh bank account?" Patsy gives a bitter laugh. "Yuh don't even have to answer dat question. You an' I both know dat we're cut from different cloth. Now you an' yuh stupid rich woman problems can wipe my ass an' g'weh. Probably di only t'ing yuh evah worry 'bout is making sure seh yuh dawta marry a white man. You is the whitest woman me ever meet in America."

B EATRICE IS TREMBLING, HER MOUTH TWITCHING AND EYES shining like glass. Shirley saunters into the park with her stroller, wearing a pair of sunglasses and looking like a tourist. "Hi, yawl!" she says with that fake Dolly Parton accent she uses whenever she's in a good mood. She stops short, the smile disappearing from her face. The glare of the three women chokes the lilt out of Shirley's voice. "Ah wha?"

Beatrice cuts her eyes and continues. Her anger glitters and sparks in every word. "Yuh want to know what's worse than di death of yuh own child, or a dead mother, fah dat mattah?"

"Who'fa mother dead?" Shirley asks, her hands flying to her round cheeks.

"Judene's brother," Patsy says.

"Oh, jeez! Delroy dead?" Shirley abandons her stroller and runs to Judene's side.

"Oonuh hush mek me talk!" Beatrice says.

"There's nothing more ah want to hear from you," Patsy says. "Judene is di one we here for. She's di one in need right now. Not you."

"Yuh don't know nuttin' 'bout pain. Nothing!" Beatrice says. "Yuh don't know what it's like when yuh only child is a gay. Every day ah pray dat she would change. How she g'wan raise dis child to believe dat two woman can get married? Dat's not even legal! Do you know what my poor grandson call Michaela an' dat white woman? Him call di both ah dem *Mommy*. Poor child. Him don't even know dat children should have a mother an' a father. I'm di one who have to account fah allowing his inno-cence to be tainted wid dis slackness. Dat's why I'm here. To help teach my grandson what's right. So, none of you know what I go through!"

Judene stops sniffling. Shirley's jaw drops. Patsy shifts uncom-fortably, remembering how Beatrice stretched the word *partner* to describe her daughter's baby's father once, which sounded to Patsy like *paaaaaat'na*. Patsy found it strange, because where they're from peo-ple either say wife, husband, boyfriend, girlfriend, baby mother, or baby father. Now it makes sense why Beatrice chose to be evasive.

"If dat's yuh only struggle an' reason fah being here, then *you* should be di one to go back home," Patsy says.

Beatrice's mouth is drawn tight, the small muscle below her trembling bottom lip seeming to pull imperceptibly at the already loosened skin under her chin. Without another word to them, she leaves, pulling her grandson off the seesaw, away from his little friend—another mulatto boy who looks like him, and whose snooty black mother goes out of her way to keep her distance from the nannies, perhaps fearing the white women would think she's one of them.

After Beatrice hauls the stroller out of the park, Patsy turns to Judene and asks, "So, what yuh g'wan do?"

Judene shrugs her shoulders with Patsy's and Shirley's hands on them. "Ah have to sen' money home fah di coffin, an' pay fah di funeral. Since ah can't go."

42

PATSY AND CLAUDETTE WALK TOGETHER IN SILENCE AFTER DINner at Sammuel's. The restaurant celebrated its three-year anniversary tonight with a party thrown in honor of the patrons who kept it open—more people than Patsy has seen in the three times she's been there. There was a deejay and a special guest, Floyd, a reggae artist who is friends with Sammuel. Patsy even saw Serge from the restaurant where she used to work. "*Dimples!*" he shouted when he saw her. Patsy recognized him from his belly laugh and his larger-than-life presence, the way he bowed to kiss her hand. It was nice to see him too. She smiled despite the heaviness that weighed on her. "*Ah neva forget a beautiful face*," he said. "*Ah always wondah wha'appened to yuh!*" He was already friendly with Sammuel and Claudette, kissing Claudette on both cheeks; they had both worked at the Palm Star Resort back home around the same time, where Serge was an assistant chef. Now he's head chef at a restaurant in White Plains. He made sure to tell Patsy that this one is owned by a yardie like them. He slipped Patsy his business card. "*Call me if yuh evah need anyt'ing. An' ah mean anyt'ing,*" he said with a wink. At that point, Claudette linked hands with Patsy and twirled her away. "*Lata, Serge!*" People were drinking and dancing, and Claudette sang the words to Whitney Houston's "I Will Always Love You" during the karaoke, hamming it up and smiling at Patsy. Patsy turned away, feeling an ineffable sadness well inside her.

Walking now, Patsy carries her leftovers. She had no appetite earlier, and may not have an appetite later either. Beatrice's words have haunted her since yesterday. Again she's aware of the dark, looming thing that surrounds her like the gusts of cold wind: New York City, stripped bare of its sheen, hollow and lonely except for the echoes of sirens and now the slushing of Patsy's and Claudette's boots in the melting snow. She turns to tell Claudette that she's okay walking home alone, but is surprised to see that Claudette is already regarding her with concern, and a glint of hurt. "What's di mattah?" she asks. "Was I too forward tonight?" She touches Patsy lightly on her arm and Patsy flinches. Claudette appears alarmed. "Patsy, talk to me."

"I jus' want to be," Patsy replies.

The wind picks up and blows flurries across their faces. Claudette lifts her fur-lined hoodie into place. She's staring at Patsy with anxious confusion, her eyes wide like she's trying to read something in the dark. "Did I do some'ting?"

"No."

"You haven't said a word to me since we walked outta di restaurant."

"I didn't like di setting," Patsy lies. Claudette's eyes narrow. Patsy's voice drops. "If it was somewhere else, dat song would be fine . . ."

Claudette laughs. "Dat's it? Dat's what's been bothering you? You really t'ink dat song was about you?"

"It wasn't?" Patsy asks.

Claudette laughs—her laughter rises and grips Patsy's shoulders with its chill. Patsy's face warms despite the cold. Giving her a sharp look, Patsy says, "It's time to call it a night."

When Claudette sobers, she says, "Ah used to pride myself on being able to figure women out. But you—ah neva met anyone like you before. Yuh hot one minute, then yuh cold. Is like Jekyll an' Hyde."

"Yuh don't know me like dat."

"Ah know enough."

"Enough?"

Claudette takes her hand and squeezes it. It warms her. "Ah know enough, Patsy," she repeats, this time more forceful, as if there were no more questions about it and Patsy only has to accept it with the finality with which she accepts the forward edge of winter. Claudette continues, "If yuh let me, ah can be there for you." There's an intensity in her eyes. Patsy looks away, strangely afraid of it. "Ah bettah be going," Patsy says.

"Dat would be too simple. Too easy fah you. Yuh not tired of running?" Claudette asks.

Patsy turns away from Claudette, who is standing against the wind. But Claudette steps closer and pulls Patsy toward her. Claudette's body is warm against hers, inciting a painful surge of what Patsy understands as a long-suppressed yearning breaking through her skin.

"Come, let's go somewhere warm," Claudette says. "We 'ave all night."

PATSY DOESN'T PROTEST WHEN CLAUDETTE OPENS THE DOOR TO her studio. She flicks on a switch and light floods the small room with its warm smell of years of candles and incense. Patsy lingers by the doorway as though unsure if, once she enters this time, she'll be able to leave again. Claudette takes off her jacket, hangs it on a hook by the door, and tells Patsy to sit. "Ah will mek us some tea. Do you want some rum in it?" Claudette asks.

"No, thank you," Patsy says.

Patsy eases into the room and out of her jacket. When the water boils and Claudette pours it onto the Tetley tea bags in her handmade ceramic mugs, Patsy takes a sip, imbued by steam. They sit in comfortable silence, drinking their tea. "You know," Claudette says very gently as if she doesn't want to break their moment. "Ah always knew you were interesting since ah first saw you." Her long fingers curve around her mug, a wry smile on her lips. "You're so secretive. Why's dat?"

"Why not be?"

"I've been open with you."

Patsy takes a deep breath. "There's so much about me dat might turn you off."

"Try me."

"Ah haven't reached out to my dawta since ah left home ten years ago," Patsy says.

Claudette is quiet. Patsy wonders what she's thinking.

Patsy continues, breaking Claudette's gaze, "My mother always told me ah child is a gift from God. But I neva could bring me self to ask har what if I neva wanted it. What about what I want? No one evah asked me what ah want, besides you." She looks up at Claudette, who appears to be looking not at her, but inside her. "Is like I was taking a present from God given to me when I was too green to say not right now. Or no t'anks."

Claudette shifts in her chair. Maybe she's judging Patsy, after all. And how could Patsy blame her? What kind of a woman leaves a child like that and dares to tell anyone about it? Patsy lowers her eyelids and gazes down at her fingers around her cup. Claudette gets up, opens a vanity drawer, and returns with a small framed photograph.

Patsy stares at the black-and-white pictures of a little girl, about five years old, with clumped dreadlocks sticking out of her head. She's in the arms of a tall, chiseled Rasta man with dreadlocks down to his waist. He's staring straight into the camera, unsmiling. The hands holding the little girl are blackened and callused. "Is dis yuh father?" Patsy asks.

"Yes," Claudette responds.

"Why yuh giving me dis?"

"We lost touch a likkle." Claudette shrugs. "He neva liked me cutting off my locs in di first place. But more than dat was how he used to treat us. Like we were aftah-thoughts. Dat man had so many women dat we didn't mattah. An' I forgave him. Took me years. But I forgave him."

"It's different fah fathers," Patsy says. "We expec' dem to be dat way. No one judge dem as harshly because ah dat. I'm a mother. Mothers, we don't . . ." Her voice trails. "Mothers don't get dat sorta pardon."

Claudette bites her bottom lip, mum.

Patsy shifts her weight in her chair. "Ah bettah get going. Ah have work in di mawnin'."

She thanks Claudette for the tea and gets up, hoping to grab her jacket before Claudette touches her again, warming her blood. When she reaches the door, Claudette is still sitting at the table where Patsy left her. "Patsy, you won't be able to earn yuh dawta's forgiveness by jus' trying to do what people expec' you to do. Do what yuh t'ink is right, from a place of honesty. She'll respect yuh honesty."

"Have a good night," Patsy says.

"You too," Claudette replies. "Same time, same place next week?"

Patsy nods and forces a smile. She closes the door. In the hallway, she stands still for a moment, frighteningly alone. She takes a few steps toward the elevator. The lights flicker above her head and the high silence screams in her ears.

She turns around and knocks on Claudette's door. As soon as Claudette opens it, Patsy kisses her. Claudette's mouth opens, kisses back. Clumsily, Patsy puts her arms around Claudette and pulls Claudette to her. She almost apologizes, almost backs away again—back to the desolation. Claudette, who must have felt Patsy's moment of hesitation, murmurs in her ear, "It's all right. Ah was hoping you'd come back. Ah didn't mean to compare your situation to my father. Forgive me . . ."

She takes Patsy by the hand and leads her to her low bed, parting the beads around it. When Claudette presses her mouth to Patsy's neck, Patsy shudders. She allows the other woman to undress her, to peel away the layers, including the flimsy girdle, which frees the excess flesh. The rolls of fat don't feel as unattractive under Claudette's gaze. Neither does the branch under Patsy's belly. With her forefinger, Claudette traces it as one does an open palm to read. She looks up at Patsy, her eyes lifting to hers with an impassioned question, but she says nothing. Patsy's skin dissolves under the gaze, becoming soft and beautiful like the colorful waist beads shimmering against the deep brown of Claudette's flesh. "Ah want one like dis," Patsy whispers, toying with the beads around Claudette's waist. "I can make one fah you," Claudette says, her lips brushing Patsy's cheek. She presses them to Patsy's and lowers Patsy to the bed as she rises above Patsy like the sea. She straddles Patsy and Patsy kisses her breasts. Caught in her embrace, Patsy smells the sweet musk of Claudette's skin. Patsy raises her face to behold Claudette in her naked beauty—openly voluptuous and thoughtfully shaped with a lovely tension to the brown skin and muscle underneath, a body so powerful and ethereal that Patsy cannot wait to experience the feel of it. Claudette kisses Patsy once again; and Patsy, as trusting as a child and as ardent as a woman, receives Claudette's tongue like she did the wafer during her first Communion.

As Claudette's body fuses with Patsy's—the long fingers that had clasped her ceramic mug curling inside Patsy and turning her to butter—the world drops away, and so does time. This, Patsy believes, is worship—to enter a woman the way one enters a sacred temple, and to be entered. Patsy frees herself of Mama G's warnings about sin—*"A chile of God mus' preserve har temple an' not give in to di dark intrusion of di Devil."* And the images Patsy has long held on to—Cicely sitting on her lap, her beautiful face emerging from the curtains of her dark, silky hair; Uncle Curtis's honey-covered secret pressed to Patsy's lips and the airy sensation of rum filling her head; Roy's permissive murmur, *"Birdie, ah t'ink I'm in love"*—fade away.

43

WHEN TRU ARRIVES FOR PRACTICE, SHE'S SURPRISED TO SEE none other than Pope himself, sitting on a stool underneath an ackee tree in the yard, wearing flip-flops and a pair of army-green pants with no shirt, showing off a very muscular torso and arms, the color and texture of rustic wood. His eyes are hidden behind dark shades and one hand is on his chin, while the other holds a ganja spliff between his fingers as he watches Tru's teammates play. Surrounded by his posse, he says nothing during the game, even as Sore-Foot Marlon scores multiple goals. The usual afternoon game has turned into a spectacle. There are men everywhere—men sitting, men standing, men talking, men laughing, men drinking. What used to be Tru and her friends' time to bond and shed their angst has now been amped with adrenaline and testosterone. No longer schoolboy soccer. Tru senses competition between her friends and the new boys, each one vying for Pope's approval. Her teammates dribble the ball with dexterity, to the surprise of the new boys and the men with purple handkerchiefs tied around their necks, arms folded across their chests, and legs apart like cowboys. "Bombaaaat! Da team yah baaaad!" they shout, and high-five each other. Tru smiles to herself, reveling in the moment, because surely Pope will want them on his team when he realizes how well they can play. But Tru's smile only lasts for a moment. One of the new boys—a tall, dark fellow from Fagan Lane with crooked teeth—pushes Sore-Foot Marlon hard to the ground.

"Who yuh t'ink yuh is, hogging di ball like dat, batttybwoy?"

Sore-Foot Marlon falls flat on his back, wincing from the sharp pain, as the other boy runs off with the ball. Not one to be pushed around, he runs after the boy and punches him in the face. The boy fights back, swinging at Sore-Foot Marlon, but misses. Three of the boy's friends dash from under the mango tree where they had been perched on rusted iron chairs from the classrooms. They surround Sore-Foot Marlon. The biggest boy among them locks Sore-Foot Marlon from behind, his elbow around his neck. Then, from out of nowhere, Albino Ricky pulls out a gun and holds it to the boy's temple. Sore-Foot Marlon's eyes widen.

"Ricky, what yuh doing?"

"Listen to me, pussy-hole," Albino Ricky says calmly to the big boy who has his arm around Sore-Foot Marlon's neck. "Touch me fren' an' me done yuh!"

Sore-Foot Marlon's fists are clenched, his chest rising and falling quickly like someone blowing and sucking air inside a brown paper bag, his face stricken. The other boys back away from him, shocked by the gun.

That's when Tru hears the booming voice.

"Enough!"

They all turn in its direction.

"Listen to me." Pope—a man no taller than any of them, including Tru—takes off his dark shades so the boys can see his eyes. "On dis team, everybody equal. Yuh hear? Fight like dis 'pon me team again, an' yuh see who g'wan get buried. Our mantra g'wan be all fah one, an' one fah all."

Tru refrains from rolling her eyes. Pope is completely hairless, save for the goatee on his chin. He stands with his hands clasped behind him in the manner of a priest. When he speaks, the inside of his mouth looks like a refrigerator with what appears to be silver braces holding his pearl-white teeth like crates of eggs. Tru wonders why a man his age needs braces. Looking at the boy who pushed Sore-Foot Marlon, Pope says, "If yuh evah pull dat stunt again, yuh off di team."

The boy nods sheepishly, wiping the sweat dripping down his clay-brown face with his T-shirt. "An' you!" He turns to Albino Ricky. "Put away dat gun an' nuh mek me see it on di field again. Yuh hear?"

"Yes, sah," Albino Ricky says, tucking away his gun in his waist.

"Oonuh shake hands, now!" Pope demands.

The boy and Sore-Foot Marlon limply shake hands without looking at each other.

"Good," Pope says when they're done, his face serious. "On dis team, oonuh g'wan train as men, not boys. Ah don't want to only mek yuh into ballers, but warriors." To the rest of the team, he says, "Watch an' learn. Wid dis team, nobody can seh nuttin' good don't come from Penny-field ever again. We g'wan show Jamaica. Ah want everyone here at four o'clock sharp. No excuse. Dis is trial period. Come late, an' yuh might as well leave. Oonuh not only playing to win twenty-five thousand U.S. dollahs. It must be earned. Undah-stood?"

They all nod in agreement. Tru senses that her friends are already tasting the decadent meals, feeling the nice clothes on their backs, and smelling the promise of twenty-five thousand dollars—an odor, she imagines like the stripped bark of a cedar tree, spicy and sweet.

Pope flashes them another caged smile. "Good."

After the boys disperse, Tru approaches Pope, who is in conversation with a few of his posse—all men.

"Pope, sorry I was late," she says.

From the corner of her eye, she sees Sore-Foot Marlon and Albino Ricky pausing to listen.

"Where were you?" Pope asks.

"Extra lessons ran late. I'm retaking the CXCs in June."

"Hm. Ah t'ink yuh was g'wan say yuh jus' come from foreign. How come yuh soun' suh proper? Yuh guh to one ah dem good schools in Kingston, don't?"

"Ah guess."

"Good money-people schools, ah can tell."

Tru pauses, not sure where he's going with this.

"What's yuh name?"

"Tru."

His gaze narrows at first as he tries to match the voice to the look. Like all the other men in the streets who have done this before him, there is a look of confusion before it transforms to something unreadable—a cross between amusement and just plain bewilderment. "You're Tru?"

"Yes, sir."

"Ricky neva mention dat you're a girl."

"I'm not."

He chuckles a bit to himself and turns to the three men behind him. "Crowbar, look who Ricky recommend as di best forward 'pon di team. Yuh evah see anyt'ing guh suh? A girl?" Tru's face warms as the men laugh. They lower their cigarettes.

Crowbar's reptilian gaze crawls all over her. "Yuh sure is a girl."

"I'm a ball player," Tru replies. "Dat's all dat matters."

Tru feels exposed. It's as if she has just walked onto a stage, all eyes on her. The men's postures change too. "Hol' on. Hol' on," Crowbar says. He stands firmly, with his arms folded across his chest. His narrow face is as dark as midnight and his eyes are gashes of yellow. Tru doesn't like him at all. "Is only one t'ing women good fah," he says. "An' balling is not it. 'Less is to jiggle it."

The other men laugh uproariously. She doesn't respond, feeling her teammates' eyes on her, the heat warming the back of her neck all the way to her face. She looks away from Pope, whose eyes are moving in a slow caress over her face as if he's observing her reaction. She suddenly wants to be invisible, annoyed at herself for saying anything in the first place. Her eyes, which swiftly cross over his, must have confessed this, because he smiles to himself. "What would yuh mother say about you playing wid boys, Tru?"

"She's not here to say anyt'ing."

"I know Patsy wouldn't like you being around me a'tall, a'tall."

"You know my mother?"

"*Know?*" He chuckles. "We almost grow up like bredda an' sistah. Yuh mother used to come to my mother's table when Mama G couldn't feed her—"

"What?"

"Dat was a long time ago. Ah guess she moved on to greener pastures, from what ah hear. She was a pretty girl like yuhself. It's a shame to see yuh waste all dis pretty. Maybe yuh should find a likkle girls team to play wid."

"Look like she already play 'pon dat team, anyway," Crowbar adds with a wink. "But we can work somet'ing out fi set har good an' straight." He grabs his crotch.

"Crowbar, not another word!" Pope barks. "Say somet'ing like dat again, an' yuh bloodclaaat dead. Yuh know who har father is? Sergeant Beckford. I see yuh want an early grave!"

Crowbar's jaundiced eyes narrow. "No, boss." He gives a slight nod to Tru and skulks away with his crew, still watchful, like a group of wildcats whose eyes glow in the shadows. Pope gestures for Tru to follow him so that they can talk in private.

Sore-Foot Marlon, Asafa, and Albino Ricky look on helplessly, since there is not much they can do or say to Pope. He leans forward, his hands on his hips. "You seem very smart, Tru. So let me ask you somet'ing—what would yuh police father seh about you playing on my team?"

Tru tries not to show her surprise or disappointment. Her mouth opens and closes.

"I—I never asked."

Pope laughs softly. "Here's some advice fah you, Tru. How about yuh sit dis one out? Ah promise it'd be di best decision yuh evah make. Right, Ricky?"

Albino Ricky looks from Pope to Tru, then back to Pope again. He gives a nervous chuckle, and Tru catches his momentary hesitation, her own distrust flaring up when Albino Ricky nods. She blinks back tears, not wanting these boys, these men, to see her cry. They'd think she's really a girl for sure. Sore-Foot Marlon puts his hand on her shoulder as they walk away, but Tru shrugs it off and stalks ahead. She can still feel Pope's gaze on her, turning and turning.

44

PATSY SITS NAKED ON THE EDGE OF CLAUDETTE'S BATHTUB. Claudette, who is also undressed, stands between Patsy's legs, one hand rested on Patsy's bowed head as though in benediction, the other hand holding a razor. They had just showered together after a morning of lovemaking. There in the bathroom, surrounded by the glow of natural light, the two women perform another cleansing ritual, undisturbed by the sounds of the city beneath them. Patsy allows Claudette to shave off the few hairs left on her head. She told Claudette to shave everything—something she would have never considered years before. She had grown tired of the wig. Tired of feeling old with it on her head.

A waft of air grazes Patsy's neck and tickles her with a giddiness she has only experienced when the man at the embassy in Kingston stamped her passport with an American visa. Slowly, Claudette runs her fingers over Patsy's almost bald head. It feels like magic on Patsy's scalp. Patsy's head is nicely shaved like a man's, though the bald look happens to be in style for women nowadays. Very gently, Claudette rests her hand on Patsy's shoulder when she's done. Patsy stares straight at the mirror, feeling as though she's sitting by a window that suddenly has a view.

45

T RU ARRIVES AT THE SEAWEED-GREEN HOUSE ON MONDAY AFTER school—the only day Pope doesn't hold soccer practice. It stands tall—a fortress wall guarding a city. A silver satellite dish squats on top of its shingle roof against the cloak of gray clouds flung over Pennyfield. Dancehall music drifts like the balmy scent of wet earth from the house and into the street.

Inside the yard, which can hold a party of fifty or more, a game of dominoes is in progress. Male voices shout from under the mango tree when someone slams down a domino. *"Seet deh! Game done!"* No one looks up or questions what Tru is doing there. She walks confidently across the yard, stepping over sleeping mongrel dogs lying on their sides. Tru imagines how Hansel and Gretel must have felt when they came across the witch's house, how their hunger must have been greater than their fear. She knocks.

Pope comes to open the grille, surprised to see her standing there.

"What brings you to my castle?" he asks in a mock-Shakespearean accent.

"I need to talk to you."

Pope lets her inside. He's wearing house slippers like Marva's, a white marina, and jeans. He takes her to his spacious living room, with expensive-looking furniture, a wide flat-screen television bigger than any Tru has ever seen, a glass coffee table, and a large couch with leopard-print cushions and covered with plastic, where he gestures for Tru to sit.

"Diane!" Pope calls over his shoulder. "Bring out some lemonade for our guest, please."

He sits across from Tru and lights a cigarette, which hangs at the side of his mouth like a forgotten toothpick. Tru notices the handle of a gun at his side, held by his belt. Just then a beautiful, petite brown girl with a mole above the right side of her mouth serves them two glasses of ice-cold lemonade. She looks about Tru's age, with a short pixie haircut, gold hoop earrings, and a gold nose ring, which she surely wouldn't be allowed to wear in school (if she even goes to school). She's wearing a midriff top and short-shorts, and Tru can see a large red rose tattooed on one thigh. "Dis is Diane," Pope says, introducing the girl, who blushes and smiles shyly. He caresses the small of the girl's back. "My heartbeat." He brings Diane to his lap, and she hits him playfully. When Diane wiggles herself free, laughing, Pope thanks her with a pinch on one of her exposed butt cheeks. Tru looks away. Once the girl scurries out of the room, managing to sway her narrow hips, Pope leans forward and lays his gun on the coffee table. The cold metal makes a heavy sound when it touches the surface. "I'm all ears," he says to Tru.

She cannot help but stare at the gun, her father's warning loud in her ears. "*Stay away from dat man!*" Pope, who must have noticed Tru's hesitation, smirks.

"Wait, wait!" he says, springing to his feet. "Where's me manners? Ah have coasters. Wata mess up furnicha. Dis is good furnicha." He disappears inside the kitchen and emerges with a coaster for her to rest her drink. When he sits back down, he says, "Please. Continue."

"You got to let me play. Football is my life," she says.

"On a girls' team," Pope replies, leaning back and crossing his legs.

"I've been playing with these boys for years."

Pope laughs. "Tru, rules are rules. 'Less yuh g'wan tell me seh yuh have superpowers to grow balls an' ah Adam's apple."

She pauses.

"My point exactly," Pope says. "Good pretty should neva be wasted. Dat shoulda been di eleventh commandment."

"So, you follow di Old Testament like dat?" Tru asks. "If dat's the case, then why yuh rob an' kill people?"

Pope laughs. "Is who filling up yuh head wid dat foolishness? Yuh policeman father?" He blows smoke from his nostrils.

"You have a revolver, an' yuh not no police." Tru sinks her fingers into the cushions beneath her, almost ripping the plastic with her nails.

"I've neva killed a soul in me life. People kill dem self . . ." Pope says with a sneer. "I'm not di crook yuh should fear. I'm just di poor delivery-man. Does dat mek me a bad person?" he asks. "Yuh see dat preacher man in di pulpit? Him is no different from me. Those politicians 'pon dem high horse? No different from me either. Yuh know why, Tru? Because people look to us fah somet'ing. An' we give it to dem. For what we offer di defeated is t'ings capable of numbing dem—be it di gospel or false promises of change. Or a likkle somet'ing fah dem nerves or headache from living on a monopoly board where dem 'ave no control. So yuh father is right not to like me. His gang—di police—rule an' con-quer using fear an' bribery. My gang, on di other hand, help people. I sell trust. Ah mek t'ings easy. Ah don't wait till people empty to break dem down wid a baton or fill dem back up wid biblical scriptures no different from a storybook wid lies." Tru discerns his wry smile. "You'll begin to see dat di world wasn't created equal, Tru. Everybody deserve di best in life, which is why it's important fah me to recruit yuh friends. Di only level playing field yuh friends will get in dis life is what ah give dem."

"An' what about me?"

"Dat's different."

"How is it different? Yuh contradicting yuhself."

Pope lights another cigarette and takes a long drag. When he lets out the smoke, he leans forward with his elbows on his knees. "Let me ask you somet'ing—you mention dat ah did bad things earlier. Yet, is me yuh coming to, begging to be on my team. How can one man 'ave all dat power? An' whose di contradicting one?"

Tru is stumped by his question.

"Tru, let me tell yuh somet'ing ah know fah sure. Ah know yuh mother. Ah know di kind a woman she is—har integrity. Years ago, ah offered to help har pay fah food, an' yuh education. T'ings was hard fah har back then, since she couldn't find a job—somet'ing no one could believe, since Patsy was di smartest in we class. Anyway, as an old friend, ah looked out fah yuh mother. Made sure nobody in di streets trouble har. Didn't know where yuh father was, an' didn't care. My priorities was di people who live in my community. We family. But yuh mother always declined my help. She knew how ah mek my money an' didn't want none of it. Ah didn't blame har. Ah didn't even get upset when she tell me which hole me mus' bury me money." He chuckles to himself and shakes his head. "Yuh mother was a proud woman. Ah always admire an' respect har fah dat."

"So what does that have to do with me?" Tru asks.

"Dis is not yuh fate, Tru."

"What does dat mean?"

"It mean yuh mus' run. Run as far as yuh can away from me. Unlike yuh friends, yuh have a choice."

"Please," she says. "Football is my life."

"I'm a businessman, Tru. Ah only compromise fah profit. I didn't make di rules. An' as often as I break dem, ah can't break dem fah you. Ah respec' yuh mother too much."

"Please . . ."

"We done wid dis convah-sation. Diane!" he calls over his shoulder. "Come walk dis nice young lady out."

"I can walk myself out," Tru says, getting up and walking away, anger boiling inside her like she's a pressure cooker resting unsteadily on a fire, the urge to dig into her flesh to let it out in the stillness of a gentle hiss overwhelming.

46

THE CITY OPENS UP LIKE DESIRE. THE CURVED STONES REMIND Patsy of soft flesh, delicate under the warm glow of sunlight. She feels more like herself, or rather, more like the women she sees on television or on Fifth Avenue swinging their purses, their high heels clicking on the sidewalks. She looks to the left and cannot see the dark thing in her periphery anymore, because everything is so bright—the racks of scarves, hats, jewelry, and I LOVE NEW YORK T-shirts that line the sidewalks. Even her sense of smell is heightened. She inhales the hot apple cider coming from a vending cart, along with something reminding her of coconut drops from the opening doors of a coffee shop. Patsy and Claudette ventured once to Staten Island on the ferry, where they pressed their noses to the window inside the warmth of the lower deck to view the Statue of Liberty, Claudette discreetly reaching for Patsy's hand, smiling, glad for the anonymity among the European tourists and the freedom of America. Here, Patsy is anonymous, inaccessible. There are no Pennyfield neighbors to recognize her. No one she knows, watching. She can afford to be careless. Do little things like brush a stray dreadlock out her lover's face, close that troublesome hook on the collar of her lover's coat, use her thumb to wipe away that extra stroke of berry lipstick she can't bear to let sit there untouched in sunlight. Here, in a place where she's alien, invisible, she can reach over to do this one thing—this one private thing without fear. The city has become an accomplice, making it so easy to fall in love.

Of all the places in the city, Patsy loves Union Square the most. The neighborhood makes her feel like she's a part of the tapestry of New York City, she and Claudette interwoven threads. Patsy enjoys watching kids flip their skateboards on the steps and rails at the entrance of the park. Patsy marvels too at the marching, chanting men and women with signs. Every time she comes to Union Square, there's a different protest going on. The protesters go around in circles like a merry-go-round as other New Yorkers walk by like it's any other day, or, like Patsy, they stop to watch a Michael Jackson look-alike moonwalk to "Billie Jean." Sometimes Patsy and Claudette watch dogs play in the doggie compound, or observe what Patsy calls "flesh-eating rats" dart like mongooses through the bushes. *"Dey eat bettah than us,"* Claudette muses. *"Dey run dis city."* Today, the couple bypass the crowded maze of the Union Square Holiday Market to sit, talk, and people-watch. After a few hours, they walk to the Whole Foods. Another thing they like to do is shop for food. Claudette's favorite place to go food shopping is the Whole Foods across the park. There, they stroll through the aisles together with a cart. Claudette likes to get raw nuts and fruit for her morning shakes, though Patsy tries to get her to save money by shopping at the farmers' market instead. Claudette, Patsy learns, is particular about foods in a way she has never considered—like buying eggs marked as free-range, drinking almond milk instead of cow's milk, picking up juice that promises no sugar or syrup, reading every last ingredient on a package before deciding whether to buy it. "Food is food," Patsy tells her. "I know people who eat anyt'ing an' everyt'ing an' live to a hundred years old."

"Yes, but it's always nice to know what we putting inside our body. American food so full ah hormones an' sugar. Everyt'ing processed."

"How yuh know the t'ings dat say organic is really organic? What if dey jus' put di sticker there, knowing people like yuhself will buy it?"

Claudette laughs. "I can tell di difference."

"How?"

"Yuh feel different aftah yuh eat certain foods."

"Rubbish. Is yuh mind an' good marketing playing tricks on yuh."

"Smart-ass." Claudette rolls her eyes.

Once they get to a quiet aisle, Patsy tickles her side. They fool around like children, playfully tickling each other, surreptitiously reaching around or under to pinch while giggling and slapping away the wayward hand. They come close to kissing, but something halts Patsy. She happens to look up in the midst of a giggling fit and into an amused familiar face staring at them. There, at the end of the aisle, is Ducky crouched, cleaning up broken eggs. Patsy freezes when she sees him staring, his face as black as night, except for the gash of pink inside his gaping mouth, and the whites of his widened eyes, pinning her. "Patsy? Ah you dat?"

The blood drains from Patsy's veins. Her hand drops from Claudette's bottom. "Ducky? What yuh doin' working here?"

Claudette is quiet, staring at both of them. Patsy notices her shifting uncomfortably too.

Ducky, whose real name is Percival Antonio Bedford, went to Sunday school with Patsy in Pennyfield. His mother, Miss Henrietta, sang the loudest on the choir, though she couldn't sing. Ducky was born on Good Friday and christened on Easter Sunday. Miss Henrietta, being religious and superstitious, believed that Ducky was a born healer like Jesus Christ of Nazareth. The whole church and community believed this too. Who knew that this man, expected all his life to one day rise to greatness despite having heel-back skin, would be a Whole Foods cleaning man? For years, Miss Henrietta told everyone in Pennyfield that her son was a senior-somebody at one of the big banks in America.

Patsy speaks up. "I—I should get going. Ah 'ave somewhere to be. Glad to see you're well."

Ducky nods. "Yes—yes. I'm busy too. Yuh know. Di banking hours can be hectic. Ah was in here shopping, an' di eggs . . . you know."

"Right."

His eyes are on Claudette. Regardless of his status in America, Ducky still has a lot of power—his ability to tell people back home that he saw Patsy pinching another woman on her rump, an act of possession. She has sinned with her hands—a sin that is hard to forgive. She cringes, remembering the crimson rage in the other man's eyes when he caught her and Cicely inside the house on Jackson Lane. But Ducky's hands are clasped tenderly around the mop, aged. No man with hands like that could kill her.

More in embarrassment than terror, Patsy averts her gaze. When she gathers the courage again to look at him, she sees that his dark eyes have hollowed and his skin has taken on the glint of coal long after the flame dwindled. Something bleak and resigned has settled in his face. Gone is the bright, motivated boy who lived on Hagley Lane.

Ducky's look of shame suddenly sets Patsy at ease; she has power too.

"I know how it is shopping wid too much t'ings on di list," she says to him, her eyes on the wet mop and bucket next to him. And just like that, above the broken eggs in the Whole Foods aisle, a silent agreement of secrecy is hatched.

47

EVERY NIGHT NOW, WHEN TRU FALLS ASLEEP, SHE DREAMS OF feathers—red, black, green, white. They slip into her dreams, the death dance of roosters. They're no different from the men cheering them on, pitting them against each other. Elbows flap like the wings of the birds, though neither man nor rooster can fly, will ever fly.

She wakes up in the middle of the night, her pillow drenched.

THERE'S SOMETHING DIFFERENT ABOUT SORE-FOOT MARLON, Albino Ricky, and Asafa since they started playing for Pope. Lately, when they think she doesn't notice, they huddle like the Three Stooges, their foreheads touching. She's reminded again of being an outsider, especially when they walk ahead. She has to run to catch up, and when she does, they stop talking. It's like they're six years old again, realizing for the first time that she doesn't have a cow's tripe hanging between her legs. Frustrated with their secrecy, Tru confronts them. "Why oonuh ignoring me?"

"What yuh mean?" Sore-Foot Marlon asks. "We jus' had a long practice."

"Yeah, but when ah come by you an' Ricky, oonuh get quiet." Albino Ricky scratches his head and looks the other way. Sore-Foot Marlon shrugs his shoulders.

"What's going on?" Tru asks.

"Nothing," Albino Ricky says, lighting up a cigarette he took from behind one ear.

"Walking away an' getting quiet when I'm around isn't *nothing*."

"Tru, jus' drop it," Asafa says.

"Shut up. Ah wasn't talking to you," Tru shoots back.

"Tru, there's nothing going on," Sore-Foot Marlon says. "Trus' me."

"How you going to look me in di eyes an' tell me dat?" Tru asks him. She doesn't wait for an answer. Strangely, the anger she feels is almost soothing. She knows that she's a liability, untrustworthy because of her policeman father. They see her as a threat. They also see her as an outsider. Pope has somehow removed the veil from her friends' eyes. She looks down at the ground, aware of the distance between them, and says nothing more. She bids her friends goodbye and watches them walk away—the silhouette of their tall, slender frames merging into one shadow.

"Goaaaaaaaaaaaal," Ras Norbert cries out in the distance, his eyes closed in sad passion, his dark face lifted to the downpouring light of the sun, lamenting to the gods for them all.

48

PATSY TILTS HER HEAD TOWARD THE SKY ON A VERY FESTIVE Flatbush Avenue where Christmas shoppers crowd the sidewalks, and notices that it might pour. Saturdays used to be errand days for her, but now with Claudette they're adventures. She and Claudette have been searching through clearance racks and holiday sales bins at the discount stores to fill Patsy's barrel—Patsy thinking of the little girl with sunbeams in her face, and Claudette picking out things she thinks a sixteen-year-old girl would like: handbags, lip gloss, perfumes that smell like fruit. Patsy has spent almost all the money she saved over the years to purchase the gifts.

"We might have to go soon. It look like it g'wan storm," Patsy says.

Claudette looks up too and sees the gray clouds. Together, they hail a dollar van to Patsy's place. By then, the sky opens up. They giggle as they run into the building, dripping wet, with their shopping bags. They make it up the steps to Patsy's room and close the door. Claudette smiles when she sees the barrel. Her eyes then wistfully survey the room. "It always feel suh comfortable here," she jokes, dropping the shopping bags on the floor.

"Glad yuh feel dat way." Patsy hands her a towel to dry off, her own body wet and chilled.

"You look cold an' tired," Claudette says. "Ah thought yuh was g'wan shop down di whole place."

"It still nuh feel like it's enough," Patsy says, looking down inside the gaping mouth of the barrel, the shopping bags lined at her feet.

Claudette laughs and comes close to Patsy, lifting her face with her hands. "Yuh heart is in it. Dat's all dat matters." She kisses Patsy, and Patsy closes her eyes to feel the warmth of her lips. They kiss deeply, pausing briefly for Patsy to pull Claudette's sweater over her head. With Claudette's help, she removes the other things. Sitting on the bed, Patsy reaches up, her fingers spread over Claudette's body, caressing the softness of her breasts and kneading the flesh around her beaded waist and hips. Patsy catches a glimpse of the barrel again, peering at them like a voyeur from across the small room. Remorse lances her and she turns from it, burying her face in the softness of Claudette's belly, then slowly sliding down and beyond, pleading with her lips for that love that would dissolve the seemingly unforgiving shadow in the corner.

49

HALF-NAKED CHILDREN PLAY ON GARRICK'S LANE, RUNNING around and sucking their thumbs while pulling on their dark, unruly hair. Tru passes St. George Furnace, where people used to sell pan chicken, roasted peanuts, and peppered shrimp before the recession. It takes her through the narrow zinc-fence aisle of Cooper Lane to the tenement yard, where washerwomen take down sheets and clothes off the lines, putting them inside buckets, and where women sit on steps, brown, fleshy legs open, combing or braiding their daughters' hair, their faces bleached near-white with cake soap and bleaching creams. Girls Tru's age move around freely with toddlers on their hips, carrying them inside boarded-up houses painted in bright blue and pink and green and yellow. There's a mini-shop with bars over the windows, selling soft drinks, banana chips, Shirley biscuits, and an assortment of liquor. Men sit on crates, on stools, on chairs, propping their chins in their hands, appearing like those gargoyle statues rich people put on their gates, watchful yet resigned, with rum bottles held between rough fingers. She feels their eyes on her as she passes them, and long after, licking the heels of her new Puma sneakers.

Tru walks to the baby-blue house in the yard closest to a standpipe where three gravely thin mongrel dogs lick the dripping water up off the sliver of concrete in the dusty yard. The breeze carries the smell of gutter water. In this area, many of the children have rashes and boils on their limbs. There is no explanation for the condition, though it's speculated that the drinking water that the people get from the foot of the hill might be contaminated with waste. This accounts for the trees dying in that area, wilted and gray. People have been told not to drink the water; but the water is free.

Tru can hear babies crying inside the house and the squeals of young children. A woman's voice shouts, "Oonuh stop di noise! Marlon, come help me wid yuh brother an' sistah dem!" Miss Olive, Marlon's mother, is a haggler who sells in the arcade downtown. Tru used to only see her at special functions at Pennyfield Primary, when she'd come dressed in one of her colorful wigs and a nice outfit that often revealed her figure.

Tru picks up a rock and knocks on the plank by the door.

"Is who dat?" Miss Olive yells. "Marlon, guh see is who dat by di door! If is Foster, tell har me nuh deh 'ere!"

Sore-Foot Marlon opens the door. He's wearing a mesh marina shirt and a pair of jeans cut off at the knees. When he sees Tru, he frowns. "What yuh doing here?"

"Marlon, is who?" his mother asks.

"It's jus' Tru, Mama!" Sore-Foot Marlon shouts over his shoulder.

"Good evening, Miss Olive!" Tru calls, biting her bottom lip and stuffing her hands inside the pockets of her sweatpants.

"Tru!" Miss Olive shouts. She appears behind Sore-Foot Marlon, a pale face—the shade of the inside of an underripe guava—bleached with the creams or cake soap the girls and boys are using nowadays. It even seems to fade her once-striking features. Her hair is already in curlers, but it doesn't matter, since Miss Olive always has a way of making everything look like it's in fashion.

"Tru! Long time. Where's all yuh beautiful long hair?" She rubs her hand over Tru's head. "Tun 'roun mek me see yuh," she says.

Tru obeys and turns for Miss Olive to examine her. "Yuh growing tall an' skinny!" Her eyes fasten on Tru's flattened chest, and Tru can almost see her mind working, the question on her parted lips. Tru folds her arms across her chest.

"Yuh look jus' like Patsy. Ah hope yuh taking good care of yuhself." Tru nods and forces a smile. "I am, Miss Olive."

Miss Olive brushes Tru's arm with her hand. "Yuh need to put some meat 'pon yuh body, gyal. Or else you an' Marlon could pass fi twin. A nice young girl suh pretty should be dressing up nice fah young men. Ah don't t'ink Patsy would like you dressing dis way. Man, dat gyal coulda dress!" She rubs Tru's arm, the slight, intimate pressure making Tru uncomfortable. "Ah thought she was sending yuh all dat American food to fatten yuh up!"

"Mama—" Sore-Foot Marlon chides. Tru's face warms.

Miss Olive fans him off, but not before stamping Tru with a do-what's-best-for-you-and-take-my-motherly-advice look. She disappears into the house of crying babies. Sore-Foot Marlon is apologetic, hunching his shoulders and hanging his head as he closes the door behind him. Before the door slams, a little naked boy with rashes all over his arms and legs runs up to Sore-Foot Marlon and hugs his leg. Miss Olive's voice is heard in the background calling him. "Barry! Come bathe!"

"Barry, guh back inside," Sore-Foot Marlon coaxes the crying boy. "Ah not going anywhere far. Me soon come back."

The little boy looks at Tru, who smiles at him and waves. The rashes cover his neck too, so much so that it looks like another skin altogether, rougher and darker. He stops crying and puts a thumb to his mouth, watching her with curiosity. Perhaps he too is trying to figure her out.

"Go!" Sore-Foot Marlon says to him.

The little boy runs back inside, and Tru turns to Sore-Foot Marlon.

"Ah want to talk to you."

"About?"

"You ignoring me."

"Tru, ah have no time fah dis . . ."

"You used to have time."

"Tru . . ."

"Why yuh keeping me out?"

Sore-Foot Marlon laughs. "I'm not keeping you out. I'm jus' busy . . . as you can see. Also, what yuh doing around here? Yuh don't want dark fi ketch yuh 'pon dis side ah town. God forbid somet'ing 'appen to you out here. Yuh daddy might neva let us live it down. Like when he—"

"Why yuh g'wan throw dat in my face?"

Sore-Foot Marlon shrugs. "Isn't it di truth?"

"We've been playing together for years. We know everyt'ing about each other. Why would you let Pope come between us?"

"What do you know about me, Tru?"

"Where's dis coming from?"

Sore-Foot Marlon is shaking his head. "Neva mind."

"Yuh not g'wan bring dis up an' drop it like dat," Tru says.

"Tru, I have to go. I have to help my mother."

"At least tell me why."

"Maybe di person yuh should be interrogating is yuhself, Tru," he says. "Yuh know how much me woulda give fi stand in your shoes? At least yuh can still afford to go to Wilhampton. Yuh father is a police-man. Yuh see dis?" He gestures with his hand to the neighborhood. "Yuh don't have to come here. Yuh neva had to. Jus' like yuh neva had to play fah Pope. So, when yuh see us working hard on dat field to win dat money, it's not about you, Tru. It's about us."

T RU WALKS TOWARD HOME, MARLON'S WORDS CLAWING AT HER. The men steeped in rum are no longer perched on stools in the shadow of dusk. The washerwomen, the young girls, the crying babies, and the mongrel dogs are all gone, because of the curfew. Soldiers holding long rifles, and police in riot gear line the edges of St. George Furnace.

"Hey, hey! Yuh should be inside!" a policeman with a rifle and bullet-proof vest roars at Tru. There are so many of them. Their shields reflect the light from the lorries and street poles.

Tru squints into the bright beams of one of the lorries. "I'm going—"

Before she finishes her sentence, the police officer heads toward her with his gun pointed. He stops suddenly when he recognizes her. "Tru?"

Tru recognizes her father's voice. When he sees the look on her face and realizes that she's visibly terrified, he lowers his gun. He used to tell Tru and her brothers to never creep up behind him or else one day he could draw his gun and pull the trigger. He's not a man who likes to be ambushed. They used to laugh at this, thinking their father was just being funny. That he would never shoot his own children.

"Tru, what yuh doing in dis area?" Roy hisses. "It's dangerous."

"I—I was—was jus'—jus' visiting a friend."

"What di hell—" Roy steps closer to her. "Yuh have no business in dis place aftah curfew hours." Another officer, whom Tru recognizes as Lieutenant Phillips, comes up to Roy from behind. "Tru? Ah you dat? Woulda neva recognize you dressed like dat! Ah thought you was one ah yuh bredda dem!" He laughs. Roy seems furious. "Stay outta dis, Joseph," he says to Lieutenant Phillips. To Tru he yells, "Go home now!"

Roy's caustic tone startles Tru, reminding her of that night she caught him and Marva having sex; the hatred in his command. "*Get di hell out!*" He signals the other officers to let her pass. And just like that, the barricades open up like a gate for Tru to walk through.

"I'm sorry . . ," she whispers to Roy. But he doesn't respond.

A T HOME, TRU TAKES A SHOWER AND THEN LOCKS THE DOOR TO her room. She sits on the edge of the bed, naked, and stares at herself in the long mirror on her wardrobe door. She has never felt so alone. The more she stares at herself, the less she recognizes who is staring back. She doesn't know any women she wants to be like. Somehow, they are all joined, it seems, linked by a sanguine chain that excludes her. Her mother, Marva, Mama G, the teachers and girls at her school. Now she fears that she will forever be afflicted with the looks and touches of strangers, their cruelty, pity, perversion disguised as gentle warnings.

Seized by a frenzy of rage, Tru stuffs her favorite Pelé T-shirt inside her mouth to muffle her groans as she presses down hard on her nipples, caught between her index finger and thumb, until the physical pain makes her forget the less tangible one.

But it doesn't help. Eventually she stumbles out of her room. Marva is home, inside the living room, fanning herself with a newspaper, her legs up on a cushion. One hand holds her belly. As soon as she sees Tru, she laments.

"Yuh father . . . did he tell yuh?"

"Tell me what?"

"You know dat woman had di baby fah him? A girl. Dat's what she gave him. A beautiful baby girl, eight pounds nine ounces. An' guess who di mother is." Marva laughs to herself like she's recounting a pleasant memory. "Iris. Can you believe it? Di same girl ah took undah my roof, fed, and send har to hairdressing school . . . she same one."

Iris moved out a few years ago, went to Portmore when Tru started eighth grade. Tru kept in touch, seeing her in passing sometimes as she waited for the bus in Half-Way Tree. She's still quiet and slight, with a shy smile. Tru remembers the days when Iris lived with them and Marva and Roy would have their fights. How the three witches came and gave Marva crushed coal and garlic to wear around her waist; how Marva stirred and stirred, her brooding figure always by the stove; how one day Iris took sick and had to move back to the country for a while; how Marva never spoke of her again, and Roy spoke very little. Marva continues, "Here I am, being a homemaker—doing everyt'ing in my power to mek sure di man come home to good meal, clean sheets, and pressed clothes—"

"Marva, I'm sorry."

"Who him t'ink him is, eh?" Marva asks Tru in a conversational tone. "Yuh t'ink God put me 'pon dis earth fi walk five steps behind a man? Yuh t'ink I g'wan spend me life kissing di ground him walk 'pon?"

"Marva, I—"

"Hell, no." She finally turns to face Tru, who is standing there in the dark, the light from the television illuminating her face. "One day yuh g'wan undah-stand. Trus' me. One day yuh g'wan know di pain of being a mule. Yuh know why? Because di sins of yuh father. Men like dat don't care dat dey have daughters. Daughters who watch an' learn an' t'ink is how man supposed to treat dem. Yuh know how much ah give up to be wid dat man?"

Tru quietly listens, silenced by Marva's rant.

"Yuh know what di man 'ave di nerve to call me? Selfish." Marva laughs again, her tirade unheeding. "All because ah tell him ah can't tek it no more. It's as if di man t'ink me is Superwoman. It's as if I mustn't complain or ask him fah help. You know, when he carried you here, him neva ask me nuttin? Him jus' tell me dat him five-year-old daughter coming to live wid us, because she 'ave nowhere else to go, an' dat was dat. His orders. I agree because ah thought I'd finally get a daughter like ah always wanted."

She looks at Tru as if noticing her presence for the first time. Her voice drops an octave, and her eyes brim with tears as she looks at Tru. "What is it wid you? Why yuh spite me, suh? Tell me. Yuh can't jus' be a girl fah once? Yuh not done wid dis phase yet?" A choked plea comes from her throat. "God already gave me three sons. Two more on di way. An' di one time ah t'ink him answer my prayer, is di one time him played a cruel joke and gave me you. Ah can't fathom you a'tall, a'tall."

Still shaking her head, she leans back on the sofa. "Dis is foolishness . . ." She flips the channel on the television to an infomercial. Tru recedes back into her room, locks the door, and retrieves the razor she hides inside her treasure box, overwhelmed by the torment of her lifelong grief. She uses it on her scarred right thigh, deftly carving three more marks that scream bright red against the quiet brown of her skin. The darkness returns. She wipes away the watery veil from her eyes, knowing that the heaviness that weighs on her has nothing to do with the dark, nor will the morning deliver her.

❦

A FTER SCHOOL ON MONDAY, SASKIA APPROACHES TRU, CON-cerned. "Yuh okay?"

She walks in front of Tru to get her to stop. Tru walks around her. "Hey, slow down. I thought you said we can walk to Half-Way Tree together," Saskia says.

"I changed my mind," Tru replies, stepping to the side.

"Tru, we can talk—"

"I want to be alone."

"It's not going to do you any good to keep whatever is bothering you in . . ."

Tru flinches when Saskia touches her.

"What do you want from me?" Tru asks, stopping to face Saskia. "All of a sudden you want to be my friend. For what?"

"Because I like you. A lot," Saskia says. "I've always liked you."

"I'm not likable."

"You are. I like you more than I've ever liked anyone . . ."

Saskia hugs her biology and chemistry CXC textbooks, shifting from side to side, barely meeting Tru's scrutiny. Tru is suddenly flooded with awareness as she watches her. She blinks. *Seriously?* she thinks to say, but doesn't. For the first time, she's terrified of what's hidden behind Saskia's shy smile, her secret gaze, her willingness to say hello despite Tru's reticence and their classmates' scorn. It surprises Tru a little and saddens her a good deal. "I—I'm—I'm sorry, I can't right now. I have to catch the bus."

Saskia nods and looks away swiftly. "Sure. Ah didn't mean to keep you. I jus' thought—" Tru senses her disappointment. "Neva mind what ah thought." Saskia moves to let Tru pass.

Tru hurries through the school gate and into the swirls of the late afternoon chaos in Half-Way Tree, telling herself that she'd rather settle for people's brutal reactions, their disgust, their disappointment, their bullet of saliva in her face as they refer to her as "*it.*"

On the bus, she looks out the window, Kingston city flying past her. Privately, she acknowledges her cowardice. Once upon a time she did everything to be liked. To be a good girl. She even lied. She would steal gizzadas her mother baked when she wasn't in one of her dark moods. Always, her mother had a thing for numbers, for counting, and if something was off, she knew immediately. Tru liked to watch her mother grate the coconut, sprinkle cane sugar on top, dip her fingers into the dough, and meticulously bend the gizzadas into shape. She stole them because it was her way of capturing those moments, remembering them, because they were few and far in between. She stored the gizzadas in a cloth and tucked it between the wall and the bed they shared. Her deeds were discovered when the cloth was mauled by ants, which crawled into the sheets and bit them while they slept. Stealing gizzadas and lying about it turned out to be a minor offense, but Tru didn't know that at the time. At the time what she feared was losing her mother's love.

50

CLAUDETTE AND PATSY ARE LYING IN BED LIKE ANY OTHER SATurday evening, watching the small television in Claudette's studio, when Cicely suddenly appears on the screen. Patsy pauses, the remote almost falling out of her hand. Cicely's image on the television screen looks pale, drained. Her graceful form under the double-breasted suit she wears seems thinner than Patsy remembers; her face, with the delicate sweep of bone under smooth cream skin, is grim but still very striking, her hair long and bleached. The bangs she wears hide that scar on her forehead—a scar only Patsy sees, because she knows it is there, as essential as a birthmark. She's standing next to Marcus as he discusses his New Brooklyn campaign with a reporter on a local Brooklyn channel. "What an ass," Claudette mutters beside Patsy, pulling the sheet over her naked breasts. "He don't t'ink him shooting himself in di leg, turning 'gainst him own people?"

"Shhh . . . let me hear," Patsy says, turning up the volume.

Marcus, who is clean-shaven and dressed sharply in a tailored suit and bow tie, is poised next to his wife, her right hand limply holding his as he publicly defends stop-and-frisk. The reporter probes Marcus on the increased police presence and escalated violence in his constituency, including the recent shooting of an unarmed deliveryman mistaken for a drug dealer on a gentrified block. Marcus deflects the question.

"What are your thoughts, Mrs. Salters?" The reporter is a portly older black man. When the camera zooms on Cicely's face, Patsy sits forward and watches, unable to move.

"Where yuh going? Yuh pulling di cover off me!" Claudette complains playfully. But Patsy ignores her. She's focused on Cicely's face. Cicely stares out at the camera with the wistfulness almost of a young girl, her blue-green eyes reflecting in that fragment of time a deep loss inside her—a look Patsy saw on more than one occasion during the days and months following Miss Mabley's death. Patsy feels a slight tug inside her when Cicely simply clears her throat. "Say something . . ." Patsy whispers to her. "You know what he's doing isn't right. I know you do . . ."

"Yuh know har?" Claudette asks from behind. Patsy almost forgot that she's there in the room. Patsy doesn't respond. What can she say? To say she knows the woman on the screen—the woman who stands by Marcus Salters—would be a lie.

"She's beautiful," Claudette says. "But why am I surprised? Ah man like dat would neva pick a black woman—wid di exception of Barack Obama. God bless him. Men like dat usually love weak trophy wives like dat woman."

Patsy yanks the sheet off of her and gets up from the bed naked. For the first time, she feels anger toward Claudette. "What's wrong wid you?" Claudette asks, stunned and bewildered.

Without another word to Claudette, Patsy walks to the bathroom and closes the door. She hears the surging sound of traffic and someone's music and scattered voices. The sounds rush in to fill the hole pierced by Claudette's words. Patsy knows that what she has been running away from has finally caught her. She's conscious of its breath on her legs, old feelings digging into her like claws. Her heart batters itself against the wall of her chest, as if in a desperate attempt to escape, understanding that there's a part of her that is willing to surrender with perverse gratification to the murderous mammoth thing capable of ripping her apart again and again.

*

Two days before Christmas, Patsy and Claudette walk down Church Avenue, finishing up their shopping for Tru. They zip in and out of bargain stores, maneuvering through the heavy foot traffic on a Saturday afternoon. The shipping date Patsy has set for herself is drawing close, and she is beginning to feel anxiety. She spends a long time in each store, deciding on every single item she chooses. Had it not been for Claudette reminding her that her gesture is the first step toward establishing a relationship with Tru, Patsy might have buckled under the weight of the pressure.

Patsy continues down the street, listing the names of the stores still on her list for Claudette, who is on her lunch break. They aren't touching, but their gestures could give away the intimacy between them.

Their banter is cut short by the sound of screeching wheels. It jolts the people on Church Avenue and incites other drivers to honk their horns at the driver of the gold Lexus with tinted windows, who had obviously pressed too hard on his brakes. Patsy gasps as the driver steers the car out of the street, almost running into a fire hydrant as he pulls up to the curb. Suddenly the door on the driver's side opens and a woman's voice yells, "Patsy!"

Patsy squints. But this can't be. It's as though seeing Cicely on the news has conjured her, and here she is, yelling Patsy's name in the street like a madwoman. "Patsy!" she yells again, jogging toward her and waving. Deep inside, Patsy tenses. Cicely must have picked up on Patsy's reserve, because she slows and takes more cautious steps toward Patsy.

"Hi . . ." Cicely says, breaking the ice. She seems suddenly nervous, her voice shaking as she comes close. Patsy shifts her purse to her other shoulder. "Cicely . . ." The name rushes out of her like air that has been trapped in her lungs.

They don't hug. She hadn't thought to practice her greeting should they run into each other. Patsy's face twitches as if trying to adjust to the myriad emotions skipping through her, trying to discern which expression is best. Esctatic? Wistful? Veiled? Patsy tries to mask all that is bubbling up inside her in this moment, still too wary about the years that had gone by—too many—without any contact. Cicely stands with her hands at her sides too, the distance between them too wide to reach over. The look Cicely has reminds Patsy of when she used to rub sinkle bible all over Cicely's skin after Aunt Zelma's abuse, shy yet curious. It's hard to tell what Cicely is thinking now. She looks better in person, though the scar on her forehead is more visible with her hair pulled back off her face. She's dressed casually in a nice jogging suit, perhaps on her way to or from the gym.

"Yuh looking good," Cicely says, taking the words out Patsy's mouth.

"An' yuhself," Patsy replies.

"It's been so long . . ."

"Too long."

Cicely leans forward to hug Patsy. Patsy's body stiffens at first and then relaxes in the embrace. "I've been looking for you," Cicely whispers in her ear.

They hug like they are girls again, lying among the wildflowers, alone in the world, together. But just as fleeting as Cicely's warm breath in Patsy's ear is the sudden rush of reality when Patsy opens her eyes and glances over Cicely's shoulder, remembering Claudette standing there, arms folded across her chest.

Patsy pulls away from the embrace and immediately gestures to Claudette. "Cicely, this is my . . . dis is Claudette. Claudette, Cicely is an old friend . . ." Her voice trails.

The color seems to drain from Cicely's face as though Patsy's words are a thread capable of strangling her right there in the street.

Cicely shakes Claudette's hand, her smile hardly reaching her eyes.

Meanwhile, Claudette scrambles to adjust to Cicely's handshake, unable to hide her annoyance.

"Claudette. A pleasure to meet you."

"And you," Claudette replies dryly.

"I'll let you two carry on . . ." Cicely says reluctantly, her eyes peering into Patsy's.

"I'm glad to see you're well. I saw you on TV. Yuh finally got what yuh always wanted," Patsy says. She looks down, for she knows those eyes can pierce her and lay her bare.

"Yes." Cicely's slim bejeweled hand absently smooths the highlighted strands in her hair.

"It was good running into you, Cicely. I—I must get going."

"Yes, yes, of course. Don't let me hold you up," Cicely replies. "An' don't be a stranger."

As Patsy walks away with Claudette, she can feel Cicely watching them until they disappear into the throng of people on the crowded sidewalk. Not once does Patsy look back. She knows she could be struck blind by the orange glow of memory that beckons her from the blue ocean of Cicely's eyes, which does very little to cool the fire crackling inside her chest.

51

SUNDAY MORNING, PATSY AND CLAUDETTE ARE AT THE LAUNDRO-mat. Stifling a yawn, she helps Claudette fold towels, underwear, and sleepwear—some of which are Patsy's left behind on the weekends since they began seeing each other. They stack the clean laundry neatly on the countertop. It's still hot from the dryer, like freshly baked bread. Patsy tries to be attentive, but she's preoccupied after a night of tossing and turning, thinking of her encounter with Cicely. She finally settled next to Claudette on the low bed surrounded by the beads and the predawn darkness, spooning her warm sleeping body. Under the watchful eye of the moon, which she could see through the window, she wondered if Cicely was wide awake too, staring at the same moon. Patsy wasn't sure when exactly she fell asleep, but she woke up to the sounds of Claudette, naked as the day she was born, moving about the studio, emptying her hamper and filling the laundry bags. She didn't kiss Patsy on the lips like she normally does when she gets up early, telling her to lie back down. All she said was that she wanted to go to wash clothes before more people decided that it's laundry day. But Patsy, not wanting to be alone with these feelings that surged overnight, got dressed too and went with her.

"Yuh still t'inking about her. I can tell," Claudette says on their walk back to Claudette's apartment. She pushes a trolley down the uneven sidewalk on Parkside Avenue, across the street from the subway station, carrying the two stuffed laundry bags. The street is busy with cars and buses, even though it's Sunday. In America there is no real day of rest. Worse, it's Christmas Eve.

"When I look at you, there's somet'ing in your eyes. You're not here," Claudette continues.

"I'm here with you," Patsy says, her breath curling. They pass by a shoe repair shop, a pharmacy, a hair salon, a bodega, a Jamaican restaurant that smells of home.

"Yuh don't have to spare me di truth, Patsy. I'm not a child. I'm a grown woman who can take it. Yuh lied about knowing her when ah asked you," Claudette says.

"I didn't lie. Ah jus' didn't answer."

"Who was she to you?"

"My best friend."

"Yuh greeting looked like it was more than dat."

Patsy furrows her brows. "Cicely and I were friends since primary school. Ah told you dat."

"And now?"

"Now she's . . ."

"Ah can hear it."

"Now she's . . ." Patsy's voice trails. "We haven't talked in ten years."

"But she clearly has an effect on you still. Patsy, don't lie to me."

Patsy sighs. "I neva talked about it. I'm not sure I can say what it was—say it right, I mean. I neva told a soul."

"You can tell me."

"Di reason why I'm here . . . di real reason why I came to America . . . was for her. I gave up everyt'ing in Jamaica hoping we'd be together. I wasn't happy dere anyway."

"An' yuh dawta? Dat's why you left her?"

"I tried. I tried to love my baby, but I couldn't. She wasn't enough, because I wasn't enough . . ." Patsy swallows a ball of guilt. "I came here hoping dat Cicely would make everyt'ing right. But it didn't work out dat way."

"Do you still love her?" Claudette asks. "Be honest."

"I—I don't know."

Claudette quiets, and Patsy immediately regrets her answer. They walk in silence toward the wide intersection of Parkside and Ocean Avenue by the big McDonald's, the trolley with the two overstuffed bags between them. Prospect Park yawns and stretches before them with its naked tree branches, taking into it joggers, dog-walkers, and people up for a frigid morning stroll, coffee in hand. Finally, Claudette says, "Go ahead."

"What?"

"I'm not gonna spend my time wondering if you'll ever have an affair with her. I was the other woman in relationships too many times to know when a person wasn't happy with their own relationship or was in search of the *what ifs* between my legs."

Patsy's heart sinks. The stoplight changes to green, a robotic voice inside the machine barking, "WALK! WALK!" But she doesn't move. "What yuh saying?"

"I'm telling you to do what yuh heart is telling you to do, Patsy. You jus' told me dat yuh came to America fah dat woman. Dere's only one way to calm those questions, satisfy whatever it is dat wasn't settled in yuh gut. Only di person who put it dere can take it out."

"You telling me to cheat on you with Cicely?"

"No. I'm setting you free."

"You're di one I love."

"Don't say dat. Not until yuh sure. Not until you've grown enough to mean it."

Patsy processes this in silence. She swallows before almost choking on her words. "Yuh don't mean dat."

Somehow it feels like a letdown that Claudette is so willing to give her free range. Roy had held on tight. At least he had put up a good fight. But he eventually let her go to America to be with Cicely. Very gently, Claudette puts her hand on top of Patsy's on the trolley. Her touch is affirming, her eyes eloquent with affection, stronger, more urgent even than Patsy's. Her gaze reaches out to claim Patsy, to confess that no matter what she chooses to do, no matter what happens, they'll be connected always. Eventually Claudette breaks her gaze and looks down at the curb. When she speaks again, her voice is a drifting, breezy music. "You'll be all right, Patsy. Yuh heart knows best."

Claudette's lips part to say something more, but she changes her mind and crosses the street alone.

52

CHRISTMAS WAS UNEVENTFUL FOR PATSY, AS IT HAD BEEN PRE-vious years. She sat inside her room, alone, drinking eggnog spiked with rum and mulling over Claudette's words and thoughts of Cicely. By the time the holiday passed, she was eager to get back to work.

Now Patsy feeds Baby his Cheerios, smiling as he chews each bite. She hovers the spoon over his head like a helicopter, making the chopping sounds, and he tilts his neck for another mouthful. They both laugh when he snatches the spoon with his mouth. Patsy welcomes the distraction from her thoughts. Claudette's final words still haunt her. She plans to call Cicely later. She tells herself that she's calling to make amends. That they can meet and catch up on the years they missed. In the next room, Patsy hears Regina's raised voice on the telephone.

"You can at least pay him a visit. Yes. But he's been asking for you. You have to tell him . . . no, you have to tell him!"

Patsy leaves Baby in his high chair to feed himself the rest of the cereal while she washes the dishes. Water gushes inside the sink and drowns out Regina's phone conversation. Finished, Patsy dries the dishes, admiring Baby, who is quietly eating his cereal, deaf to his mother's shrieks in the other room. The bedroom door slams and everything quiets. Patsy helps Baby down from his high stool with ease and tousles his hair as she stares at the closed door down the hall. "Let's go out," she says to him gently. "We can't waste such a nice day."

She bathes him, dresses him, and takes him for a walk down Columbus, bypassing the park today. The sun shines bright through the bare tree limbs. Patsy sits on one of the benches facing the street. She allows Baby to count the yellow taxis, waving along with him in the cold. She then takes him to a small park with swings and pushes him. He squeals, delighted by the force and the sight of his legs in the air. When they return to the apartment, Patsy sees a note from Regina that she's gone out and won't be back until later after a reading.

Baby tugs at Patsy's skirt. "Where did Mama go?"

"She didn't say where."

Suddenly her annoyance flares up. "Gone to write . . . gone to meet someone . . . gone to do everything else but be—" Patsy stops herself. Her angry burst, it seems, encompasses not only the woman and her abuse of Patsy's long day, but the pain that occasionally blazes up from her past and has now become her daughter's too. Baby gazes up at Patsy, quietly listening as though waiting for her unspoken words. At the sight of his angelic face, the words tangle inside Patsy's throat. Slowly, her anger fades. "All right. Yuh g'wan have me for longer today. Yuh know what dat mean?"

"Soldier Ronald!" Baby shouts, clapping his hands in delight.

"Yup!"

"Now, help me out by packing away yuh other toys. Soldier Ronald need space to drive around an' look fah enemies."

When they're done playing, Baby naps for an hour. She watches *Oprah* while she mops the floors and vacuums the drapes. Oprah is interviewing a former porn star and talking to a woman—an expert of some sort—about the growing number of women interested in pornography and erotica. Patsy switches off the television after the hour and busies herself with putting away Baby's toys and cooking dinner.

After the sun sweeps across the sky before vanishing, she feeds Baby his dinner. She then reads him a bedtime story. "One more!" he says when Patsy closes the book. "All right." Patsy reads to him again, and every time he requests another story, then another. It's almost eight p.m. She stops when Baby nods sleepily in her arms. The toy he was holding falls from his limp hand. Patsy gets up with him and walks toward his bed, where she lowers him and covers him with his blanket. Finally, the only sounds inside the room are his light snores.

Suddenly the front door opens; Regina's heels are loud across the hardwood floor. Patsy listens as Regina pauses to take them off.

"Is he asleep?" she asks once Patsy emerges from Baby's room, locking the door behind her.

"Out like a light."

Regina appears relieved. "I can't thank you enough for staying."

"No problem," Patsy says. "No problem at all."

PATSY SLEEPILY OPENS THE DOOR TO HER ROOM. HER WORKDAY had begun at six a.m. and she's now just getting home at nine p.m. She limps to the bed, feeling the effect of squatting for long periods on the hardwood floor to play with Baby.

She has to look for Cicely's number in an old address book with the words *National Commercial Bank* stenciled on it, the whites of the letters almost rubbed off by the years. It was buried at the bottom of Patsy's suitcase—the one she has kept since she came to America. The suitcase is tattered, the leather stripped, but inside it are the memories between the yellowed pages of the address book: a few scriptures given to her by Mama G, the numbers and addresses of people she once spoke to, like Ramona, Vincent, and Roy, and the letters that Cicely wrote her years ago, carefully folded in yellowed envelopes.

Listening to Cicely's phone ring, she wonders if she's calling the wrong number. What if Cicely changed it? Patsy looks at the clock by her bed. It's nine-thirty p.m. She would've called earlier if she hadn't worked late. Maybe Cicely is asleep, or busy. After all, she's still a married woman. Her heart races. Patsy's thumb hovers over the end button on her phone, but before she hangs up, she hears Cicely's voice. "Hello?"

Patsy holds her breath.

"Hello?" Cicely says again.

"Hi, Cicely. It's me."

‹

W HEN CICELY ARRIVES AT PATSY'S APARTMENT, SHE SMILES and tells her how much she loves it.

"It's not di American Dream," Patsy says with a hint of sarcasm.

"It's yours," Cicely says, smelling of expensive flowers and looking resplendent in a long purple peacoat sinched at the waist with a belt, a colorful silk scarf wrapped around her neck, still holding on to her Chanel handbag on her elbow. Patsy suspects the bag is not from the fake piles in Chinatown where Patsy and Claudette went two weeks ago to get bargains on T-shirts and accessories for Tru. Cicely inspects the small room. Patsy offers to take her coat. She apologizes for not having a coat hanger, but Cicely tells her she can just put it on the chair.

"Yuh sure?" Patsy asks.

"I'm positive," Cicely replies.

Patsy runs her fingers over the wool. "Dis is really nice."

"Not as nice as having yuh own place. It mus' feel so good to have somet'ing dat's yours."

"Well, if yuh husband have his way, in no time I'll be homeless."

Cicely delicately puts her hand to the base of her throat and clears it. "Uhm, yuh know what I'd like? Ah glass of wata."

Patsy likes that she still doesn't pronounce her *r*'s. She was worried that Cicely would've completely swallowed her native tongue by now. In the kitchen, Patsy fetches a plastic cup and bottled water she finds inside the refrigerator.

When she returns, Cicely is staring down inside the barrel that Patsy and Claudette are working to fill, her hands spanning the circumference.

"Is this for Tru?" she asks, taking the water from Patsy.

"Yes."

Cicely takes a sip of the water.

"Do you want more?" Patsy asks.

"No, thank you." Cicely smiles.

"You can rest it anywhere yuh like."

Cicely sets the cup on the vanity. Patsy watches her move to the window, where the pigeons are nesting, and where the faint sunlight shines through the curtain, making even the dust in the corners of the room appear gold. She's looking out at the vacant lot and the bare trees forming an arcade toward the cemetery. Patsy examines Cicely in the silence: Her dark roots are growing in, along with some gray at her temples. She's even thinner than she looked on television next to Marcus, her chest fuller.

"How is Shamar?" Patsy asks.

Cicely folds her arms across her chest, her eyes still on the vacant lot outside. "He's fine." She shrugs, looking tired all of a sudden. "He dropped out of Cornell after his freshman year, so he's home now, looking for a job. Supposedly. From valedictorian of his class at Stuyvesant High to Ivy League college dropout who smokes weed all day." She laughs a bit to mask the sarcasm in her voice. "I can't say ah didn't try." When she looks at Patsy again there are tears in her eyes.

"I'm so sorry, Cicely," Patsy says.

"Don't be. His father an' I put a lot of pressure on him, yuh know. Especially his father. My son hates me."

"Yuh don't know dat . . ."

"He does. My own son hates me. Ah couldn't protect him from his father."

"Yuh did yuh best, Cicely," Patsy says, swallowing her own guilt. She puts a hand on Cicely's shoulder. Cicely smiles through her tears. "I'm not here to cry ovah my failure as a mother."

Patsy squeezes her shoulder. "It's okay."

Very slowly Cicely reaches into her purse and takes out a small jewelry box. "I have somet'ing special for you." She gives Patsy the small box. "Open it."

Patsy obeys and opens the box, surprised to see the familiar tiger's-eye pendant on what looks like a shiny new sterling silver chain. She smiles. "Yuh kept it."

"I bought the new chain from Tiffany's when the old one rusted."

"Tiffany's?" Patsy asks with an incredulous stare. "Cicely, you didn't have to."

"I wanted to."

But then Patsy remembers the hurt, the disappointment, and gives it back. "Ah can't accept."

"I'm so sorry," Cicely says.

"It's okay."

"No. It's not okay."

"Is wata undah bridge."

"Ah was fooling myself," Cicely says matter-of-factly, setting the gift box down. "I always loved you." Cicely steps closer—so close that Patsy can smell the mint on her breath. "You have no idea how hard I looked for you over the years. Every Saturday I drove through these streets, hoping to find you. I was so desperate to see yuh face, yuh dimples, those eyes." Cicely cups Patsy's face—her eyes a deep blue wall of ocean rising before Patsy, the tender caress of waves like a baptism. "An' now here you are."

Patsy closes her eyes and allows herself to be carried by these waves, her caution floating up, buoyant and ethereal as a piece of cloth in water. She sinks into Cicely's embrace. Patsy imagines Cicely driving slowly through Brooklyn, her Lexus rolling down the different streets of Crown Heights, maybe taking Utica Avenue all the way out to Kings Highway and circling back down Linden Boulevard toward the Caribbean ghetto of East Flatbush, which leads into wealthy, white Park Slope. Or maybe she drove over the bypass of Atlantic Avenue into Bed-Stuy, and through the rough parts of Bushwick and East New York, where women might look twice at her, the street ones with breasts up to their necks and big behinds, wondering if she's a john willing to take them in the backseat;

and black and Latino boys on the corner might pause, wondering if she's their dealer, since her windows are tinted.

"All I could think about were the *what ifs*. Ah sat in dat car for hours, thinking about yuh fingers in my hair. Of all things! Ah realize dat my feelings for you never went away. I wanted to apologize to you fah being a coward. I—I was jus' so afraid, Patsy." Cicely buries her face in the crook of Patsy's neck, and the feel of Cicely pressed against her, her hands caressing Patsy's back, Cicely's murmuring lips against her neck, arouses Patsy. In her fantasies of Cicely, before Claudette entered her life, Patsy's primal instincts would've gotten the best of her; but she already knows deep down in this moment that the memory behind their bodies together only brings pain and anguish.

"Cicely—" Patsy slips from Cicely's embrace, lacing her fingers with hers.

"I made my fear get di best of me," Cicely says.

"It's all right."

"I was hoping we could—"

"Cicely, I—"

"We could start over. Jus' di two of us."

"Cicely, I've moved on. I'm in love wid somebody else."

This confession startles them both. Patsy allows Cicely's hands to drop from hers. In this moment, she acknowledges that though she still has strong feelings for Cicely, they aren't enough. She had used them as fuel to sustain her over the years—but she's found new sustenance.

Quiet falls over the room. Cicely looks to the window again. "Dat woman you were with dat day?" she says finally, her eyes not on Patsy but on the barren trees.

"Yes."

Cicely cups her mouth as if to suppress a sob. Patsy watches her take a deep breath and hug herself. "It's my fault. Ah waited too long. Ah thought ah sacrificed too much to let my guard down. Give up what ah thought was safe."

"Sacrificed what, Cicely?"

"My soul."

"What yuh talkin' about?"

"Twenty years ago, I helped Pope."

"What yuh mean, yuh helped Pope? How?"

"I—I sold drugs for him. He used me to get his stuff into hotels he couldn't get into without a pretty face. I was eighteen . . . I didn't know what ah was doing, and once I was in, I didn't know how to get out. So on one run, instead of delivering Pope's money to him I took it and ran. I used drug money to buy my way into America. Dat was how ah was able to come to dis country. Dat was why ah disappeared for so long without writing. Ah was afraid to let anyone know where ah was. Because ah thought ah was a dead woman when ah lost everything. All of it . . ."

How could Patsy not have known this? She knew her friend had dated Pope, but this? Patsy remembers the envelope she clutched at the embassy with her dreams inside it. With the taste for sweetness in her mouth, and without shame, Patsy had boarded that plane hoping for the release she had always dreamed about with the woman who is now standing in her room—a stranger. How she had yearned to be face-to-face with the scar on the forehead she planned to kiss and unleash the mammoth love that swallowed everything, including love for her own child, and herself. An elephantine love that took her breath away and yanked her under the covers for days despite her baby's crying. It hung over the child's crib, thick and dark. *"You're my home in this world."* It was only with this promise that Patsy was able to care for Tru with the dedication of a woman about to take flight.

And now she looks at the stranger before her. The taste sours in Patsy's mouth. Finally, she says, "You need to go. Your husband might be waiting."

Patsy watches Cicely button her jacket and wrap her scarf around her neck. Before Cicely goes, she pauses by the door. "Can we still be friends?" she asks.

"I don't know," Patsy replies.

Patsy waits until the door closes to sink to the bed, her gaze on the barrel in the corner.

53

EARLY IN THE YEAR, IN MOST PARTS OF THE ISLAND, THE WIND from the north brings a cold front. It's when birds make their migration, descending on the island for warmth, and when the waves lash violently at the shores, digging into the white sands and leaving behind seaweed and other detritus dredged from the ocean as they recede, brooding. Fishermen know not to go out too far, for they might get carried away and find themselves far out in the Atlantic, or worse, might encounter the sharks that migrate to the Caribbean Sea. But recently, something more unusual arrived onshore. A barrel. It was addressed to Tru, with a telegram. Roy was called by the wharf to collect it and bring it home.

On that day, Tru comes home from school and sees the barrel waiting for her in the living room. Kenny is at the table doing homework like any other day, and Roy and Marva, who is nursing her twin boys, are sitting on the couch. Somehow, they all seem small in comparison to the newly arrived four-foot-tall barrel. Tru is transfixed by it, not knowing what to do with ten years' worth of sorry. Her hands drop to her sides and her eyes wheel over the room in a desperate search for an answer in the familiar faces around her. Her gaze meets theirs as her hands lift uncertainly. But they each look away, as though the decision to act or react is hers alone. As if on her way to meet someone for the first time, Tru adjusts her uniform tunic and runs her damp palms down the length of it. With one hand, she smooths her short hair. The others watch as she peers over the barrel. Finally, she lifts the seal, and there, at the top of the pile, is a bag full of girlie accessories—glittery nail files, a pink Babe pouch, big sparkly hair bows, press-on gemstone earrings, flower clips, a notebook that reads *Happy Girls are the Prettiest*. And as if that's not enough, there's a white JanSport book bag with pink flowers all over it, and lots and lots of stationery with girlie flare like Hello Kitty this and Hello Kitty that.

Tru peers up at Roy and Marva. "This is . . . this is not . . ."

Before her next word, Marva and Roy look the other way. Only Kenny, who by now has stopped his homework, meets her searching eyes. Something resembling pity (or is it apology?) lances Kenny's eyes. It reaches across the room to assure her that despite their differences, he understands they are now linked by something stronger. Tonight is the first time she experiences a side of rejection that Kenny has always known—Kenny, the son the father acknowledged but never saw.

She turns and runs from the room. Roy doesn't go after her when she slams the door.

54

PATSY JUMPS UP, AWAKENED BY THE SOUND. AT FIRST SHE thought it was pigeons. It sounds like wings beating in that space so empty of light. But at ten o' clock at night those birds are usually quiet. She's at Claudette's studio, and she's tempted to go back to sleep, too exhausted to raise herself up and part the beads. But she notices that the window is open, and that the sound is coming from tiny pebbles desperately raining from Heaven accompanied by bolts of lightning and thunder. A hailstorm. Patsy has never seen such a thing. The impact is so hard that it's a miracle nothing has shattered. Some kind of omen, some kind of premonition, she thinks, to be woken up this way. Claudette doesn't stir. Patsy closes the window and goes back to sleep, snuggling in Claudette's warmth, glad she has been forgiven.

THE NEXT EVENING, AN UNFAMILIAR NUMBER CALLS PATSY'S phone. Usually she's not home this early. As soon as she sees the 876 area code, she picks up. She has been waiting on this call. She doesn't know if she should take the call standing up or sitting down. And would it even make a difference? Her breath rushes ahead of her thoughts when she answers, "Hello, Tru?"

But it's a distinct baritone voice she hasn't heard in ten years. All the memories rush in with the familiar tenor. "Roy," Patsy says, suppressing any emotion.

"Birdie. This is jus' a courtesy call." His voice is tight, as though wound in the base of his throat with something heavy. "It's Tru."

A dull throbbing begins behind Patsy's eyes at the sound of Tru's name, and all the air rushes from her lungs with one exhale. "Wha' 'appen to Tru?"

"Dat barrel yuh sent." Roy's voice cracks.

"Di barrel?"

"Yuh couldn't even call to ask what Tru like from what she don't like? Yuh couldn't even give har di courtesy? What kinda mother—" He stops himself.

"G'waan, say it," Patsy urges. "Finish yuh sentence an' get it ovah wid. Crucify me now, Roy!"

"Ten years, Birdie. Ten years. An' fah those ten years yuh neva t'ink of picking up a phone to call or a pen to write yuh dawta. Yuh really t'ink one barrel could erase dat fact?"

"I tried . . ."

"Clearly not hard enough."

"Ah wasn't ready."

"Yuh had no choice, Birdie. Many 'ooman raise children dey thought dey wasn't ready for. Who were you to t'ink yuh could run away from yuh responsibility?" The edge in his voice is exposed.

"We not g'wan go down dat road again . . ."

"Yuh neva even made an effort. Yuh don't know one t'ing 'bout our dawta, Birdie. Dat barrel is evidence—"

"When did you become an expert 'bout what a girl want?" Patsy asks, suddenly defensive.

"When yuh left me to raise one," Roy spits. "But dat's not di point. Dat broke har, Birdie. You promise har dat you'd be back. Yuh neva intended to come back a'tall. Yuh shouldn't have sent it."

"Jesus Christ, Roy! Is a stupid barrel!"

There's an abrupt silence on Roy's end. Finally, he says, "Jus' a stupid barrel, huh?" He chuckles to himself—a chuckle that sounds empty, a mere echo that taunts Patsy. "You said it, not me. A stupid barrel. Dat's all it was to you. A selfish guilt trip. A Band-Aid fah di deep wound yuh cause."

"Ah didn't mean it like dat . . ."

"You said what yuh said. Well, yuh know what, Birdie? It back-fired. Yuh should've kept to yuhself like yuh did fah ten years. T'ings was a lot bettah dat way. Our dawta wouldn't be fighting fah har life now."

"Oh, my God . . ." Patsy cups her mouth. "What 'appen to our dawta, Roy?" Roy doesn't immediately answer. "Roy!"

"She's in di hospital," Roy says. "She lost a lot of blood. Went ino hypovolemic shock. She need a transfusion." As Roy fills her in on the details, she only hears bits and pieces, the questions in her head even louder. Roy found their daughter bleeding. "Hol' on, hol' on!" Patsy screams. "Who did dis to her? Yuh found him? Who did it!"

"She did it to harself, Birdie."

"When did it happen?" Patsy asks, barely breathing now, her voice a wheeze.

"We found her yesterday evening . . ."

Yesterday evening. While Patsy had been working, looking after Baby, her own daughter had nearly bled to death.

"My biggest regret in all ah dis is dat ah didn't know what was going on wid Tru—di one person who mattah to me di most . . ." Roy cries.

Patsy remembers how Roy appeared out of nowhere inside the house on Jackson Lane—the shattering of the rusted mirror now loud in her ears as if she's back inside that moment. It was Roy who fought the man off of Patsy and Cicely with his bare hands; his blood splattered when the man slashed his fist with a shard of glass. It formed a puddle, a river, deep like their secret. Roy had to get twenty-nine stitches. Because of some nerve damage, he almost didn't make it into the police academy. Patsy felt she had no choice then but to love him for it—never once asking Roy what he was doing at the house on Jackson Lane to begin with, too ashamed to ever bring it up again. She closes her eyes now to fight the tears as she listens to Roy tell her how their daughter, the fruit of their temporary union, their baby, had punched in the mirror inside her bedroom and dug into her own flesh—her own flesh!—with the broken glass. *How could this be? How could the same man who once saved Patsy from such a fate at the hands of a hateful person be telling her that he could not save their daughter, too?*

Patsy stares out the window, where the sun seems low and drained as it sinks into the hollows of the clouds. Her stomach is taut with the oldest fear she has ever felt. "You're right. It's my fault," she says to Roy. "Ah shouldn't have made dat promise. Ah shouldn't have assumed ah could jus' sen' t'ings like dat without—"

She looks around the room, her eyes sweeping out through the window, where the evening sky glows red-orange. She thinks about Tru harming herself, remembering her mother's gaze toward Heaven when Patsy was just a girl. How she felt a deep sense of loss then, watching her mother's eyes move away from her, toward twilight. How she had looked around the clutter and the empty cupboards her mother left behind inside the house crowded with Jesus figurines. Patsy was reduced from a child to one of the things her mother left behind. Maybe that's why her tears are unrelenting now, spilling from a hidden reservoir. *"Di Bible seh children are di heritage from di Lord. Di fruit of di womb. Yuh reward!"* Mama G had once said to Patsy. *"Ah hope yuh not t'inking 'bout leaving di chile God bless yuh wid."* Patsy lowers her head. She wonders now if that was her mother's attempt at an apology, an acknowledgment that Patsy was worth more than those damn figurines and her God. She searches her memory, desperate now to see the remorse in her mother's eyes. How she stood there on the outskirts of Patsy's girlhood and watch things happen to her, how her back was always turned as if she had given permission to the night to swallow Patsy, to touch her with coarse hands.

The memories come back in a scale of colors. Before they were merely just black-and-white. They now coalesce into a prism of clarity—a light that reflects the shadows that have always been there. Patsy always thought they were hers alone, but as she remembers the frail hope that died in her mother's eyes and emptied all the rooms of her presence, Patsy realizes that the shadows were her mother's too. And Patsy, unaware, gave Tru every reason to believe she too had no worth. *Be a good, obedient girl, an' ah promise I'll be back fah yuh.* It was a lie. A trap. How is Patsy different from her own mother?

"Oh, Tru . . ." she whispers, choked. Slowly, she raises her head toward the sky again, which is now a brilliant violet and silvery blue. "Oh, Tru, forgive me. I didn't know how to be a mother to you . . ." Her voice is a whimper. How powerless she feels now. "Oh, Tru, forgive me! Ah wasn't there for you."

"We both failed Tru, Birdie," Roy says now, softening. It's not like

Roy to do this, to absolve Patsy of her crime. "Don't take all di blame." It also dawns on Patsy that Roy now calls their daughter Tru. How the years have made a difference. The name has taken on new meaning, a purpose.

The door unlocks. Claudette walks in with a bag of groceries and bouquet of fresh flowers. Patsy meets her lover's gaze. She appears like the sun itself, shining on Patsy's left, and on Patsy's right is a large black cloud of uncertainty, threatening rain in the distance. No rainbow on the horizon. "Is it too late?" she asks Roy. The tearful question hangs in the air, unanswered.

55

SINCE THE INCIDENT, TRU EXISTS ON THE PERIPHERY OF EVERY-thing. She feels like she's looking down at herself—a puppet on a string, going through motions with *antidepressants*, as the doctors call them. Tru has to take them like vitamins each day. At times she feels like an exotic fish inside an aquarium under constant surveillance at home and at school, where everyone—Marva, Roy, Kenny, Mama G, the teachers, and her classmates—gawks at her every move. It's as though they are holding their breath.

Her mandatory meetings with the school guidance counselor, Miss Fairweather, are a waste of time. She sits and doodles—Miss Fairweather's voice muted by the clamoring of Tru's thoughts. Tru feels no obligation to fill the silences. Surely the young, hip, half-black, half-Chinese counselor with her wild curly Afro, the flowy linen African print dresses and conch-shell earrings, and her fancy foreign degrees in psychology, probably deems Tru a lost cause. The psychiatrist at Bellevue Hospital probably thought the same, too, when she asked Tru how she was feeling, and Tru's only complaint was that she could no longer masturbate. Maybe that's the reason why they decided to release her back to her father's care, though they never thought to take her off the numbing meds. Though Tru is even more alone than before, she avoids Saskia and refuses to answer Sore-Foot Marlon and Albino Ricky's text messages. Her mother has tried calling, and Tru refuses to speak to her. *How ironic. After all these years in America, she finally acknowledges the existence of telephones.* She sends Tru a letter that Tru refuses to open. The white envelope with Statue of Liberty stamps is still sitting on Tru's nightstand, collecting dust in the same position where Roy placed it last week.

TONIGHT, THE HOUSE IS QUIET. TRU FINISHES HER HOMEWORK and is now pretending to read the Bible Mama G gifted her. *"Fah comfort,"* Mama G said when she placed it at Tru's bedside. She has pestered Tru ever since about reading a few chapters a night. When she caught Tru taking the pills that the psychiatrist prescribed, she snatched them and handed Tru the Bible. *"Dere's nuttin' more powerful fi cure whatevah dey claim wrong wid yuh than prayer an' di Good Word."* Mama G's doting is more than Tru can handle. Mama G has come to stay with Roy and Marva after Tru got out of the hospital—an arrangement made so that Tru is never by herself. The door to Tru's room has been removed, which means she has absolutely no privacy.

"Mine yuh strain yuh eye," Mama G says to Tru now in that gentle voice she has taken to using since Tru's release from the hospital. Tru is sitting at the dining table. She watches as Mama G hauls herself to the kitchen on her bad leg to make her tea.

"Ah don't want any, Grandma," Tru says.

"But yuh haven't eaten. Yuh g'wan get gas in yuh belly if yuh nuh drink somet'ing warm."

Tru is too tired to protest. Too tired to do much these days. With both her wrists still bandaged, she doesn't like to look at her hands. They're just reminders of her failed attempt, and, subsequently, a source of pity.

Marva, like Mama G, acts like Tru is a baby again. It's Marva who wakes Tru in the mornings, coaxes her out of bed, walks her to the bathroom. Marva stands there by the bathroom door and waits until Tru finishes her bath. Tru senses that Marva would bathe her herself if she could. Tru remembers how Marva reverentially washed her back, her head, her face on the first day of Tru's arrival to her father's house. She turned away to give Tru some privacy to wash between her legs. They did this in comfortable silence with just the sound of the water slushing around in the bathtub. There was such tenderness in Marva's touch—a tenderness Tru would welcome now. Each caress expressed to Tru that Marva was handling something of great value, something she regarded as her own.

The outside sounds of crickets give way to the patter of the water heating up on the stove. The smell of peppermint leaves floats up into the dining room, blown by the electric ceiling fan. Soon there is the tinkering of the spoon as Mama G mixes condensed milk into the tea. She places the cup with steam rising from it on the table, then pats Tru on the shoulder with her bony hand. "Mek sure to turn out di light when yuh finish."

"I'm not supposed to be alone, remember?" Tru says with a hint of sarcasm in her voice. This rule is so stupid, since everyone is asleep at night anyway. If Tru really wanted to hurt herself again, she would've done so by now.

"Then yuh need to finish up yuh reading before ah leave," Mama G replies.

Mama G takes her time to pour her nightly glass of water that she keeps by her bedside in case she gets into one of her coughing fits. She's now sleeping in Iris's old shed. She hums as she fetches the water jug herself from the refrigerator. Her housedress sweeps the floor, whimsical-like, as she moves. Tru listens to Mama G's humming and her movements without raising her head, the crickets outside getting louder and louder with the amicable—though slightly off-putting—silence between them. Tru closes the Bible.

"Grandma, can I ask you something?"

"Anyt'ing m'dear." Mama G pulls out one of the chairs at the table and sits, seemingly glad to be engaged by Tru, who has been quiet with everyone else. *Would you love me this way if I didn't almost die?* she wants to ask. But when she gets her grandmother's undivided attention, Tru opens and closes her mouth, the words turning back to settle inside her gut. Instead, she asks, "At what age did you get saved?"

Mama G lets out a big sigh like she intends to blow down the whole house and straightens her back. "Is thirty-t'ree years now since God delivah me."

"From what?" Tru asks.

Mama G makes a face. "How yuh mean, from what? Di Devil himself. Ah was a very misguided young woman."

Tru can't imagine her grandmother as a young person. There was never a time in Tru's life that her grandmother alluded to her past.

"What did you struggle with?" Tru asks, her eyes trying to search for the young woman behind the scowling mask. Mama G looks at Tru, but Tru can tell by her eyes' glossy veil that they've looked past her, beyond the dining room. She doesn't know how far her grandmother's gaze stretches, but it's definitely not here.

"T'ings was hard raising yuh mother by me self wid di chump change ah was getting as ah helper," Mama G says. "Har father left me for ah ole wench him used to cut grass fah up Stony Hill. Di stupid brute thought a high-class woman like dat would want him fah more than him—" She clears her throat, though it is obvious from the way she does it that it does not need clearing at all. "Di woman husband found out about di affair an' shot him dead two months before yuh mother was born. Ah used to seh serve him right. But dat was before ah got saved. God took care of it." Her head bobs up and down despite the words of forgiveness she speaks. "Anwyay, only God was keeping me from going mad, raising a chile by me self. Di only other time ah felt suh powerless an' weak was when me daddy, Papa Joe, die." She pauses and shakes her head, her face darkened by the memory. "Ah neva found peace till ah surrendered it all to God. Once ah started looking to Heaven, everyt'ing else became easy. Nuttin' else mattah aftah dat, because di good Lawd let us know dat Him will come in di night like ah t'ief an' tek di worthy ones back to Heaven wid Him. Dat we mus' prepare we self fah di day of salvation. Di Devil taunted me even more. Tell me all sorta t'ings to discourage me. Him even tempt me a few times. But ah was ready fah him. Ah prayed an' fasted. One time it got suh bad dat ah had to fast fah forty days an' forty nights like Jesus in di desert. Yuh mother was small, but she knew we had to work hard fi keep di Devil away. When ah die, ah know my Almighty God is waiting to congratulate me."

Tru frowns. "Soun' like yuh waiting to die, Grandma."

"Di good Lawd say to wait faithfully. Everyt'ing shall come to ah end. Dere's ah bettah place than here, my chile," Mama G says, looking off again beyond the patch of blackness by the window.

"What if dat place don't exist?" Tru asks.

"How yuh mean? Dere's a place fah people like us. It's definitely not 'ere on earth. Earth is fah di sinners—di ones who get dem riches in ways di Lawd condemn. Yuh don't know? Well, mek me tell yuh—we might be piss-poor, but God done promise we paradise in di sky, way above those hills weh di rich people live. Dey t'ink dem looking down on us, but we are di chosen ones—di ones God pick to carry di weight of mankind 'pon we back 'cause we black an' strong. Our reward is in Heaven. God choose di poor to be heirs to di Kingdom, 'cause we rich in faith."

"Yuh don't think we deserve our reward here too?" Tru asks, remembering her conversation with Pope. "What if—what if while we busy looking to di sky, people steal from us?"

"What we got fah dem to steal?" Mama G asks, her eyes boring into Tru's. "Tell me."

Tru shrugs. "Ras Norbert say we sitting on gold."

"Screw what dat ole dutty mop-head brute seh. What him know 'bout anyt'ing? Since him 'ooman lef' him, all him do is sit an' smoke him ganja all day. Gold? Which pa'at? If we 'ave gold we woulda been rich by now as a people, as a country. Black people don't got nuh gold fi claim, 'less we sell we organ dem. As me seh, our riches is in Heaven. Not here. Yuh must not question God," Mama G says. "In fact, yuh should be grateful dat Him spare yuh life. I'm happy you survive because yuh wouldn't get to Heaven by killing yuhself. Dat woulda been a path straight to Hell. Suh give t'anks."

The memory of the darkness that had skipped through Tru's veins moments before she smashed the mirror with her bare hands and dug into her flesh returns. She realized then, as she does now, that the darkness lives with her; crouches in certain corners of her room; lingers well after the rain stops on an overcast day; persists in the silences when she doesn't have music blasting through headphones to drown it out. She wishes she hadn't survived. Her heart laps fiercely in her throat as she sits at the table with her grandmother, listening to her go on about Heaven. Tru swallows, barely able to suppress her anger. She balls her fists tightly. Mama G doesn't care about her at all. It's clear now that all Mama G is concerned about is getting to a place that may not exist.

"Was Mama saved too?" Tru asks. She doesn't know what prompted her to ask this. Maybe it's Tru's failure to imagine herself as a young girl being forced to fast for forty days and forty nights, trapped in her mother's fears of going to Hell. *Was Mama told she'd go to Hell too?*

Mama G is shaking her head. She turns the water jug, which by now has formed a large puddle on the wooden dining table. She has a pained look on her face as if Tru has asked the wrong question. In the room's dim quiescence, Tru hears her grandmother catch her breath as though to speak, but she says nothing. Tru waits patiently. Suddenly Mama G's voice comes, so quiet that it seems distant.

"Some people jus' can't be saved," she says. "But not ah soul can say me neva try. Di war between God an' di Devil is not fah us to undah-stand."

❦

UNDER THE WEIGHT OF THE DARKNESS FLUNG LIKE A CLOAK wide over Rochester, the lights inside the house glower as Tru opens the letter that arrived from her mother a week ago. *"She's still yuh mother, Tru."* Perhaps Roy knew that her anger would eventually drop. He was right. Now, after speaking to Mama G and realizing that her mother might have been escaping something more than just Tru, Tru picks up the envelope.

Dear Tru,

i hope this letter finds you well. i know it's well after many birthdays and Christmases. There's a lot to say . . . a lot i don't know if i can put into words. i'm not much of a writer, which is why i always liked numbers. But here i am, relying on words, hoping they will get through to you. i can't leave America to come see you, because my papers not straight here. But Tru, if i could travel, i'd be there in a heartbeat. i know you're probably wondering why it took me so long, after all these years, to reach out. i'm writing you now because it's long overdue. Truth is, i didn't know what i would have done with myself if you died, god know. i know i didn't make the best decision, leaving you like that when you was young, but i wouldn't forgive myself to know i could hurt you even more. i wasn't a woman when i had you. Although i was twenty-two years old, i was still a young girl who wanted so much more. i was terrified of raising another human being, feel-

ing complete responsibility for how you'd end up. Not everyone can handle that pressure so young. Speaking for myself, i could not handle it. i also didn't think it would've been fair to raise you and end up putting all my dreams and aspirations on your back. i've seen way too much children crushed that way, too. When you was a little girl, i didn't have the heart to tell you how sad i was. It was a sadness i never knew how to explain—one that made me feel like i was being buried alive. i felt stuck, believing a black ghetto girl like me would never mount to anything.

Then you came. A beautiful baby whose beauty i couldn't see, because you looked so much like me. i was afraid to look you in the face, knowing there wasn't much i could do to save you. My biggest regret is that i didn't figure out how to love you sooner. i couldn't even love myself. i was guilty, because i had brought you into a world i could not change—a world i feared would break you, too. i also could not bear to pretend that motherhood was for me.

A wise woman told me that you'd respect me more for my honesty. This is why i am baring my soul to you. When you were born, they called you a miracle, because doctors thought i couldn't get pregnant again after a miscarriage i had when i was young. You were a miracle i was reckless enough to take for granted. A miracle i was too broken to appreciate. You're alive for a reason, Tru. You're here to prove people, including myself, wrong. You can be the one to change things. i know i've scarred you with my absence. And for that, i am truly sorry. However, life scars make us warriors. You're a warrior, Tru. i know this, because i left you with the best person, your father. He's a good man. And Marva is a better woman than i am.

i know i may not be qualified to call myself your mother at this stage, or even try to pretend that i know what's best for you or what you like, but i can only hope that one day you will find it in your heart to forgive me. i also may not be the best at shopping for gifts, but i will leave you with these words that i wish someone had told me when i was your age: Never let anyone define you. Always know that you matter. Your thoughts, feelings, and your desires matter. Your happiness matters. As your mother-in-training, the least i can do is set you free.

i'll always be here if there ever come a time when you need me.

Love always, Patsy

BOOK VI

WHAT IS TRUE

56

T RU CROSSES THE PARKING LOT OF THE NATIONAL STADIUM, breathing in air thick with the smell of ripening mangoes. Her teammates have just emerged from the school bus with their gear. She spots Saskia, who waves at her. She's standing by a big lignum vitae tree not too far from a cluster of palm trees. Tru slows down. Saskia's smile broadens when Tru comes closer, squinting in the Saturday morning sunshine.

"Look at you," Saskia says, appraising Tru's athletic gear with Wilhampton blue and white elephant logo on the jersey.

Saskia is wearing her hair out today. It's neatly curled with a curling iron and glistens in the sun. She attempts to tuck strands of it behind her ears. Tru does it for her, her hand lingering just behind Saskia's right ear. They stare at each other, suddenly shy again, their mutual bewilderment confessing they have reached a certain level of intimacy. "Who yuh waiting on?" Tru asks with a smirk, removing her hand.

Saskia shrugs. "Hm. Someone wid a nice fade an' big brown eyes. She's di forward everybody's been talking about on di school's football team. You know her?"

"Is she cute?"

Saskia blushes. "I dunno. Maybe."

"You say she plays? Does she have di best game ever?"

"Today we're about to find out dat she's di best high school football player in all of Jamaica, playing fah di best team. Those St. Andrew High School girls look like giants out there, but I bet she can beat them."

"Really?"

"Really."

"Hm. Sounds like you really like her."

Saskia shrugs. "I think so."

"You think?"

Saskia nods and smiles shyly. "I really like her."

"I'm sure she really likes you too."

Saskia looks down at her shoes. Tru does the same. "Let's do something nice aftah di game. Maybe we can go to Devon House fah ice cream."

"So dat yuh can eat up all ah mine when I'm not looking?" Saskia laughs.

"Sharing is caring."

Mrs. Rosedyl, who's on her way to the VIP section of the bleachers with an older black man dressed in all white, stops to greet Tru. Mrs. Rosedyl is smiling, looking extra tanned from the sun. She's wearing a visor, a white polo blouse buttoned all the way up to the neck, and a salmon pleated skirt, looking very much like she's about to play a game of badminton or tennis with the royal family.

"Ready for the game, Tru?" Mrs. Rosedyl asks.

"I was born ready."

"I'd like you to meet Mr. Andre Porter. He's a recruiter from Cambridge University."

The man smiles with perfectly aligned teeth—the straightest teeth Tru has ever seen besides her mother's. He shakes Tru's hand.

"You have a good handshake," he says to Tru in a clipped British accent that also surprises Tru, who has never met a foreigner who isn't white. "Firm," Mr. Porter says. "I like you already and I haven't even seen you play. A woman with a man's handshake!"

He turns to Mrs. Rosedyl, who laughs. Her laughter seems apologetic to Tru and Saskia. "Ur . . . uhm . . . and Saskia here is our exceptional net-ball team captain!" she tells him, quickly changing the subject.

"Hello." Andre bows slightly when he gently takes Saskia's hand like a prince greeting a princess. But Saskia grips his hand and shakes it.

Mr. Porter, who seems caught off guard, says to Mrs. Rosedyl, "You're making some firm handshakers at this school. I'm impressed!"

Tru thinks she sees her headmistress flush red. If her blouse wasn't buttoned all the way, Tru would've probably seen that reptilian vein she gets in her neck whenever she's upset as she says, "They're all amazing and exceptionally gifted, Mr. Porter."

Following her successful CXC pass last year and admittance to sixth form, which is now co-ed, Tru had gone to Mrs. Rosedyl about starting a soccer team at the school. She made the case that girls can be good and competitive at male-dominated sports too, and given that the school has so much money already set aside, why not put it to good use? Mrs. Rosedyl didn't appear too thrilled at the time, dismissing Tru with, "I'll think about it." Next thing Tru knew, Mrs. Rosedyl made an announcement on the intercom for Tru to come to see her in her office. Her classmates oohed as Tru gathered her things to go to the principal's office. When Tru arrived, Miss Thelwell, the PE teacher, and Miss Fairweather, the guidance counselor, were there, all three women smiling. "*Tru, Miss Fairweather told me how much it would mean to you if we start this new program at our school. I was telling Miss Thelwell about your proposal. Her father, Ronnie, was a soccer coach at St. George's College. He'd love to come back and coach our team. But there's one catch . . .*" Mrs. Rosedyl pursed her lips in a thin line. "*You'd have to help recruit.*"

Tru gleefully took on the task, designing flyers with Kenny's help and handing them out all over campus. She even spoke onstage at assembly, encouraging girls to try out for the team. To Tru's surprise, girls from every form signed up, more girls than Tru thought would ever be interested in soccer, girls willing to try out despite their status as Branded or Uptowns.

After Mrs. Rosedyl walks away with Mr. Porter, the girls turn to each other and giggle. "That skirt is hideous!" Saskia says.

"And aren't visors outdated?" Tru laughs, shaking her head.

"Also, what's up with that man and handshakes?"

"His hair says it all. Old school."

Saskia laughs. "Well, I showed him!"

"Yes, you did."

"A scholarship to Cambridge University in England goes a long way," Saskia says.

Tru smiles. "And if I get it, you can visit me, since yuh mother is there. Dat would be nice."

"What yuh mean, if you get it? You will. Good luck," Saskia says, echoing Patsy when Tru spoke to her over the telephone this morning. "*You'll show dem. I'm so proud of you.*" They have been talking a lot more lately, at least once a week. It took almost a whole year for this to happen, for Tru to begin to forgive her mother. She's not sure if she's fully there yet, or if she'll ever get to that place of complete forgiveness. In her quiet times, there is still an unexplainable ache she feels, which throbs like the nerve of a phantom limb. She is secretly relieved that her mother hasn't been pushing the possibility of having Tru come live with her and her girlfriend, Claudette, in America, though Roy has put in the paperwork for a visa application for Tru to visit. "*At least you'll 'ave di option. Ah could introduce you to Claudette,*" her mother said. Tru only nodded, leaving quiet on her end of the line.

"*Yuh mother has a girlfriend? Dat's so cool,*" Saskia mused when Tru confided in her. Tru felt guilty about lying, since her mother has never uttered such words to Tru. Tru has only inferred that the woman living with her mother might be more than her roommate. "*Claudette sen' har love too"; "Claudette an' I not g'wan be home on Sunday, we going on a boat trip"; "Me an' Claudette saw a good movie di other day"; "Claudette fried fish today an' it remind me suh much of Port Royal. Dey still fry good fish an' bami ovah dere?"*

By then, Tru and Saskia had been going steady for a couple months. They had gone all the way, Tru finally surrendering to the all-encompassing feeling of being girl and boy, hard and soft, powerful and vulnerable at the same time. Tru loves Saskia's muscles moving under her damp skin, and her heaving chest against hers like she's breathing for her, her heart beating for them both. Patsy doesn't know about Saskia. Tru doesn't like the idea of pinning things down, defining them. She relishes this ambiguity of liking who she likes. And besides, Tru wants to take it slow. She's not at that stage where she feels comfortable disclosing her personal life and desires to her mother. But she will tell her about the University of Cambridge and her plans to study psychology there, if all goes well.

Before she goes off to the locker room to prepare for the game, she looks both ways, making sure the coast is clear before she draws close to Saskia for a small kiss. In that pause, Tru's heart ceases and she knows that after the game all she wants to do is sit in Saskia's cool room or lie across Saskia's bed with her to listen to music together, or make their own, the sun spread over them through the window. But it's only a moment. Saskia blushes and steps away a little. The world has intruded once again. With a shadow of caution covering her face, Saskia gives Tru's hand a squeeze, then stalks off to the stands, her white Wilhampton High School T-shirt merging quickly with the crowd.

"Don't be tardy," Sore-Foot Marlon whispers from behind, nudging Tru.

She jumps and clutches her chest. "Yuh coulda given me a heart attack!"

"Jus' a warning. Yuh standing out here looking lost when yuh have a game to play."

"So? How yuh know ah wasn't meditating?"

"Meditating, my rear end. Di word is tardy. Yuh face right next to it in di dictionary. Look it up." He winks.

Tru cuts her eyes at him. "Your dictionary needs an update. 'Cause I'm here, aren't I?"

"Who is di cute girl?" he asks.

"None ah yuh business," Tru replies.

"Yuh looking kinda sad. Everyt'ing all right? Is wha' she do yuh?"

"Mind yuh business, Marlon." Tru laughs.

"Yo, Ricky!" Sore-Foot Marlon hollers across the lot. "Check out Tru Juice friend."

Albino Ricky's eyes expand, growing in circumference to fit the width of his face when he follows Sore-Foot Marlon's crooked index finger to Saskia, who is now sitting cross-legged in the bleachers. He tosses his cigarette and stops. "Wah? It g'wan pour to rhaatid!" he jokes. Asafa comes over too to stare, all three boys gawking, their curiosity pressed up against her.

"Can I get har numbah?" Albino Ricky asks.

"You all should get a life," Tru replies. "Is jus' a classmate."

"Jus' a classmate?" Sore-Foot Marlon smirks, his comment private.

"Stop it!" Tru says.

"Stop what?" Sore-Foot Marlon asks, playing clueless. "Tru Juice, ah haffi give yuh props. Neva knew di day would come . . ."

"What's dat supposed to mean?" Tru asks, reveling in the indecent delight. "Yuh know I got more game than you, Marlon."

"Ooooooooooooh!" the other boys hoot, cupping their mouths.

Bewilderment and intrigue lance Sore-Foot Marlon's eyes. "You do, huh?" He brings his face close to hers like he wants to kiss her. "We'll see about dat, Tru Juice."

She stares boldly in his face; something in it triggers her—the slight twitch above his thick eyebrows, maybe. Or his light eyes reflecting an image of her in their deep centers. With a strong graceful lift of her head and squaring of her shoulders, revealing an almost irrepressible vitality, she says, "I'm very good at other t'ings yuh won't know about."

"Heresy!" Sore-Foot Marlon's astonished laugh joins hers. "Di dictionary has yet another word bearing yuh beautiful-ugly face."

"And yours . . ." She smiles at him.

When the other boys leave in a bevy of laughter to find their seats in the bleachers, Sore-Foot Marlon stays. He reaches for her hand. "Now more people will get a chance fi see what ah always know—dat you's di real deal."

His playful smile returns, followed by the gold flecks of mischief in his amber eyes, as he holds his face at an angle to get a really good look at her, his laughter leaping out. "Actually . . . you's second best to di real deal." He stretches both arms toward the blue of the sky like Rocky at the top of those steps in the movie. "I am di real champ."

Tru laughs out loud. "Now, dat's tacky—"

"What?"

"Show-off!"

Brushing his lips across her cheek, he says, "I'm quite disappointed, Tru Juice, because ah thought yuh got more balls than dat. How yuh g'wan say yuh got good game an' not act like it?"

Without waiting for her reply, he strides jauntily across the parking lot toward the bleachers, leaving her smiling and shaking her head. "Arrogance!" she calls out after him. "Yuh face right next to it in di dictionary!"

He waves her off, and she stares after him, her hand cupping his breath on her cheek.

INSIDE THE LOCKER ROOM, TRU PULLS OUT THE NECKLACE HER mother sent her from her godmother Cicely—a tiger's-eye pendant for good luck. *"I'm passing it on to you wid yuh godmother's blessing, 'cause yuh need it more,"* her mother said over the telephone. Tru puts it to her lips and then latches the silver clasp around her neck, letting the pendant fall inside her jersey so it can be next to her skin.

From the soccer field, Tru sees her friends sitting in the bleachers next to Roy, who is beaming with unbridled pride. Beside him, holding one baby to her breast while the other dozes in a stroller, Marva is pursing her lips as if she's trying to hold back tears. Her face shares the same look of hope that burns in Kenny's and Miss Maxine's and Miss Foster's and Miss Belnavis's and Mr. Pete's and Sir Charles's, and the faces of Tru's other old neighbors from Pennyfield. Only Mama G has refused to come, because her church forbids her to go to movie theaters and stadiums.

Roy had taken the initiative to invite most of Pennyfield, like he had taken the initiative—finding his calling—to start a soccer camp sponsored by the Jamaica Constabulary Force for inner-city boys and girls, which also provides scholarships from money donated by local businesses and major corporations. Sore-Foot Marlon, Albino Ricky, Asafa, and many of the boys on Pope's team are involved. *"It reduces crime rate by giving these boys an' girls somet'ing to do. Somet'ing to hope for. Somet'ing dat build their confidence an' prove to them dat dey have a future,"* Tru heard Roy telling a reporter in an interview he did over the telephone. He was written up in the *Jamaica Observer* with his new title: "Superintendent Roy Beckford Changes a Troubled Community with Football." When Tru told her father about Pope's team and what he's trying to do with it, Roy became interested. Pope gave the team over to Roy, trusting that Roy can take the team a lot farther with his reputation and ability to get sponsors to grant them more and better opportunities. Today, Pope is in the stands too. Today, he nods discreetly at Roy, who nods back, before nodding at Tru—his braces glistening in sunlight. Today, he points his index finger at Tru and mouths, *Your turn.*

Tru scores two goals for her school. All of her training seems to funnel to this moment: her father teaching her how to kick that makeshift ball with all her might, the many games she played in the dwindling emerald light surrounding the bald patch of land behind Roman Phillips Secondary with her friends. How Sore-Foot Marlon kicked the ball to Albino Ricky, who bumped it on his knees and kicked it to Asafa, who head-butted it to Tru, who did a horizontal kick, her right leg almost touching her forehead, straight into the net. She repeats the move now, to raucous hoots and hollers. Miss Maxine and Miss Foster, who had brought their Dutch pots, bang them with metal spoons. Roy hugs Kenny, almost lifting him off the bleachers, and then turns to kiss Marva full on the mouth.

"Pennyfield to di werrrrrrrl!" Albino Ricky shouts, grinning from ear to ear.

THE END.

ACKNOWLEDGMENTS

MY MOST HEARTFELT THANKS AND LOVE TO:

My wife, Emma Benn, whose encouragement helped me to finish this book; my agent, Julie Barer, who had been sold on this project from the very beginning; and my editor, Katie Henderson Adams, Cordelia Calvert, Michael Taekens, and the Liveright team, who fell in love with Patsy and made it possible for her to enter the world.

I am also very grateful to those who helped me along the way as I worked on this project—my mother, my grandmother, my sister, and my dear friend Janae Gaylyn, who has read every draft. I am also truly grateful to my nephews, Logan and Jayden, for being such gifts during this process; my best friend, Tina Whyte, for listening and for your tremendous help; Alistair Scott for your wealth of knowledge; Latoya Blackwood for your motivation and support; Tracy-Ann Ferguson for your keen eye and insight; and Miss Claudette for your wonderful spirit. Also heartfelt thanks to Sharon Tucker-Gordon, Wayne Gordon, Tameka and Lionel Taylor, Juliet Jeter, Louie Benn, Benny Benn, Lavern and Linda Adger, Aunt Lillian, David Watkins, Cheryl Benn, Carolyn Horton, Nancy Kirby, Iris Bonner, Eugenia Benn, Charlie Benn, Sheldon

Shaw, Craig Wooten, Sharon Gordon, Marcia Wilson, Anna Masilela, Richa Deshpande, Chengcheng Tu, Shayaa Muhammad, Krystal Brown, and Debbie Hardie for being true angels of love. And special shout-out to Lamont and Alicia Adger for going out of your way to cook some good food for the soul when I needed it the most. And Rowena Hunter for your prayers.

Many thanks to Hedgebrook and Sewanee, especially Richard Bausch; the New York Foundation for the Arts; the MacDowell Colony; Lambda Literary; and *Kweli* literary journal, *Mosaic* literary magazine, Kimbilio, and the Hurston/Wright Foundation for your constant support of black writers.

I'm forever grateful for my predecessors, beginning with my great-grandmother, Addy, Zora Neale Hurston, Toni Morrison, Edwidge Danticat, Audre Lorde, and Paule Marshall.

Much gratitude to Marva and Danville for the inspiration. And to all the mothers who have helped me during the birthing process of this book. I couldn't have done it without your insights and encouragements. You know who you are! This is for you.

Last but not least, thanks to Jamaica, my homeland and beloved country, for the lush, but mostly untold stories; and my second home, Brooklyn, for the opportunity to tell them.

© Jason Berger

Nicole Dennis-Benn is the critically acclaimed author of *Here Comes the Sun*, winner of the Lambda Literary Award and a finalist for the 2016 John Leonard Prize National Book Critics Circle Award, the 2016 Center for Fiction First Novel Prize, and the 2017 Young Lions Fiction Award. Born and raised in Kingston, Jamaica, she teaches creative writing at Princeton University and lives with her wife in Brooklyn.

www.nicoledennisbenn.com

Also by Nicole Dennis-Benn

A finalist for the New York Public Library Fiction Award, the NYPL Young Lions Fiction Award and the Center for Fiction First Novel Prize

A Grand Prix Littéraire of the Association of Caribbean Writers Selection

Named a Best Book of 2016 by the New York Times, NPR, BuzzFeed, San Francisco Chronicle, The Root, Book Riot, Kirkus, Amazon, WBUR's 'On Point' and Barnes & Noble

In this radiant, highly anticipated novel, a cast of unforgettable women battle for independence while a maelstrom of change threatens their Jamaican village

Capturing the distinct rhythms of Jamaican life and dialect, Nicole Dennis-Benn pens a tender hymn to a world hidden among pristine beaches and the wide expanse of turquoise seas. At an opulent resort in Montego Bay, Margot hustles to send her younger sister, Thandi, to school. Taught as a girl to trade her sexuality for survival, Margot is ruthlessly determined to shield Thandi from the same fate.

When plans for a new hotel threaten the destruction of their community, each woman – fighting to balance the burdens she shoulders with the freedom she craves – must confront long-hidden scars. From a much-heralded new writer, *Here Comes the Sun* offers a dramatic glimpse into a vibrant, passionate world most outsiders see simply as paradise.

'Stuns at every turn... It's about women pushed to the edge, Jamaica in all its beauty and fury and more than anything else, a story that was just waiting to be told.' Marlon James, author of *A Brief History of Seven Killings*

PATSY

NICOLE DENNIS-BENN

Nicole Dennis-Benn's second novel is an urgent story of race, migration, motherhood and belonging. Like her debut, *Here Comes the Sun*, this is a fiercely engaged, sometimes uncomfortable novel that confronts the reader with important questions.

This reading guide is intended to broaden your discussion of some of *Patsy*'s major characters and themes.

QUESTIONS FOR DISCUSSION

1. What do you think about Patsy's characterisation?

2. How do you think Patsy understands motherhood, in relation to herself and to her own mother?

3. Discuss Nicole Dennis-Benn's portrayal of immigration.

4. What do you think of Tru as a character? Do you think her struggles with identity, sexuality and abandonment shape who she is? To what extent?

5. What do you think of the representation of LGBTQ+ and POC characters in this novel?

6. Discuss whether in the current political climate you think this book is creating positive conversations about immigration.

7. What do you think of the examples of xenophobia and racism in this book?

8. Do you like that the book is told from two different perspectives? Whose point of view do you relate to most?

9. Why do you think Nicole Dennis-Benn chose to tell this story with two unconventional women?

10. Do you think that Cicely and Patsy's relationship is a source of joy for Patsy? If not, how so?